BRENDA JOYCE

DARK RIVAL

HQN™

ISBN-13: 978-0-373-77219-3
ISBN-10:   0-373-77219-X

DARK RIVAL

HQN Books is excited to introduce
A Dangerous Love
Brenda Joyce's latest historical romance
Coming in spring 2008

DARK
RIVAL

PROLOGUE

Long ago, somewhere in the Kingdom of the Picts

TODAY HE WOULD DIE. He did not care, even though he was but three and twenty. For he would not die alone.

He stood on the ridge amidst oak and pine, panting like a hunting hound, sweat pouring down his body. He had been hunting Kael for two endless weeks, ignoring all advice, all counsel and every warning. Now Kael was within the fortress on the other side of the glen, atop the adjacent ridge. He did not have to see him to know. He felt his black power.

But he could not sense Brigdhe, his bride.

Pushing tendrils of gold hair from his face, he started down the ridge, his strides long, determined. His linen tunic stuck to his young, hard body, soaking wet, clinging there. His longsword bumped his thigh with every step. He left the security of the tree line, and saw men gathering on the wooden watchtowers, which were spaced evenly about the palisades. A horn blew. He smiled. Let them shout a warning!

He reached the barred doors of the fortified manor and did not hesitate, although he was new to his powers. He had been summoned to Iona six months ago by his father's friend, MacNeil. He hadn't understood then what a

summons by an abbot to a monastery had to do with him.
But he had quickly learned that he hadn't been summoned
by a true abbot, and that there was far more than a monastery on the island.

He'd been aware for most of his life that he was stronger,
more virile and more sexual than other men. His intellect
was sharper, his sense of danger far more acute. And physically, he was at least a head taller than his friends.

When he made his vows to old gods he hadn't paid attention to until the choosing, swearing to protect Innocence
through all time, suddenly his powers were released. He
remained unsure of just how strong he was, but nothing
would stop him now. He reached for the bolted doors, each
one as tall as two men and as wide as a warhorse. He ripped
them off their iron hinges.

Above him, on the towers, the men shouted in alarm.

Arrows rained down on him. One pierced his skin and
stung. Another went deeper, embedding itself in his flesh.
He ripped it out, feeling no pain.

He collected his mind and instinctively put his power
around him like a shield, never breaking stride, heading for
the largest of the buildings in the fort. The arrows fell uselessly around him now.

A dozen giants rushed him, carrying lances and leather
shields. They were human, but evil possessed them.

He kept walking, drawing his sword. Metal hissed.

The giants rushed him, throwing their spears all at once.

He found more power and thrust it boldly at his assail-
ants; the giants fell as if pushed by huge winds, their spears
falling backward, past them.

He lunged up the steps and into the darkened hall.

Kael faced him.

But he saw only Brigdhe, lying naked on the rug before

the fire, her long red-gold hair streaming about her slender body, her hands bound. He faltered.

She turned her head listlessly and looked at him. Her eyes widened—and then he saw the accusation on her face.

The blow took him by surprise, sending him flying backward. He landed hard on his back by the door, but did not drop his sword. As Kael's sword descended, Brigdhe's accusatory expression remained engraved on his mind, and with it, so much horror arose in his heart. Instead of parrying the blow, his own weapon yielded uselessly and Kael's blade rent his shoulder, all the way through muscle and bone.

He forgot his bride. He rolled away as Kael blasted him with more energy, the second blow as stunning as the first. He was not used to men fighting this way. Pushed against the wall, he felt Kael's sword coming, and this time, he struck upward with his blade, blindly, by sheer instinct.

Steel met steel. Metal screeched, rang. He leapt to his feet, bleeding heavily. Kael thrust more power at him.

He was hurled backward into the wall again. As he crashed into the wood as if thrown from a cliff to the glen below, he gathered his wits. He had power now, and surely he could fight this way, too.

"A Brigdhe," he roared. And he struck at Kael with all the power he had.

Kael was flung across the entire hall, landing on his back, not far from Brigdhe. He rushed after him, ignoring the burning pain in his shoulder. Kael rose and he thrust his blade savagely through his heart, the tip piercing out the other side of his back.

A human would have instantly died. Kael gasped—and then smiled. "Your suffering just begins."

He could not understand and did not care to. He pulled his sword free, took Kael by the neck and cruelly snapped it in two. The demon's red eyes glowed another time—and then they were sightless.

Instantly, a pain arising in his shoulder, he ran to his wife.

She sat with her back to the wall, hugging her knees to her chest. His heart now breaking for her, he knelt, reaching for her, about to enclose her in his embrace. The pain in his shoulder suddenly screamed, making him dizzy.

"Don't touch me!"

Stunned, he jerked back, the floor becoming level once more. Somehow, he dropped his hands; somehow, he did not touch her. "T'is over now. I'll take ye far from here," he soothed. But in his own heart, he was sick, frantic and ashamed of his failure to protect her.

"No."

He tensed, stunned, searching her eyes, but she wouldn't look at him now. "I'm sorry, Brigdhe."

"Sorry?" Her tone was scathing and hatred filled her eyes. "Get far from me. He did this to me because of ye. Stay away from me!"

Her words delivered the blow that Kael had not been able to wield. He tried to breathe and failed. She was right. Kael had used his bride against him. He had vowed to protect Innocence, and he hadn't even been able to protect his own wife.

In that instant, he knew his marriage was over.

"Can ye stand?" he asked, his tone rough with emotions he must not yield to.

"Dinna touch me," she cried furiously.

He stood and stepped aside, just as his brother and MacNeil arrived. Horribly grim, he watched Brogan lift her and carry her from the hall. He stared after them, refusing to feel the aching in his heart. He had been a fool to think he could keep a wife and uphold his vows as a Master. He did not blame Brigdhe for hating him now. He hated himself.

MacNeil beckoned him from the tainted hall's threshold, his handsome countenance set in grim, severe lines. "Ye disobeyed me, Ruari. Ye were told not to hunt Kael alone."

He was in no mood to argue. "Aye." From where he stood, he could see the great Healer, Elasaid, tending to the woman who had so briefly been his wife. Never again, he thought.

And MacNeil had been lurking in his mind, because he said, "Aye. Yer a Master, lad. Ye'll stand alone like the rest o' us. A Master stands alone, fights alone, dies alone."

"Dinna fear," he said grimly. He had no intention of ever allowing another woman into his life, much less taking one as a wife. He would not condescend to any pain in his heart. Not now, not ever. The vows he had made would be his life.

MacNeil softened. "I dinna think ye could vanquish Kael. I'm proud of ye, lad."

He nodded curtly. MacNeil clasped his shoulder, indicating that they should leave. The fortress would be razed, the ground consecrated. Human prisoners would be taken, demonic ones vanquished. The humans would be exorcized, if possible.

He heard a woman's soft cry for help.

He stiffened, because the afternoon was entirely silent outside the dark hall.

"Ruari?" MacNeil asked.

The air moved around him. A woman whispered his name.

He glanced at MacNeil. "Did ye hear the woman?"

MacNeil looked aside. "There's no one here but ye and me."

He was wrong. A woman had called to him from the hall—he was certain. Leaving MacNeil, he stepped back into the dank chamber, glancing into every shadowed corner, but no one was present. Then he saw a trap door set in the floor.

Please.

Royce.

He had heard a woman calling for him, as clear as day. He rushed to the trap door and lifted it. And he heard the hissing of snakes. "Get me a torch!" he called.

"There's no one down there," MacNeil said firmly. "I'd sense life if it was here."

"A torch," he demanded.

A moment later MacNeil handed him a burning torch. He lowered it and saw piles of black, writhing snakes—but the pit looked empty otherwise. Still, he could not be sure. For he felt the woman now, and she was afraid.

He leapt down into the pit, waving the torch, scattering the snakes away from his bare feet. He looked around the small manmade cellar, and realized MacNeil was right. There was no one down there.

He tossed the torch to MacNeil and reached up. A moment later he was walking from the manor, but he remained uncertain and uneasy. He looked back.

The air inside the dark hall fluttered and beckoned. A woman's fragrance suddenly enveloped him. And he heard her again. *Royce...*

He seized MacNeil, halting him. "Who is she? Where is she? What does she want an' why does she call me by my English name?"

MacNeil stared. "She's not here, lad."

"Then where is she?" He did not, could not, understand. And he turned back, overcome. "I must find her."

MacNeil took his arm, forestalling him. "Ye canna find her now. She's in the future—yer future."

CHAPTER ONE

South Hampton, New York—September 4, 2007

SHE STOOD NAKED at the window, aware of her lover's deep, even breathing coming from the bed behind her. The Long Island night was blue-black and star-spangled, the moon full and bright, and she could hear the ocean's rhythmic roar. A sea breeze caused the upholstered shades to knock softly against the windows. As she stood there, clouds gathered. She tensed.

The sky darkened. Shadows crossed the moon's bright face, scarring it. The shutters began banging against the walls, almost frantically.

Allie stared at the moon, watching as it turned black.

She strained. And she felt evil intent forming.

Her pulse accelerated. She hurried across the room, about to step into her walk-in closet, when Brian stirred. He murmured, "Hey," his tone drowsy

She smiled and swiftly returned to his side. "I'm starving. Want me to bring you some goodies from the kitchen?" She hated lying to him, but he would not understand.

He was snoring.

She waited a moment, impatience gnawing at her. One of her best friends was a whiz with spells, but Allie didn't have any powers like that. It was unfortunate at times like these, when a sleeping spell would have been great. Reassured that he was deeply asleep, she quickly stepped into a black tank top, black cargo pants, and black Nikes, picking up a black backpack. She didn't bother to open it; it was loaded and ready to go. As deftly as a cat burglar, the sleeping man now forgotten, she slipped out the window and climbed down the trellis, as if she'd done so a thousands times, which she had. Then she ran across the lawn to the driveway where she'd left her Mercedes SL560.

Allie jumped in, but didn't turn the car on. She sat very still, focusing her sixth sense.

A shadow of darkness and death was gathering in the north.

She felt malice; she felt lust.

Allie turned the ignition, adrenaline flooding her. Aware that she couldn't peel out of the driveway, because that would wake up the entire house, she focused on the gathering storm of violence, needing to pinpoint the location. She slowly cruised down the drive, the lust in the night intensifying. Allie felt its heart thudding, thick and strong, hot blood pulsing with evil carnal intent.

She turned onto the two-lane road and hit the gas. Rubber burned and screamed. *She was going to save this vic.* She drove by instinct, feeling the monster's evil energy. She ran two stop signs. The damned monster had found its prey. She could feel it watching, about to pounce, to take, to kill. She was guessing both the predator and his or her victim were outside of one of the bars or restaurants on Highway 27. It was the weekend, and the nightspots were hopping.

A wave of pleasure began.

Allie cried out, because she could actually feel their sexual pleasure. It quickly began to escalate. Murder was always the outcome of these crimes of pleasure. The car ahead of her was obeying the speed limit and doing forty-five. Allie stomped on the gas and veered dangerously past the car ahead of her—and narrowly by an oncoming truck. The truck driver blared his horn at her.

The pleasure became ecstasy, rapture. It flowed over Allie in waves—both victim and criminal were having orgasmic sex. It didn't turn her on—it couldn't. Her rage knew no bounds. It was going to be too late....

Allie sped into a parking lot adjacent a popular bar and restaurant overlooking the bay. Although the lot was full, she knew exactly where to drive.

In the back, far from the restaurant's entrance, she saw them. A couple was in the throes of sex on the ground. And it wasn't rape....

As she stared, the man turned his head in her direction, sensing her white power.

Allie jammed on the brakes and leapt from the car. As she did, she felt dark power exploding in the night. It was too damned late!

For it was blinding and briefly, her senses were diminished. It was hard to see and she could not feel the victim; all she could feel was the triumph of evil and death.

She stumbled as she reached for her backpack, pulling out a gun with a silencer. Then she turned, bracing herself as she aimed.

The man stood, smiling, blond and beautiful, his features perfect, like a movie star's. In fact, for all she knew, he *was* a movie star. Dressed like a model in expensive trousers and a beautiful shirt, he hurled his black power at her.

Allie cocooned herself in her white light, but it was a healing light, so it didn't do a lot. Instead she was slammed against the car so hard it felt as if he'd broken her back. She somehow lifted the gun and fired.

She was a good shot, but not after that kind of blow; still, she got him in the shoulder. Bad news was, he had so much power after taking the life from a victim that a shot wasn't going to do much except cause a bit of inhuman bloodshed. He laughed at her and vanished into the stars.

She hoped his shoulder hurt like hell!

Allie reeled, still in pain from the blow. Then she flung the gun into the convertible's backseat and staggered to the prone victim.

Her senses began to work. The night was still and dead—lifeless.

Allie knelt, knowing it was too late. Had the woman still been alive, she would feel a flicker of her life.

The vic lay unmoving on her back, clad in a pretty halter top and skirt, eyes sightless. Allie cried out, because she couldn't be more than fifteen years old. *It was not fair.*

She was so tired of the malicious murders. For every human being she healed, there were hundreds of victims like this one, their lives stolen by the monsters who stalked the innocent in the night and then used that power to cause even more mayhem and death.

But there was no end in sight. Social commentators kept talking about the breakdown of modern society, how the murder rate was sky high—and ninety percent of all murders now were pleasure crimes. That is, the victims did not struggle. Somehow, they were seduced by complete strangers, and bodily fluids showed numerous orgasms. But the victims all died. As if old and feeble, their hearts simply stopped during intercourse.

But the victims were always young and beautiful and in perfect health. There was no reasonable medical explanation for heart failure.

Of course there wasn't.

Because science could not explain evil and it never would.

The far right wanted the death penalty for these perverts. The far right blamed law enforcement and the state and federal governments for the failure to apprehend these perps and for the rising crime rate. The far left wanted more studies and more research; they wanted better inner-city education, health care, hospitals, dear God, as if the inner cities bred the perps. They did not.

The left and the right and the general public thought the criminals rapists, even though there wasn't rape. They thought the perpetrators were human. But they were wrong.

It was a huge government cover-up. These sexual criminals did not have human DNA and Allie knew it for a fact. Not only did she know it because her mother had taught her to sense, feel and understand evil the moment she was toddling, but Brianna worked in CDA—the Center for Demonic Activities.

CDA was secret, too.

The perps looked human, but they were a race of evil, preying on mankind, sent by Satan himself centuries ago. Crimes of pleasure existed in every century; what was new was the growing numbers of the demonic hordes. Their population was expanding at a terrifying rate. Something was wrong.

And she, Brie, Tabby and Sam couldn't do this alone, nor could the handfuls of healers and slayers around the world. Why, *why* didn't the good guys have extraordinary powers, too?

There were some in the Center who believed that a race of men existed who did fight the demons with superpowers, some of the agents swearing they had seen these warriors. The stories all varied—they were pagans, they were Christian knights, they were modern soldiers—but one thread ran through every rumor: they could travel through time and they had sworn before God to fight evil. Allie grimaced. If such a race of überheroes existed, why didn't one of these pagan or medieval or modern warriors appear to help her out?

She needed someone to hold the line while she healed victims like this one.

As badly as she wanted to fight, it was hard to do so when a simple energy blow could send her across half of a football field.

Allie felt tears rising. She took the girl's hands and showered her with a healing light. "I'm sorry," she whispered, wanting to soothe her soul before it went to the next world.

And as she looked at the beautiful girl's face, her outrage knew no bounds. She showered her with more light, because she foolishly wanted to bring her back to life.

Of course, she couldn't do so. She could not resurrect the dead. She had begun healing insects and fish as a toddler, with her mother's encouragement. Every year her abilities had become stronger. By the time Elizabeth Monroe had suddenly died, when Allie was ten, she'd been easily healing the flu and the common cold. At fifteen, she could heal broken bones. At sixteen, she could heal an older person with severe pneumonia. At eighteen, she had given a boy run over by a car the use of his legs back. At twenty, she had healed a case of critical skin cancer.

She had to be careful—she had to be anonymous or she'd wind up being studied like a lab rat. Her mother often warned her to keep her powers secret.

There was so much she couldn't do—she couldn't give the blind their sight back, and she couldn't raise the dead. But Allie wanted to try.

She threw all the white power she had into the girl. She sat with her, tears streaking her face, straining to give her more and more white healing light. The girl remained still; her eyes remained sightless. Her heart did not beat. Allie screwed her eyes shut, refusing to quit. If only she could resurrect this girl, and save one of the demon's innocent victims! But it was hard to grasp her power now and bring it forth and send it to the girl. Still, Allie somehow sent another shower of healing power through the girl. It hurt to do so and she moaned. Allie realized she was at her limits; she felt depleted, drained, exhausted, and she knew she had no more power to give.

She hadn't realized she was lying down, on her belly, until she clawed the dirt, seeking her healing power. But it was finally gone...

The ground began to spin.

Allie closed her eyes, dizzy and faint. She heard voices coming from the bar but she was too weak to even tense. They were coming her way and she couldn't move—she was utterly defenseless. She strained her senses—there was no evil. Allie moaned and collapsed.

Her last conscious thought was that she had tried, but she hadn't resurrected the dead.

ALLIE AWOKE, feeling heavy and drugged.

She opened her eyes, feeling as if they'd been glued shut, and tested her fingers and toes, her hands and feet, relieved that, although weak, everything was in working order. She'd been asleep, but not in her own bed, and she felt nauseous, too. She started, suddenly realizing that she was in a hospital room, hooked up to various monitors and an IV. What the hell?

And instantly, she remembered trying to bring the dead

girl back to life and finally passing out. Someone must have found her and called 911.

She sat up. She was seriously exhausted from the effort she'd made, but not so much that she couldn't get up and leave. She grimaced, imagining the questions she'd be asked when she summoned a nurse. Questions were to be avoided.

Allie tore the tape off the IV and was removing the needle as gently as possible when she felt warmth filling the room. She tensed, recognizing the white power, and looked up.

Her mother appeared by her bedside. Allie gasped in shock. Although her mother had died fifteen years ago, Allie had never forgotten her. Her legacy—and her compassion— had been far too great. There was no question that her mother had come to visit her from the dead, for the first time. She was as fair and blond as Allie was dark, with an oddly ageless appearance. Now she smiled at her, but her eyes shimmered with urgency.

It is time now, darling. Embrace your destiny.

Stunned, Allie reached out—but her mother was already fading. "Don't go!" she cried, sliding from the bed to stand.

But her mother kept fading, becoming a vague shadow. *Golden.*

Her mother was speaking again! Allie could hear her, but her voice was weaker, nearly inaudible, as she drifted away.

But of course she was fading—it would be almost impossible for her to come back to this realm after being dead for so many years. "Mom! Don't go! What is it?" She was shocked, thrilled, but she was also alarmed. If her mother was trying to communicate with her from the dead, after so many years of absence, something had to be terribly wrong.

Trust....

Her mother's image was gone, and she was alone in the

small, curtained cubicle. "Who do you want me to trust? I trust you!" she cried.

The golden Master.

Allie stiffened, confused and doubtful she had heard correctly—until a stunningly clear image formed in her mind.

One of the most gorgeous and masculine men she had ever seen took over her mind. Allie saw a bronzed hunk with disheveled, dark gold, sun-streaked hair—and he was stark naked. Her interest escalated. He was a mass of bulging muscles, interesting slabs and amazingly defined planes. The man was built like the mythological Hercules—and he was packed. He was drop-dead gorgeous, with nearly perfect but oh-so-masculine features set in a very strong face. His expression was terse and hard, with stunning silver eyes that were piercing.

His body belonged on a knight from another time. In fact, she could envision him with a sword in hand. At the same time, he looked ready to rock and roll.

She swallowed, terribly breathless.

What was she doing? She was hearing her mother, speaking from the dead, and fantasizing about the kind of man she'd never meet, except maybe in a romance novel. But his expression wasn't one she could ever make up, not in a million years. What did that mean? And did it matter? She had to get the hell out of the hospital before someone tried to question her.

"Allie?"

Allie tensed as one of her best friends stepped through the curtains. Brianna Rose was a dead ringer for Jennifer Garner, but it was almost impossible to realize that, because she wore shapeless suits and black eyeglasses, and pulled her hair severely back. She was the shyest person Allie knew. She was also the smartest, a true techno-geek. Their gazes locked as Brianna hurried to her.

"Why did you cruise alone?" Brie whispered, her pretty green eyes clearly visible in spite of the serious spectacles she wore, which only enhanced her nerdy appearance. "I saw what happened!"

"I'm okay," Allie whispered. Brie had the Sight. She was also highly empathic. Of course she'd have rushed to Allie's side after she'd made herself so sick. "Aren't you late for work?"

"It's six in the morning," Brie returned. "They brought you in at 3:00 a.m. I'm sorry! I was at HCU all night—I was so engrossed in a case—or I'd have known sooner. Sam and Tabby are outside. C'mon. Let's get you out of here before CDA gets wind of this."

Allie seized her hands. "Brie. I just saw my mom."

Brianna hesitated. "We'll talk later," she said after a significant pause.

ALLIE STUDIED HERSELF critically in the mirror. Her father was holding a political fund-raiser and she had to be downstairs in a few moments. Concealer hid the dark circles that remained under her eyes. While she was feeling better, she was not herself and she knew it. She had gone too far, trying to raise the dead.

The sea-foam chiffon evening gown floated sensually down her body and made her olive complexion and dark eyes glow. Allie had used some serious teal eye shadow, dark liner and now she added pale gloss to her lips. For someone who'd awoken in the hospital that morning, she looked okay.

"Alison Monroe, you are late!" Her other best friend, Tabby, sailed into the room, looking drop-dead gorgeous in a bronze evening gown. She'd recently divorced and Allie knew the smile was fake—she'd been dumped for a younger woman and her heart was badly broken.

"You look awesome." Allie smiled.

"Thanks. I almost feel pretty again," Tabby said, closing the door. Tabby was of medium height, slim and blond; when she wasn't practicing spells and scrying for evil, she was practicing yoga. She was a first-grade teacher and her ex was a Wall Street high roller. It had been a Cinderella story—or so they'd both thought. "I'm giving you a heads-up. Brian wants to know why you walked out on him last night."

Allie grimaced. "I guess I got caught."

"Not for the first time," Tabby said softly. "I hate it when you cruise alone! You could get hurt! You *did* get hurt. Thank the gods Brie felt it so we could rescue you from the clutches of the police."

Tabby no longer smiled. Tabby, Sam and Brianna knew her secret—they'd known she could heal since they'd become friends as children. But Allie knew their secrets, too. As Rose women, they all had powers, which they used to fight evil. Tabby and Sam were sisters, and Brie was their cousin. Although Brie worked in CDA, no one knew her ability to see the future, and they all kept the lowest profile imaginable. "I guess another one bites the dust," Tabby remarked.

Allie glanced away. Brian had started to act like he was really interested in her, and that was not a good thing. Men had always swarmed to her like bees to honey. Yet she'd never been able to do more than go through the motions of being in love. She was twenty-five and she'd never been in love, not even a schoolgirl crush.

And she was always getting caught sneaking out in the middle of the night—and it was still just as hard trying to make up excuses. That behavior ended every relationship, sooner or later. Allie knew she didn't have time for love. In fact, love would probably interfere with her destiny as a Healer.

"I'm so tired of lying—and hiding who I really am," Allie said, sitting down on the bed. "But of course I'll tell him you called with a broken heart and I had to come right over."

"At least you're not in love," Tabby said significantly, referring to her own broken heart.

Before Allie could answer, Sam came in without knocking. While Tabby was as elegant as a woman could be, Sam had really short, choppy blond hair and favored distressed denim and biker boots. She had slipped on a very tiny, very immodest black dress for the affair, revealing the fact that she was as buff as a personal trainer, with a lot of black eye shadow and really pale lips. She was so beautiful that no amount of Rocker-Meets-Biker attitude could change that. "I heard that. Some of us are liberated women who need a guy for one thing only." She winked at Allie.

Sam understood her—she always had. Sam was really tough—the kind of tough that happens when tragedy strikes in front of your face when you're young, but old enough not to forget and move on. Unlike her sister, she was not romantic at all. Allie got it. She was on her own quest— hunting demons—and love would never get in the way.

"I wish I could be like you and Sam," Tabby said very seriously. "I wish I could date and have a good time and walk away whole."

"No one can change who they are," Allie said softly. "You're perfect the way you are." She wasn't going to reveal that sometimes she wondered what love felt like, that sometimes she was tired of being so damned alone.

Tabby snorted inelegantly. "Well, as I'm swearing off men forever, I guess that will be our secret."

"Just swear off Mr. Right—because he's always Mr. Wrong," Sam said, sitting on a chair and crossing her long, chiseled legs.

Allie said, "You'll meet someone who is as perfect for you as you are for him." She smiled and went to the mirror, pretending that she wanted to touch up her makeup. She didn't want to keep talking about love.

Tabby said softly, "Hey, are you forgetting I'm pretty telepathic?"

Allie glanced at Tabby's reflection in the mirror. She wouldn't trade her gift for anything or anyone, but her life was hard and isolating. She didn't know what she would do without such incredible friends. She said firmly, "My life is helping others, not falling in love. I have never been in love—and I doubt I ever will."

Allie turned and silently warned Tabby not to reveal her secrets. Tabby squeezed her hand. "On a more sober note, Brian's pretty upset about last night, Allie. He asked me if you're cheating on him."

Allie bit her lip. "Can you send him into the arms of a really hot babe? By dawn he won't remember me."

Tabby gave her a look, but Allie knew she'd cave. No one was as kind or caring as Tabby and she'd never let Brian walk around heartbroken. Tabby finally smiled, just a little. "It's against the rules to send him his soul mate, but I'll try to set Brian up."

Sam stood. "Duty calls, ladies."

Allie didn't move away from the bureau. "Any chance Brie's here?" Allie asked.

Sam gave her an incredulous look. "Brie wouldn't come to a party if her life depended on it. If she's not at work, I guarantee you she's at home, by her lonesome, with a glass of wine, buried in classified HCU files."

HCU was the Historical Crimes Unit of CDA. "I need a favor from her," Allie said.

Tabby stared, reading her thoughts. Allie had mentioned her mother's visit that morning when they were in Sam's SUV, on their way home from South Hampton Hospital. Now she thought about her mother's strange words and the warrior-hard muscleman with a suntan. She tensed, actually feeling the stirrings of desire. "I need to know what she meant."

Sam snickered. "No, you want to know if a golden sex machine is in your future. Man, I can always use one of those—although I prefer my men dark."

Allie had to smile. "He's mine, girl."

Sam shrugged.

But Tabby was serious. "How many times have you wished for a warrior to help you while you healed? I do recall that being your exact word—warrior. I have this sense that your mother is sending you someone." Her eyes were bright with excitement.

Allie's heart raced. "Maybe she's sending me a CDA agent."

"Those guys are ex–Special Ops. That'd do the trick," Sam said.

Tabby whispered, "I'm not Brie, not by a long shot, but should I get my cards?"

Allie tensed. Tabby was gifted with the Tarot. She didn't have Brie's incredible Sight, but the cards usually spoke to her. "Use mine."

A moment later, Tabby had laid out a simple seven-card spread. While Allie was familiar with the cards, she never read them like Tabby, but she saw the Knight of Swords. "Is that him?" she asked quietly, the hairs rising on her neck as she looked at the knight on his white charger, sword in hand.

Tabby looked up. "No. That's him." She pointed to the Emperor. He had been dealt upside down.

Allie's eyes widened. "Are you sure?"

"This spread is about him, Allie—and it is Fate." She pointed. "Five of these cards are from the Major Arcana."

Allie trembled. "I see that."

"Someone is coming from the past—not your past. There is another woman here, and she's hurt. The man is older, with great authority. He has power and faith, and his quest is Justice." She added, "Allie, he is blessed."

Allie breathed. It was hard to believe that her golden warrior would be an older man. "Is the other woman my mother? Is my mother hurt?" Had her mother become trapped between worlds? She'd heard it was possible and that might explain her odd visit.

"I don't know who this other woman is, but like the Knight of Swords, she is a bridge between you and this man. She is very important to you both. She's come up as the Queen of Cups. Allie? Your life is about to be turned upside down." Tabby pointed at a card showing the Tower, which was being struck by lightning, people jumping from it. It was next to the Death card.

Every interpretation claimed the Death card did not symbolize death. Most readers refused to read literal death in the cards, but not Tabby. In her world, the Death card was just that, if juxtaposed correctly to other cards. "Does someone die?" Allie wasn't chilled—the innocent died every day. Death was a fact of life.

"Someone dies," Tabby whispered seriously. She pointed at the Sun, lying beneath Death. "But from the ashes, comes a new day."

Their gazes locked.

Brianna stepped into the room, clad in a shapeless black pantsuit.

Allie started.

Brianna didn't smile. She walked over to them and stared at the reversed Emperor. "He is here."

IT WAS MIDNIGHT when Allie stepped outside onto the flag-stone patio by the pool. She'd had enough of the fund-raiser. She didn't give a damn about politics except when the politicians fucked up and the little guy suffered because of it.

She'd stolen out, leaving Brian at the bar with Tabby and a few other guests, not having had a chance to really talk with him. She had a rare headache, and knew she was still off from last night.

She wanted to get past the guests who were lingering at the brilliantly lit-up pool without being waylaid. She crossed the lawns, leaving the pool and her father's guests behind, thinking about her mother, the golden warrior and Brie's stunning statement. She paused by the split-rail fence so she could watch their Thoroughbreds grazing under the moon-light. Was her golden warrior really present?

Was her mother sending someone to her, someone to help her in her ambition to heal those in suffering?

Allie smiled almost sadly. On the day of her death, as if she'd known she was going to pass, Elizabeth Monroe had asked Allie to make vows. She'd sworn to keep her powers secret and worship as she'd been raised, in her mother's ancient religion. And she had sworn to never turn her back on any suffering creature, great or small, human or beast, if it was Innocent.

Her father hadn't ever gotten over his wife's death. Her father was a Fortune 500 entrepreneur, as different from Eliz-abeth as anyone could be, and maybe that was why he'd loved her so. Unlike his friend Trump, he paid people to keep his name—and her and her stepbrother's—out of the news.

William Monroe hadn't remarried, although he had many model girlfriends.

Allie loved her mogul father, but didn't understand him very well. She had learned long ago not to let her father see her spiritual side, just as Elizabeth had hidden it from him when she was alive. He didn't have a clue that she was a Healer. He expected her to serve on various boards and marry Brian or someone just like him. Allie didn't mind being on the Board of Directors of the Elizabeth Foundation, which gave away huge sums of money to philanthropies and charities with her direction. She'd barely made it through high school, and while healing could easily be a full-time job, she didn't dare do so openly. She was the Monroe heiress, and the media watched her pretty closely. She had to be careful, always.

She had to pretend to fit in with everybody in his world when she didn't really fit in at all, except with Sam, Tabby and Brie—and the evil monsters who wanted to murder them all. Allie sighed, staring at the grazing horses. Even in bed with a great guy like Brian, she had to pretend to be something she was not. Allie was certain her father suspected that his wife had been far more than your average socialite; she was determined he'd never guess the truth about his daughter. But hiding out most of the time was *hard*.

And then she felt Brian, even before he called her name.

She shoved her brooding aside. Brian was approaching and she smiled at him, hoping Tabby would put a love spell on him really soon. He was going to be hurt and that went against her very nature. Unfortunately her sex drive was too high for her to avoid men and be celibate.

"Hey. Are you okay? First you split on me last night and tonight you've been quiet. You're never quiet."

Allie hesitated. "I have a headache. Are you still mad about last night?"

"You cut and ran, Allie," he said quietly, but not with accusation.

"I couldn't sleep so I went out for a drive." That was, she thought, a part of the truth.

His gaze was searching. "You're an amazing woman, Allie." He hesitated. "It's not happening, is it?"

He knows, she thought, saddened but relieved. She touched his arm. "I am awful at relationships, Brian. They never last. It's not you. It's me. I'm not like other women. I've never been in love."

He shook his head. "That makes you even more desirable."

It was time to tell him it was over, she thought. But then Allie tensed. *A huge power had settled around them, hot and male.*

She was stunned. She had never felt such power in her life. The power wasn't dark or demonic. It was pure and white—but it was not a healing power, for it was charged with testosterone. It was aggressive.

Stunned, she tried to see across the pasture, past the horses, into the night. *The power was holy. It came from her gods.* But hadn't Tabby said he had faith—that he was blessed? A terrible excitement consumed her.

And then she saw his aura.

Orange and crimson burned, powerful and bright, and she saw the man at last. The world around them vanished. Brian was gone, the horses disappeared, it was only her and him and the night. *She had found her golden warrior.*

And that was *exactly* what he was—the golden warrior she'd envisioned earlier, except he wasn't naked. He wore a pale tunic and boots, his thighs bare, along with two swords and a plaid, which was pinned over one shoulder. *He was a Highlander.* He could have stepped out of *Braveheart.*

His gaze unwavering on her, he started to approach.

No, he had stepped out of time, she somehow thought. Allie trembled, her heart accelerating so wildly she felt faint. There was so much power emanating from him, and finally he was bathed in moonlight. Allie breathed hard. He was even better than she had dreamed. Big, bronzed, beautiful.

Their gazes met and locked.

"That guy's a loon. Let's go." Brian took her arm.

But the man's gaze held hers and Allie didn't even feel Brian's grasp; instead, she felt desire fist in her gut. His silver gaze widened as if he was startled by her somehow, too.

Then his face hardened. "Lady Ailios," he stated, using an old Gaelic version of her name, speaking with a heavy brogue. "Dinna fear. MacNeil has sent me. T'is time."

His words washed through her with such warmth she realized he was attempting to enchant her. But she didn't mind. She smiled at him. "Okay."

His gaze narrowed with suspicion.

"I am not afraid of you," Allie whispered.

And she felt the dark coming. She froze—and he half-turned, stiffening. She knew he was sensing them, too.

A cloud turned the moon bloodred.

The warrior said firmly, in a tone of command, "Ailios. Go into the house with yer man." And as he spoke, she saw his aura erupt in a blast of more intense red and gold light. It was savage determination, explosive and hot; it was the battle readiness of a warrior.

But Allie wasn't going anywhere. "Are you kidding?" Allie cried. Real concern for Brian began. He'd get hurt if he stayed to fight. She whirled. "Hey." She smiled and pressed close. "I know this guy from high school. Yes, he's weird, but he's harmless." She could barely believe such a lie. "I know we have to finish our conversation. Let me get his number and I'll meet you in my room. Bring a bottle of Dom," she added with another smile.

Brian's eyes widened. "I don't like leaving you with him, Allie. But we do need to talk."

Allie wanted him to rush off and she almost hopped up and down. "He's on his way to a costume party at the Grussmans' in Bridge Hampton."

He stared suspiciously at her.

"Go to her room an' take her with ye. Go now," Mr. To-Die-For said.

And a terrible chill fell.

"Allie, let's go." Brian took her arm, clearly enchanted.

Allie tried to pull free but failed, for she was too small to succeed. "I am *not* going," she told the golden warrior, their gazes locked. "I will fight, too. I'll help!"

His eyes widened incredulously. "Ye think to fight?"

And black clouds filled the space between them.

The chill became arctic.

The warrior seized her, pulling her behind his huge body as if he meant to be her human shield. The demons formed, all blond and perfect. They were the highest level of diabolical power. Allie took a stiletto from her garter as one demon was flung backward by the Scot's energy blast. Allie was jubilant—he had the kind of power the demons had! She tried to step past him as Brian was thrown to his back by a demon. But more energy was being hurled at them and she was flung back herself, landing hard on the grass. For one moment, pain exploded in her back, and she was stunned. Then she rallied and looked up and saw the golden warrior, sword in hand, behead two demons almost simultaneously. Only one demon remained—somehow, while she'd been flung backward, he'd vanquished the third.

Allie got up. *He was like a frigging superhero, and just what the world needed.* She wanted to jump and cheer but she saw Brian, lying facedown in the grass.

The single remaining demon was almost as tall and muscular as the warrior, but he wore long, dark robes—like a friar or a monk. Allie was certain he'd come from a past era, too. He murmured, "Ruari Dubh, ciamar a tha thu?" He grinned. *Black Royce, how are you?*

Allie crept closer, grasping the knife, understanding every word of the Gaelic the demon spoke, although she had only ever translated the prayers bequeathed her by Elizabeth. Brian wasn't dead, but he was hurt, bleeding internally, and his life was compromised. Rage engulfed her. She was not going to let him die, too.

The demon looked at her. "Hallo, a Ailios. Latha math dhulbh."

"Fuck you," Allie cried, and she lunged past the warrior, intending to stab the demon in the eye if she could. It would not be the first time she had blinded a demon, at least partially.

But the golden warrior seized her arm, pulling her back into his embrace where she writhed furiously, wanting a chance to murder the demon. "Stay still," he roared at her. "Or do ye wish to die?"

The blond demon laughed at Allie. "Latha math andrasda." He vanished.

Allie stopped struggling and began shaking wildly instead. *Goodbye for now.* What did that mean?

As sick with fear as she was for Brian, she was shockingly aware of being in the warrior's thick, impossibly strong arms. His body was huge and hard and powerfully male—and she felt a very large package stirring beneath her.

She closed her eyes—she had to heal Brian. It was hard, because her body began screaming at her, delicious sensation rushing across her skin, inflaming every fiber of her being. "Let me go so I can help Brian," she said hoarsely.

He released her.

She met his hot, glittering gaze and that fist slammed her again, hollowing her more acutely than ever before. And he knew. A slight, smug smile tilted the otherwise still line of his mouth.

He wouldn't be so smug in another hour, she thought. Because he was going to have the time of *his* life.

She turned and ran to Brian and dropped down beside him, reaching for him, flooding him with her white healing light. Even as intensely focused as she was, she was acutely aware of the warrior as she felt him as he came to stand behind her. Instantly she knew he was standing guard over her so she could heal.

Her heart thundered. When this night was over, she was going to thank all the gods for answering her prayers.

"Can ye heal him?"

She swallowed. "I'll die trying." But her temples throbbed. It almost hurt to heal Brian. Releasing her white light felt like pulling out her own teeth, one by one.

He was silent, but not for long. "Are ye hurt?"

She panted and took a short break. "Last night...I got hurt." She glanced up at him.

He did not seem happy to hear that.

She breathed deeply and turned back to Brian, flooding him with her light. Brian's life flickered and blazed.

Allie was swept by an intense wave of dizziness. She felt the land tilt wildly and she was dismayed. The huge warrior knelt, embracing her from behind and holding her steady against his chest.

She gasped. His scent was overwhelming. Man, sex, power, the clean Highland mist and more sex. His body could have been honed from steel, and the thighs beneath her ass were even better than a soccer player's. This man rode horses and ran hills.

Allie opened her eyes and shifted to meet his gaze. The night had changed. It was charged. She was weak but she needed this man—and she wasn't thinking about a partner to combat crime. Oh, no. In fact, suddenly, strangely, he was all she could think about, and she sensed he was using his powers of enchantment again.

His eyes hot, he moved away from her, standing. "Who are you?" she whispered, forcing her gaze to his eyes.

But Brian sat up. "Allie?" He was alarmed. "What happened?"

Allie jerked with dismay. She'd been so mesmerized by the warrior she'd forgotten about Brian.

The Highlander stared at Brian. "Go to the house. I'll bring her soon enough."

Brian stood and left without a word.

Allie met his gray gaze and this time, she knew her eyes were wide. "It's all true, right? You're one of them...a warrior who can travel through time...with superpowers...defending mankind."

His gaze dropped to her mouth, and it slid lower, to her breasts, which were barely covered by the corset-style, push-up bodice of the evening gown. "I dinna ken," he said softly. But his silver eyes were hot and an arrogant smile played on that incredible, chiseled face.

And a shadow fell over the night.

Allie glanced up in alarm; the moon was gone again, covered by black clouds. She tensed, glancing at the pool, but it remained brightly lit. It didn't matter. Huge and heavy, blackness swiftly approached them again.

Incredulous, she looked up at the warrior. She was too weak to fight more demons now! She scrambled to her feet, not as steadily as she'd have liked, as an arctic chill fell.

Fear and anger warred in her heart. Allie looked at the warrior. He looked at her and she knew something bad—really bad—was about to happen. "I'm okay," she lied. "Where's my knife?"

He shook his head, jaw flexed. "Ye canna fight again," he said firmly. His grasp tightened. "Ye need to hold me tight."

Allie was about to say that was fine by her, when they were flung across the pastures, over the horses, into space. If she could have, Allie would have screamed. Instead she gasped as her body was ripped apart, into shreds of hair, tissue and skin.

CHAPTER TWO

Carrick Castle, Morvern, Scotland—September 5, 2007

HE WOULD NEVER GET used to the pain.

Leaping through time was like being tortured on the rack, and even though he'd leapt a thousand times, he still fought not to give in to the urge to cry out like a woman would. It was like having the skin flayed from muscle and bone, like having one's organs ripped outward by a human hand. Fire burned inside him. Landing, there was a final explosion of pain, and then there was a stunning darkness.

He held her tightly in his arms, briefly left powerless by the leap through time. His ability to sense evil was so well honed, however, that he knew they were not in danger. He focused on recovering his powers, given to him centuries ago by the Ancients, when the old gods despaired for mankind's Fate and decided to create a race of warriors to defend them. From experience, he knew that in a moment or two he would recoup.

But the Healer was small, soft, warm and womanly in his arms.

He'd never leapt with a woman before—much less one like this.

Although she was unconscious, he could not forget her stunning white light, the purest power he had ever sensed or seen. And to make matters far worse, she was as stunningly beautiful as she was powerful, with a tiny but lush body; that dark, silken hair, and dark eyes that seemed to look into his most secret thoughts. Her buttocks were soft and full, spooned into him, and he rapidly swelled.

It was usual to want a woman in every possible way after the leap. Every Master had many godlike powers; the greatest power of all was the ability to take life at any time, from anyone and anything, like a god. Taking some of the force of life from her would instantly restore his powers. And taking power was also pleasurable. In fact, there was no rapture like that which came from power.

He looked at the woman and knew that her white power, swelling his veins, his body, would be like no other.

But he was a master at self-control. Except in war or when facing mortal death, "taking" was forbidden. The young Masters were always tempted to test the Ancients, to taste power and to experience the sublime rapture of La Puissance. He had been upholding his sacred vows for over eight centuries and he would not touch this one's healing essence, ever.

Royce closed his eyes tightly, more aroused than before, but determined to ignore it. And then any internal battle was over. He felt all of his extraordinary strength settle over him, in him, through him, in one vast wave. Breathing naturally again, he could look at her face.

He stared, his heart lurching anew at the sight of her beauty. *She was so beautiful, so pure that he felt the Ancients near her—and she was so terribly brave.* She had tried to fight the deamhanain as if a warrior. She would never be a warrior—it was a physical impossibility, for she was so small. Yet she had intended to attack Moffat with a knife!

Too well, he could recall his horror in that moment.

And now the question loomed—had Moffat leapt to the future to hunt him, or did he hunt Elasaid's daughter, a powerful Healer and great prize in her own right?

Moffat had been an annoyance for centuries. Whenever Royce had an interest at stake, whether in land, finance or politics, Moffat took the opposing side. Periodically Moffat's soldiers attacked his lands, his men, and once, an innocent village. Royce's retribution was always swift and severe—he'd besieged the Cathedral where Moffat held reign as bishop with bombards and battering rams, and had destroyed three of its four walls. That had been decades ago. The Regent Albany had ordered him to cease before he'd beaten down the Cathedral itself.

Three months ago, in the darkest winter days of late January, the stakes had increased. Royce had encountered a deamhan in the throes of taking life from an Innocent— Moffat's new and favorite lover. He'd vanquished Kaz with little effort, but too late to save the Innocent's life. And ever since, Moffat had been enraged, harassing his people at every turn, bringing death and destruction as he could, without arousing the King's complete ire. That is, he did not dare openly declare war.

It was too soon to know Moffat's intent. The answer would eventually become clear.

She stirred in his arms. His body remained hot and hard, but he ignored it easily enough. Slowly, he looked around.

He had leapt forward a single day into the future, to his own home in Scotland. Although she was a powerful Healer, he'd felt her weakness and pain the moment she'd begun to heal her lover. Aware of her being somehow hurt and compromised, he'd made certain to only leap forward slightly, hoping to lessen the torment for her.

He had never been to the future before, as there had been

no need, and a Master wasn't allowed to leap for his own pleasure or gain. He was in the Great Hall at Carrick Castle, but he barely recognized his home. Everything had changed. There were so many fine furnishings, many of which he did not understand, such as the posts with cloth heads on the small tables. Even the rugs and paintings were different. The room was beautiful—the kind of home his friend Aidan would enjoy. Who was lord of Carrick now? He would not bother to furnish this room so luxuriously. Or would he? For there was a collection of swords on one wall, and he recognized every one. They belonged to him. If there was a new lord and master now, why did that man own his weapons?

He considered the possibility that he was still lord of Carrick and earl of Morvern. If so, it would mean he had lived another five hundred and seventy-seven years. He didn't know how he felt about the prospect. But the Code was clear. It forbade in the most certain terms a Master leaping forward or back in time to a place where he could encounter his younger or older self. He felt certain no good would come if he walked into the corridor and encountered his future self there. If he remained the lord of Carrick, he must exercise caution.

He glanced at the woman, Ailios, again. Her thick, almost black hair was covering her cheek and without thinking, he slid his hand beneath it and pushed it back over her shoulder. Instantly more lust began. It was impossible not to keep thinking about sex and pleasure with such a woman in his arms. So much desire was almost inexplicable—and he sensed it could even threaten his vows.

No man would bed this woman once and walk away. Yet that was how he lived. A Master must refuse all attachments, and he had learned that lesson the hard way, when the deamhanain had captured and tortured his wife.

He should leave this one alone.

He lifted her and stood, then glanced into the corridor and saw that it was empty. He started down it, intending to go up to the North Tower, where he had his rooms in the fifteenth century. A housemaid appeared, coming down the stairs. Royce tensed, awaiting her scream of alarm, but she smiled at him, pausing to curtsy. "My lord."

He smiled grimly back. *He was still the lord of Carrick.* Had he somehow sensed he would be alive on this day in the future? Had he thought to take her to his *future* self?

Satisfaction began, hard, primitive and male.

He strode into the bedchamber, laying her in the center of a large canopied bed with no hangings, which pleased him. His chamber had hardly changed. The bed was new—larger, and more convenient, as sometimes he enjoyed several women at once—but two chests had survived the centuries, as had the shield on the wall. The thronelike chairs in front of the hearth were new but their fashion was not, and he approved of the severe beige-and-brown-striped fabric covering them. He liked the brown and black rug on the floor. It looked like an animal skin, but it was wool.

He stared at her now, as if enchanted.

This one could tempt the Pope and seduce the devil.

For not only were her face and figure so perfect, she knew her allure. She knew the gown she wore revealed her every curve and hollow; it thrust her bosom out, it cupped and caressed the plump mound of her sex, and nothing was left to the imagination. She had chosen it to increase her beauty. And he felt certain she wore nothing beneath it, not a single undergarment, to make a man insane with his desire.

His heart thundered and so did the pulse in his loins. He reminded himself that she was unconscious and ill—at least for now. But sooner, not later, she would wake up. He needed to have control and when she did awaken, he needed to be gone.

He tore his gaze away from her full, bowed mouth and for the first time saw the portrait on the table beside the bed. It was a perfect rendering.

He picked up the small framed portrait. He stood with his nephew, Malcolm, Malcolm's wife, Claire, and Aidan. He stared at himself with some curiosity. He looked very much the same—hard, distant, bronzed from the sun—but his hair was shorn like a penitent monk's. He wore the modern style of clothes—a black, shapeless surcote and black, equally shapeless stockings. He was not smiling.

Royce looked closer. His eyes held no light—whatever he was thinking or feeling, it was impossible to tell. Although he appeared but a human of forty or so, his stance was that of a man ready for battle. Even in the dark, somber, modern fashion, he seemed dangerous.

Apparently his life would not change.

He remained a soldier of the gods.

Then he looked at his nephew, Malcolm, and his wife and half brother. Everyone was smiling.

They were all happy, five hundred and seventy-seven years into the future. He was happy for them.

He put the portrait down, wishing he hadn't been in it. The future felt bleak and loomed as if endless. It was all the same. Nothing would ever change. Good and evil, battle and death. For every vanquished deamhan, another would rise in its stead.

Then, slowly, he turned and gazed down at the woman.

Everything had changed, hadn't it?

He was accustomed to a hard, ready cock—but not to the wild beating of his heart. It was almost as if the floor he stood on was tilting, and wouldn't ever be quite level again.

He looked back at the framed portrait. The man in that

rendering, the man who was over fourteen hundred years old, did not appear to have a single weakness, character failing, or human flaw. The man in the portrait had been at war for so long, only the warrior remained, and that was why he looked into his eyes and saw nothing at all. In the future, he would be able to bed the woman and walk away; he would also give his life to protect her.

Oddly he felt savagely satisfied.

She would be safe here.

And in five hundred and seventy-seven years, he'd have the pleasure of taking her to bed, of pleasuring her time and again, of watching her come, feeling her come—and coming inside her, again and again.

He'd learned patience long ago. He'd wait.

Royce gave her one last look, and leapt back to the fifteenth century, where he belonged.

ALLIE AWOKE, cocooned in down, aware of being in one of the most comfortable beds she'd ever slept in. She had been so deeply asleep, she felt groggy. So many different birds were chirping outside the window, she became confused. She blinked against warm, strong sunlight, searching for the familiar sound of the ocean echoing on the beach, but she did not hear it.

She was widely awake, staring up at the unfamiliar beige silk pleats of an unfamiliar canopy over the very unfamiliar bed she lay in. Her heart lurched and she jerked to sit up. She took in the bed, with its brown paisley coverings and striped sheets, the fleur-de-lis pillow cases, the larger brown velvet pillows behind them. Her gaze lifted, bewildered, and she saw the entire sparsely furnished stone chamber—and it hit her, hard. She was not at her home in South Hampton.

She was still clad in the sea-foam evening gown; now, she saw her silver sandals on the floor.

The events of the night rushed over her—she'd been at her father's fund-raiser and a powerful warrior had appeared, thwarting the demonic attack.

She breathed in hard. Last night had been *real*. A warrior from another time, blessed by the gods, had come to help her fight the demons. Her mother had told her to embrace her destiny and trust a golden Master. Tabby had seen him coming, powerful and blessed, from the past. *The CDA rumors were true.* She trembled with excitement. She couldn't wait to tell Tabby, Sam and Brie.

Ye need to hold on to me tight.

Allie gasped, because the last thing she recalled was being flung across the pastures and horses, the velocity ripping her body apart.

Where was she? She was obviously in someone's ancestral home—she had toured Europe and Britain extensively enough to know an old manor or castle when she was in one. Allie threw the covers aside, stumbling from the bed to the window. The panes were golden glazed glass. She jerked hard on the latch, and the moment she opened the window, she breathed in crisp, scented air that was unmistakable.

She was in the Highlands.

She stared out of the window, stunned. She was on a high floor, and she saw castle walls to her left, ending at a round tower. She realized she was in another, similar corner tower. The castle itself was perched on the top of a high hill, and she saw the sparkling blue waters of a loch or river far below. Across the body of water were the barren, harsh hills and higher mountains of the Highlands. Clouds shrouded the peaks.

Her mind raced with dizzying speed. She'd been to

Scotland many times, but not until after her mother's death. Her mother had been born in Kintyre, her father's parents in Glasgow and Aberdeen, so curiosity had brought her to the land of her ancestors. She was definitely in the Highlands now; she just wasn't sure where.

Calm down, she told herself, but it wasn't fear which clouded her mind. It was excitement.

Her golden warrior had brought her here. But the plaid he wore marked him as a Highlander, too.

She stared out of her window, at the lake or river below, and her senses took over. Allie realized she was looking south, but slowly, she leaned out of the window and gazed to the west.

She breathed harder now.

The magnetic pull was familiar and timeless.

The Ancients were near—in the west.

Allie trembled. Every time she'd visited Scotland, she'd been drawn to the small, quaint island of Iona as if a nail to a magnet. There, she'd wandered the ruins of the late medieval abbey and the Benedictine monastery, aware that the ground below had been hallowed by the great St. Columba, who had raised the very first monastery on the island's shores. She'd become entirely unaware of the other tourists. Beneath her feet, the ground had throbbed. And above her head, whispers from another time, another era, seemed to beckon her. She felt as though if she reached up into the sky, she might pull someone down to stand beside her; or if she reached into the ground, she might lift some past person up.

Later, lying awake in her bed at the Highland Cottage Hotel on Mull, she had laughed at herself for almost believing that she had heard people from another time. But she was certain of the power and purity of the ground itself. Iona was a holy place, even if she was one of the few people to realize it.

Now, Allie felt the same magnetic pull. She knew, beyond any doubt, that the small island lay somewhere to the west and that it was not far away.

She turned back to the room, regarding it closely again. Her warrior had been a medieval Highlander, but she was in the present—except for two antique chests, the room was a modern one. There was a cheetah-print wool rug on the floor, two impressive armchairs before the fireplace and she'd bet a small fortune the bedding was Ralph Lauren. She crossed the room and thrust the bathroom door open.

It was beige marble from floor to wall, the ceiling mirrored. This was *his* bathroom. Everything about it, from the sunken marble tub, surrounded by a wall of glass windows, to the plush brown towels, was masculine. She stared at the sink where an electric razor was plugged into the wall, alongside an Oral-B toothbrush.

Allie could scent him now and she felt dizzy, overcome by his power and masculinity. She opened the mirrored cabinet, beyond curiosity now—compelled. She scanned the contents, noting all the usual items, and saw that he used Boss cologne. She almost smiled at that. She closed the door and then jerked it quickly open again. She couldn't help herself. She looked at every single item inside, but didn't see condoms.

What are you doing? she asked herself, her mouth dry, her heart pounding. She closed the door and backed out of the bathroom, trying to get her bearings. It was impossible, because she was too consumed with her warrior now.

She forced her mind to work. Her golden warrior had *not* been in costume. But she was in a man's bathroom, and that man was as contemporary as she was.

What did that mean?

A quick look into the closet confirmed that she was in a modern man's room, and that he had impeccable taste. She riffled through Armani suits, expensive button-down shirts and elegant silk ties; she saw Gucci loafers and Polo Tees. But the jeans were no-nonsense Levi's and he wore tighty whities…

Her heart exploded at a few very interesting, tempting and graphic mental images far too racy for any Jockey ad. She was off track again. She could not resist walking over to the bedside table and looking in the single drawer. No condoms. Did this guy live like a monk?

Stop it, she told herself, her heart accelerating impossibly. The real question was, why was she in a modernized castle? Her warrior was the real deal. He'd had supernatural powers. He'd been able to use energy the way the demons did. He could sense evil the way she did. And he'd used that sword like a medieval knight, making movie action heroes seem inept.

Had she imagined being hurled across the pastures?

She walked over to the other bedside table and searched it, with no results. And the photo caught her eye.

Allie picked it up and saw her warrior and was so relieved she sank onto the bed. *It was him.* She felt as if she'd just found her long-lost best friend—no, her long-lost lover. He had a buzz cut in the photo, but he was still the hottest hunk she'd ever laid eyes on. And he looked as strong and capable as he was, like a commando who wouldn't think twice about crossing enemy lines to take out a terrorist leader.

His friends were drop-dead gorgeous, too. The pretty woman was clearly with one of his friends, not that she was really worried about competition.

She stared more closely and her confusion renewed itself.

He looked different. He was only in his early thirties, but in this photo looked ten years older. He seemed harder, as if he'd lived through so much and had no soul left....

Damn it, had he been in costume after all?

The warrior who'd appeared last night had been a genuine überhero, but had he been from the present, in spite of the swords, the tunic, the boots?

A knock sounded softly on the door. From the light, tentative sound, she knew it was a woman outside the door. "Come in." She glanced at the photo a third time. *That was her warrior; was he medieval or not?*

A plump woman in a domestic's uniform smiled at her, bearing a tray. Allie smelled the coffee and warm bread and realized she was starving. "His lordship didn't leave instructions. I must say, I was surprised to realize we had a guest." But she smiled very pleasantly. "I am Mrs. Farlane."

His lordship, Allie thought, realizing he was titled. A nice little perk. "I'm Allie." She smiled. "My visit wasn't really planned. I mean, one minute we're at a party in South Hampton, the next, here we are! Thank God for jets," she added quickly. This woman couldn't possibly know her employer traveled through time and fought the evil monsters of the night.

Mrs. Farlane placed the tray down on the ottoman by the bed. "Lord Royce doesn't have a jet. I hadn't realized he was in South Hampton. He told me he'd be in Edinburgh for a few days." She seemed unhappy to be out of the loop.

His name was Royce! Of course it was, for the demon had called him Ruari, the Gaelic version of such a name. "My dad has an Astra." How could Royce be in Edinburgh when they'd been at her Long Island summer home last night? Or had she been sleeping for days? "I'm sorry, what day is it?"

Mrs. Farlane gave her a queer look. "It's the sixth, dear. I didn't see any suitcase."

She had only slept for half of a night. "It was very spontaneous. I'm afraid everything I have with me is on my back." Clothes, Allie thought, her heart sinking. "Um, where exactly am I?"

Mrs. Farlane blinked.

Allie said quickly, "Royce is a tease! He said he was taking me to the Highlands, and that it was a surprise!"

"We're at Carrick Castle, my dear, in Morvern—a bit north and west of Glasgow."

Allie breathed hard—she had been right. "Iona is to the west."

"Yes, and it's a lovely island, just a few hours by car and ferry."

Allie's heart raced. She'd make a detour before she went home—whenever that was. "When will Royce be back?"

"In the early evening."

She went still, except for her heart, which now thundered with unbearable excitement. He was coming back and she couldn't wait to see him. "Are there any shops nearby? I am going to need a change of clothes." She realized she wanted to find an outfit that would knock him senseless. She had never worried over what to wear to impress a man before.

"The best shopping in Scotland is in Glasgow. Tom can drive you. His lordship pays him a fine wage to be his chauffeur, but then he drives himself everywhere." She shook her head. "All those cars. How can a man own so many cars? He's got three garages down the hill!"

"My best friend is that way with shoes," Allie said. She'd have to call Tabby. She turned to the silver pot and poured coffee and took a sip, black. It was heaven—and that night would be heaven, too.

Every inch of her quickened. She was as excited—and as nervous—as a teenager. It was absurd. It was wonderful!

But she did need a change of clothes and she didn't have her purse. On the other hand, she was very recognizable. Designers often begged her to *take* their clothes and were always sending her items, like the gown she was wearing now. She refused to spend ridiculous sums on clothes and accessories, not when that money could go to charity. Maybe she could find a new designer and buy what she needed on credit. She'd figure it out, one way or another.

But there was one more problem.

Mrs. Farlane, however, solved it. "My daughter is about your size, dear. She's fifteen, but you can borrow some jeans and a T-shirt. Tom will show you the best shops. As his lordship's guest, our merchants will be thrilled to help you."

Allie wanted to hug her. "Thank you so much." Then she gave in and embraced the woman, who started and then smiled.

IT WAS ALMOST seven o'clock, and Allie's stomach was in knots. She was sipping a glass of white wine in the great room, clad in a beautiful shamrock-green jersey dress that skimmed her body, one she hoped Royce would really appreciate. She hadn't had any trouble making her purchases. Her driver was well-known, and a few merchants had eagerly charged items to Royce's account, while others had given her what she wanted. She had been recognized by everyone and when she got home, she would send thank-you notes and checks. She'd also called Tabby, but she hadn't been home, and Allie had left a message that she hoped was coherent.

She felt like she was fifteen and about to go on her first date.

But considering she had never felt this way about anyone, maybe that was normal.

Barely able to stand the anticipation, she stared across the large room and out the windows, into the cobbled courtyard outside. As she did, a small, dark sports car appeared from the gatehouse, clearly having just entered the castle walls. Allie stood, her heart turning over hard.

He was driving a Ferrari; of course he was.

He probably had a Lamborghini, too.

She couldn't breathe.

The car stopped and the door opened; she saw her warrior get out.

Desire hollowed her. She felt faint.

His unmistakable aura blazed, red and gold, with some blue and green, the aura of a powerful warrior blessed by the Ancients. This time, it was bursting with sexual heat.

He was clad all in black, in a fitted tee and easy trousers. As he closed the car door, he glanced at the window—and Allie knew he was looking into the room and right at her.

Allie didn't move. She felt his excitement—or was she feeling hers? *Hurry,* she thought.

He started around the car and vanished from her view. A moment later, he appeared on the threshold of the hall and his desire made her feel weak and faint. It was explosive. And there was no doubt. *It was him.*

His silver eyes locked with hers, blazing.

She wet her lips to say hello, but then said nothing at all.

"My lord, when will you be sitting down to supper with Miss Monroe?"

Allie couldn't look away from him. He was as big and hunky as she recalled, maybe six foot three, the feather-weight tee clinging to his broad shoulders and sculpted chest and to his hard, tight torso. Beneath the short sleeves, his biceps bulged. His hips were small, but what was encased below was not. Fabric bulged and rippled. Allie swallowed.

He kept his gaze on her. "Are ye hungry?"

Allie shook her head.

His gaze glittering, never looking away, he said to the housekeeper, "Ye may retire for the night."

His hot gaze moved over her dress and her legs, lingering on her brightly painted pink toes and the pair of retro platforms she had bought. The shoes added five inches to her diminutive height. Then it lifted. "Hallo a Ailios," he murmured.

No tone could be more arousing. She felt her heart trying to push its way out of her chest. She felt heat and liquid slipping down her bare thighs. "Hi…Royce."

He strode forward, into the brighter light of the great room.

She now realized he had the same buzz cut as in the photo. Some confusion began. "I…charged a few things.… I hope you don't mind."

He smiled seductively. "I hope ye charged that dress."

She nodded. "You cut your hair."

His eyes flickered.

But now, she looked from the marine-style cut to his eyes—and the lines emanating from them. She tensed. He was the same man who had helped her fight off a demonic attack last night, but he looked older—or had she imagined him looking younger in the dark of the night? And he was modern after all. "I don't understand," she whispered. "Last night, I thought you were a medieval man."

He paused before her. "It dinna matter. I'm the lord o' Carrick, Ailios. And tonight, yer mine."

It was hard to think after such a confident statement, not

when he stood an inch from her, not when she knew she could shift her body oh so slightly and be in his arms. But he was not, exactly, responding to her question.

She searched his gaze and he stared back, with a promise that told her she was going to heaven really soon. "You helped me last night in South Hampton, didn't you?"

He took her wineglass from her and set it down on the table behind him. "Ye talk too much."

She wet her lips. "I almost thought…I'd wake up in an earlier time."

He didn't laugh. Staring into her eyes, he said softly, "Aye. I helped ye, but not last night." And he clasped both of her shoulders, his hands large, strong and unyielding, like the man she somehow knew he was. Every fiber in her tightened. She could barely stand it.

"I helped ye…six centuries ago."

Allie tried to understand him. How could he mean what he had said? But his grasp had tightened and he pulled her close, so her breasts were crushed by his rock-hard chest. His body was aroused and strained for hers. She began to blank mentally as his massive erection brushed her abdomen. "Oh."

"I have waited a long time for this moment," he said bluntly.

Her gaze lifted to his.

"I have waited five hundred an' seventy-seven years for ye, lass."

CHAPTER THREE

HE COULD NOT BELIEVE she was finally there with him, in his home, in his arms. Her memory had haunted him for the past five centuries, a confirmation that he had been correct to leave her in the future and return to the fifteenth century alone. She was the sexiest woman he'd ever beheld, but there was so much more. Her pure white power brought forth an intense desperation; even now, he felt her shining light warming him when he had been cold inside for so long.

He moved his hands to her face, held her head steady and finally, after so many years, he kissed her.

He was already swollen and hot. His body clamored to move inside hers and it needed release. But just then he was stunned. All he could think about was the taste of her lips, the caress of her tongue and the warmth seeping from her to him. His heart beating almost frantically, he drank from her mouth. *Ailios.* And the deep, wet kiss just wasn't enough.

His body shrieked at him, but so did a part of him he never listened to. He wasn't sure if it was his heart or his soul. In another moment, he was going to take her to the heights of ecstasy, joining her there in orgasmic release after orgasmic release. But he almost wanted more. Her power already seemed to touch him, and it almost felt like a relief....

It was forbidden, of course. He wasn't going to touch her power, even if his bones felt old and in need of her healing. Nothing in him was broken. He was old, but powerful and strong. He had never broken the Code. He would not start now.

Her small hands on his waist, she trembled in his arms, kissing him back as frantically, as deeply, her mouth and teeth tearing at his. He felt how swollen and wet she was.

Her lust matched his and he was hardly surprised by the enormity of it for them both. He had known it would be this way. He could control her desire, if he wanted to—he'd learned that skill long ago—but he wasn't feeding her passion now. It belonged to her and her alone. He was savagely pleased.

Expanding even more, hugely aware of an impending release for them both, he slid his hands down her narrow, slim back and clasped her buttocks, lifting her high. He could feel her pleasure cresting and couldn't wait. He turned her against the nearest wall and with his thigh, pushed her right leg high.

She hooked her leg high up on his hip.

The wool of his trousers ripped.

He reached and jerked the zipper down, jerked the briefs apart. Her glazed gaze met his. "Ailios, I wish to show ye real pleasure."

"Hurry," she whispered, dazed, her palm on his cheek. Then she slid it under his T-shirt, caressing the slab of one of his large pectoral muscles.

As he gasped with desire, it crossed his mind that she deserved to be pleasured in bed. But he had her jersey skirt in his hand and he lifted it out of their way, all patience gone. He smiled at the sight of peach lace straining over wet, waxed flesh and he slipped his fingers past the G-string.

She cried out as he thumbed her soaking, throbbing lips. And he shifted, pushing the huge head of his penis against her, rubbing sensually back and forth. She clawed his back, panting, "Yes. Please!"

He was throbbing dangerously, on the precipice of release. He could make her come this way. He knew it—he felt it with his body, his mind. But it was too soon—and he controlled the cresting wave of her pleasure with his mind and refused to let it break.

She started to weep. Eyes wide, a plea formed there. *Why?*

He wanted to tell her that they had all night and she would have more pleasure than she'd ever known—so much she'd never think of any other man again. Instead, slowly, he pushed deep. Her pleasure doubled, intensified, roiled over them both. His pleasure surged. One more moment, he thought, and savagely satisfied, moving very deliberately, he controlled the cresting wave in her, allowing it to soar a bit higher, and then higher, bit by agonizing bit.

She called his name, panting, clawing his chest.

Sweat poured down his face and chest. And then he gave in.

"Ailios."

She met his gaze, panting and writhing, trying to ride him when he was the one riding her, satisfying her.

When he had her attention, he poured his power into her. She cried out—stunned—and he let the dam break.

She sobbed in ecstasy. He closed his eyes and drove hard over and over again, coming with her, encouraging her to come again. She did. He did. She shouted as he roared. He had waited so long…he would pleasure her like this, all night.

ALLIE LAY LIMP and exhausted in Royce's bed, acutely aware of her wildly pounding heart and the man who lay on his back beside her. Finally her mind started to work.

Was it really dawn? For pale gray light was slipping into the bedchamber.

Her heart refused to slow. She covered it with her hand. They had made love for hours—since early last evening— and for the first time in her life she was sated, oh, yes.

Royce hadn't tired, flagged, or even softened, not a single time.

She was a Healer but she was very human; clearly he was not. Because he'd climaxed as many times as she had, and she wasn't sure if she'd had dozens of orgasms or one single, endless one.

And she was pretty certain he'd had some kind of control over her orgasms, too.

She turned her head. "Tyrant," she whispered, smiling.

He lay on his back, too, but his breathing was slow and even, and he was staring at her. Their gazes locked.

And he smiled at her. It was a surprisingly soft look from such a hard man, and it changed his entire face. He became too beautiful for words. "Are ye pleased?"

She beamed and turned onto her side, aware of his gaze instantly moving to her breasts and belly and legs, before lifting. She laid her hand on his magnificent chest. She traced a frightening scar. "Very pleased. How can you even ask?"

Was he relieved? Surely he knew he was supersexed. He simply shrugged, as if indifferent, but his gaze was intense and searching. "Are ye pleased enough to break off with yer man?"

Allie was confused.

"Brian," he said softly.

Her eyes widened. She felt as if an entire lifetime had passed since the fund-raiser the other night. "He's not my man."

He absorbed that. Then, "Since when? Tonight?"

She grinned and rubbed his rock-hard pectoral muscle, then scraped her nails over his nipple. "I was going to break it off with him the night of the party."

He nodded at that.

Allie realized, in shock, that his large but flaccid member was stiffening. How was it possible?

"Yer touching me," he said softly, as if reading her mind.

"I want to touch you," she said, staring and stroking the tight skin over his ribs. "Who *are* you? What just happened isn't humanly possible."

He sat up against a number of pillows, another beautiful smile playing. "Aye. No man can bed a woman in such a way. Ye should remember that."

"As if any woman would ever forget!" Becoming serious, she sat up, too. She wanted to snuggle, but she didn't—this was too important. "You vanquished three demons the other night as if it were a piece of cake. But you used a sword as well as your energy, not a gun." Her mind began to really get into the game. "You said you waited five hundred–odd years for me." But hadn't Tabby said he was an *older* man?

He shrugged casually again. "Well, I'm a patient man."

"How old are you?"

"It doesna matter, Ailios."

But she was sorting it out. "Last night, in South Hampton, that was you, but younger, way younger—five hundred and seventy-seven years younger."

"Aye."

"Wow." Allie sat back against her pillows, stunned and uncertain as to the significance of having met him a day ago, when he had been almost six hundred years younger—when he had come from the fifteenth century—and their being together now, a day later for her, but five centuries later for him. She'd been apart from him for a day; he'd lived through almost six centuries. She had a million questions. "How many of you are there? Is the sex always like that? Are you immortal? Why do you guys keep such a low profile?"

His smile flickered brightly again. "Yer so young, so pretty, so passionate." He reached out and touched her cheek, then let his hand drift across her breast. Then he dropped it. "I am mortal. I will die one day."

Allie thought about that. "I worship the Ancients. And when I see your aura, I can feel their presence—they are with you. You are blessed. They favor you."

"Aye. Long ago, the gods wanted to save mankind from evil. They feared for their creation. They sent a great warrior goddess to the kings, an' men like me were born." He spoke as if it was an everyday occurrence and not a huge deal.

Allie laughed. "You don't mean that your mother is a goddess, do you?"

He gave her a look. "My grandmother is the great warrior goddess, Faola," he said softly.

But of course, Allie thought. He looked like a grandson of the gods. And how else could he screw all night like that? How else could he have the kind of energy to throw around that the demons had? "The demons are descended from Satan, aren't they?"

"Some, an' some are fallen Masters."

Her mother had told her to trust a golden Master. "Is that what you call yourself? A Master?"

"We're the Masters of Time, Ailios. I made my vows before the Brotherhood and God on Iona long ago. We exist to keep mankind safe an' to serve the Ancients."

Allie was intensely interested. "I have always been drawn

to Iona. Even today, the ground there is holy. Wow. I felt you—the Masters—every time I was there!"

"Ye have great powers. They'll become greater with time."

Allie barely heard. She shivered with excitement. "Sworn before God—meaning, sworn before the gods, plural?"

"Aye. T'is one an' the same." He smiled a little at her again, this time sliding his hand down her arm. "Defend God, Keep Faith, Protect Innocence—our vows are simple but strong. A Master serves God and Innocence, first an' last, always."

She snuggled up to his hard chest and lean torso now. "That almost sounds like a warning," she said, thinking about where she wanted to put her tongue.

His gaze blazed as if he sensed her intentions. He moved his large hand into her hair and grasped it.

Her heart went wild at the forceful gesture. But she was still and their gazes locked. "I'm not done," she said softly. He'd teased—even tortured—her all night. A little payback was in order.

He almost smiled. "Ye talk too much."

"Admit it—you love it."

"I'm nay fond of great conversation."

She slid herself halfway over his body. "Why are you guys so top-secret?"

He pulsed against her quad and sighed. "There's a Code. T'is vast an' even today, our scholars debate its many rules an' meanings. But some rules are clear. The Masters are secret, Ailios, the Brotherhood is secret, an' that is our law." He slid his hand down her back, cupped her buttock and hiked her into a very appropriate position. She gasped with pleasure; he grinned. "Do ye still wish to talk?"

It had become really difficult to think, but she whispered, "Did you control my orgasms last night?"

His eyes widened with innocence. "How can a man do that?" He grasped her waist and gave her a lazy, sensual look.

"Hmm...someone needs a comeuppance."

He gave in to a chuckle. "It's up, lass, and ye ken."

She sat on his hips and his eyes turned even lighter and brighter. "Why did the Ancients forbid your telling the world about who you are and what you do?"

He was now annoyed. Instead of answering her, he nuzzled her breasts and caught her nipple with his teeth. He tugged.

"Be good and I won't tease," Allie breathed.

He sighed. "The Code was written afore St. Columba, lass, an' I dinna ken the reasons behind it. But in past ages, 'was a grave heresy to consort with the old gods—an' to have godly powers. In that time, men were outlawed, excommunicated, hanged or burned for such sins. No Master then would walk openly. Today, we dinna walk openly, either."

Allie slid off of him, ignoring his surprise. This was too damned important. "We need you guys, desperately!" she cried, startling him anew. "Damn it, Royce, more of you guys need to be here, in the twenty-first century, helping us, helping Healers like me, even helping CDA! Forget the antiquated rules. It is so hard healing when I have to worry about another demonic attack behind my back. It's so hard watching so many innocent people die." She added grimly, "I can't save everyone by myself."

He was sitting, too, a magnificent sight. "Evil preys on the Innocent in every age, Ailios. Pleasure crimes have been sung about by the ancient bards an' there's a need for

Masters in the past, too. There are Masters in every time."
He added softly, his gaze locked with hers, "I'm sorry ye
have been alone so long."

Allie looked up at him and saw his intense, searching stare
and couldn't decide what it all meant. But there was so much
hope. The good guys had superheroes on their side, too.
Battles had been lost, but the war wasn't over, not by a long
shot.

And she wasn't alone anymore.

Her heart seemed to be singing a very happy song.

A seductive smile began. He said softly, "Ye may be holy
an' ye have the gift of white power, but yer Innocent, too."
And he reached for her.

Allie went into his arms, astride his hips. As he pushed
slowly against her buttocks, she felt faint with impending
pleasure. "What does that mean, exactly?" she whispered.
She shifted and began rubbing herself over his massive
length.

"I'm sworn to protect Innocence. I'm sworn to protect
ye." He grasped her hips and held her still.

She seized his wrists. "I like your idea of protection."

"I thought ye might," he said, holding her so she could
not move. Very slowly, he began to penetrate upward.

So much pleasure crested, hollowing her. "It's my turn,"
she gasped, "to be the tyrant."

He laughed and flipped her onto her stomach, pushing
even deeper as he did so. "I dinna think so," he said.

Allie couldn't protest. There was too much rapture trying
to explode. "Let me come!"

"Aye," he gasped.

WHEN ALLIE AWOKE the second time that day, his side of the
bed was empty and she was alone. The sun was high beyond

her window. She grinned and wiggled her toes. She was a very feminine and sensual woman, but she had never felt so sexy and so desirable.

And she had never felt so happy, so light. But why not? She had the hunk of all ages, literally, as a lover—and he was also an überhero. In fact, they could go cruising together tonight. He'd fight the demons while she healed their victims. It was going to be *perfect.*

And her silly heart was grinning, too, swollen with happiness.

It felt suspiciously like love.

She slid from the bed, realizing this delirious high was just that. She was falling in love with her golden, not-so-medieval hero. She had thought herself immune to love, and had even wondered if her heart was somehow defective. She had rationalized that love was not a part of her very definite Fate, but apparently she had been wrong.

She laughed and as she showered and dressed, she hummed her favorite country songs, off-key and uncaring of how awful she sounded. She'd had the best sex of her life. Royce was to die for, and she couldn't wait to see him, exchange smiles and ask him to cruise with her that night. She couldn't wait to be in his arms and tell him how she felt—and that this was so new for her.

A tray had been set outside the bedroom door with coffee and scones and several newspapers. As it was half past four in the afternoon, the coffee was ice cold. She retrieved the papers, then headed downstairs for hot coffee and a gargantuan breakfast. She was famished.

She did not know the house, and she wandered from the great room past several salons before stumbling across the dining room. Royce was seated at a long wood table, reading a newspaper, apparently waiting for her. Her heart tried to burst from her chest and she felt happy enough to float to the ceiling. He looked up and smiled at her, then shot to his feet.

She walked up to him, thinking about his body, his kisses and how damned great he looked in a dark polo shirt and Italian trousers; he took her hands in his and pressed them to his chest. "Hi," she breathed.

"Hallo," he murmured back, his gaze terribly warm.

Absurdly it made her think about lots of great sex—not that she'd ever really stopped thinking about last night. "Wanna cruise with me tonight?"

He didn't seem to understand.

"I need to heal—you can fight the demons," she said softly.

"I can think o' better things to do tonight," he murmured.

She flushed. "I'll bet you can."

He guided her toward a chair. "Come have lunch with me. Then we'll plan our day. If ye like, I'll take ye on a tour of the country."

Our day. Allie sat, realizing eating would be impossible, because all she wanted to do was stare at him, drown in his masculine beauty and pinch herself to see if she was dreaming. He grinned, as if he guessed her thoughts. "Mrs. Farlane? Miss Monroe has come down to dine," he called. Then he poured her coffee.

IT WAS LATE when they returned to Carrick, having spent the entire day touring the Highlands in his silver Lamborghini. He drove well but fast and they hadn't talked very much—there was no need. Allie had been so happy just to be with him. They had stopped for lunch at the magnificent Dunain Park Hotel in Inverness, where the proprietors had fawned over them both—she had been recognized. And they had wandered about the ruins of Urquhart, where they'd also made love behind a ruined stone wall. Now, as Royce parked the car in one of his garages, Allie wandered back into the castle. Supper would be a late affair, but she didn't care.

She was about to go upstairs to freshen up and call home when she caught a flash of brilliant color from the corner of her eye. Posed to go upstairs, her heart leapt and she turned around to face the aura that had caught her attention. A strange man stood in the great room. He emanated the same warrior power as Royce: holy strength vibrated from him in red and gold waves of light. Testosterone charged his aura, too. But he also radiated a white, healing light, even if faintly. Most importantly, the blue and purple in his aura told her that his Karma was huge—but far from mastered. In fact, he would pay a high price for it.

Allie knew she was meeting another Master, and excitement began. He stared at her, as well, smiling. She came forward curiously. Taller than Royce, he had fair skin, dark hair and he was Hollywood-leading-man handsome. He was wearing a slick black leather jacket with distressed jeans and he was young—maybe her own age.

He grinned more widely at her, revealing two dimples, while his gaze slid over the ivory corset top she wore with a print circle skirt. "Hallo."

Her interest peaked. He appeared modern, but she had a sudden sense that he was not from the present, in spite of his clothes. "Hi. You're a Master, too."

His eyes widened. "Royce has talked very freely in yer bed."

"I can see your aura and it reeks of a few pretty specific traits. I'm Allie." She came forward and held out her hand.

He took it and, instead of shaking it, lifted it to his lips. "I'm the lord of Awe, the earl of Lismore. But ye may address me as Aidan." A grin followed his rather arrogant tone.

Allie wasn't all that surprised by the gallant, Old World kiss. Definitely for Tabby, she thought. "How old are you?"

He dropped her hand, amused. "I'm old enough for ye, lass."

"I'm with Royce."

"T'is evident. I'm pleased for him. But I willna mind much if ye decide Royce is too old for ye." His smile flashed. "I'm *only* thirty an' two years of age."

This man was wearing modern clothes, but he was not a modern man. "What year did you come from?"

He stared, his smile fading. "That's an odd question." Then, "I followed Royce from 1430."

Before she could decipher that bit of startling information, Royce strode into the great room. And it was *her* Royce, the modern, insatiable, supersexed lover she had spent the past twenty-four hours with. Even though they'd spent the night and day together, her heart raced madly as he approached.

But Royce was grim and unsmiling. "What are ye doing here, Aidan?" he asked.

The dark Highlander came forward, unperturbed by the cool greeting. "Have ye lost yer mind? Ye canna recall that I followed ye to help ye if ye needed me?"

Royce looked him up and down, disapproval on his face. "That was six centuries ago. I see that you've broken the rules again."

"Ye ken I hate rules. They cage my poor soul."

"Ye followed me five centuries ago when I was a younger man—but ye dinna help me fight Moffat in South Hampton. My memory hardly fails me." Royce was sharp and cold.

"Ye dinna need my help. Ye battled Moffat alone easily enough. I decided to go to Rome." He shrugged. "I thought to come to Carrick and see what ye decided to do with the Healer." He grinned. "Finally ye come to yer senses, eh, Royce?"

Royce seemed annoyed.

Allie said, "What does that mean?"

Aidan looked at her. "It only took him hundreds o' years to find some pleasure outside o' bed with a woman."

Royce's stern expression did not ease. He turned away, walking over to the sideboard as Allie deciphered the conversation. In South Hampton, Royce had appeared from 1430 to help her fight the demons. Aidan had followed him from that time, but had not helped them in the battle. Instead he had gone to Rome. Then he had stopped by Carrick to check on her, which did not make sense. But Royce was clearly not amused. "Ye need to go back to yer time as the Code requires—without the jacket an' jeans."

"I spent hours shopping in Rome!" Aidan exclaimed. "But I see ye have barely changed—ye remain far too grim. I'll go." Aidan turned to her. "At least ye make him smile. T'is a vast improvement."

Allie wondered at that and said, "FYI, there's better shopping in Milan."

"Dinna encourage him," Royce told her. "The Code is clear. He travels for his own pleasure...t'is strictly forbidden."

"But he looks so cute in black leather," Allie said, smiling at Aidan.

He winked at her. Then he turned to Royce. "Ye have done well, Royce." Aidan's smile was male and knowing. "I never thought I'd see the day when ye'd take a mistress."

"Keep yer eyes in yer head," Royce warned softly.

"A man must look, if he lives an' breathes."

"You'll never change," Royce retorted, and then he

clasped Aidan's shoulder hard, with great affection. He turned to Allie, who was highly interested in the somewhat avuncular exchange. "He's the rogue of all rogues, Ailios...dinna fall for his pretty smile an' prettier words."

"Don't worry," Allie said. "I've already fallen—for the first time in my life."

Royce started, and he wasn't smiling.

Allie was surprised she'd said such a thing so openly, but she meant it. She never led guys on, but this was different. She was falling in love, even if it wasn't a part of her game plan. And she was certain he reciprocated her feelings, and not because every guy she'd ever dated became serious with her sooner or later. She thought she could feel Royce's emotions.

Then he touched her hair. "I like ye, too."

Allie was briefly dismayed, but his eyes were so warm that the confusion vanished. Lots of men could not say the *L* word.

Aidan cleared his throat. "Mayhap a glass of wine before I leave? To celebrate matters o' the bed—an' the heart?" He was amused.

Allie didn't quite get it, but Royce seemed a bit annoyed again. However, he started to turn back to the massive sideboard where a wine rack was placed in one of the glass cabinets. He faltered.

Aidan's shoulders stiffened.

Darkness descended at lightning speed—and so did an arctic cold.

Aidan rushed to the wall display of swords, lifting one from its sheath. He took one look at the dull blade and flung it aside. As he lifted another, Royce opened a chest and withdrew a semiautomatic. "Aidan." He tossed an unsheathed sword at him.

And Aidan caught it easily by the hilt. Allie ran to Royce as the demons formed in their midst.

"Stay back," he said.

She was about to argue when the blow came, taking her by surprise, before she could even try to shield herself. She cried out, hurled across the entire great room, slamming into the stone of the fireplace.

Royce roared in fury, firing.

Allie got to her hands and knees, watching Aidan beheading a half a dozen demons with so much skill and speed it might have been the final cut from a Hollywood movie. Royce was firing at the same demon that had attacked them in South Hampton, but the demon had put up his energy and the bullets were deflected, scattering everywhere.

She took up a poker but remained where she was. Aidan was doing a good job with the remaining demons, and Royce and the blonde from South Hampton seemed to be intent only on each other. This time, though, if he came close, she'd get more than his eyeball; she was going for his unfeeling heart.

Royce now threw the useless semi aside. He blasted his energy at the demon, who blocked it and grinned, revealing white, gleaming teeth.

Allie tensed in alarm, thinking, *No, Royce!*

A dagger had appeared in his hand, but as if he'd heard her cry out silently, as if he knew she was desperate to go to his side and help him, Royce turned to look at her. "Ye stay back."

The demon threw a knife at Royce. Allie saw it; he did not. She screamed in warning.

Royce whirled back but the blade impaled him in his chest as he moved.

Allie froze in horror.

For one moment, Royce stood upright, unmoving—and he threw the dagger. He threw it with unbelievable accuracy and Allie realized he would nail the sonuvabitch. But the blond demon vanished the instant the blade seemed to pierce his chest, and it fell to the floor. The two remaining demons also disappeared, leaving behind the dozen dead on the great room floor—and Royce.

He reeled and fell over onto his back.

The hilt of the knife protruded from his heart.

Allie rushed to his side and fell onto her knees, pouring her white light over him. He was not going to die, no matter how bad it looked! He couldn't die—he was a hero, a Master, the savior of mankind and the love of her life!

She hadn't raised the dead girl, but surely she could save Royce!

Panic began.

Royce took her hand. He was deathly white. But he smiled. "Nay, lass. Let me go."

He was *dying*. She felt his life spinning away. But she could heal him—she *would* heal him. In panic, she poured all the white light she could muster on him, trying to hold her terror at bay.

"Ailios!" Royce's grasp tightened, his gaze on hers. "Let me die."

Allie looked at him in horror. "Don't talk. You don't mean it. I won't let you die! I love you!"

"Please," Royce said softly. And his grasp loosened.

And she felt his life soaring away from him. She saw a white-gold light lifting from him. "No!" Frantic, she poured white power over him, through him, but everything was happening too fast now.

Royce looked up at Aidan. *Let me go. T'is time.*

And strong hands seized Allie from behind.

But she had heard Royce, and she screamed, furious at Aidan, terrified, struggling, but Aidan wouldn't release her. Panicking, she flung white light at Royce, but Aidan was interfering with her powers—and Royce was leaving rapidly now.

Aidan, take her away, protect her.

"No!"

Royce smiled at her—and the white-gold light swirled upward, into the ceiling—his gray eyes becoming sightless.

Allie screamed. *"Nooo!"* And she fought to go to him, the white-gold light hovering above them, but Aidan pulled her away.

ALLIE WEPT AND WEPT.

The paramedics had Royce's body on the stretcher, covered with a cloth, and were wheeling him from the room. Two local police cars were parked inside the courtyard, the officers in the hall with Aidan and Mrs. Farlane. The housekeeper, who was crying, clearly knew about her employer's secrets. The dead demons, of course, were gone. Their bodies had started disintegrating immediately, and unless there was a crime scene investigation, no traces of them would be found. But from the murmur of voices, and the snippets of conversation she'd heard, Allie knew the police knew the truth. One officer was already talking about the Highland gangs run amok these past few years, a favorite cover-up for these kinds of battles. The other had already called Scotland Yard. The British government probably had their version of CDA, too.

How could he be gone?

Allie doubled over from the sheer pain of her grief. Too late, she understood Tabby's reading. Then she heard footsteps.

She looked up. Aidan stood there, his face ravaged, a single tear tracking down his cheek. She didn't hesitate. She jumped up and ran at him, fists balled. He caught her arm as she swung; she lifted her knee, wanting to emasculate him, but he twisted and easily avoided that assault, then caught her in a viselike embrace.

She fought him, wanting to rip his handsome face apart. She wanted blood. He had prevented her from healing Royce—she could have saved him. "I hate you!" she screamed. "Let me go! I will never forgive you—you bastard!"

He released her and she pounded his chest, hurting her fists because he was a wall of muscle. He caught her wrists. "Lass, cease. I love him, too." His voice broke.

Allie collapsed against the solid wall of his body, weeping again. This could not be happening. Royce was a great man, a great hero, a Master. He deserved to live! Aidan held her loosely now and she needed the comfort he could offer, when there was no real comfort to be had.

Let me go.

Why had he wanted to die?

How old are you?

It doesna matter, Ailios.

So much grief and pain, such a beautiful man…

I have waited a long time for this night.

Allie trembled, but stopped crying. *He had waited five hundred and seventy-seven years for her.*

Aidan released her and walked away.

Allie wiped her eyes, her heart slamming, turning to gaze after him. He was pouring two huge glasses of whiskey. He drained most of his, then started toward her with the other tall glass. "You're a Master, too."

He faltered before offering her the glass.

Allie shook her head. "You can travel through time, don't even try to deny it. You said you followed Royce here from 1430."

His eyes were wary now. "Does it matter?"

"Oh, yes, it does."

He stared, then murmured, "MacNeil asked me to follow Royce. When he left ye here, I should have gone home to Awe, to the time where I belong, but I went to Rome. I need to go back to my time."

She stared, her mind scrambling.

Sympathy had filled his blue eyes. "Lass, I will take ye home. I just need to think a moment because ye need a Master to aid ye now, here, in yer time."

She didn't know what he was talking about. "Take me back in time!" she cried, trembling wildly. "I am not going home! I need to go back in time, to earlier today or even to last night. I'll tell him what will happen—we'll stop it this time! I'll go back in time to stop his murder!" This was the answer; of course it was. To go back in time—and prevent his death.

Aidan paled. "Ye canna go back in time an' change the future…t'is forbidden."

"Who cares?" she cried. "I must stop Royce from being murdered! You must help me!"

"I canna break such a rule."

"What?" She was shocked. And then she was furious. "You hate rules. They're a cage for your soul!" He would refuse her now? What was wrong with him?

"Lass, the rules I break are the petty ones. MacNeil will take my head if I take ye back so ye can change this day." He was dark and grim now. "Besides, Royce wished to leave this life. I have heard him say, many times, that he's tired o' the fight. Ye'll nay change his mind, not in a single day."

Allie stared at him, incredulous, disbelieving. Her mind spun and raced. He wasn't going to take her back to earlier that day or yesterday; she could see it in his eyes. Royce had wanted to die. She had to accept that, even if she couldn't understand it. *And he wasn't going to change in a single day.*

She breathed hard. Her senses told her that Aidan knew Royce well and he was telling her the truth. Instantly Allie changed her plans. To undo his death she needed time with him—time to convince him he had a future worth fighting for.

And she wanted time with him—a lifetime—even if it was in the primitive past.

He must have sensed what she intended, because his eyes went wide. "Nay."

"I haven't asked you yet!"

He shook his head and then drained half of her drink.

"Take me back with you." A wild determination hardened.

He stared back. "To 1430? Royce will have my head."

"No, you don't understand. When we met the other night, he came to me from the fifteenth century. He left me here— but waited for me for almost six hundred years. Don't you get it? There's a reason we met that way. He loves me. I love him. You're going back—take me to him. Take me to him in your time!" she begged fiercely.

He inhaled. "Lass, lust an' love are hardly the same."

She seized his hand. "I am going with you!"

And Aidan hesitated.

Allie knew an opening when she saw one. "Please. I will do anything, *anything,* to go back with you to Royce.'

"Ye offer me yer bed?" He was incredulous.

"Anything…but that!"

He shook his head, still ready to refuse. "Ye willna like my time. Ye willna like Royce very well in my time, either."

"You can't deny me. Please." Her grip tightened. Panic began. He had to do this for her.

He looked into her eyes. "Are ye certain, Lady Allie? Are ye truly certain? What if yer wrong? What if Royce doesna love ye as ye love him?"

"I am certain!" she cried, clinging now to his large hand with both of hers.

He drained the drink, murmured, "Royce left ye here fer a reason. I dinna ken," and pulled her into his embrace. Allie held on tight. And they were flung across the room, through the walls and into the universe—back to 1430.

CHAPTER FOUR

Carrick Castle, Morvern, Scotland—1430

SHE OPENED HER EYES, the torment finally receding. Allie somehow breathed. This time had felt even worse than the previous one and she was amazed she was alive. While in the throes of bone-breaking pain, she'd thought she would actually die. Now she became aware of a pounding headache threatening to split her skull. Allie stared up at a high ceiling with timbers. High on stone walls, stunning stained glass windows radiated from the sunlight outside.

"Rest a moment more."

She blinked and saw Aidan standing above her, arms folded, and all recollection returned. Royce had been murdered and she had gone back in time. Grief rose up, choking her, but she fought it. Instead she thought about the fact that traveling through time was hell. She hoped to never do it again, at least, not until there was no other choice in order to return home. And the gods only knew when that would be.

She sat up, still somewhat weak and very shaken. Her body felt as if it had been stretched out like elastics and pounded with hammers. But since the night before the fundraiser, when she'd tried to bring that girl back from the dead, her body had been through hell. Making love to Royce had to have taken its toll, too. "Did we make it? What time are we in?" she managed to ask. She sounded hoarse.

He gave her a look. "T'is May 15, 1430."

She started. "And you know that how?"

"I dinna have to look at a calendar, lass. T'is almost two weeks since I followed Royce to the future." He added, "I decided to give Royce some time to forget ye."

Allie got to her feet. "He isn't going to forget me in a week or two. He waited six centuries for me, remember?" She glanced around. They were in a beautiful church or chapel. There were rows of highly polished wood pews on either side of the knave, and an altar at the far end. She stared, confused, at a beautiful, gilded, bejeweled crucifix with Jesus hanging there. "Why are we in a Catholic church?"

"We're in Carrick's chapel. Everyone's Catholic, lass, even the Masters."

Allie just looked at him. The Masters were blessed by the Ancients, not Christ; he had to be wrong. But she didn't really care. Her heart began to accelerate and she started down the knave, toward the oversize wooden door.

She heard Aidan following.

But before she could pull the heavy door open, he laid his hand on it, keeping it closed. "Have a care, lass," he said.

She turned. "I haven't forgiven you, but thank you for bringing me here. Now, let go. I have to find Royce."

Aidan said softly, "I'm very sure he willna be pleased to see ye."

Allie dismissed his comment as absurd and pulled open the door. She stepped into Carrick's inner ward—and she faltered.

She had asked to go back in time. But she hadn't really had a chance to think about what to expect. Vaguely she recognized the courtyard, even though it was not cobbled. She saw the entrance to the largest building across from her and knew that inside was the great hall. The corner towers were the same. But that was it.

The courtyard was filled with people—medieval people.

The women wore simple linen dresses and had bare feet. Two women had plaids pinned to their shoulders. The men she saw crossing the ward wore the same tunics, but only to the knee, and they were barefoot, too—and armed with swords and daggers. A pair of pigs wandered about, and a milk cow was being led by a little boy. Animal droppings abounded. Huge hounds were barking from across the ward, chained to a wall. They were barking at her and Aidan.

The passing men and women turned to look at her and Aidan.

Allie tensed. They stood out like sore thumbs. He was still clad in his jeans, T-shirt and leather jacket; she was wearing her knee-length skirt and linen corset top and her platform shoes. Surprise was becoming suspicion.

"Are we in trouble?" Allie whispered to Aidan. She wasn't afraid—not exactly—for these were people, not evil demons. On the other hand, every medieval movie she had ever seen seemed to tumble through her mind. Ignorance caused people to do really bad things to other people.

"They have seen stranger sights, lass," Aidan said. And even as he spoke, Allie saw men and women firmly turning away. In that instant, she realized that life in the Middle Ages wasn't very different from life at home. The average person preferred ignorance and chose not to think too hard about all the events and phenomena they saw but could not explain. She and Aidan being unusually dressed couldn't be half as disturbing as seeing one's friend or relative murdered in a crime of pleasure, or witnessing a battle between Masters and demons when the weapons were invisible—kinetic power.

"They're wary because we're strangers," Aidan said to her. "In this time, yer friend or foe, an' no man can be in the middle." Then he raised his voice, speaking to a pair of men who had their hands on the hilts of their swords.

"I'm the Wolf of Awe an' a great friend o' Black Royce. Release yer swords." He stared at them.

Instantly Allie saw their eyes glaze. She looked at Aidan and saw the glittering light coming from his gaze and realized he had great powers of enchantment.

Both men released their swords, but they glanced at Allie now.

Aidan moved so quickly Allie didn't know what was happening until it was done. He suddenly had one of the men's swords laid against that man's throat. "Ye show the lady *respect*," he said softly. "She's Royce's guest."

Allie wet her lips. What had she been thinking? He could flirt and charm, he liked trendy clothes and was a bit arrogant for her taste, but he was as fierce and powerful as Royce, maybe even more so, for the red in his aura was almost blinding. There was something else present in his aura that she could not understand, either—a black streak, like black rain. But she had forgotten all that. She had dared to curse him and strike at him.

A horn blew.

Allie jumped in surprise and almost twisted her ankle. She whirled to look up at the tower above her. She didn't have to ask, she knew.

Royce was returning. She could feel him, his energy huge and hard and powerful, impossibly male, impossibly in-domitable. He was somewhere beyond the castle walls.

Excitement seized her and made her breathless, caused her body to ache and swell. This was not the time—but maybe it was. Because after she leapt into his arms, she could think of nothing she'd rather do than be in his bed, making love, celebrating his life, and afterward, cuddling and talking, kissing.

Joy and relief warred.

Ahead was the gatehouse with its four towers, the one that he'd driven through in his Ferrari the other day. She rushed forward.

"Ye wait for him here," Aidan called. "Ye let him accept what we have done."

Allie ignored him, stumbling in her tall shoes, wishing she'd had the foresight to wear her Nikes. She stepped into the dark stone corridor that formed the passageway through the gatehouse—and came face-to-face with iron bars.

Her heart slammed. She was barred by a closed portcullis, because this was the fifteenth century, not modern times. Another portcullis was closed at the other end of the passage, and beyond that, she saw an outer ward, a smaller gatehouse and a drawbridge that was slowly lowering. Instantly she realized a large group of horsemen was approaching the drawbridge, the sun glittering wildly on their armor.

She seized the cold iron bars, her heart leaping.

His aura burned hotly red, dominating the orange and gold, making any blue and green invisible. He was at the band's forefront, and he'd come from battle. The energy given by the planet Mars and the war gods was bursting in him still.

She swallowed, uncontrollably excited now and very aroused.

She hadn't thought about what it would be like to see him again, in this century. Although they had first met when he was from this time, they'd exchanged no more than a dozen words, fought a single battle before they'd leapt time. The memories she had of him now had nothing to do with a Highland warrior standing in mail and a plaid, his legs boot-clad but bare. She would never forget the sight of Royce getting out of his Ferrari in his black T-shirt and trousers; Royce in bed, surrounded by Ralph Lauren pillows and sheets; Royce offering her wine, his 18 karat gold Bulgari watch glinting on his wrist; Royce smiling at her from across a table covered with linen and crystal.

The man riding across the drawbridge was on a huge, wild charger and wore mail over his tunic. Both horse and man were spotted with blood.

And then the bars started lifting.

She swallowed hard, telling herself it was silly to be uneasy. She shouldn't be surprised to see him dressed like a medieval knight, because she'd seen him dressed as strangely at the fund-raiser, yet this *was* different—in his time, it was strange and somehow disturbing. It was hard for her mind to reconcile this Royce and the one she'd spent twenty-four hours with. The man approaching looked almost like a stranger. But he was the same man, when push came to shove, and she needed to remember that. He was her golden warrior, her lover, the man who fought demons no matter the time, the golden Master her mother had told her to trust.

The portcullis was waist high; Allie ducked through it and ran down the stone passageway. As she did, something made her look up and she saw gaps in the ceiling above. A face appeared, shocking her.

Allie ran faster, sensing hostile intent. Just before she made it to the second portcullis, this one almost the height of her head, an arrow whizzed past her. And then a dozen arrows scorched her path.

They were shooting at her.

Frantic, she ducked beneath the last portcullis, and she heard Royce shout, "Cease yer fire!"

She burst into the gray Highland daylight.

His gray eyes wide, he galloped his horse across the dirt ward, thrusting himself between her and the gatehouse. Allie halted, shaken by the attack, but so overjoyed to see him. The horse reared and Royce jerked mercilessly on its reins, making it submit to his halt. His gaze slammed to hers.

It was hard and incredulous.

Allie smiled, trembling. The moment he took her into his arms, all of her anxiety would vanish. Wouldn't it?

But his hard eyes slammed down her rather exposed bosom to her skirt and bare legs. The sexual appraisal was raw, ruthless. Then he leapt from the horse, which reared again. Royce turned and kicked it in the ribs, hard.

The animal stood docilely, head down.

Allie tried to breathe. He didn't look at her now, his expression strained, and she wasn't sure she'd liked how he'd looked at her before dismounting. He was handing his helmet to a boy, then his gauntlets, his gestures forceful, almost angry.

They needed to speak. She tried to assimilate what was happening. He was the same man—she would swear it— but he was so different, too. He was so *medieval.* "Royce?" she asked uncertainly.

He whirled to face her, eyes blazing.

He was angry, she realized, shocked. But he couldn't be angry with her. He might not know they were lovers, but he was in love with her. She had no doubt he'd told her he'd waited so many centuries for her.

And then he closed the short distance between them, towering over her. "I left ye in *yer* time," he ground out.

What was this? As Allie stared blankly at him, her joy really faded. "Royce." She wet her lips, terribly uncertain.

Where was her warm welcome? She laid her hand on his chest. His strong heart thundered there. "I am so happy to see you. I have so much to tell you."

His eyes widened with surprise. For one moment, he stared at her and she stared back, waiting for him to smile and erase all her doubt and confusion. Instead, slowly, he said, "Ye touch me as if we're familiar." His gaze had narrowed with cool speculation.

A sick feeling began. This was Royce five hundred and seventy-seven years before they'd made love. He didn't know they were lovers, but he did love her, right? "We are very familiar," she whispered. "In my time."

His expression changed. A satisfied, smug and hard look settled on his gorgeous face. But then he said, "Ye need to go back to yer time."

Allie dropped her hand. "You're not…happy to see me?" She was shocked. It was hard to wrap her mind around the fact that she knew him intimately, but he did not know her.

Then she added silently, *yet*.

"Do I look pleased?" he demanded.

He did not look pleased at all. What was happening? Where was her lover—the man she had traveled through time to be with?

"Yer lover," he said, his eyes glittering, "awaits ye in yer time, not this one."

Allie could not react. Royce was cold and rude, terribly so. He was not welcoming, and he had put her in an uncomfortable and defensive position. She was far more than off balance, she was starting to feel rejected. But men did not reject her. They courted her, chased her, fell in love with her. Why was he being so harsh, so mean? Could he be so different from the man she'd slept with last night?

"Royce." Aidan approached from the gatehouse.

Royce stiffened and turned. "Of course it was ye, Aidan. Ye brought her back. Are ye very amused?"

Aidan did not smile. He looked so incongruous, standing there in his jeans and leather jacket, confronting Royce in his mail and plaid. "There has been nothin' amusin' about this day. Ye need to be pleasant to the lady."

Royce stared, his gaze narrowing. Allie saw the red in his aura explode. "So ye defend her?" he asked very softly.

Aidan shook his head, grimacing "Ye fool! Dinna start. I brought her to Carrick, not to Awe."

Royce folded his arms, biceps bulging, a gold cuff glinting on one arm, a terribly dangerous expression on his face. His smile was ruthless. "Then ye be the fool. Take her with ye when ye leave."

Allie bit her lip, aghast. *He didn't want her there.*

Aidan flushed. "Ye dinna mean such cruel words."

"If I'd wished to bring her back with me, I'd have done so," he told Aidan. "I left her in her time for my reasons— I dinna like being crossed." He glared at Allie.

Allie wanted to cry. He acted as if he hated her. He wasn't even the same man as the Highlander who'd come to her aid at the fund-raiser.

"I dinna cross ye!" Aidan erupted, seeming as angry as Royce now. "Ye left her behind because yer afraid."

"I left her behind at Carrick to protect her," Royce said as furiously.

"Stop," Allie cried. "Stop fighting like small boys."

They ignored her. Aidan said, "There's no one at Carrick in her time to protect her."

Royce stiffened.

Allie looked back and forth between the two men, certain Royce had instantly understood Aidan's inference. And he slowly faced her.

Uneasy, she tried to decipher his feelings. Most men would be shocked to learn of their death. Most men would be distressed to learn of the event, and the date. Royce's gray gaze met hers.

And she saw the stark comprehension in his eyes. She wanted to ease any distress he might feel, to soothe any anxiety, any fear. She wanted to tell him that it was not the end, that they would fix it, change it somehow.

But a mask settled over his face. "I die in her time." He was still looking at Allie as he spoke to Aidan. And he did not seem to care.

"Aye," Aidan said. "Ye died in bravery for her, as any Master would."

He nodded at that.

Allie still wanted to comfort him, not that he looked as if he needed comfort from her or anyone. He didn't even seem upset. She laid her hand on his hard chest again, hating the feel of the sharp mail. And in spite of the vest, she felt him tense. "It was a mistake. An awful mistake. It doesn't have to happen that way." She tried to smile. Instead, horrified, she felt tears well. It was going to be a long time before she got over his death.

His thick, dark lashes lowered. "Yer fond of me. Ye grieved."

Allie nodded slowly. "You're fond of me, too, Royce."

He made a harsh sound, and it was dismissive. Only then did he look up. Allie forgot to breathe. Everything was the same—she felt his lust, huge and bold, a presence throbbing between them, and she was overcome by it. It was as if a bond was there between them, connecting their desires, their bodies. She moved her hand lower, across the sharp mail, toward his waist. A terrific fold had appeared near the hem of the mail shirt.

"I need wine," Aidan said. He wheeled and strode back through the gatehouse.

Allie was alone with Royce, although several knights remained at a distance. She trembled and waited for him to take her into his arms, hold her and tell her everything would be all right. Then they could go inside, upstairs. And by the dawn, everything would be back to the way it should be. She knew it. It wasn't too late. They could get past these first few awful moments.

He took her hand and removed it. "Dinna tease me."

Her eyes widened. "Royce, I am not teasing you."

His smile twisted. "Yer lover is *dead*."

She inhaled. "No, you are very much alive," she cried. "And I thank the gods for it!"

"Ye mistake," he said grimly, "two very different men."

Allie backed up, shaking her head. "Why are you doing this?"

"Why did ye follow me to my time?" he shot back.

Allie tried to control the hurt roiling through her now. "You don't want me here?"

"Nay, I dinna."

His words were a blow. She could not begin to fathom what he meant, or why, and what this meant for her, for them. She had never suffered such cruelty before. "You're not making sense," she said thickly. "You told me you waited six hundred years for me! You are not acting like a man in love."

His eyes widened. "I am a soldier of God," he said sharply. He nodded at the gatehouse, a gesture that was clearly a command for her to follow, and he whirled and strode that way.

Allie didn't move. The man striding away from her was not the man she was in love with. It had become painfully clear. What had she done, coming back to his time? And what should she do now?

Allie wiped at some moisture on her face. Her world was spinning now. And the grief came back, hot, hurtful, fresh. With it, there was so much confusion.

"I can please ye, lassie."

Allie tensed. She hadn't paid any attention to his men. Several stood in a half circle around her now.

The giant who had just spoken to her smiled, revealing mostly missing teeth. He was huge and unshaven, and blood stained his tunic. He had no mail and he wore a longsword, a dagger and carried a spiked club. He was dirty and reeked of body odor.

Five other men stood with him, each as gross and primitive and dirty, and they were all leering.

Alarm began.

She was used to being admired. Men looked at her lush boobs all the time. Suddenly Allie wished she was not wearing a supersexy corset top a size too small, much less such a feminine skirt and high heels. For the first time in her life, she was not the center of admiration; she was the center of savage, primitive lust. She felt as if the men were rabid wolves about to fight over her carcass before ripping it apart while devouring it. And she felt a flicker of fear, when she was never afraid.

Suddenly Royce was striding past her, his face livid.

Allie was so relieved, although instinct made her jump out of his way. He didn't stop to ask her if she was fine or look at her. Enraged, determined, he went to the first giant, who backed up quickly.

Royce suddenly had a dagger in his hand—and he pressed it between the giant's thighs, beneath his tunic.

Allie clapped her hand over her mouth, not daring to cry out.

"Take another look," Royce taunted softly. "Dare."

The giant was white. "I be sorry, my lord. I'll nay look again."

"Ye look at her one more time, ye ever speak to her again, ye'll be looking at yer balls, hanging from my walls, drying in the sun." He straightened, sheathing the dagger.

The giant got on his knees. He bowed his head. "Aye, my lord."

"Lady Ailios is *my* guest, under *my* protection," Royce said harshly. "Ye tell every man in the keep." He turned and his heated gaze locked with Allie's.

Allie was frozen. He meant it. She was no stranger to evil, but she was a stranger to this kind of violence. Royce was a holy warrior, but she had not a doubt he would emasculate the man who had dared to look at her with lustful intent without thinking twice. And as gross as that man was, he wasn't evil, he was just a savage.

This was a primitive, savage world.

And this man was not her twenty-first-century lover.

There was *nothing* civilized about him. He was utterly ruthless, terribly chauvinistic, a barbarian. A product of his primitive, savage time.

What had she done?

His jaw flexed. An odd light came to his eyes. "T'is late for regrets."

She swallowed hard. "I have made a mistake."

His face hardened. He gestured for her to precede him through the gatehouse, even more displeased than before.

Allie did.

THERE HAD BEEN a huge battle with a rival clan, and his body was still hot and hard from the fight. Like most men, he always enjoyed fucking after fighting, and he had returned to Carrick intending to do just that. Instead he had discovered Ailios in his home, waiting for him, her eyes filled with love.

He was furious! He had left her in the future for a clear purpose! He did not need such temptation now—or ever.

There would be such a respite when buried in her warm, quivering flesh, from this life....

She shined with that pure, holy, healing white light. He could bathe in it....

He was so tired of the fight....

He steeled himself against such weakness, against her. He stole a glance at her now. The light around her was stunning and bright, as if the air surrounding her was infused with moisture after a Highland rain. His pulse drummed harder and he looked away. Even with the entire hall separating them, he could almost taste her purity and power; he could almost feel its warmth seeping into his sore, aching flesh.

Except he was hardly sore, anywhere, and he did not need healing. He had never beheld such power, and that must be the reason for his fascination. For he had never spent even an entire day, much less two weeks, thinking about a woman—not even Brigdhe in the days when he had just taken her as a bride and they were still exploring their passion. He was a Master. He dwelled on great matters of good and evil, life and death. Lust belonged in the bedchamber, the stables, or the wood on a quiet afternoon.

But ever since he'd left her in modern times at Carrick, he had been restless, annoyed, short of temper and irascible. In general, everyone and everything had displeased him. He had thought about her frequently, in spite of his better intentions. His interest hadn't waned—it had *increased.* He had thought about her even while in bed with other women. But this was worse, oh, yes, to find her here, in his home, in his time, a temptation that would lead him astray from the life he had so carefully forged.

But Aidan had made the decision to bring her there because he had died in the future last night.

His heart drummed hard. He would live for almost six more centuries, and he did not know whether to rejoice or despair. He strode across the hall to the long trestle table, his mind grappling with the fact of his future death. He did not know the details, although he soon would. All men had to die eventually, even Masters. But that left the gaping question of how to best protect Ailios now.

Filled with tension and heat, he ignored his friend Blackwood at the hearth, talking in a low voice with Aidan. He poured claret into a mug, his hand trembling. His mind could spin and race, but he felt the woman at the far end of the hall as if the air was a bridge of desire and emotion between them.

She was so small and so beautiful. He felt the waves of hurt emanating from her, washing over him.

Damn it all! He did not care if her feelings were hurt because he hadn't welcomed her with warmth and smiles into his home—and into his bed. When would she understand that he was not her lover? Her lover was dead. And if she spoke the truth, if he had somehow come to love her, then there was the proof that he must avoid her seduction at all costs. His recollection of her these past two weeks was proof he must avoid her or find an entanglement that would endanger her—and him. He must never take a mistress, much less care for one. She must never be another Brigdhe. Although his wife's features were faded beyond recognition now, he would never forget how she had suffered because of him; nor did he want to.

At least he'd had her before dying.

That knowledge gave him a savage exhilaration. But he didn't know the details of their time of passion. He didn't know what had happened, what it had been like. He didn't know how she sounded when she was coming, or how she felt, climaxing around him. Could he really wait five hundred and seventy-seven years to find out?

He cursed and drained his wine. His frustration knew no bounds. He would have enjoyed ripping McKale apart and hanging his balls out to dry. He felt like doing so now. *She* was the reason he was as frustrated as a twenty-year-old. It was inexplicable.

He refilled the mug and turned, staring against his will. Instead of lusting for what he could not have, he must dwell on the hard facts. Moffat hunted her and she was out of her time. She did not know their Highland ways. She could not strut about Carrick in such clothes, with her chemise missing, inflaming all men. His men would have raped her had he not come out and made his law clear. She came from a soft time, an easy place. This time was hard and savage and she needed protection more now than ever, and not just from Moffat and the deamhanain.

He would never hand her over to another Master, because his brethren were ruthless when it came to seduction and she would wind up in another's bed in the brief moment it took for her to become entranced. He had not meant it when he'd told Aidan to take her to Awe; he'd never let Aidan do so. MacNeil had chosen him to protect her, and he could not do so in her time, when his future self was dead. Iona would be a safe haven for her—but he'd have to convince MacNeil of that. Somehow he would do so. Until then, she would have to remain at Carrick, under his protection.

He returned to the bottle on the table. It was not his wish to hurt her. He was not a cruel man. But he was not going to feel guilt, either. He owed but one woman guilt—his wife. This was Aidan's fault, and he would gladly blame Aidan for disobeying him and creating such a predicament. However, she was in his home now and he should treat her as he would any other valued guest.

Having a clear, determined course of action calmed him somewhat. Almost soothed, he decided to offer her wine. He poured a new mug, and walked over to her. Her eyes widened.

"Will ye have some wine?" he asked brusquely. He could not risk showing her any pleasant manner beyond politeness. Oddly, though, he wished she would smile. Her smile was like the Highland sun rising from behind Ben More. "Ye'll feel better. A maid will show ye to a chamber."

She took the mug and cradled it in both hands against her full, soft bosom. He stared, not bothering to hide his avid interest. Any man would look at what she displayed in such a garment and think of being pillowed there in various ways.

"Are you being nice to me now?" she asked thickly.

He dragged his gaze upward. "Ye need to rest." Surely she knew his suggestion was a command? "Ye can eat first," he added, realizing she might be hungry.

"I'm not hungry and I'm not tired," she said, staring at him, her gaze terribly moist. "And I have no intention of staying here—with you, an ogre like no other."

Her words stung. He reminded himself that he did not care—and no matter what she claimed, he never would. "Ye'll stay here. Ye need protection. I'll see if MacNeil will allow ye to stay at the Sanctuary. Then ye go to Iona."

Her stare intensified. "The only place I'm going is home! Ask Aidan to take me. I don't want—or *need*—your protection."

She seemed ready to shed tears. It was time to end the

conversation. "Ye have my protection, whether ye wish it or ye dinna wish it." And he started to walk away.

"And to think I thought you were a tyrant in my time," she whispered.

He did not pause, but he did not understand. Curious, he lurked in her mind. He inhaled, seeing her very graphic thoughts about his prowess in bed, seeing him slowly entering her, purposefully teasing her, as she wept and begged. He even heard her cries of pleasure. His pulse raged, almost blinding him. He tried to think of something else, but it was simply too late. *He had given her so much pleasure.* He was pleased—he was tortured. He whirled.

Their gazes clashed, hers wide, as if she knew his thoughts, too.

When he could push the erotic images aside, he spoke. "I am lord here, Lady Ailios, an' I demand to know why ye remain so hurt. I saved ye from my men. I'm taking ye under my roof when I never wanted ye here. Ye dinna have to find shelter or food. Ye willna sleep in the rain. Ye should be pleased," he added firmly. "Another lord would turn ye to the wolves—or force ye into bed."

"I should be pleased?" She laughed, the sound shrill. "I came back to this barbaric time to find you.… Instead I find a ruthless stranger with no heart whatsoever! What would please me is some courtesy, some respect…and some sign that the man I made love to all night really exists."

He wondered if this was her way of seduction—to remind him at every turn of the pleasure she'd enjoyed—pleasure and satisfaction he would not have for six centuries. Now, he refused to lurk in her thoughts. He did not dare.

"Where are you, Royce?" she cried.

Her desperation to find his future self washed over him. He stiffened. Why did she want him so? "I'm here in my time, an' the man ye love doesna exist. I dinna believe he ever will."

She inhaled raggedly.

"I'm sorry," he added, meaning it, "that ye grieve so. I'm sorry ye think me cruel, but ye'll never find yer lover here. Aidan shouldn't have brought ye back with him."

She wet her lips. "Is that an apology?"

He was surprised, even confused. "Why would I apologize? I have done nothin' wrong."

Dismay twisted her mouth and she fought for her composure. "I don't believe," she finally said, low and slow, "that you are indifferent to me. We both know how manly you are, but there is more—I am certain."

He tensed. She was right—and she must never know. "Think as ye will." He shrugged. "But tonight ye willna be the wench in my bed."

She turned starkly white and he regretted his words. "That's right! Because I won't be here!" She leapt away, spilling the wine. She shoved the glass at him, red wine stained his leine. "Aidan? Would you mind?" She stared at Royce, her eyes filling with tears.

Annoyance quickly rose. "Ye go nowhere, Lady Ailios, not until I give ye permission, an' then I'll be tellin' ye where to go. Leave Aidan be."

She gasped. "I beg your pardon. I decide what is in my best interest. I always have.... I always will."

He was incredulous. She was arguing with him—defying him—and not for the first time. "I am lord an' master here," he said, holding his anger in check.

"No one is my master," she cried.

He felt his world still as it always did when he was poised for battle and ready to attack. Did she not understand that she would obey him? Did she wish to war with him? She was a maid! Did she not obey her father or her man, Brian, in her time? "Those are words o' great disrespect."

She shrugged. "Sorry! Here's more disrespect. You are a nice, pleasant person in the future. Right now, you are a cold, cruel, uncaring, selfish *ass.*"

He smiled without mirth, fighting to hold his temper in check. "Another man would strike ye for such words."

Her eyes widened in alarm.

"I dinna beat women an' children—or dogs," he shouted. Then he leaned close. "I must be very different in yer time, eh? Otherwise ye wouldn't love me so greatly."

"You are a hero, my hero," she said, "and it's unbelievable that you are the same person. A woman would be mad to love you right now!"

He turned away, wanting to strike something, anything. Why had she fallen so deeply in love with his future self? It enraged him, it pleased him—it terrified him. He preferred her hating him now, didn't he? It was better for them both. "In this time, women fall in love with me after a mere *moment* in my bed."

She flushed.

He slowly smiled, lurking, and his suspicions were right. "Perhaps, Ailios—" and he used his most seductive tone "—ye were nay different, even in yer time. Like all women, ye confused lust with love."

She inhaled, but he saw more hurt rise in her eyes, and he didn't like it—or that he'd caused the hurt again. "You fell in love with me, too," she said thickly.

"Is that why I died?" he demanded. He had to know. "Did I die for ye apurpose—or did I die because I loved ye to distraction?"

She just stood there, stricken.

She had been the death of him. He'd given his life for her, and he was certain he had done so gladly. He saw tears tracking down her cheeks. She was grieving for him and mourning his death.

It was sobering, confusing, dismaying. It was a moment before he could speak. He didn't mean to touch her, but he laid his hand on her tiny arm. Her warmth slipped over him. When he did speak, he softened his tone. "Ailios, enough argument. I dinna wish to war with ye. Ye canna triumph here. Ye'll stay at Carrick, an' here, I decide yer life. Ye'll leave when t'is safe—an' only when I say so."

He released her, not wanting to break the physical contact. Warmth seemed to curl about his insides. It seemed to infuse his bones. Was her white power stealing into him somehow?

"Will you force me to stay here, against my will?" she demanded to his back.

He whirled. "At Carrick yer will bends to mine."

"Like hell!" she cried, dismayed and furious.

"There is one will here." How could she fail to understand this fundamental fact of life? At Carrick, he was king.

She stared at him in disbelief. Then she said, "I am *not* going to stay here. I am not going to stay here while you *cavort* with other women. You will have to make me a *prisoner.*"

He was incredulous again. "Yer my *guest.*"

"I am your prisoner!" she shouted, trembling.

"Only if ye make it so!"

"No, you are the one making it so!"

That she would outdebate him was stunning. In that moment, he did not have a clever reply. "Then consider yerself imprisoned," he snapped. He turned away. "Blackwood," he called. "Aidan." He stalked to the table and slammed his fist on it.

Blackwood came over, his eyes filled with amusement. Royce had not a doubt he'd spied on their entire conversation. He was a tall, dark Lowlander, and his rakish ways were well-known—but he was a Master, and it was to be expected. His father had been a great English nobleman, his mother a Highlander, and he dressed in the English court style, his estates close to the borders there but half a day from the great cathedral at Moffat. His dark blue gaze now went to Allie. "Such a clever wench. A bit outspoken, don't you agree? Do you really wish to converse now?" He snickered, enjoying himself immensely. "Mayhap she needs a lesson in the ways of masters an' mistresses."

Royce was not in the mood for his taunts. But he was right. If he took Ailios to bed, he'd subdue her in *seconds*. He'd put her defiance to a quick death—replacing it with her lust and her love instead. "Our dear *friend* Moffat hunts the woman."

Blackwood's smile faded, but it was a moment before he tore his gaze from Ailios. "She is a Healer. I can see her white light. How great is her power?"

"Great." Royce turned to look at her. "She is Elasaid's daughter."

She had climbed into one of the two thronelike chairs, the arms and back carved ebony wood, the seat red velvet. The chair dwarfed her. She was heartbreaking in her beauty and if he did not know better, he'd think her fragile. But she wasn't fragile; she was fierce, with enough courage for ten men.

She glared at him.

He realized that Blackwood was staring at her, and so was Aidan. Both men had admiring and speculative looks in their eyes. He lurked, even though it was the height of rudeness to do so to another Master, and he saw both men thinking about her naked and in their beds. His temper exploded; he saw red. "The woman is mine," he said softly. And he could not regret his words, no matter how he knew he must somehow do so.

"T'is obvious." Blackwood shrugged, as if indifferent. "She's too bold an' conversant for my tastes. Of course, if you change your mind, I'll change mine."

"The lass is in love with Royce," Aidan said firmly.

"She loves the future Royce," Blackwood corrected. "I don't think she cares very much for Royce now." He smiled with vast amusement. "Don't you wish to take back your cold, heartless words?" He laughed again. "Most men would greatly wish for such a woman's *love*."

Royce happened to know he was speaking to one of the most conscienceless Masters when it came to seduction and women. "Yearn for her love, go ahead," he said dangerously. "But go near her an' suffer my will—an' my blade."

Blackwood chuckled. "I won't steal your woman, Royce, upon my vows. But I will happily escort her to Iona."

"She stays here until I say otherwise," Royce snapped, aware that Blackwood was playing him. "Moffat hunts Ailios, but whether to hurt me or have her, I dinna ken."

"The bishop," Aidan said softly, referring to Moffat, "was the one who attacked us at Carrick in her time. He killed ye, Royce. He put his dagger right through yer heart when ye were tryin' to keep Lady Allie safe." He added, "He seemed to be from the future, too, for he was dressed in that fashion."

Royce stared, refusing to have any feelings about his own death. But was it possible that his enemy had vanquished him—six centuries from now? Was it possible they would war this way for what felt like a near eternity?

Blackwood's amusement had vanished. "I'll send for my

spies—an' place new ones in the cathedral an' town. I'll learn what Moffat intends."

"If he thinks to use her," Royce said quietly, the idea enraging and terrifying, "she must never fall into his hands."

Both men became silent and he knew they were both thinking of the rumor that long ago, he'd had a wife who'd been destroyed by the deamhanain. He would not discuss Brigdhe with them or anyone else, and he would not confirm that the rumor was partly right. His stomach sickened with dread. Ailios must never be put in such a position. *Ever.* He dearly hoped Moffat still sought revenge for Kaz's death and that it was nothing more.

Blackwood knew Moffat well, considering the proximity of their lands, and he said, "The deamhan is clever. T'is rumored he has discovered pages of the holy Book of Healing. If so, he would want to capture a great Healer an' have her use her powers with the Book."

Royce had heard the whispers that Moffat had procured parts of the Cladich, the Book of Healing, stolen long ago from its shrine. That might explain why his armies kept growing. A deamhan with some healing ability would be a terrible thing. "Find out if he has parts of the Book. If so, he must die now."

Aidan spoke grimly. "An' how will he die now, if he lives to hunt an' fight in the twenty-first century?" He was referring to the part of the Code that specified no Master could change what was written in the past or the future.

"I'll see what I can discover," Blackwood said, standing. Then he grinned, his severe expression gone. "So you will protect the innocent Healer until this war passes?"

Royce scowled as Aidan also stood, speaking. "MacNeil asked Royce to protect her for his great reasons, which I dinna ken. But he sees the future, when the Ancients allow it. This is written." His face was oddly bland and he shrugged.

Blackwood shook his head. "Aidan, the woman is wasted on Royce. He won't find comfort in his black soul with any woman—even this one. The only comfort he'll have is in a bed." He gave Royce a slanted glance and languidly strolled from the hall, pausing only to nod at Ailios with an engaging smile.

She nodded back at Blackwood, smiling just a little, and then glanced hesitantly in Royce's direction.

He thought about the fact that it would soon be dark and that he was sitting there, as hot as a man could be, because of her. But that could be changed. He rose.

Aidan clasped his shoulder. "Dinna play the fool."

Royce shook him off. "Ceit, a chamber for Lady Ailios," he told a passing maid as he started across the hall. As he passed Ailios, she jumped to her feet, wide-eyed.

"Where are you going?" Ailios asked, appearing stricken.

He didn't answer. She wouldn't be pleased if she knew.

CHAPTER FIVE

"WHAT CAN I BE OFFERIN' YE, my lady?" the pretty blond housemaid asked.

Allie looked grimly around the stone chamber. A plain bed with four thick posts, covered with wool blankets and a thick fur, was against the wall. Two rustic wood and wicker chairs faced a hearth, where a fire burned. A small wolf skin was on the floor near the bed; the rest of the stone floor was bare. The only attractive piece of furniture in the room was a handsome carved chest by the bed, with brass studs in an interesting design, a pitcher and mugs set on it. The windows were small and narrow and the light outside was dull, indicating that the sun was finally setting. She shivered, already cold in her heart as well as her bones.

"My lady?"

Allie turned. A plaid in Royce's colors—hunter-green, black and silver—was folded over the back of one chair. She took it and wrapped it around her trembling body. She thought about how dirty she was. "Is a hot bath at all possible?"

The blond smiled, as if relieved. "Aye, ye'll have yer bath an' a good supper, too." And shyly, she curtsied. "My name be Ceit, if ye need anything else."

Allie raced after her as she went to the door. "Wait."

Ceit paused, surprised.

Allie had to take a breath. All of her composure was in shreds and worse, she felt despair. "Which of you is his mistress?" Every maid she'd passed on her way upstairs had been young and pretty. It was quite the coincidence.

Ceit's eyes widened; she blushed. "He doesna keep a mistress, my lady."

Allie didn't believe it. "Are you going to tell me he lives like a monk?"

Ceit's color increased. "He be a man, lady, an' our lord. He has whomever he wishes."

Allie hugged herself. She should not care. The medieval Royce was not even remotely like Royce in the twenty-first century. A gulf of six hundred years separated them, and in that time, a man could and would change, becoming entirely different. The Royce she had left a moment ago was barbaric to the bone. He gave new meaning to the word *heartless*.

When he had left the hall she had known, with all of her being, that he had gone out to get laid. And she was in disbelief.

He didn't want her. He emanated hot, sexy lust every time he came close. Virility dripped from his body like sweat dripped from other men. But he didn't want *her,* otherwise, a barbarian like that would have come on strong. It was the final straw.

Ceit hesitated and left.

Now what?

She stumbled to the chair and curled up there. The fire could not warm her. She had never had such heartache. But she had never been in love before. Was this how her boyfriends and lovers had felt, when she had eventually ended things? She hoped not! She had always tried to be kind when saying goodbye. She had always cared. And Tabby had put a few of her exes under a new love spell.

No one should have to feel this way.

She started to cry.

She tried to remind herself that the man who was down-stairs somewhere, undoubtedly with another woman, in the heat of really amazing sex, was not the man she loved. The man she loved was dead. She had watched him die before her very eyes, fighting the evil Satan had sent to hunt them all everywhere, in every time. The only problem was, she knew with her heart that they were one and the same.

What was she going to do?

She had spent less than twenty-four hours with the modern Royce, but she had fallen in love with him. He was the love of her life; she loved him even now and she would never get over him—nor did she want to.

There wasn't ever going to be anyone else. No one else could possibly compare to her golden warrior. She'd remain faithful to him and his memory until she died.

Except, she wasn't dead yet and this wasn't over. Time travel opened up all kinds of possibilities. Her tears ceased and she sat up straighter. That love was worth fighting for. Why was she wallowing in hurt?

What had Tabby said again—exactly?

Allie breathed deeply, trying to think, her determination returning. Tabby had said her life would be turned upside down—and she had been right. She had said someone would die—and Royce had been murdered shortly thereafter. But the Sun had lain beneath Death on the table. *From the ashes, there will be a new day.*

Allie groaned and stood. Of all the times for Tabby to be cryptic! What the hell had that meant, exactly? She was one hundred percent certain she was knee-deep in ashes right now.

She looked at the fire burning in the stone hearth. She was

in a small, cold chamber in a fifteenth-century castle. Time travel was a fact.

She had not expected such a cold, even hostile welcome, or that Royce would be a chauvinistic and heartless pig. Currently he was the jerk of all time, but one day, he would be her lover—and the love of her life. She corrected herself. He *was* the love of her life, he just didn't know it yet.

There was hope.

She was a Healer before anything else, but she was a fighter, too. She'd been fighting demons since she was thirteen, and she'd managed to survive evil, in spite of her small size and her lack of warrior power. Fighting was instinctive for her. She was going to fight for a future with Royce. She was going to figure out how to prevent his murder in September 2007. And somehow, she'd survive his current and very unpleasant self.

Allie breathed hard. Her composure had returned, and so had her optimism. But then, she was an optimist by nature. Every time she failed to save a vic, it hurt and she cried. But the next night, she was out cruising again, trying to save the next Innocent. Giving up was not in her nature, not now, not ever.

She just couldn't help wishing she'd see a glimmer of her Royce somewhere behind that tunic and plaid. She loved the modern Royce, but she didn't like his antiquated self at all. Did Mr. Medieval even *know* how to smile?

And why wasn't she the one in his bed? Not that she'd let him touch her, after he'd been such a complete jerk!

She groaned. He was with another woman, she was still in love with his future self, and obsessed with his present self. Not good, but considering the high stakes, she'd have to deal.

Her door opened. As two lanky boys lugged in a wooden

tub, keeping their eyes firmly on the stone floor, Allie smiled, her attention turning to her imminent bath—which she desperately needed. Their shyness amused her. Two men carrying buckets of steaming water followed. They kept their gazes averted, too, and Allie became suspicious. Surely these men hadn't heard about Royce almost emasculating that giant outside of the gatehouse?

"Thank you." She smiled at them. "Thanks so much."

They nodded but didn't look at her or even speak as they left.

Allie decided she should not be surprised—Royce probably instilled the fear of the gods in everyone at Carrick. Then she looked at the steaming bath and realized she'd have to put on her dirty clothes when she was done. Either that, or dress like the Highland women in those long, shapeless linen dresses.

She had a moment of doubt. Would Royce even look twice at her in such clothing?

She told herself that she was pretty no matter what she wore—and a good, decent person with a big heart. But Mr. Macho Man didn't give a damn about any woman's heart—he was interested in their bodies. She was sure of that! And she was shocked because she was suddenly uncertain and insecure. She had never worried about appearing attractive before, or about attracting anyone.

If at all possible, clothes from the future would be a big help. Instantly she thought of Aidan, who liked to shop. He hadn't seemed bothered by her anger toward him. Maybe she could convince him to help her out. She was pretty certain he was the Knight of Swords in Tabby's reading. In fact, he was truly decent—it was too bad the medieval Royce didn't have any of his charm or consideration.

A knock sounded on her door. Allie sensed male power,

but not Royce's. She wasn't surprised to find Aidan standing there, smiling. There was a slight, mischievous gleam in his very blue eyes. He was still wearing jeans and his beloved jacket.

Allie grinned. "Telepathy? You knew I want to talk to you?"

"I heard ye thinking my name—quite a few times." He shrugged but his bright gaze veered to the hot tub. "I do hope ye need someone to scrub yer back?"

Allie laughed. "When have you ever scrubbed a woman's back—without doing anything else?"

He grinned back at her. "Did I say I'd only wash ye?" But his gaze was direct.

This man could seduce a nun, Allie thought. "I'm taken, otherwise I'd share the bath with you."

His smile flashed. "Aye, I ken. Royce is a fool in this time, eh?"

Allie tensed, imagining him with another woman.

Aidan touched her arm lightly. "I warned ye."

"Yes, you did." She couldn't smile now. "What is his problem?"

"Ye ken, he has no heart. Not yet."

"I can't even imagine how that is possible. You have a heart."

Aidan's dimples deepened. "I like women, lass. I canna help but be nice to ye. Otherwise my bed would be cold."

Allie hoped Royce did not become charming when he was intent on seduction. She hated the idea of even his medieval self charming anyone but her.

And Aidan seemed to read her thoughts. He said quickly, "He's cold in his soul, lass. He doesna speak warmly to anyone."

"Why?"

Aidan shrugged. "Ye'll be stayin' on a bit, then?"

She became serious. "I won't let Moffat kill him in the future."

Aidan sobered. "That be six hundred years from now—a very long time."

"So you won't help me?"

"I dinna believe ye can change the future. When the Ancients write a man's Fate, t'is in stone." His smile appeared. "So ye love him even if he is an ass?"

She flushed. "I do not love the jerko that just left the great room. But, one day, he will be the man I do love." She hesitated and added, "Hopefully sooner rather than later."

Aidan folded his arms. "And if ye dinna wish fer me to wash yer back, ye want what from me?"

"Don't you want me to apologize first for attacking you?" she asked softly.

His smile faded. "Lass, ye watched yer man die. I dinna need an apology."

"You are so reasonable!" she exclaimed. She wished Royce had an ounce of Aidan's compassion. Then she smiled at Aidan again. "You do know that you're my Knight of Swords?"

Aidan looked mildly at her, amused. "I dinna think Royce would care to hear ye say so."

She took his hand. "I have a huge favor to ask of you."

He looked at their clasped hands. Allie felt his male interest escalate and she released his palm. "Could you please bring me some clothes from my time? I am not giving up on Royce and I need a few secret weapons." She thought about Brian. He had really liked her. All of her boyfriends had adored her—and wanted her. Why should a medieval warrior be any different? Maybe a few sexy things would tame the beast.

Aidan's mouth curved. "He's a Master, lass. He doesna care what garments ye wear."

She smiled grimly. "Actually you're wrong. All men respond to the right red flags—just like bulls."

Aidan laughed. "I'll do as ye wish. I dinna mind seeing Royce acting like a bull."

Allie sobered. "Why is he so angry? Why is he so set against me? Why is he with another woman, when I know he still wants me?"

"I dinna comprehend Royce at all. If I were him, I'd be in that bath with ye, now. But, lass, he has made it clear he willna allow another man near ye. And he dinna have to speak so boldly. I'd lose more than my head if I did share yer bath."

Allie didn't hesitate; she touched his cheek. "Thank you," she said softly. "Thank you for being so generous of nature, so kind and for helping me through this really hard time. I can't thank you enough."

Aidan's eyes gleamed. But he stepped away from her. Softly he murmured, "If ye decide to give up on Royce…"

"I will never give up on Royce."

Their gazes locked. "Ah, well, a man must try." He saluted her. "I'll find yer clothes."

Allie watched him walk out.

ROYCE LAY IN BED, on his back, naked, hands beneath his head. He was more irate and frustrated than earlier, and the maid creeping out of his room did not help matters.

He sighed. "Peigi. I'm sorry…another time I'll be more pleasing."

She blushed, facing him, and curtsied. "Ye be pleasin' all the time." That was a lie and she fled.

He hadn't been pleasing—he had been selfish and crude.

He had spent ten minutes with her, no more, unable to stop thinking about Ailios. And he had the terrible suspicion that if he hadn't been thinking of the Healer, he might not have become aroused enough to climax.

That was unbelievable. It was all unbelievable. Bedsport was meant to last for hours—or an entire night. And he was always aroused. What the hell was this failure?

He was immune to witchcraft, otherwise, he'd think Ailios had put a spell on him.

He wasn't even sated; how could he be? He felt even hotter than before.

But now, he had to make amends to the wench, who was a good maid. She worked hard and never complained. She was lusty in bed. He'd find her a husband with a small farm. She had to be eighteen, maybe twenty. She was ready for bairns.

As he sat up, the door opened. Only one man would enter without knocking. He considered Aidan the son he'd never had, as he did Malcolm, so he merely frowned.

Aidan glanced at him and grinned. "I wanted to thank ye for yer hospitality," he said, clearly about to depart Carrick.

Royce stood, stalking to a huge chair and shrugging his leine on. His heavy leather belt followed. He never went unarmed, so his shortsword and a dagger were added to the ensemble. "Since when do ye ever bother to say goodbye— or to thank me for anything, much less my hospitality?" He was annoyed and suspicious as he sat and yanked on his boots. And he did not like the amused look on his friend's face. It was as if Aidan knew he'd just had the one and only single failure of his life in bed with a woman.

"Yer guest asked me for a few things, so I'll be back in a few hours," Aidan said innocently.

Royce stiffened and looked into Aidan's eyes, then lurked.

Ailios lounged naked in a steaming bath tub, speaking to Aidan, smiling at him, as he stood admiring her face and figure.

"Ye watched her bathe?" he cried, aghast.

"Nay, I spent a moment with her *before* her bath, but Royce, for the gods, o' course I am thinkin' about her in her bath." He grinned and vanished.

Royce just stood there, hot and hard, *steaming*. Did Aidan want him to go to the tower and seduce the Healer? Did he desire such a union? If so, why?

Or had the sultry little Healer somehow seduced him to her will? Was she in her bath now? Did she think he'd fall for such a ploy? Did she think to seduce him against his will? Did she not trust that he had a damned good reason for staying far from her bed?

He grunted and hit his fist against the wall. His stiff body cried out for release, but he was not going to Ailios now.

He knew a conspiracy when one was formed.

THE FOLLOWING MORNING, Allie hesitated on the threshold of the Great Hall. After a huge meal with a ton of meat—which she rarely ate at home—two glasses of wine and that steaming bath, she'd crawled into bed and passed out, the sun still in the sky. Not only had she slept deeply, but her sleep had been dreamless, which had to be a good thing.

Royce sat with Aidan at the table, having breakfast. He was already staring at the threshold when she paused there, clearly having sensed her coming downstairs.

Her resolve had strengthened from the afternoon before. She could survive the beast, and maybe even tame him. She would change the future, no matter what. She was well rested and she felt good, although she'd finger-combed her hair and wished she'd had clean clothes, a good brush and a mirror. She had known he was still in the castle. She'd felt his power below. What she hadn't expected was his eyes to turn bright silver when he saw her.

Her heart sped wildly with excitement and anticipation, as if he was her lover, not some nameless, faceless woman's. And damn it, medieval version or not, he looked so good—and his heat and power pulled at her. But he was not her Royce, and she damn well knew it. So she stared and her heart eventually got it and began to slow.

As if he knew of her initial excitement, a satisfied look settled on his face.

She smiled grimly, to herself. He had been impossibly rude last night, but she wasn't holding a grudge. They were going to have to get along, somehow, for the moment.

His gaze turned wary.

"Good morning," she said, a bit too brightly. She crossed to the table, Aidan standing, as did Royce. That he would get to his feet in this persona surprised her.

Aidan smiled. "Ye look rested."

"I slept like a log," she told him, but she kept one eye on Royce, who merely nodded at her. However, he was acutely tuned to their every gesture and word. "Did you know my mother was from Kintyre, my father's parents from Aberdeen and Glasgow? This feels like home. The air is amazing. The views are amazing." She turned her megawatt smile on Royce. She refused to let it falter, but now, she saw that he looked tired.

Of course he was tired—he'd been up all night with a housemaid. She increased the wattage. "How are you? Did you sleep well?" she asked in a sugary tone.

He gave her an odd look. "I spent the night thinking about the deamhan," he said, and abruptly sat down.

She sobered. What did that mean? She glanced at Aidan,

who gave her a heavy-lidded, enigmatic look. Was he telling her that Royce hadn't been amusing himself with a lover? Was he encouraging her? She walked around the table and sat down on the bench next to Aidan. Royce stiffened, seated alone across from them.

She ignored him and smiled at Aidan. "Did you sleep well?"

He grinned. "I had dreams," he said. "Very pleasant ones."

Allie got it and laughed.

Royce shoved his plate at them both. "Ye seduce her at the breakfast in my home?"

"If I wished to seduce her, I'd have done so last night."

"Are you always so suspicious?" Allie was actually amused. If she didn't know better, she'd think Royce was jealous. "We're just having a friendly conversation." She kept glancing at his strong, bare forearms. He wore a huge gold cuff on his right bicep. It was damned sexy. She knew what that arm felt like, too. He might be a helluva lot younger than her Royce, but she was pretty certain his body hadn't changed at all. "I am a friendly person."

His eyes narrowed. "Ye weren't so cheery yesterday."

"Yesterday I was dealing with a boor. I'm cheery now."

Royce shook his head, his eyes filled with annoyance. "Ye called me an ass yesterday, an' now, ye call me a boor?"

If the shoe fits, she thought. A perplexed expression crossed his face. "You are my gracious host. You do know what that means?"

Aidan laughed.

Royce flushed. "Do I appear the village idiot? I ken yer English words, even with yer strange accent."

Allie hesitated. "I don't want to fight. I'm sorry." She finally smiled, meaning it. "I didn't travel back in time to fight with you." She thought about her previous expectations that she would find him alive in 1430 and leap into his arms and his bed. "I was hoping we could start over, you know, have a truce."

He started. "A truce? There's no war."

"Good." Allie smiled again—and this time, their gazes met and held.

Her heart turned over hard. He continued to stare, not searchingly, just boldly and simply. He didn't smile. Allie felt his pulse rising in his loins. She would never understand his decision last night to forsake her for someone else. Of course, it was for the best.

"Did something happen last night?" she asked. He tore his gaze away from her eyes. "I always sense evil. I can't imagine sleeping through a crisis."

"No deamhanain attacked—the deamhanain will never attack Carrick." He lifted a jug, filled a mug and handed it to her.

Allie was surprised by the gesture. She smelled beer. "No, thanks." His gaze lifted and their eyes held again. "Then why were you brooding last night?" She almost added, *if* you were brooding.

"Ye have enemies." He reached for a trencher laden with bread, smoked fish and cheese. "Will ye break the fast?"

Having eaten the equivalent to about three meals the night before, Allie wasn't hungry. "I beg your pardon. I don't have enemies—not human ones. I'm a Healer. I have friends—tons of them, in fact." She added, "Because I'm a nice person, in case you haven't noticed."

His gray gaze had drifted to the edge of her corset top. She hadn't been able to help herself and she had pulled it down as low as possible when getting dressed earlier. Another half inch would be immodest even for her. Tearing his eyes away, he said, "Moffat, a great deamhan, hunts ye or thinks to use ye against me."

Allie looked at him, ready to laugh. Then she sobered, because Royce was dead serious.

Allie became alarmed. Moffat had killed Royce in the future. He was shrewd and dangerous. He'd seen one moment of opportunity—a moment she had inadvertently created—and he had taken it. "Moffat can't possibly have any interest in me."

Royce's brows lifted. "Yer a great Healer. He may have powerful pages from the Book o' Healing, which belongs to the Brotherhood."

"It was stolen centuries ago," Aidan told her, "from its shrine on Iona."

Allie tried to put the puzzle together. "I'm a Healer, but I don't know anything about the Book of Healing. I am certain Moffat isn't after me."

Neither man appeared convinced. Worse, they exchanged looks she did not comprehend. "Moffat needs to die," Royce said flatly, brooding now.

"I don't think you should hunt Moffat, Royce!" Allie was so alarmed at the notion that she seized his hand. Touching his skin was electric. Instantly she released him. "Please." She tried to smile but was so worried, she failed.

He stared. "Ye dinna think me strong enough to vanquish him?"

She knew when to soothe ruffled male feathers. "Of course I do!"

He made a harsh sound. "I'm nay afraid to die, even now, an' I'll do what I must do." He stood.

Allie looked helplessly at Aidan.

As if reading her mind, Aidan said, "He kens Moffat murdered him in the future. I willna let him hunt the deam-hanain alone."

"Thank you," Allie whispered. Surely, surely, Moffat would not murder Royce now, in 1430? And in the moment, her fear knew no bounds.

But Royce had turned and he stared coldly at them both.

Allie realized she was holding Aidan's hand. She let go and said, "Royce's murder was *not* Fate. It was a mistake."

Aidan returned, "Then why are ye so afraid? Why do ye believe Royce canna kill Moffat—that Moffat will live to kill *him?*"

Allie wrung her hands. "How can I not be afraid when I watched Royce die? Are you reading my mind?"

"Aye."

Royce slammed his hand on the table, causing the jug, mugs and trenchers to leap. "The two of ye are fast friends? Since when? Since last night—when she bathed? What else happened last night?"

Allie gaped at him. *He was jealous.* Aidan didn't seem perturbed. "I like the lass. An' she's worried for ye, jackal, not for me."

Allie stood. "Royce, Aidan is my friend," she said carefully, still stunned and wondering if she was misreading him. "And he is becoming a good friend."

Aidan smiled and said softly, "I'm her Knight o' Swords."

Royce's face hardened so she said quickly, "In my time, men and women are often friends!"

"Now ye'll tell me men an' women are friends an' they dinna sleep in the same bed?"

"Yes, actually, most men and women do not share a bed, just conversation, supper, wine."

He rolled his eyes. "Aidan leaves today. Yer *good friend* has his own lands an' affairs. And, Ailios? He keeps a mistress, one he is fond of."

Allie said stubbornly, wishing she had something to knock over Royce's head, "He's my *friend*. A friend for conversation, nothing else."

"Unfortunate as that may be," Aidan murmured.

By now, Allie had realized he loved being an instigator. She gave him a dirty look.

"But ye wish to share wine with him!" Royce shot. "An' what else do ye wish to share?"

Allie shook her head in denial—when torment racked her.

She gasped, the flood of pain taking her by surprise, doubling her over. *She could not breathe. Pressure crushed her. She was trapped. She could not move.*

"Ailios!" Royce crouched beside her, holding her shoulders.

She was breathing without any difficulty, but she knew someone had just been terribly hurt, and whoever that person was, he or she was suffocating under a terrible weight. She looked up into Royce's wide eyes. And now, she felt the bleeding, inside his or her chest, and she felt sharp, stabbing pains, from the ribs. "Someone is hurt." She stood. "Really badly hurt. He or she is going to die." She stepped back from the table, Royce moving in unison with her.

"No!" She warded him off and moved into the center of the room, alone and sweating. She focused intently. *So much pain. A lack of air. That awful crushing weight. And fear, gut-wrenching fear.*

She opened her eyes. "There's a village, close by, below us. Take me there!"

Royce took two strides and confronted her. "I'll go. Ye'll stay here at Carrick, where it's safe. Whoever is hurt, I'll bring him to ye."

Allie shook her head, trying not to erupt in anger. "There

is no time, Royce. Someone has been crushed by stone. He or she will die, soon. I have to go!"

"Ye'll stay here," Royce said harshly. "Aidan—let's go." He wheeled, Aidan already halfway to the door.

Allie was in disbelief. "Damn it! I'm coming, too!" She ran after them.

Royce caught her arm. "Ye willna heal in any public manner! Or do ye wish to be accused of witchcraft?"

She tried to free herself from his ruthless grasp. He gave her a dangerous look and followed Aidan outside, slamming the door in her face.

She gasped, reeling. Didn't he understand? Who cared if the damn villagers thought her a witch? She flung the door open and saw Aidan and Royce galloping through the gatehouse. She ran after them and tripped in her platforms, falling hard. She spit dirt and got to her knees, watching the portcullis closing.

She began to shake wildly. The fear had escalated—and there was so little air!

"My lady, let me help ye," Ceit whispered.

Allie looked at her. Then she unbuckled her shoes and stood without them. "Help me get out of here."

Ceit paled. "His lordship—"

"His lordship is just a man—and he is *wrong*," Allie cried.

Ceit turned even whiter.

Allie took a deep breath. It did not take a genius to know that Ceit was programmed to believe Royce as flawless as a god. She said, "Ceit, look at me."

Ceit met her gaze.

"A boy has been hurt in the village. I can help him. I have skills with broken bones! Please help me."

Ceit nodded. "I can help ye, lady. Come."

Her heart leapt. Ceit led her past the large, four-towered gatehouse, where both portcullises were closed. A huge circular corner tower was ahead. Allie realized it was another entry point—for through its passageway, she saw a closed portcullis and a second raised drawbridge. "Aye," Ceit said. "But ye'll never get out that way."

Ceit led her into the tower, but not to the passageway leading through both iron gates to the bridge. They passed to the farthest corner, out into the next ward, and Allie saw a wooden door set in the castle's stone outer walls. It was so small that a man Royce's size would have to really squeeze himself through.

They darted to the door and leaned close to the wall, in the shadows cast by the still-rising sun. Allie trembled. "What do I do when I get out? Isn't that a ravine surrounding the castle?"

Ceit nodded. "Go left. Follow the castle walls. There's a small bridge hangin' by ropes. Ye can cross the ravine that way."

Allie nodded, adrenaline pumping. "Is there a road to the village?"

Ceit nodded. "Keep goin' down the hill. The road will be on yer right. The village be but moments away, if ye hurry."

Allie hugged her and opened the door. She slid out, closing it, and then she hurried left along the castle walls. She knew there were men in the watchtowers, but she didn't dare look up. She prayed to the Ancients for their blessing, hoping one of them might hear her and put a spell of invisibility upon her.

She saw the bridge and stopped short. *Holy shit.*

It was made of planks of wood, hanging by two ropes, and it looked about as secure as a tightrope—no, less. The frigging ropes looked old and worn and rotten. But she had no time to linger and worry. A life was at stake. She started forward, and as she did, she could see into the ravine.

She faltered.

It was a hundred feet below the grass ridge where she stood. And she took one look at the jagged, deadly rocks at the bottom and she knew that if she fell, it was over. Those rocks were not an act of nature or of God. Men had put those rocks there, to kill anyone who fell from the bridge or castle walls.

She sucked air, seized the upper ropes and started crossing.

The wood groaned. The bridge swung. Something snapped.

Allie hurried across, the bridge swinging violently now, hoping that snap had not been the rope but one of her joints instead. She saw the other side. She ordered herself not to look down. She'd never minded heights before, but now, she hated them.

A plank broke away beneath her right foot.

She screamed and seized the upper rope, her heart thundering, and she watched the plank hit the rocks below, breaking into pieces as it did so.

But the bridge remained suspended. Breathing hard, she crossed the remaining distance, and hit solid ground.

Allie ran.

IT WAS A ROCKSLIDE. Allie stumbled into the village, a collection of thatch and wattle huts, and saw the mound of rocks. Royce and Aidan were throwing boulders aside with their superhuman power. A dozen other men were helping, and no one seemed to care about the Masters' exceptional strength. A big woman stood weeping, two small girls holding on to her skirts. The entire village was probably present, perhaps two dozen men, women and children having gathered about the slide.

Allie ran forward, ignoring the sharp pain that every step caused her. Her experience of being barefoot was on the beach or at a picnic on a manicured lawn or while at the Korean pedicurist.

Royce straightened and looked over his shoulder at her. His gaze went wide with disbelief.

Allie ran to the pile of rocks and knelt there. And she felt that the boy—it was a boy, perhaps fifteen—was now unconscious. She poured her white light on him.

Royce started tossing more rocks and boulders aside.

Allie was vaguely aware of him and the other men. There was almost no air left and there was so much blood. She pushed more white light through the rockslide onto the boy, into him, healing his broken bones and crushed chest.

"I have a hand," Aidan said sharply.

Royce and Aidan redoubled their efforts.

Allie redoubled hers.

Suddenly Royce bent over her. "Can ye move for a moment?" he asked.

She nodded, stepping back, but she kept her light flowing over the boy, who was about to become exposed.

They tore at more rocks and his dirt-encrusted, bleeding face was revealed. Then she saw his shoulders, arms and chest. The woman screamed. "Is he alive? Does my Garret live?"

Allie scrambled to him. She held his young face in her hands and showered him with more white light. His eyelids lifted. His fingers moved. His gaze met hers.

She reached deep. The ribs were healed, but the lungs were sore and straining. She covered his chest. And she felt them begin to pump, at first faintly, then more distinctly. She saw his chest rising and falling now in a normal pattern. *He would live.* His pain finally vanished. She closed her eyes, filled with relief.

Royce laid his hand on her shoulder.

It crossed her mind that he was standing over her while she healed, a powerful guardian, and it was right. She smiled, eyes still closed.

"Garret!" the woman cried, kneeling beside Allie and seizing her son's hands.

Allie opened her eyes as Garret muttered and began to sit up.

"Yer alive!" The woman wept.

Garret sat up, seeming dazed but otherwise unhurt. Allie felt Royce's hands on both her shoulders now. His grasp was warm, strong, impossibly reassuring. She twisted to look up at him and she smiled.

His gaze was unwavering, searching, and then his mouth softened. He slid his hands to her waist and lifted her to her feet. Allie turned so she was in his arms. She reached up, clasped his huge shoulders and laid her face on his chest. His tunic was soaking wet.

She smiled again. The sexiest man in the world, she thought. Desire began.

She had just saved an innocent life and her blood started to pump. Yeah. It felt good.

"Are ye weak?" he asked roughly.

"Give me a moment," she murmured, not wanting to move. She didn't care that he was covered in sweat. His sweat was sexy and exciting. *He* was sexy and exciting. In fact, she felt his manhood full and throbbing between them, but that was right, too.

"Mum, I couldn't breathe!"

Allie lifted her cheek so she could smile at Royce, but

this time, with promise. She needed him now, as soon as they got back to Carrick. She'd never had a man with her when she'd healed, much less one like this one. She'd given back life and now, she wanted to take something from him—pleasure.

He tensed. His eyes turned silver.

There was always a feeling of euphoria after a healing. Royce was going to make it a million times better.

His hands tightened on her waist.

"I be crushed. There be nay air. There be pain, blackness—I be dyin'!"

Allie turned slowly, so she remained in Royce's arms. She was about to tell the boy that it was over now and he was fine.

But the boy was staring at her as if fascinated—or horrified. He pointed. "Ye did it. Ye saved me!"

Royce's grasp on her shoulders tightened. "God saved ye," he said firmly. "T'was not yer time to die."

But the boy shook his head. "My lord, I think she be a witch!"

The crowd gasped as if one. Murmurs began, disbelieving and even frightened.

Allie tensed.

"Lady Ailios is my guest," Royce said, sounding like a king, not a knight. No, he sounded like the emperor. "If ye accuse her, ye accuse me."

The boy paled.

Allie pulled away. "Royce, it's all right."

He gave her a hard look, which said, be quiet.

The heavy woman grabbed her son's hand. "His lordship and the Wolf dug ye out, Garret. They be good Christians. Thank ye, my lords, thank ye." She bowed her head, flushing. But when she lifted it, she looked right at Allie.

Her eyes were wide, bright and scared.

CHAPTER SIX

THE BOY'S SUSPICION had reduced her euphoria. So had the woman's unpleasant, frightened stare. They thought her a witch—and not a good one. So much for gratitude.

Once again, Allie wished she knew something about the Middle Ages. What she did know came from Hollywood, and she was pretty sure it wasn't accurate. But ignorance was ignorance in any time. Ignorance led to prejudice and that's when bad things happened.

The last remnants of her euphoria vanished.

She sat alone on Royce's mount—he had put her there because her feet were bare and sore—but she didn't mind. She'd been riding horses since she was four. However, he didn't know she could ride like the wind, and he led the horse up the hill. She didn't mind that, either. In a medieval way, it was gentlemanly. He wasn't being a jerk and telling her to hike up the hill alone.

But his face was hard and tight. Royce was very disturbed and if the truth be told, she wasn't thrilled with the way that woman had looked at her. She'd been caught using her powers many times, and usually, after the shock wore off, there was fear. The entire village had watched them leave, no one making a sound. She had been outed.

Should she worry?

The drawbridge and first gatehouse were ahead. Allie

said, "I was the worst student in high school. In my senior year I didn't open a single book! But what I do know is that in Salem, Massachusetts, in the 1600s, witches were burned at the stake. And I'm pretty sure they weren't even witches, just young girls *accused* of being witches."

He turned to look at her. "I dinna ken any witch bein' burned in Alba in this time."

She exhaled. "Well, that is a relief." She smiled at him.

He did not soften. "Yer never to display yer powers again."

Her smile vanished. "I am a Healer. It's what I do. If someone is in need, I will heal. I can't pick and choose the victims."

"Witches are imprisoned, stoned, outlawed. Take yer pick!" he exclaimed in agitation. He now led the bay horse over the drawbridge, Aidan abreast of them but quiet and thoughtful.

He was really concerned about her. And she'd be a fool not to listen to him, considering she didn't have a clue as to how dangerous such charges could be in the medieval world. "Okay. How worried should I be?"

"I'll do the worryin'. Ye dinna need fear. I said I'd protect ye an' I will." They entered the middle ward.

Allie stared at his broad shoulders from behind. No one had ever told her not to worry, except for her mother, and that had been in her dreams—and her mother had been dead. She worried all the time. She worried about evil hunting Innocence and about getting to its victims in time to save their lives. She tried to imagine not worrying and letting Royce worry for her, and she felt as if a hundred pounds were being taken off her shoulders. But could she trust him enough to hand that burden over to him?

Her heart was racing. No matter how medieval he was,

there was a bond between them. The one thing she was certain of was his strength. She could lean on him, count on him. She wasn't alone—and it was a relief. "Maybe I will let you worry for me," she said softly.

Royce pulled the horse to a halt and faced her. "How can I protect ye if ye defy me foolishly—thoughtlessly?" he demanded, as if he hadn't just heard her.

She stared, becoming dismayed. "Don't do this," she tried. "Not when we're becoming friends."

"I told ye to stay at Carrick. Ye disobeyed me."

She tensed with dread. They were going to fight—just when she was beginning to think she could adjust to his being a macho man. Unhappy, she slid from the horse and winced. She had been immune to the discomfort of being barefoot while racing over a rocky dirt road to save the boy, but now, her feet hurt.

Royce cursed and swept her into his arms. He bellowed for someone to take his horse and strode into the next gatehouse.

Surprised, Allie held on tightly. Her senses began to fire in delight. *Being in his arms was so right.* "Let's keep the truce," she whispered. "I am trying so hard to understand you."

"Ye disobeyed me," he exclaimed, but with far less anger, his strides long and hard.

"I don't take orders from anyone," she tried to explain. "In my time, women are their own bosses."

"T'is my time."

She sighed. "Has anyone ever told you that you are macho to the core—and as difficult?"

He glanced down at her, his mouth in kissing range. "I dinna ken macho."

She didn't smile or reply. He wasn't all that angry now,

and she bet she knew why. She slid her hands into the dark gold hair at his nape. She felt him tense; she smiled.

"You are always giving orders—and treating me as if I am weak," she said softly. "I'm not weak at all. I am trying to understand you. Why don't you try to understand me?"

"Yer a woman an' ye talk too much," he said, as if that explained everything, and in his mind, it probably did. But his gaze was on her mouth.

She smiled again. She could manage macho. She was getting used to it. It was more bark than bite. And she didn't want to argue with him. Besides, he wasn't a very reasonable man so a debate was pretty pointless. In the end, the only way to get her way was through feminine manipulation.

Yesterday had been awful. Today wasn't awful at all. "I liked having you with me while I saved the boy," she said softly.

He gave her a dark look, but his eyes were silver. "Will ye try to seduce me now?"

"You're the one who put me here," she said, and their gazes locked. "And sometimes, I don't talk at all."

He halted and she felt the tension in him explode. "Do ye think o' sex all the time?"

"I'm twenty-five," she said swiftly. "What else should I think about—especially when I'm in your arms?"

He made a sound and continued on, crossing the inner ward now. His face was set ruthlessly with determination. His temples were throbbing. Allie felt his pulse rioting, strong and thick, and bet a lot more than that was throbbing, too. "Can you deny that's what you think about—half of the time?" she asked, teasing now.

"Aye—half o' the time. The other half I have grave matters to contemplate!"

She laughed and hugged him harder. Hugging him felt *great*. "Well, that's the difference between a twenty-five-year-old and someone who's…how old are you?"

"I'm eight hundred an' fifty-five." He kicked open the great room door. "Ceit! Peigi! Bette!" he shouted in annoyance, but he put her in one of the two thronelike chairs as if she were a china doll that was about to break.

She'd had no idea he was that old. She touched his handsome face, wanting to stroke a lot more than his cheek. "I won't break. I'm sorry I had to disobey you." She actually was. "But that boy needed me. You know he would have died if I'd waited for you to bring him to me."

His face tight, he made a harsh, grudging sound—possibly one of admission. Then, "Yer feet are bleeding."

"It's only cuts. I'll have that beer now." She smiled at him. Had she just won a battle with him?

He gave her a cautious look. "I dinna ken the word."

"Ale?" she tried.

"T'is mead," he said. He turned to the three maids who'd run breathlessly into the hall. "Warm water, soap, bandages."

Allie now crossed her legs so she could inspect her feet. She had a few cuts and blisters that were no big deal. "I'll be fine. I bet I'll be as good as new in the morning." She'd be better than new if this moment led to where they both wanted it to go.

Royce gave her a look that said she was not off his hook, and he walked away. She had been right—his tunic had that terrific fold in it. Most importantly, he wasn't acting like an enraged medieval beast.

Allie watched him pour mead into a mug, pleased. He could act like an ass, but he was really concerned about her being accused of witchcraft. He was even concerned because she had slightly bruised feet. He could act like he didn't care, but he did. In poker, it was a called a "tell." Actions were everything.

Amazingly she had been in the fifteenth century less than twenty-four hours, and they were on the verge of friendship. It might be an unusual friendship, but his anger of yesterday had been diffused. What they had just shared in the village had somehow changed everything—for her, anyway.

Aidan walked in. "Ye have a powerful white light," he said.

She grinned. "I'm glad you approve."

He smiled back. "How could a man nay approve, lass?"

"Pour it on," Allie said happily.

Royce returned, handing her the mug of mead. He gave Aidan an intense, cool stare.

Allie had the feeling he felt left out. And he was still jealous. She took a sip and reached for his hand. "Aidan is gorgeous, but we both know it's you I want."

He just shook his head. "So you admit ye lust after him, too."

"No, that's not what I said. I said I lust after *you*."

Royce met her gaze and she felt his sexual tension rocket, sky high. So did his temper. "This is a game for ye!"

Aidan laughed and left the room.

Her smile faded. "No, Royce, this isn't a game. I wouldn't have traveled back in time five entire centuries if this was a game."

Royce stared at her, unsmiling. Allie stared back. He hadn't moved his hand. She said softly, "Doesn't it feel right to hold hands—to touch?"

He pulled away. "I need to save ye—from yerself."

Allie started. "What does that mean?"

"Yer the most reckless woman I have ever seen. Yer more reckless than Aidan." He gestured at the open doors leading to the corridor and staircase.

Allie saw Aidan returning—with two large Saks bags. She cried out in delight. "You did it!"

"Aye." He handed her the bags.

Allie forgot about her feet. She dug in and gasped in more delight. A green print jersey dress. Matching shoes. A long floral print skirt in white and rainbow hues. A tiny white tank to go with it. A denim mini. Cute tops. Skinny jeans. Jeweled low-heeled sandals by Giuseppe Zanotti. A white halter dress—summery, sexy, innocent, perfect. Oh, yeah, and a red drop-dead number by Escada, floor length, with red satin evening sandals.

She looked at Aidan. "I love you."

He beamed.

Royce turned red.

"Not meant literally," she told him, now standing, sore feet be damned. She reached deeper and pulled out a pink lace bra. She looked at Aidan in amazement. "I am not going to ask how you knew the right size."

"Lots of experience." His eyes gleamed.

Royce seized the bra. "Ye'll not wear this chemise—a gift from him!" He threw it furiously aside.

Allie grinned. "I need to wear something!" She grabbed the bra and returned it to the bag and produced a handful of Hanky Panky lace thongs in assorted jewel tones instead. "Perfect."

Aidan was silent.

So was Royce.

Allie looked up. Aidan had a very sexual look in his eyes—he knew what a thong was for. He'd probably seen it on a mannequin—or he'd seduced a pretty salesgirl and had her model it. But Royce was bewildered. His gaze kept going back and forth between the very tiny pink thong she held to her face. His expression was comical. He didn't know what it was or where it was supposed to go.

She bit back a laugh.

He finally said, "Is that a garment?"

Aidan choked and walked out of the room.

Allie said, "Oh yeah." And she heard the sexy note in her tone.

Royce looked at her face again, frustration covering his features. "Where, pray tell, do ye wear it?"

"You'll have to wait and see," she murmured.

His eyes widened. He stared at the scrap of spandex lace as if waiting for it to speak up and identify itself. "Is that for yer hair?" he finally asked.

Allie choked on her own laughter now. "Not exactly." She turned away. She owed Aidan, big-time.

He seized her shoulder—and the thong. "Ye owe him nothing. I dinna like yer laughin' at me."

Allie tried to stop smiling. "I'm not laughing at you—not really. But in my time, many women wear the garment—and everyone knows where."

He was red. "I'm from this time."

"Do you want me to show you where it goes?"

He became wary instantly. "Aye."

"Now?"

Very wary, he said, "This is a trap, aye? That little scrap of lace is an undergarment—it has two holes—for yer breasts."

She kept her face straight. "Sorry. But if you come upstairs with me, I'll show you. I'd show you here, but you will be really pissed if I do, especially if Aidan walks in."

His expression was bewildered again, but he nodded at the staircase just beyond the hall.

Allie shoved her Saks bags at him and, thong in hand, hurried out. Behind her, she could feel how intense Royce was. He did not like being out of the loop. Her amusement quickly faded.

Maybe this wasn't fair. He wanted to know what the dumb thong was—and she was certain he'd take one look at her wearing it and cave.

Men were visual. And Royce had enough testosterone for a dozen men. He would cave—she had not a single doubt. The thong was a trap.

Allie became somber. They walked into her chamber and Allie hesitated for a reason she could not comprehend. The most macho man she had ever met was determined to stay out of her bed. But she was about to wave a red flag—no, a pink thong—at him.

Making it about her, and what she wanted, and not about him, and what he wanted.

An hour ago, he'd stood behind her back while she healed an Innocent, and it had been beyond right.

Royce had dropped the bags, staring grimly at her. "Show me."

Her doubt escalated, intensified. She didn't want to trap him into her bed. She wanted him to take her there because he cared and could admit it.

Allie turned slowly. "I'm sorry. Maybe another time. You're right. It is a trap."

His face was chiseled hard and tight. *"Show me."*

She tensed, swallowing, desire hollowing her, at war with her morals, her mind. *Did her sudden hesitation mean that she cared for the medieval Royce, too?*

Allie was afraid to answer her own question. But she didn't want to railroad him now. It didn't feel right.

"Royce, you'll be angry when I do. And…you'll take me to bed."

He smirked. "Ye canna seduce me with a scrap of lace." His eyes burned. "Aidan has seen the garment."

"Not on me," she said quickly.

"Show me."

Her mind drummed. He wasn't going to take no for an answer, and she sensed a part of it was that Aidan knew the joke. But damn it, if he didn't resist her in that thong, she was forcing him to her will—and her bed—and he'd be really angry when they were done.

"I'm losin' patience," he said harshly.

And Allie realized some degree of pride, for God's sake, was at stake. *This was all her fault.* Filled with uncertainty, she reached under her skirt and slipped her lace boy shorts down. As swiftly, she slipped on the thong. She unzipped the skirt and dropped it.

His stare was wide and surprised. He hadn't had a clue.

So much tension filled the room she felt the blast of his sex and heat and she staggered.

He made a harsh sound. His leine swelled and lifted high up his thighs. *"Turn around."* His gray eyes didn't turn silver—they turned lightning white.

In spite of having misgivings, she was taut and breathless. It was almost impossible to think now. She turned slowly.

He was breathing hard when she faced him again. "Ye win."

She inhaled.

"Ye wanted to seduce me. Yer the victor here. Yer weapon is the scrap of lace." He strode to her and seized her waist; Allie cried out. Not with fear—she wasn't afraid—but he was furiously angry and furiously aroused. He jerked the tunic out of his way.

Allie looked at his huge, gleaming manhood and she was faint. She knew what he felt like; she knew every detail of being in his bed, of riding him for hours and hours. But this wasn't what she intended. Everything was spiraling out of control. "Royce," she tried, "I didn't mean this."

His eyes blazed. "Aye, ye did. Ye meant to seduce me. An' yer seduction will destroy us both." Suddenly her back was against the wall.

He caught her face in his hands and it was déjà vu. Allie was trying to decipher what he meant, but when she met his blazing gaze, she gave up. He kissed her.

Hot, hard, hungry, deep—and anger filled his kiss.

His thigh lifted hers high. She seized his arms. "No, wait!"

He pushed against her, slick and hot, huge, and her body spasmed uncontrollably.

But she clawed his arms. "I can't do this—this way!"

He tensed, panting against her mouth.

Allie slid her hands to his linen-clad chest and his heart thundered there. Suddenly she was ill. "Not this way. Not with anger."

He lifted his face and stared at her, his expression taut and angry. "Now ye tell me to wait? When I am ready to come inside ye?" He was incredulous. "I dinna like yer games."

She was ready to faint and come, too. It would be so easy to give in. They'd both find pleasure, rapture, ecstasy—and then he'd be furious with her for her seduction.

Something had begun that morning—in spite of his death yesterday—in spite of his medieval macho chauvinism. Something wonderful had begun between them in the village. *He'd stood behind her, defending her so she could heal. It had been so right.*

"Royce, I'm sorry."

He stared at her and his grip tightened; Allie thought he wasn't going to listen. Instead he pushed her back and released her, stepping away. "Dinna ever play me again."

"Royce!"

"Ye amused yerself—ye and Aidan, with the fucking

lace." He was furious now. He wheeled, striding for the door.

"I thought we could become close this way!" she cried, aghast.

He paused, his face livid. "Ye thought wrong!"

Allie cried out. He stormed from the chamber and she started to run after him, then stopped herself. She had done the right thing.

Trapping him was wrong.

Sex in the heat of lust and anger was wrong.

Because she was falling in love with the medieval Royce, too.

ALLIE SAT ALONE at the trestle table in the great room, having eaten a midday meal. Royce was gone. He'd left Carrick with a band of armed men, but no one had been in armor, which was somewhat comforting. Ceit said he had clan matters to attend.

She owed him a huge apology. And she didn't have to know him well to guess that he wasn't going to be inclined to accept it, either.

But she wasn't going backward. They'd formed a bond, a partnership of sorts. One step at a time, one day at a time, and no more rash seduction. Too much was at stake.

She hated herself for hurting his pride with the stupid thong.

Allie took a sip of wine. Then she tensed, aware of discomfort. Somewhere at Carrick a young child was feeling ill and running a low fever. In fact, the child was close by.

She stood. There were probably a few ill people on the castle grounds. Suddenly she was serious and intent. Like a doctor, she'd make rounds.

"Lady?" Ceit hesitated on the threshold of the room.

Allie smiled. "Yes?"

Ceit seemed nervous. "A woman from the village wishes to see ye."

Allie was alarmed. "Is it Garret's mother? The mother of the boy who was caught in the rockslide?" But the sick child was even closer now.

Ceit shook her head. "Nay, t'is Magaidh an' her bairn."

Allie's eyes went wide. Instantly she realized that the boy was the sick child she had been sensing. "Send them in," she said quickly.

A moment later Ceit showed a thin woman Allie's age into the great room. The woman was carrying a sick toddler. Recalling Royce's orders not to heal publicly, she firmly asked Ceit to leave them alone, and when she had stepped out, Allie closed the doors. Then she turned to Magaidh, who was gaunt and worried.

Allie smiled reassuringly at her.

Magaidh bit her lip. "Lady, thank ye for seein' me." She trembled and Allie felt how nervous she was.

"It's all right," Allie said, taking her hand. "Your son is sick. But he won't die."

Magaidh's eyes shot to Allie's. "Can ye heal him? He's been poorly fer days," she whispered.

"Can you keep this a secret?" Allie asked, thinking about Royce again. She owed him. If he thought she should be discreet, she would try.

Magaidh nodded.

Allie took the toddler in her arms. He started crying. He did have a fever, but it wasn't terribly high. He had a sore throat, though, and Allie knew it could be strep—which could be fatal without the proper care. Allie stroked his brow and smiled at him, sending a white healing light through him. As he wasn't very sick, he was easy to heal. The little boy started smiling and playing with her hair.

Magaidh's eyes were popping. She touched her son's brow. Her eyes went impossibly wide.

Allie looked at her. "I am not a witch. I am a Healer."

"Thank ye," she cried. She kissed Allie's hand, took her son and hurried from the room.

Allie followed her to the open door. Magaidh paused before Ceit. "She healed him." Then she ran down the corridor and outside.

Ceit turned and looked at Allie, her eyes wide with fear.

Allie sensed so much suspicion and wariness. She walked determinedly over to her. "I haven't thanked you for helping me get out of Carrick this morning."

Ceit shook her head, backed up, turned and ran.

"Great," Allie muttered. She folded her arms and stood there grimly. Making rounds was not a good idea. Not right away, anyway. Besides, no one was seriously ill. If someone was suffering and in danger of losing his or her life, she would feel it.

She really hoped Ceit or Magaidh did not start a nasty rumor.

HE WAS EAGER, too eager, to return to his home.

He had been anticipating the moment for the entire day. Now, his foolish heart sped and raced, for he was riding across the drawbridge.

Images of the little Healer were suspended in his mind, and no matter the issue at hand, even as he settled a dispute with a rival chief, she remained there, hovering, like a tiny, sultry, tempting fairy. He was beginning to think himself enchanted.

He could not cease recalling her in the low-cut, linen bodice and that tiny scrap of pink lace.

And he recalled her kneeling at the rockslide, too, straining to heal the stranger buried below.

He had been stiff with lust for most of the day. Now, uncomfortable and more displeased than he could ever recall being, Royce leapt from his steed and handed the hotheaded white charger to a young lad. "Cool him well," he said. He smiled at the boy, Donald, even though he barely saw him.

"Aye, milord," young Donald said eagerly.

His displeasure was double-edged. Aidan had joined her in the jest, and the jest had been on him. He flushed. No man from his time would have ever dreamed she wore it as she did.

And she had ruthlessly played him. He had broken his resolve and had been able to think of nothing other than getting her into bed and beneath his body. He had been about to finally experience her very warm depths. She had then *refused* him. Women did *not* refuse him. They fought for his attention. Then they begged for more.

But she had broken him and then turned him away.

The warmth in his cheeks increased. Hadn't he known, from the very start, that she could seduce the Pope? She was the victor here. She was lord and master, not he!

He did not like being made a fool of and he did not like being played. He could have had his way with her because she had been as hot as he was. With another woman, he would have stroked and caressed her and had her crying out in a climax before they'd ever gone to bed. He had walked away from this one, but he was still the defeated party.

He'd walked away, but not because he'd wanted to. That morning, in her chamber, he'd wanted to fuck her a hundred times—and watch her take her pleasure a hundred times, too.

Not this way. Not with anger....

He had walked away because of the torment, doubt and regret in her eyes. Was he now twice the fool? Had he really seen such emotions? And why, the gods damn it, did he care?

He strode through the gatehouse and into the inner ward. If he cared, it was because she was a Healer and she was a part of the Ancients' plan. If he cared, it was because she was an Innocent under his protection, and he felt her pure white power every time she was near. All Innocents were good. She was far more than good; she was angelic in her motives. He had never met anyone who wanted to help and heal more than she did. Not even Elasaid.

She deserved more than his protection; she deserved his respect. Especially because his accusations of her being ruthless were a complete and selfish lie.

She was in love with him. He had lurked shamelessly in her mind, wanting to know her every thought and care and did not even try to respect her privacy. Nor would he. She had loved him in the future, and she was starting to love him now.

The gods could only know why.

He should not be savagely satisfied, but he wanted her foolish, romantic emotions! He cursed. He had to keep the greatest distance possible now.

Royce slammed open the door to the hall. And he halted in his tracks.

Ailios stood in the center of the great room with one of his peasants, an older man who, when younger, had been a great soldier. She had cocooned Coinneach's face with her white light and it pulsed there.

And three more villagers stood in a line, as if awaiting their turn to be healed.

He was deafened by the roar of his heart. Her pure white aura pulled at him, entrancing him, the way her hot sex and stunning beauty did.

She wore a long skirt in a bold, bright pattern of black,

red and blue flowers on white, and the smallest bodice once again, although this one covered her shoulders, barely. And he knew she wore the chemise Aidan had brought for her, the pink lace garment that would only cover her breasts, the one he was going to burn, for the beaded and lace straps stuck out from the tunic.

His blood rushed to his loins; it heated his mind. He knew she felt him but she did not look his way. She was completely focused on healing Coinneach.

He fought the blinding urge to stride to her, gather her up in his arms, and end this mad mating ritual of pursuit and flight, seduction and denial. *Why not?*

He could not go on much longer this way. He had needs— and only she could relieve them, he was certain. All he had to do was put a stone wall around his heart.

They could share rapture—and nothing else.

His mind felt peculiar and dizzy now. He focused, fighting past the blinding red lust.

She was healing a toothache?

He breathed hard a final time and strode forward, in some small degree of control. "Ailios."

She now clasped old Coinneach's face in her hands and smiled at the aged warrior. "It will never bother you again," she said softly.

Coinneach's face burst into an expression of amazement. "My lady! T'is been over a year and now, there's no pain!"

Ailios smiled sweetly at the old man. As if she'd smiled at him that way, Royce's heart turned over, hard.

"It was quite the infection. It will not come back. Go home and enjoy your evening," she said.

Highlanders were proud and hard, every last one of them, high or low, but he dropped to his knees and kissed the hem of her skirt. "Thank ye. Bless ye. Yer a saint."

Ailios laughed, the sound like shallow spring water rippling over moss-strewn stones. "I am not a saint." Her smiled faded. She touched his shoulder, encouraging Coinneach to rise, and finally, she turned her large, dark eyes on Royce.

He stared back. He had asked her not to display her powers. Three villagers had just watched her heal old Coinneach. And he was certain they were waiting their turn to have their particular ailments relieved.

She bit her lip. But something eager and bright flickered in her eyes, a beautiful light, like joy, and he lurked and saw how happy she was to see him, even after only a few hours. "Hallo, a Ruari."

He tensed impossibly. They had been speaking English together. He knew, however, that she understood every word of Gaelic he or anyone else spoke. His heart lurched at the sound of the old tongue flowing like honey from her lips, just as it thundered in pleasure that she was joyous to see him.

He looked more closely at her. Her lips were painted with something pink and shiny. He wondered what it tasted like.

He wondered what she tasted like, and didn't feel like waiting another five hundred and seventy-seven years to find out. "Yer healin' a tooth."

"The infection was severe," she breathed, worry crossing her face. Her gaze drifted to his bulging leine. She wet her lips.

He lurked.

She was recalling the taste of his manhood. She was recalling how very close they'd come to "making love" that morning.

He took another calming breath. "An' the rest o' them?"

She was reluctant. "I don't know how this happened. They've been coming to see me all day. Toothaches, the common cold, cuts, bruises, aching backs!" And now, the joy that had lit up her eyes was gone. She was filled with apprehension.

He counted to three. He gestured at the three waiting villagers. "Is anyone severely ill?"

"No."

He turned. "Lady Ailios willna see ye today. G'day."

The two men inclined their heads and the girl curtsied. They all seemed disappointed, but they left immediately. Royce folded his arms across his chest and slowly turned to face her.

He tried not to think about how beautiful she was in the bright skirt and the small white bodice with the daring chemise beneath. He tried not to think about the fact that he'd bet his life she wore the tiny pink *thong,* too. "Ye heard the boy calling ye a witch this morning."

She breathed deeply. "You know I did. If you are angry— and I know you are…your aura is flaming red—you are doing a great job holding your temper."

He was angrier about this morning. His priorities were not straight. Let her try to play him. He had to swiftly quell any gossip about witchcraft and sorcery. He did not want the rumor of her healing power.

Moffat would realize she was there, in this time.

The royals might take an interest in her, too. The King was fervently devout, and he could see Ailios as either an omen or a dangerous sign of the devil; the Queen was ambitious and she would think only to use power for royal ends. He did not care to have Joan Beaufort ever interested in Ailios.

"I dinna wish to argue," he said to Ailios. "T'is clear ye

obey no one." He gave her a look. "If ye disobey yer own father, I'd be a fool to think ye'd be obedient to me, even if I am lord here. I'm no longer insulted by yer defiance." He meant his every word.

He walked over to the hearth and stared at it. How was he going to get through this evening—and every subsequent one—when his lust was raging like an inferno?

He could smell her scent. Something floral, something crisp and pure, like the Highland water, but mostly, it was woman and sex.

She was wet and full beneath that surprising skirt and that tiny, shocking garment.

He rubbed his temples.

"Okay," she said cautiously behind him. "You were really pissed this morning. You should be pissed now. What's going on?"

He didn't want to face her. "I ken ye canna help yerself. If someone is ill, ye'll heal him."

"Yes."

He did turn. "Yer like yer mother that way. She never turned her back on anyone, as long as he was a Master or an Innocent."

Her eyes widened.

"You know—knew—my mother?" she gasped.

He became cautious. "Aye, I did."

Her mind whirled in shock; it raced incoherently. "How…you mean—wait! You haven't become the twenty-first-century Royce yet! You couldn't have known my mother!"

His instinct was to soothe her. Her anxiety was profound, and dread was beginning. *She didn't know anything.*

He lurked but her thoughts were still not coherent. He hesitated and touched her arm. "Ailios. Let us sit."

"I don't want to sit!" she cried. She was pale, except for two bright pink splotches on her cheeks. She opened her mouth—and no words came out.

He took her hand firmly. "I'm sorry that ye dinna ken the truth about Elasaid."

She pulled away. "Her name was Elizabeth! Elizabeth Monroe!"

"Aye, Elizabeth is the English translation." He smiled at her. "Come an' sit with me, lass." He increased the seductive note in his tone.

"Oh gods," she whispered instead, oblivious to his male allure now. "When? When did you know my mother? What time was it in?"

He took her hand and pulled her close to his side. His body screamed in pleasure at him; he ignored it. When she learned who and what she was, she was going to be shocked. He recalled, too well, his own shock upon discovering that his Fate was the Brotherhood, and that his grandmother was a goddess. "I first met Elasaid in the sixth century."

Ailios cried out.

"Yer mother was a great Healer, an' yer so much like her," he offered softly.

She looked at him, tears rising. "Why didn't she tell me? What does this mean? Was she the granddaughter of a god, too?"

"Nay, her father was the greatest o' the gods."

Ailios stared at him, her eyes huge. And abruptly, she sat down on the bench. "My grandfather," she said slowly, "was a *god.*"

"Aye." He wondered if he should tell her the rest of the truth now, or later.

She whirled. "What else is there? I can hear you—debating what to tell me, what to hide! All this time, I thought my mother was a Healer and a pagan. I even thought she might, possibly, be a good, powerful witch. I thought that explained our religion—the prayers, the healing, our sense of evil!"

"Elasaid was not a witch. Yer nay a witch, Ailios."

She stared breathlessly at him.

"She was our Priestess, in the days when we still had one."

CHAPTER SEVEN

ALLIE SAT THERE IN SHOCK.

Her entire life, she'd thought her mother a woman blessed with extraordinary healing powers. Not once, however, had she guessed or even considered that Elizabeth Monroe might not be entirely human. Although she believed in the Ancients, it hadn't occurred to her that one of them could sire or mother a child with a human being. Her heart thudded painfully in her chest. *Her grandfather was a god. Her mother had been a High Priestess centuries ago.*

"Have some wine," Royce said softly.

She jerked, having been entirely unaware of him. He sat beside her, a mug of wine in his hand, offering it to her. He was grim, as if her shock upset him. "I had no idea," she whispered unsteadily. She met his gray, searching gaze. It was *kind*.

And she felt his concern, a soft, comforting wave, undulating in the air about her.

But she was too stunned to dwell on Royce's sudden sympathy now. Her mother was the daughter of a god. *What did that make her?*

And she thought about how her mother had hidden their powers and their religion from her father, so carefully, so deliberately. She thought about the secret room where they'd prayed. "She made me take vows of secrecy," Allie whispered. "My God, did Dad ever suspect the truth about her? About me?"

Royce clasped her shoulder. "I dinna ken, Ailios."

She began to feel sick. Her father had been a no-nonsense, ambitious, brilliant man. And while he had been Episcopalian, Allie was pretty certain he didn't really believe in any god at all. He had been a workaholic and as different from her mother as possible. Had he suspected anything? How could he not—he had been so smart! Allie tried to recall his life with her mother, but all she could remember was his grief over her death. "He loved her," she whispered. Royce didn't answer and she met his searching gray gaze. "What does this make me?"

"A great Healer," he said softly.

She had the odd urge to cry. But was she crying for herself—or for William Monroe, who had been betrayed by them both, in a way? "How long will I live?"

"I dinna ken." He handed her the mug. "Take some wine, lass."

The endearment rolled off his tongue like smooth, aged Scotch whiskey. Allie stared, then set the mug down. "Did you know her a long time?"

"Aye, for centuries."

There was so much comfort in his presence and she felt like going into his arms. She did not. Instead she thought about how much the gods meant to her. "I'm not a Priestess, too, am I?" Was this why he was intent on refusing her advances?

His gaze was serious, moving over her face. "Yer a Healer. There has nay been a Priestess in centuries. Worshiping as we do is a grave heresy, so we follow the Catholic ways in public. Yer mother was our last Priestess."

"Can you tell me about her? And how on earth did she wind

up with my father? They were so different!" She was starting
to worry about that marriage. Her mother had lived through
centuries, and of all men, she had chosen someone with no faith
whatsoever.

Royce began to speak, distracting her from a new, great
unease. "She was a great beauty, like ye, but fair. An' she
was always spilling her pure light on those in need. Had she
been ye, today, she would have healed old Coinneach, too."

Allie smiled. "I remember that. We couldn't even step
into an ice-cream parlor without her showering someone
with healing light. She died when I was ten years old—and
no one knew why." She wiped her cheek with her hand.
"Was it her time to die, Royce? She died in her sleep! Can
the daughter of a great god die that way?"

"If she died in her sleep, it was the will of the Ancients.
Mayhap she was very old. The Masters are nay immortal,
Ailios, even if it sometimes seems so. Yer mother was nay
immortal, either."

Allie smiled sadly, in that moment missing Elizabeth
very much. "I never grieved when she died. That night, she
came to me in my dreams, comforting me. And it was the
first of many visits while I was a child."

Royce was silent.

"The night we met, she suddenly appeared again—telling
me to trust you."

Royce started. "Ye saw her? Ye heard her?"

Allie nodded. "I was pretty alarmed. I hadn't had a visit
from her in at least ten years. She told me to trust a golden
Master—and that night, there you were."

Royce stared. "Mayhap she dinna come from the dead.
Mayhap she came from the past."

"Could she time travel?" Allie demanded.

Royce nodded.

Had those visits from her mother been from another
time—and not from the realm of the afterlife? She began to
shake. "She wore white flowing robes in my dreams. But
how could she come to me from the past? How? She
wouldn't know about me. Or did she also have the Sight?"

"She dinna have the Sight an' I dinna have the answers
ye need, lass."

He was being so kind. "She could live centuries, like
you." She took both of his hands in hers. "If I went back in
time, I could find her, couldn't I? She'd be alive, in the past.
You'd know where to find her!"

Royce stood. "T'is forbidden to leap for personal gain."

"And what if she has been trying to contact me from
some past century—because something huge is going
down? When she came to me in South Hampton and told
me to trust you, her eyes were filled with urgency. I sensed
that something was wrong!"

Royce stared, silent.

Allie hugged herself. He wasn't going to take her back
to her mother—at least, not yet. Maybe there was no point—
or maybe it meant everything. "When did you last see her?"

"In the thirteenth century." He added, "No one has seen
her since then."

Allie sat up straight. What did that mean? "Do you think
she leapt from the thirteenth century to my time?"

Royce glanced aside. "I think it possible."

He was suddenly being evasive. "What happened?" she
asked with alarm.

He was slow to respond and her dread increased. "Her
husband, William Macleod, an' his eldest son, from
Macleod's first marriage, were murdered. No one has seen
Elasaid since the murders, not even her own son—yer
brother."

Allie gasped. Her mother had been married in the thirteenth century. Once she could wrap her mind around the fact that she'd had another husband—or even other husbands, given her life span—she wouldn't be so stunned. She'd also had a half brother. And no one had seen Elizabeth since the thirteenth century—almost two hundred years ago.

Had she leapt after the murders to the twenty-first century? "What are the facts? Who murdered her husband and stepson?"

"There are no good facts," Royce said softly. "Only Macleod an' his heir were found. Elasaid vanished that day. The murders weren't evil—they were political, a part o' border wars. At first, we thought she fled the murderer. But she never returned."

"If she witnessed the murders, she wouldn't have been safe anywhere," Allie said. "Maybe she went to my time, where she met my father and had me." But why had Elizabeth married William Monroe? And now, Allie realized the strange coincidence that both her husbands had the same first name. "Did she love her husband, Macleod?"

"Deeply. William the Lion was a mortal man, a great an' powerful English baron. Still, Elasaid wasn't meant to love a man, Ailios. Like ye, she was meant to serve the Ancients an' mankind."

Allie tensed. Suddenly she sensed the power of her mother's love for Macleod. It had been huge, consuming, the love one found once, if ever, in a lifetime. "Don't try to tell me the gods willed Macleod's death in some kind of holy reprisal for her daring to find love! And by the way? She loved my father, too." But she couldn't recall her mother's love for her father; all she could recall was her father's grief after her death. And she somehow knew that love had been a mere shadow of Elizabeth's love for her English baron.

Allie rubbed her throbbing temples. Her mother had never recovered from William Macleod's death. She was certain. "Please tell me about my half brother."

"His name is Guy Macleod." He added, "He's known as Black Macleod. Most men fear him mightily."

Allie realized Royce was speaking in the present tense.

Royce put his arm around her. "I ken yer in so much shock."

She twisted and clutched his shoulders. "My math sucks, but he was born almost two hundred years ago. If he's still around, that makes him godlike, too!" But it was a question.

"He's a Master, lass."

She had a brother, a holy warrior like Royce. Allie held on to Royce and felt him hold her in return.

"Ye need to lie down."

Allie did not want to lie down. She wanted to think! Another brother…her mother the daughter of a god and married to a Highland baron in the thirteenth century, a man she had truly loved…her mother possibly fleeing the assassins of her family, into the twenty-first century…meeting her father and giving birth to her.

And a few days ago, her mother had tried to contact her. What did it all mean? Allie's headache became explosive.

"What should I do now?" she asked desperately, clinging to Royce's strong arms.

"There's naught to do now," he said firmly. "Ye need to rest. Tomorrow yer head will clear. Ye think too hard, Ailios. Let me take ye to yer chamber."

Their gazes locked. His power was the safest harbor she'd ever been in. "Why are you being so kind now?" she finally asked, embarrassed by her emotional upheaval. But her world had been turned upside down in the past few moments. "Where is Mr. Macho? Don't be kind if you don't mean it." She didn't know what she'd do if his cold, even cruel medieval side popped up just then.

"I had the same feelings—the same kinds of questions—ye have now," he said.

She grew more confused. What was he talking about?

"I dinna ken the truth of my ancestors until I was chosen," he said quietly. "I'll never forget the shock."

He understood. Allie collapsed against his chest. It was a moment before his arms went around her. She closed her eyes and tried to think, but it was impossible.

"Ye may never ken the truth of yer mother's disappearance," he warned quietly, her head tucked under his chin. "She fled after the massacre. Mayhap she lived in other centuries for years. Does it matter, Ailios? Yer mother died in her sleep in her own bed. Ye buried her as a child. T'is the past. Let her rest in peace."

It took her an instant to rebut. "But she may not be resting in peace," Allie whispered. She looked up at him.

He was grim. "Ye need patience. We willna find the truth tonight."

Allie held on to him, their gazes locked. Her mother wasn't resting in peace—she knew it in that instant the way she knew she loved the medieval Royce as much as she did the modern man. Something was wrong—and for some reason, whatever it was, her mother had led her to Royce.

Royce had just said "they" wouldn't find the truth. He was in this with her. And she didn't care if it was his sense of duty or the vows he'd taken. "Thank you," she managed.

Royce hesitated. She felt it in his big, warm frame. Then he pulled her close and held her tightly, just for a second.

ALLIE SAT UP.

It was the middle of the night, but she hadn't been asleep.

She had been thinking about her mother and both of her brothers, the twenty-first-century one and the medieval one. She loved the former, Alec, even if he was a new soul like their father and even if he thought her soft spirituality silly. She didn't know the latter, Guy Macleod, but she damn well was going to meet him one day soon.

Royce was right. As far as her mother's life went, she might never learn all the answers, but she was damned well going to make sure her mother was resting in peace. Unfortunately she didn't have the faintest idea how to proceed.

Tension crept over her, darkly, with stealth.

Outside, the night was studded with white stars and a half-moon. Inside, a fire blazed in the hearth, as if it were a winter night. Allie pushed all her musings aside, all her emotion, as wild as it was, and she focused.

Evil stalked them, not far from Carrick's walls.

She leapt from the bed, still in her white tank and colorful skirt. She skipped her sandals and ran across the tower. She didn't have to guess which chamber belonged to Royce, because she felt his power as she went. Like quicksand, it sucked her toward him.

But she would not relish seeing him in bed with someone else. His kindness earlier had been shocking, and she was afraid she had imagined it.

Arriving at his chamber, Allie only felt Royce. She was about to seize the door handle when it opened and Royce came out so swiftly that they collided.

He seized her elbows. "Evil."

"Human," she said quickly.

He stared at her, then lifted his head. She watched him sense the night. Then he gave up and looked down at her. "Yer senses are stronger than mine. I canna feel if they're human or deamhanain."

"They're human, but possessed. I can feel them on the walls. They're not inside yet."

Royce's face twisted. "Ye stay inside yer room." He strode past her. He seized a bell cord and pulled. The bell began to toll. *Bong…bonggh…bongghh…*

"I need a weapon," she cried.

"Not if ye hide," he snapped, not looking back. He thundered down the stairs.

Allie followed, the stone ice cold beneath her bare feet. Evil and malice were seeping into the castle, but it was still only intent.

"I said ye stay back," he shouted over his shoulder.

Arguing was pointless. He was ruthlessly intent on the pending battle. Allie saw it in his flaming aura and she felt his power and purpose in the night.

In the hall, he donned both swords and flipped open a chest with weapons. Two men thundered into the hall. Allie reached into the chest as he said, "The walls have been breached."

Taking a knife, Allie responded, "Only six of them are possessed. Capture them alive if you can!"

He sent her a furious and incredulous look, and rushed into the night.

Ceit ran in with Peigi. "What happens?" she cried, her reddish hair flowing to her waist, clearly having been asleep.

"Both of you should hide." Allie turned her back on them and closed her eyes and focused.

She felt them on top of the ramparts. She gasped as a knife went through a man, his pain flowing around her.

She opened her eyes and ran out into the inner ward. Above, on the ramparts illuminated by torches and starlight, she saw three possessed humans knifing the watch to death. The soldiers' cries faded.

Royce leapt onto the stairs, sword raised, six men with him. "A Carrick," he roared.

But the humans who'd just murdered his guard were not coming down the stairs. The walls were over two stories high, but Allie sensed their intentions. "Royce!"

He turned.

The three attackers leapt from the walls into the court-yard, landing below Royce, who was now halfway up the stairs, and just a dozen yards from Allie.

And she met three pairs of maddened eyes, glowing red. All evil was focused on her and their death lust rose up, its scent sickening. In that moment, she knew they were after *her*.

"Ailios," Royce cried, clearly sensing their evil need, too.

Allie gripped her knife, tensing.

Royce thundered back down the stairs.

One attacker leapt at her with his demonic power, crossing the entire dozen yards with a single bound, a dagger gleaming. Allie jumped aside and he landed on the ground, not far from her. He leapt to his feet and Allie crouched, waiting to dodge his next attack.

He smiled, teeth dripping saliva, and sheathed the dagger.

Allie started, realizing he didn't wish to murder her. He wished to *seize* her.

Behind her, she heard the furious exchange of sword blows. She felt male might and male fury; she felt pain. A man cried out, dying instantly.

Allie jerked and saw it was one of Royce's men.

Her attacker reached for her with demonic speed, like a striking snake.

Allie leapt aside, but he caught her arm, and she was flung back against his body so hard she saw stars. He was a giant; her head barely reached his chest. His strength was demonic and Allie went still. She could not struggle her way out of his clutches and didn't bother to try.

Dazed by the impact, she saw Royce violently behead one human monster. Three of his men lay dead at his feet.

The last of the monsters stood behind him—and as Royce flung his glance over his shoulder at her, the possessed giant struck.

It was déjà vu.

The sword descending toward Royce from behind…Royce shouting her name, blind to the thrust…her watching from a short distance, helpless to intervene.

As if the Ancients intended his death this way, no matter the time, no matter the moment.

Allie screamed, twisting in the man's foul, inhuman grip, as the sword sliced cleanly and deeply into Royce's shoulder. She screamed again, almost expecting to see his left arm fall to the ground, severed from his body.

Royce turned, thrusting. The swords met, screaming.

Allie saw his left arm hanging oddly, and she sought his pain—but felt nothing. Either Royce was too enraged and adrenalized to feel such a blow, or he was immune to the kind of pain that would cause other men to pass out.

And then he seized his shortsword with his left hand, stunning her that he could use his arm at all. And he thrust the shorter weapon across the man's neck, slitting it. Blood sprayed.

Bleeding heavily, Royce seized the dying man's ax and turned to face her captor. His silver eyes blazed. He dropped the longsword and shifted the ax to his right hand.

Allie went very still.

She didn't feel pain now. She felt murderous rage.

And she felt her captor hesitate. His fear welled.

Royce smiled and it was terrifying. He was breathing hard, and still bleeding heavily. The upper part of his tunic was crimson. But it was the ruthless look in his eyes—the ruthless heat in his soul—that made her hold her breath. Nothing was left of Royce except a barbaric warrior.

He strode forward, still smiling.

Her captor's heart rushed and he pressed his dagger to her throat.

Allie choked.

"Draw her blood and ye die," Royce said, not stopping. He closed the distance rapidly, ax in hand.

Her captor hesitated, and Allie felt his fear escalate wildly.

"Ye die anyway," Royce snarled, and he hurled the ax at them.

Allie froze as the blade whirled at them, whizzing through the air. The ax sailed over her head—she felt it brush her hair—and it cleaved the man's face in two.

He staggered backward and screamed, releasing her.

She leapt away, tripping. Royce strode past her and with his sword, he impaled the monster through the heart. Then he stood there, breathing hard, leaning on the blade, his left arm hanging uselessly now.

Allie got slowly to her feet.

He turned, jerking his sword free of the corpse. He sheathed it and looked at her, his eyes glittering insanely— like a warrior maddened from battle.

"Let me help you," she whispered, shaking. She wasn't sure the old Royce was present anywhere in the medieval warrior now. She wanted him to come back to her, but looking at him, she wasn't certain that he would.

But he was very badly wounded. Another man would be unconscious now. She had to save his arm—and his life.

But she couldn't find his pain.

Royce stared at her, his eyes hard and wide and bright. Allie felt small, female, defenseless. Then the hot silver rage began to glitter less furiously. That wild sparkle began to dull. She felt his frenzied heartbeat slowing slightly. He didn't speak but he was coming back to her and Allie knew he was seeking sanity.

He breathed and said, "Did he hurt ye?"

"No. You're hurt, not I." She had to heal him, but she was wary. She wasn't sure what would happen if she walked up to him.

Royce nodded, panting, and turned to his men. Now that the brief battle was over, every knight in the garrison had surged into the ward, bearing arms. "There'll be nay more attacks on Carrick. Triple the watch. Take care o' the dead." He looked at Allie harshly, his gaze still overly bright. Abruptly he strode past her.

His pain blinded her.

Allie breathed hard, shallowly, shocked that he was still standing. Then she ran after him. Royce was still in a savage, warrior mode, but he was feeling the effects of that terrible blow and he was bleeding badly. Now that she could feel his pain, she was pretty certain his arm was partially severed from his body. He was just too enraged to feel it completely yet.

He stood by the table, draining the jug of wine.

Ceit and Peigi looked ready to faint.

"There'll be no more trouble this night," he told them harshly. "Bring linen, water. Good night."

Ceit didn't hesitate. She and Peigi fled.

Allie walked slowly toward Royce, now standing in a puddle of his own blood. That blinding pain went through her again.

Royce looked at her—and then tore his blood-soaked tunic from his body, flinging it to the floor. Allie bit her lip at the sight of his body—muscular, scarred and shockingly, fully aroused. He gave her a heated look.

He was still in the throes of bloodlust, she thought uneasily.

"Come here," he said. And it was the kind of order he'd give to one of his men.

She had to heal him but she hesitated. Even badly wounded, he was a magnificent sight. And she felt his lust—not around her—in her. It seethed and begged for release.

She was almost afraid of him. But her body was humming and vibrating with an intensity of its own. Her gut was hollow, aching. "You're bleeding to death."

He sent her another heavy, hot look. "So heal it." Then, he spoke in a murmur. "Come an' heal me, Ailios."

She trembled and poured her white light over him, into him.

His eyes widened, as if he hadn't expected it.

But then, had a Healer ever healed him before? She knew her power was warm and that it felt good. She knew the moment he received her white power, his pain would begin to diminish.

He stared at her in surprise, but his gaze remained intently male and predatory. Allie felt the sharp pain going through him, through her, but it wasn't blinding now.

She poured more light over him, into him, focusing on his shoulder and the deep wound. He grunted. The sound was one of release.

Then he gave her another long look. His gaze was coherent now.

Confident that he was not about to leap on her in a very bestial manner, she walked up to him and laid her hands on the wound, ignoring the blood. More healing power flowed from her hands, surging now because of their proximity.

His gaze held hers, watchful and intent. "It feels good," he said roughly.

She smiled but didn't speak. She could not focus while having a conversation. She threw more healing power directly into the wound this time. She became aware of his bulging bicep, just above her eye level, and his bloodstained chest.

He grunted again as more pain was released. He sat down.

Allie was so short it was easier to stand with her hand on his shoulders while he sat. The bleeding had stopped. She felt the flesh inside the wound binding and renewing itself. His pain had dulled to a mere ache. She smiled, pleased, and then her heart lurched.

She had almost been the cause of Royce's death—again.

"I'm fine," Royce said thickly.

Allie saw that he was even more fiercely aroused than before. But of course he was. That shocking, savage, murderous frenzy was gone. The barbarian was gone. But she'd stopped the bleeding, meaning his blood supply was going somewhere else. His gaze was on hers, oddly uncertain and searching.

Her heart turned over, hard. "Don't move," she said softly. "Let me finish."

He just sat there, staring at her face.

Allie went to the door and stepped into the hall, hoping to find Ceit for the linens and water. She'd set a basin of water and clean linens next to the door. Allie gathered up the items and returned to the hall.

Her steps slowed. Royce sat naked on the bench, fully aroused, looking exactly like what he was: a supernaturally virile, superpowerful holy warrior with a godly ancestry. He turned and stared at her. His gaze sizzled.

She came forward, her entire body flaming. Was he inviting her to bed, finally? Or was this still about the battle from hell? She cleaned the blood from his shoulder with the wet linen, pleased to see an angry red scar there. By the morning it would be pink, and in another day or so, white.

She wrung out the linen and ran the wet rag down his arm, cleansing the blood there, too.

He breathed deeply and threw his head back. His eyes closed. The pulse in his throat throbbed. His abdomen tensed, the muscles hard and tight.

She rinsed the rag and laid it on his shoulder, so swollen she couldn't stand it. Everything had changed in the past few hours—and there was no anger between them tonight.

Aware of what he was asking her for, aware of what she wanted, she moved the moist linen slowly over his chest.

He said, without opening his eyes, "Oh, dinna think I'm nay angry."

She had to smile, removing more blood. "Hush." She ran the moist rag lower, over his ribs, removing the blood there.

His gaze opened, hot and heavy, languid with intent. He remained arched backward against the table. "Ye can disobey me anytime," he said softly, seductively, "but nay in battle."

Allie hesitated. Her gaze was not on his. He was straining for that moist rag. "I think," she said, and she slid the wet linen low, all the way down his belly, even though there was no blood there, "I may have learned my lesson."

He sat still, breathing hard, watching her now.

Allie took the wet cloth and flicked it up his long, thick shaft.

He made a very harsh sound of enjoyment.

Allie met his gaze and smiled at him, her heart hammering with excitement. His gaze flared and he seized her hand.

He took the rag and tossed it aside. Allie sank to her knees, pleasure building wildly now, nuzzling his perfect length. He gasped and she teased him with her cheek. She thought she heard him ask her to hurry. She rained kisses on his hot skin.

Suddenly he seized her hips, lifting her to her feet and anchoring her between his legs. "Let go," Allie gasped, because she had been about to do something she'd been thinking about for days.

"I'm master here," he said, and he pulled her hips forward. Suddenly she was on his lap, his turgid erection against her side, and he was clasping her face in his hands. "I'm tired o' this game."

"Me, too," she said, her heart ready to explode from her chest.

He looked at her and their eyes met. She saw wild excitement and hot lust, but also something else, bright and light. Then he lowered his face to hers.

Allie gasped with pleasure, with joy, because he claimed her lips with such hunger, such need and desperation that for one moment, she thought herself back in 2007. She reached for his shoulders and clung. He thrust his tongue deep while he kept her face still in his huge, uncompromising hands. Allie came to her senses and started kissing him back.

He finally grasped her skirt, the gesture brutal. Allie knew he was about to rip her clothes from her body. She seized the zipper and frantically pulled. He never stopped kissing her, but his mouth softened and she felt a smile.

"Yer precious garments," he murmured.

"Very precious," she gasped. Somehow she wriggled out of the skirt. He seized it and tossed it to the floor.

And he stopped kissing her.

Allie opened her eyes, breathing hard, her body positively in flames.

He stared down at her thong—and the soaking-wet flesh beneath. Then he gave her a sensual look. He slid his thumb beneath and Allie almost wept from the delicious pressure. Smiling, he rubbed deep, deeper, firmer, knowingly.

"Oh," she gasped.

"I want to watch ye come, right now."

Allie didn't think it was a problem. She was about to crest and break. And then something stopped her—*he* stopped her, with some kind of force over her mind, her body, her sex.

Just as he'd done that first and only night.

"Except," he said, his gaze blazing, "I want ye coming the first time with me inside." He lifted her and laid her on the edge of the table, a knee on each side of his hips as he stood.

Allie began to hyperventilate. "Hurry."

He smiled and dipped between her thighs and rubbed against her. She couldn't stand the exquisite pleasure and she writhed. He restrained her.

"Be still," he murmured. "Let me do the fucking. Lie still an' enjoy it."

She looked at him.

He was dead serious. "This one time, ye can obey. Let me pleasure ye, Ailios."

She nodded—or thought she did. It was really hard to respond because he was starting slowly, with agonizing deliberation, to push inside—only to pause after every single inch.

She lay as still as she could, starting to cry from the pleasure and pressure, and she let him stroke her, bit by bit, until it was long and slow, deep and deeper still. Madness began. She was blinded by the need for a release. She didn't know how she could hold so much pressure inside her—or how he could do so, either. Because she felt his pleasure, too. It had crested into a tidal wave, one about to crash down on the shore—on her. And finally, she couldn't stand it; finally, she wanted to beg.

"Aye," he said, and he gasped, surging deep.

Allie felt the block being lifted. She felt the huge damn break. She cried out, exploded and flew farther, higher, than she'd remembered, weeping his name, shattering a hundred times, each time more intense than the one before. He came with her, each time, violently, long and endless. *"Ailios."*

CHAPTER EIGHT

ALLIE AWOKE IN A BED twice as large as her own. She lay naked beneath a fur and instantly she thought about Royce's very hot, very endless lovemaking. She smiled, reaching for him, to move into his arms. He was gone.

That was okay. She looked up at the ceiling, grinning so widely her mouth hurt. Wow. Those first two times hadn't been a dream. She hadn't imagined all that supernatural sex.

Mr. Medieval was *hot*.

She lay still, thinking about the heated night—thinking about his passion and her own. For her, loving him now as she did, it had been even more intense than in her time. That first night it had been only sex and desire; she'd begun to fall in love with Royce after spending that night with him. As for his passion, it had been so off the charts there was no way she'd believe he wasn't in love with her, too. In fact, unless she was imagining it, she felt that he was even more insatiable than he'd been in 2007. That was pretty impossible, though.

Or was it? Everything had changed and so swiftly, at the speed of light. In the future, he'd waited almost six hundred years for her. Last night, although he hadn't had to wait centuries for her, they'd shared a lifetime in a few days—a very dangerous, intense lifetime. They'd fought and argued, they'd saved Garret from the rockslide, they'd fought demons, she'd healed him from a mortal wound—and he'd comforted her while she tried to adjust to the shock of the truth about her mother.

Allie sat up slowly. That last action meant as much as anything, if not more. He was a very complex man, with so many sides—he could be savage and barbaric, but he could be caring and kind. She thought about the way he'd used the ax to destroy the giant who'd captured her and her stomach vanished. He'd been scary. He could have used an energy blast but he'd preferred an ax. She'd been afraid to rush up to him to heal him. But hadn't she needed someone that ruthless, that brave and that determined to hold the line, her entire life? Royce had the savage intent *and* the strength to fight the most powerful demons and win.

Allie shivered and lifted the fur. She almost wished she hadn't recalled his savagery and bloodlust. But she had to admit that she had a primitive side, too. She was fascinated with the savage warrior. She *admired* his intensity.

Still, she would have never dreamed in a hundred years that the same man would hold her while she unraveled. He had probably been just as surprised. Now she could see how the medieval version would evolve into the modern man she'd first fallen for. However, it was a bit presumptuous to think he was starting that transformation already. Maybe, *maybe,* he could do it in a hundred years.

Allie got up, wrapped in the fur, smiling. She wasn't sure what her life span was; apparently her mother had lived at least six hundred years. It would be interesting to watch Royce embrace his softer, kinder side. Her heart leapt impossibly as she imagined long nights like the last one, times spent before the fire or on the ramparts, gazing at the stars.

She was falling for this Royce, and she had better slow

down, because Mr. Medieval might be back at any moment and he was not ready to hold hands. Her smile faded a little. One thing had been missing last night. He hadn't cuddled and he hadn't talked.

Allie focused. She needed patience—she'd be his teacher now. It was okay. All that sex was coming from his macho side. He needed a bit of time to learn how to be intimate and about the enhanced pleasure intimacy could bring.

Maybe she'd start teaching him tonight.

In any case, things were looking up. They were becoming friends, and they were lovers, too. The beast wasn't as scary as he'd seemed, and he was starting to eat out of her hand. Now she had to figure out why he'd wanted to die in 2007. It was time to get to know him—she needed to get inside his head.

Allie was eager to know him better, but she was not at all deluded. If he didn't like talking—and he had made it clear he did not—figuring him out might not be that easy. That was going to take time, no matter his kindness last night.

Her heart wanted to float up to the ceiling like a hot air balloon. Last night made up for his initial hostility; it sure did. And she had time, didn't she? There was no rush to go home, even if Royce changed his mind and let her do so.

Allie walked over to the hearth, wishing a fire flamed there. She'd assumed her stay in the past would be a brief one. In fact, she'd assumed her future with Royce would be *in* the future, too.

They were meant to be together, that was clear—he was the one for her. But in which time?

Allie became uncertain. She would stick around in the fifteenth century for a while, but at some point, when they had a way to prevent his murder, she was going to the future to be with the modern Royce, wasn't she?

Unease began. She would leave her medieval man there at Carrick, in the fifteenth century, and with a leap through time, she would be reunited with Royce instantly. But he'd be left behind in his time, and he'd spend centuries without her—until he aged into his fourteen-hundred-year-old self and was reunited with her.

How could she leave him for five hundred and seventy-seven years? They were embarking on a new relationship. He'd become her guardian as well as her lover. He needed her, here and now, and she needed him.

Allie looked around at his chamber, thinking about the bedroom in her Manhattan penthouse. Then she shoved the memory of her luxurious room aside. The Middle Ages weren't as bad as she had expected. Nothing at Carrick was that dirty, and while there was a lot of body odor, Royce smelled great. She would bet a fortune that he swam in one of the lochs every morning.

She wasn't going to be able to leave him, she thought. And the moment she realized that, her heart began to dance and sing, rejoicing. Grudgingly she smiled. Man, she was getting in deep!

A knock sounded.

Allie was glad for the interruption. She knew Royce would not knock—it wouldn't occur to him. She called out to enter, curious.

Ceit came in with a maid Allie hadn't seen before, a pretty blonde. Ceit smiled at her. "I thought ye might be awake, finally. T'is hard to open yer eyes after a night with his lordship." She held a trencher in her hand.

Allie stiffened. Some dread niggled as Ceit set the trencher down while the blonde, who was very young, blushed and giggled.

It had sounded as if Ceit knew all about Royce's lovemaking. Allie told herself to breathe. Ceit was a nice woman, and not the type to catfight. She knew she hadn't meant anything and she counted to ten. "Did Royce tell you to send that up?"

Ceit looked surprised. "He left hours ago, my lady. He be an early riser. He dinna say a word, really, this morning. He seemed to be considerin' weighty matters. He dinna seem all that pleased, either." Ceit gave her a curious look.

Allie felt her smile vanish as the blonde began to start the fire. She folded her arms. "Last night was great."

Ceit went to the bed and started pulling off the covers.

Allie gave up. "So you have shared Royce's bed, too?"

Ceit looked at her, eyes wide. "Not in two years." She added hastily, "Only fer a short time, my lady."

Allie reminded herself that Royce's days as Don Juan were over. She knew he was in love with her—she felt a blazing connection between them, even out of bed. He had her in his life now, and that changed everything. Didn't it?

She hated knowing that he was a medieval lord and pretty much had a castle filled with pretty women to hurry to his beck and call. But he had shown her how much he cared yesterday—and how much he loved her last night.

Knowing she should not ask, she couldn't stop herself from speaking. "Did he make love to you all night long—as if the world were ending?"

Ceit's eyes widened. "There be no love at all, my lady. He's a man with strong needs. Ye dinna need look at me with such fear."

Allie tried to smile. "What did he do? Tire of you? Find someone younger, prettier?"

Ceit was puzzled. "Of course he tired of me. I knew he would, for he tires of all the maids. Lady, what is this? Dinna be saddened! Ye should enjoy his attentions for the moment."

"For the moment," Allie echoed, uneasy now. "But he won't tire of me." Royce was falling for her. Why couldn't Ceit see that?

Ceit glanced at her and quickly looked away.

But Allie had seen pity in her eyes. "I'm different—and you know it!"

"Ye be very different. But that look on yer face—I've seen it before—hundreds of times—in this very chamber."

Allie felt ill. "Okay. He's had a lot of lovers. And they all fall for him. Great."

"T'is hard not to think ye love such a man after such a night," Ceit said softly. "But, my lady, dinna be so foolish. All men tire of their mistresses. T'is the way of the world. Men like young, new sport. He'll only break yer heart."

"I am in love with him," Allie said firmly. "I will love him until I die. And he loves me, too. I am here to stay."

Ceit smiled kindly, but worry was reflected in her eyes. "So ye think to marry him?"

Allie didn't hesitate. "Yes, I do, when the time is right."

"Yer a foreigner, English be my guess?"

Allie hesitated. "Close enough."

"Are you an heiress?"

Allie was confused. She was about to say yes when it occurred to her that in this world, she had not a dime. "No. I'm dirt poor." It was weird saying it—and almost meaning it.

"If his lordship marries, he'll marry a great heiress. He doesna need more land or another title. But all men need more wealth." Ceit started making the bed.

Allie walked up to her, aware that Ceit believed her every word. "What about love?"

"Love? What does love have to do with marriage?" She shook the covers for emphasis. "When a man needs power, wealth or sons, then he marries."

And briefly, Allie was disturbed. She wasn't going to claim that she knew very much about the medieval world—how it worked, how a man like Royce might think, or what he really wanted. But love was timeless, wasn't it? Or didn't love matter in the Middle Ages? Could Royce really look at the world the way Ceit was describing? "Does Royce have sons? Why isn't he married?"

Ceit shook her head. "Nay a single bastard, an' that be strange." She then said, "No one knows why he's unwed. There's gossip, of course."

Allie seized the bait. "What kind of gossip?"

"I heard it said there was a wife, long ago, but that doesna explain why he hasn't married anew."

"Royce was married?" Allie gasped in surprise.

"T'is said the marriage did not last." She shrugged. "I have even heard it said that his wife be the reason he's unwed to this day."

"Why?" Allie cried.

"I dinna ken." She smiled kindly. "And that be gossip, my lady, an' mayhap untrue."

Allie stared unhappily. "Where there's smoke, there's fire."

ROYCE HAD BEEN GONE all day. Allie learned he'd had to inspect some lands belonging to Morvern and that he would be back by supper and that was fine with her. But she hadn't gotten over the morning conversation with Ceit. The maid's assumptions that she was no different from his previous lovers worried her. Ceit had to be wrong.

When the sun began to lower, Allie went into the courtyard. She was wearing her jersey print dress and high heels, aware that Royce would be inflamed by the tiny, clingy dress, and she made her way up to the ramparts so she could watch for him. Every man she passed avoided looking at her; Allie felt ridiculously safe.

One long day apart after last night felt like weeks, no, months. She stared past the crenellations, across the small midward and the outer walls, across the dangerous ravine. When she went into his arms—when they made love—she would forget about the confusion Ceit had raised. A group of horsemen were approaching and she recognized the huge white horse at its head. Her heart leapt and sped.

As the band got closer, his aura blazed, dwarfing everyone else's. Allie tensed, fisted with desire. His aura was red-hot and she knew what it meant. He was coming for *her.*

She hung on the crenellated wall for one more moment, as the riders trotted over the main drawbridge. Royce glanced directly up at her, clearly sensing her presence on the walls.

Allie was still, an act of great self-control, because she wanted to rush down to the courtyard and leap into his arms—and then be dragged to his bed. She couldn't wait. He kept staring until his charger disappeared beneath the gatehouse towers.

Allie finally gulped air, wet to the core, and carefully descended the stone stairs. Anticipation made her feel faint. Royce had already dismounted and his steed was being led away. He hadn't been wearing armor, just the belted tunic and plaid, and his swords. He looked every bit a warrior of the gods. Not glancing her way, he started for the Great Hall.

Allie tensed. He hadn't looked back at her, not once. But his senses were acute, like hers. He had to have known she was there. "Royce!" She hurried after him.

For one moment, his strides didn't slow. Then he faltered, but as he turned, he beckoned to one of his men. "Neil."

Allie was confused, because he was facing her now, but not looking at her.

A big man with flaming red hair approached. "My lord?"

"At dawn, take five men an' pursue the poachers. Yer to bring them to me. I wish to stare in the eye the man who dares break my laws."

"Aye, my lord."

Allie stood beside Royce and the giant, waiting for Royce to acknowledge her. Why was he avoiding looking at her? Where was his sexy, knowing glance—and an even warmer smile? Her heart beat so hard it hurt. What was happening?

Neil left and they were alone. Royce finally looked at her in such a way it was as if he didn't wish to really see her at all. In fact, his glance was so brief, so cursory, that Allie would bet he didn't even know she wore a sexy green and white print dress that hugged her every curve. "Good eve," he said, staring at the great room door instead of at her.

What the hell was this? Allie's confusion became uncertainty. "Hey. Hi," she managed, staring up at his profile. But it was an expressionless mask that could have been carved of stone.

He nodded, his gaze briefly flicking over her, avoiding her eyes. "I'm hungry. The day has been long." But he waited for her to walk inside before he did so.

Allie couldn't understand. Why wasn't he looking at her? What was wrong? His aura remained hot and ready to go. "Hey." She reached for his arm and touched it. "Are you okay? What's wrong?" Had something terrible happened?

He shifted and her hand fell away. "Let's sup," he said, and he walked inside, leaving her standing alone.

Allie tried to remain confident. There was no reason for Royce to reject her. She didn't care what Ceit had said earlier. His aura told her he was hot for her. He couldn't possibly have tired of her.

But he was cold and impersonal, as if last night hadn't happened, not any part of it.

SHE WALKED INTO THE HALL behind him, terribly unfamiliar with her anxiety. Most of her life she had cruised through any and every situation with no doubts at all—especially if the situation was social or romantic. Any anxiety she'd ever had had been related to her academics. She felt so odd. He was going to have a drink and turn and smile at her, wasn't he?

Royce was shouting for Ceit to bring the meal, while pouring a mug of wine. Then he hesitated, his back to her. Finally, Allie thought, trembling.

Ceit came running in with Peigi. She laid a trencher of meat and fish on the table, while Peigi went to Royce and unpinned his plaid, taking it from him. When Royce didn't turn to her to smile or even speak, Allie began to breathe hard. Moisture came to her eyes. *Was he rejecting her? Had Ceit been right?*

Both women left, only to return with bread, cheese, grains. Royce, his shoulders stiff, finally turned. "Here." He extended the mug of wine.

The last shreds of her optimism and confidence vanished. She walked up to him when it felt like she was walking into the mouth of an erupting volcano. "What is going on? Why aren't you looking at me? What kind of greeting is this? I have missed you so much!" she cried, trembling.

He was looking at her now. Still offering the wine, his gaze moved from her eyes, where a tear slipped free, to her mouth and down the sexy jersey dress, right to her green suede high heels. He lifted his gaze, and before his lashes came down, Allie saw bright heat. "Do you wish for some wine?" he asked with so little emotion that he could have been asking a stranger.

Allie trembled, the urge to strike the wine from his hand huge. "No. I was thinking along the lines of a hug and a kiss."

He drained the wine and refilled it, his back to her once more. "Tomorrow ye go to Dunroch."

Allie tensed impossibly. Everything was wrong. He was not the lover she'd had in her bed last night; she didn't know who he was. "Dunroch?" she managed to say. She wiped another errant tear. But why would he do this?

"Aye. My nephew Malcolm an' his wife are there. Ye'll be safe with them."

Allie gasped. "Are you getting rid of me?"

He sat down at the table, heaping meat and salmon upon a trencher. "Ye need protection. I trust Malcolm. He's a powerful Master." He didn't look at her, just started eating.

Allie was in disbelief. "Royce," she began.

"Sit down an' eat," he said, shoveling food into his mouth.

Allie realized he was intent on ignoring her now. She stepped to the table and pulled his trencher from him, so abruptly that some meat and bloody gravy sprayed over the table and his lap. He looked up, his face hard. "Last night we made love. Today we're done?"

"Aye."

Shock began.

"Ye need protection an' Malcolm will protect you with his life," Royce said.

This could not be happening, Allie thought. "You did not use me," she managed to say.

"I'm sorry."

He had used her?

Allie did not have a temper. Now, she saw red. She hit him across the face, as hard as she could. And pain blinded her, bringing the tears she so wanted to release.

He leapt up and seized her throbbing hand, holding it tightly, to ease the pain. "I am sorry. I dinna make any promises...nary one." Then he bellowed for the maids.

She tried to jerk her hand free, but it was impossible. "Let go." *But he hadn't made a single promise and he hadn't said he loved her—or anything even close.*

He held on tightly for one more moment, as the maids came running in. They gasped at the sight of his stained tunic and the spilled food. "Get seawater for Lady Ailios. She has hurt her hand. I need a leine."

As Ceit and Peigi vanished again, Allie jerked on her hand and he let it go. "Am I a fool?" she said, still reeling.

"Last night Carrick was attacked. The deamhanain want ye an' they want ye alive," Royce said flatly. His gaze was searching, but Allie couldn't look at him.

"We had an incredible night, and you want someone else?" she asked.

He said, "I dinna ken if Moffat is behind the attack. He's one o' the greatest deamhanain in Alba, an' has been so since the earl of Moray was vanquished three years ago, by Malcolm an' his wife. Some say he has the Duisean but I dinna think so."

"Have I totally misunderstood? Have I completely confused you with the man I fell in love with in my time?" Allie cried, feeling like a pathetic fool.

Royce stared. Then he turned and walked to the fire. "Even if Moffat wasna behind the attack, that only means other deamhanain want ye—alive. Yer nay safe here. Malcolm will defend ye with his life, an' ye will like Claire. She's like ye. She's from the future."

Allie cried, "Last night was about love!"

Royce whirled. "Last night we fucked." His eyes were finally ablaze. "I ken yer in love with me. Do ye wish to

share my bed tonight—knowing that on the morrow ye'll go
to Dunroch an' that I'll leave ye there?"

She gasped again. *He was ditching her.* She could barely
think. "You're supposed to protect me."

"Aye, protect ye—not take ye to bed."

"Are you purposefully trying to hurt me? All I have ever
done for anyone, everyone, including you, is to be kind and
caring. I healed you last night! But you are throwing these
words at me—and you might as well be throwing knives! Do
you want to see me broken? Is that what you want?"

His face was taut. "I want to see ye alive. I want to see ye
home, to yer time, where ye belong—when yer nay in
danger."

Allie stood there, trembling convulsively, as Peigi dashed
in with a clean tunic. She had made a terrible mistake. Mr.
Medieval wasn't at all like the modern-day Royce, and from
what she now saw, he never would be that man. He was the
cruelest man she had ever met—and the most indifferent.
In that second, it seemed impossible that he would ever
become the man she had fallen for.

Royce stripped off the tunic, revealing his hard and
muscular, scarred body, and the fact that, in spite of his
words, he was ready to take her upstairs as he had suggested. Handing him the tunic, Peigi blushed.

Allie turned away. She was ill, really ill—heartsick. How
could this be happening? Had she imagined him being kind
last night? She stumbled from the hall.

"We leave an hour after dawn," Royce called after her.

She almost whirled and strode back to him to tell him
she wasn't going anywhere with him. But she hurt too
much now to fight.

Outside, she sat down on the steps and curled up, her
heart shattered and broken. How could this be happening?

She had been ruthlessly used. The medieval Royce didn't love her *at all*. He didn't care *at all*. She had never realized heartbreak could be so painful. How could she have confused the two men with one another? How could she have been so drawn to, and have fallen for, the heartless barbarian? It didn't make sense, because the cold bastard who was currently inside the hall had held her last night as if he cared—as if he had a heart. But he didn't—and he had just made that clear.

Allie let the tears fall. And the worst part was, now that she'd given her heart to this Royce, she suspected there was no taking it back.

ROYCE GAVE IN TO HIS RAGE and swept his arm across the table, sending every trencher, the wine and mugs crashing to the floor. Peigi cried out and fled.

Then he grasped his throbbing temples and sat down. He leaned his arms on the table and held his head in his hands, his appetite gone.

Was she crying? Would he ever erase that look of hurt from his mind? He was doing what was best. She was not going to become another Brigdhe. And he had an odd ache in his chest now, for having caused her so much anguish. She was one he never wished to hurt. She had said it herself—she was kind and good and she did not deserve such cruelty.

Why did she have to love him? Had he asked for love or any affection? He'd only wanted sex! He hadn't made a single promise! He was a man of his word and when he made a vow, it was forever.

That morning, as he slipped from their bed, he'd had the oddest urge to slide back in beside her and hold her, watch her while she slept. It had made him pause.

He had never met such a selfless woman. He had never seen such courage—all of it reckless, but well-meant. She emanated not just her white light, the power of all that was good, but her happiness. When he looked at her he saw more than her beauty, he saw so much purity and joy. He saw hope.

She looked at the gray world as if it were a brave white dawn.

She was everything he was not.

No good could come of the confusion he felt. He'd never held another human being except for the woman who was in his bed and then only during fornication. Holding her last night—and wanting to hold her now and tell her he was sorry—was unacceptable. He had made vows. His duty was to God and Innocence. There was no room in his life for affection for a woman. It would make him weak and she would become a terrible target the moment his enemies knew.

He had to remind himself of that fact now.

He had been fond of Brigdhe. When his father had died, leaving him the great responsibility for Morvern, he'd decided to marry and beget sons. His older brother, Brogan, had suggested he consider Brigdhe. She was pretty, her lineage ancient, her dowry pleasing. He was a dutiful man and she had been a good woman. But he had learned his lesson well. Brigdhe had been captured, imprisoned, tortured and raped because of his love. He had failed to protect her. And when he'd freed her, she'd hated him for his failures. He was not going to repeat the mistake.

He reminded himself of Brigdhe's terrible ordeal and his equally shameful failure once a year on the anniversary of her death. She had died in old age, well loved by her sons from her second marriage and their grandchildren. Before her death, her presence in his time had been enough to make him remember the lesson he must never forget.

She had died in the spring, and it was autumn now, but it was time to remember. It was time to remember her and never forget. He let his mind open and, with the memories, the guilt began, crushing him.

When he'd found her, she'd been battered and bruised, her face swollen and ugly, her lips split. There'd been lash marks on her back. Demonic seed had been all over the room.

She learned later that she carried Kael's seed—and she had almost died getting rid of the demon spawn.

Royce laid his head on the table and let the torment wash over him.

THE WAVE OF ANGUISH was so huge it knocked Allie back against the wall where she sat. Instantly she righted herself, eyes wide, shocked.

Royce.

In disbelief, she felt the waves coming, hard and fast, cresting. With the sorrow she felt regret, but mostly a crushing guilt.

Allie stumbled to her feet, her heart racing. What was happening?

She shouldn't care; she was helpless not to. It was in her genes to heal those who were suffering. And Royce, whom she loved even if he was a ruthless bastard, was in the throes of torment now.

She staggered into the hall, fighting her way through the waves of his pain. She stopped abruptly, for he sat hunched over the table, his head on his arms, his big body shaking, as if he was weeping. But he wasn't weeping, not with tears.

His aura was split in two.

It was mostly blue, but pure black divided it in a jagged line.

Allie cried out, shaken to the core. All self-control and self-mastery were gone. She wasn't looking at a warrior or a Master; she was looking at a broken man.

His soul bled.

Allie couldn't help herself. She raised her hands and threw a wave of white healing light at him. She had never healed a man's heart or soul before, but she had to try.

He was so parched, it was like watching a dry sponge in the desert on a midsummer day; his body sucked up the white light instantaneously.

He leapt to his feet. "What do ye do?" He roared, furious and incredulous at once.

Allie sent more white rain showering down upon him.

He lifted up his forearm and blasted his energy, sending the white rain spiraling back toward her, and it fell uselessly to the floor, vanishing. "Ye think to heal me?" he cried. But now his aura had repaired itself and it blazed mostly red, orange and gold. No jagged black chasm divided it.

Her mind raced. Royce was suffering and he had been suffering for centuries. This wasn't about her. The guilt she'd just witnessed was so vast, it had to be the product of something unspeakable.

Somehow she knew it was a woman. And that meant it was his wife. The idea hurt her impossibly—but she ignored it. Royce needed her—desperately.

He drew himself straight. His blazing gaze held hers. "Save yer healing power for those that need it."

"You need it."

His smile formed, cold and twisted. "I need no white light. Besides, ye hate me now."

She hugged herself. "I don't hate anyone, and I don't hate you." How dense could he be? She had given him her heart. No matter what he did, no matter how awful he behaved, she'd never be able to take it back, because she knew the man he'd become one day.

His gaze flickered.

"You are in pain. I can help. Why won't you let me?"

He stiffened. His smile was forced. "I'm nay in pain. Ye imagined it."

"Let me help," she begged, and she went to him and tried to take his large hands in her smaller ones.

As if burned, he drew away. She'd sent a rush of white light into him before he could suspect what she meant to do. "Cease," he shouted at her. He paced away.

He blamed himself for whatever had happened. She stared up at him. She had to know. She could help.

He whirled. "I dinna need yer help, Ailios," he warned. "Leave me to my affairs."

She tensed. "You can read my mind, can't you?"

"Aye." He stared without remorse at her.

She'd analyze that later. "If you can read my mind, you know what I want to know. Who is she?" she asked, sure he would explode.

His face was grim. "My wife."

Allie tensed, even though she had expected the answer. "Where is she, Royce?"

"She's dead," he said without emotion. "Dead an' buried, as she should be, these past eight centuries."

Allie somehow nodded, shaken to the core. He was consumed with his dead wife—after eight centuries. How could she compete with that? What had Royce done—or what did he think he'd done?

And when his aura roiled and started to split, as the blue rose up, the color ruled by Uranus, the planet of change and transformation, the planet of Fate, everything became so clear. She loved the medieval man as much as the modern one and she could never turn her back on either one. He was breaking apart before her very eyes. She had to try to save him.

Trembling, she walked bravely to him and laid her hands on his chest. "How did she die, Royce? What happened?"

He seized her hands, hard. "So ye think to seduce me tonight? Ye wish to heal my *bleeding soul* with yer hot little body? Aye, fine, let's go up to bed."

Very softly, she said, "Be a jerk. You're forgiven. You're forgiven for everything you said today and for all of your despicable behavior. I understand what you're doing—but you can't change the subject."

He started and dropped her hands. "Ye mean it. Ye forgive me for being a bastard. Ye don't hate me. Ye would never hate anyone."

"No, I can't hate anyone—and I can't hate you. And, Royce? You could pay me ten billion dollars—enough wealth to buy all of Alba in my time—and I wouldn't sleep with you."

He flushed.

She smiled sweetly. "The next time I sleep with you it will be because you tell me that you love me—and you mean it."

His high color vanished. Their gazes locked.

He smiled slowly at her. "Ye challenge me?"

"No," she said quickly, "I do not."

"So ye retract yer words."

She wet her lips. Her heart pounded wildly. This was so important, because one day, she wanted those words! "No, I do not."

He nodded. Softly he said, "Then we won't be sharing pleasure, will we? Not unless ye back down."

"Maybe you'll be the one to see the light."

His expression became taut. "I will never say such words.

Ye have my word on that." He was so furious his aura spit fire.

"We are not rivals," Allie insisted, meaning it.

He shook his head. "Then ye shouldn't have challenged me." And with those harsh words, he vanished.

Allie cried out. She had not a doubt that Royce had just leapt into the future—or the past.

She sank to the floor, terribly worried now. Royce was in the throes of unleashed torment and she was afraid he was vulnerable to his enemies in such a state, wherever he was. God, she hadn't meant to confront the wounded beast in his den. It felt like a miracle that she had survived the encounter.

She hugged her knees to her chest. One thing had become crystal clear. This man needed her as no other ever had. And that meant she wasn't going anywhere.

CHAPTER NINE

595 AD

HE LANDED SO HARD his head exploded and he welcomed the pain.

Royce lay still, seeing stars. He did not move or even think to fight the pain, until the wracking waves of torment and anguish had entirely receded. He was on his back, staring up through a canopy of pine so thick that he could barely see the sky. When he was breathing normally, when it felt like his body might have some strength and he might be able to sit up and even stand, he focused.

Kael.

Eight hundred years had so honed his senses that he could scent his enemy just below him. The glen reeked of evil and lust. He focused even more intently, and felt Brigdhe's pain. Then he recognized her utter hopelessness.

She did not believe he was coming.

He stood, his heart beating slowly, with the utmost calm. He was a hardened warrior now. There was no fear, just a sense of what he must do to triumph over a mortal enemy. However, as much as he wished to do battle now, this was not his fight to fight. It was Ruari's.

Very slowly, intent, he walked through the wood, down the ridge. And he thought about two women, not one. For

Ailios's image had crept into his mind, as crystal clear as Brigdhe's was not. Let her love him—it changed nothing.

When he reached the tree line he paused, staring down at the timbered palisade and manor, knowing what his younger self, Ruari, would find when he broke down those wood gates and fought his way into the hall. His gut roiled. He fought it.

He must not ever forget what had happened to her, even if the Healer wished for him to do so—even if her smiles and happiness tempted him to do so.

Brigdhe's pain and defeat wafted from the glen, sickening him, as he had hoped it would. He tried to recall her beauty and failed. He could not quite attach a clear image to her energy. Time had blurred her features, making the real woman impossible to envision.

He recalled her bruised, battered body, though. Time had not faded that image, not at all, and that was good.

And although he was a rational man, although he was a centuries-old Master, the urge to rush down the hill and break down the gates to destroy Kael was overwhelming. He stared at the palisade and somehow restrained himself. Although he knew the horrors Brigdhe was suffering, he must not break the Code. It was forbidden for him to change the past—or the future. Ruari must rescue her, vanquish Kael and bless her union to another man—and lose the last of his naiveté and hope.

The Code was also very clear that he must not encounter himself in a past or future time, either. He did not intend to do so. He had come back to remember, and already he was recalling the events of this day with terrible clarity.

Royce glanced around and saw his younger self emerging from the wood farther along the ridge. Stunned, he realized he hadn't timed his leap with enough care—he had been so furious. He stared with great interest and realized this was an even better way to relive the horrid day.

The boy strode down the hill, soaking wet with sweat, his leine clinging to his lithe, muscular body, his face a mask of determined rage. Royce simply watched, refusing to feel for him.

Tell me what you want.

Soft laughter, her warm body, and a slow, sweet entry. You know what I want, Ruari.

Male laughter, an exchange of kisses as he moved deeper and deeper still, the first ones gentle and playful, the last one deep and urgent. Can ye come fer me now, Brigdhe?

Oh, aye! Aye!

Her soft, female cries filled their bedchamber, and he allowed himself to join her. She was a passionate woman and this pleased him; he had chosen well. And perhaps they had conceived a son—he wanted a son. And she snuggled in his arms...

Royce couldn't breathe. Where had that terrible memory come from? He wasn't that boy anymore—he would never be that boy again. He didn't want to remember! There would never be any sons!

Ruari was at the gates. He reached for them.

Royce trembled, wanting to see him savagely wrest the doors from their hinges.

He breathed hard.

Ruari tore the gates from their hinges.

As he did, Royce knew that the bombard of arrows would begin. He knew one arrow would pierce his skin, another a tendon. Ruari did not know, but it would not stop him, anyway....

Royce gave in. As Ruari threw the doors aside, as the arrows hailed, he blasted the archers with his energy to deflect every iron-tipped shaft. The arrows rained down on Ruari, and one pierced his arm. Oblivious, he jerked it out and kept going into the palisade, sword drawn, as the giants swarmed him.

Stunned, Royce looked at his hand. *He'd sent a huge blast of energy at the archers and nothing had happened.*

And in that instant, he suddenly understood the rule to never encounter oneself in the past or the future.

He glanced into the fortress. Ruari was engaging the giants. He hurled a blast of energy at the closest watch tower.

Nothing happened.

It should have come down.

He turned, seized an overhead branch—and failed to tear it from the pine.

He breathed hard. Although he was physically solid, with his own self there, below, on the same temporal and physical plane, he was but an ordinary man.

He had no power now.

POWER AWOKE HER.

Her sleep had been light and fitful, determined as she was to wait for Royce to return. Allie felt his male power in an oddly gentle wave and she jerked awake, curled up in one of the two large chairs before the fire. She turned, looking over the chair's high back.

The fire still blazed, clearly fed during the night by maids. Royce stood not far from where she was seated, his face a cold, hard mask, his gray eyes so dull they were almost lifeless. His aura was split distinctly in two, one side red and gold, the other blue, a black chasm between. It did not blaze or burn. Every color was faded and muted.

Only his pain blazed.

Allie slid to her feet, trying to hide the fact that she was concerned for him. "Are you all right?" she asked softly, knowing he was not. His torment cut into her like knives, slicing her skin, flesh and tendons into ribbons.

He did not answer, and she felt the vast resolution in him. He was not going to budge. In that moment, she sensed he embraced his anguish and would keep it hidden from her at all cost. "Ye should go up to rest. T'is late an' we leave in a few hours."

Allie walked over to him, her heart thudding. "What happened? Where did you go?" She tried to caress his cheek.

He jerked away. "I'm tired. If ye want to stay up all night, then do so." His mouth twisted with unhappiness, he turned and strode from the hall.

And she sensed another woman's presence clinging to him, the way one might scent a woman's fragrance after she had left the room. Allie didn't have to ask to know the identity of the woman he had just been with. She hugged herself, certain he had gone to see his dead wife.

CLAD IN JEANS and a lace-trimmed cotton tank, Allie stepped somewhat cautiously into the courtyard. She was barely awake, having been roused urgently by Ceit and told that his lordship wished to depart and she must hurry. Instantly her gaze found Royce.

His aura was whole again, fiercely blazing with his warrior power and his sexual heat. He stood with a man Allie now recognized as his estate manager, not that she knew if that term was used or not. Royce was apparently giving some instructions, his face set in serious but not severe lines. His white charger was being held for him just beyond, as was a big black mare. His mood had obviously improved from the night before. He had buried his pain.

Finally finished, he turned to her.

If only he would let her help him, she thought. Allie smiled at him. "Good morning."

His gaze swept over her tight jeans, then up her tiny, frilly top. His expression wary, he gestured and Allie came over. "Good morn," he said quietly, not meeting her gaze. "We go to Dunroch."

Allie knew it was a test. She had no intention of being left behind there, but she wanted to meet Royce's nephew and his wife. She had very personal questions about Royce, and she might find the answers at Dunroch. She smiled brightly. Besides, she was not fighting with Royce, hopefully not ever again. He needed her—last night was the proof.

"That's fine with me. I have had the urge to see the countryside since we last spoke."

His gaze narrowed, lifting to hers.

Allie said seriously, "Did I really hear you say that Malcolm's wife is from the future?"

"Aye."

Allie hid a smile, turning quickly away. She needed an ally and a friend. This was an incredible stroke of luck. Then she faced Royce. "The Masters seem to go for us strong, modern women."

"Claire is very strong," Royce said as if discussing the weather. Then, "Yer brother married a modern lass, too."

Allie was very surprised. "Have other Masters met their soul mates in the future?" she asked, eyes wide.

"There are only the two." Royce was brusque. "We have a long day ahead." He nodded at the big mare.

Allie's heart leapt with excitement. The mare was clearly strong and athletic, and some kind of Warmblood. "She's for me?"

"Aye. She's quiet. Ye'll manage."

Allie didn't try to hide her smile this time. As a child, she'd spent hundreds of hours riding without stirrups or without reins, and she'd learned to take small fences with her eyes closed. She still rode frequently, and she loved jumping—the mare or any mount would be a piece of cake. "Then let's go."

Royce turned. A boy handed him a folded white garment, and Royce handed it to Allie. "If ye please. Ye canna ride about Alba dressed as ye do."

Allie took one look at the long linen caftan and sighed. "We have a truce. A pleasant one—I like your mood. Do you want to start a war?" Then, softly, she added, "Do you really want to look at me in such a sack?"

Royce seemed to want to smile. He did not. "T'is a shame," he admitted. His gaze skidded away. "Ye can take it off at Dunroch."

He still wouldn't look her in the eye. Allie realized suddenly that he was embarrassed about what she'd seen—and what he'd revealed—last night. But of course he was uncomfortable with any kind of intimacy. He probably thought his emotional torment a sign of weakness on his part.

Allie touched his bare forearm. He flinched. She said softly, "The only way to heal from heartbreak is to work it out. Talking is highly recommended. I'm not a shrink, but—"

"Ye talk nonsense." He cut her off, taking the mare's reins and leading her forward.

Of course he wouldn't talk about his pain, at least, not yet. Allie slid the huge garment on, thoughtful. His having opened up to her, even if he hadn't wanted to, was a first step toward the cleansing and healing of his soul. He'd been afflicted with grief and guilt for eight hundred years. He could not go on this way. He had cancer—and it needed to be eradicated. "Just so you know, we are friends," Allie said firmly. "I get that a medieval hunk like you thinks a woman is only for bedsport, but I am your friend—no matter what, through thick and thin. If you ever want to talk, I am here."

He gave her a disbelieving look. "What man speaks o' his dead wife with the woman he takes to his bed?"

"Ah, but we're friends now—not lovers," Allie reminded him.

Royce gave her the hottest, most promising, most significant look she had ever received. In one heartbeat, he told her it wasn't over, not by a long shot.

Heat washed through her.

"Can ye ride at all?" Royce asked, changing the subject.

Instead of answering, Allie took the mare's reins and led her to the stairs that went up to the ramparts. Climbing the stairs, she grasped the stirrup, designed for a tall man, and swung onto the mare. Then she gathered up her reins and trotted back to Royce.

Royce stared as if surprised—or impressed. "O' course ye can ride. There were fine horses at yer father's home."

Allie shrugged modestly. He hadn't seen anything yet.

Royce swung up into his saddle and waved his men on. Royce said, "Ye stay with Neill."

Allie recognized the big redhead from the other day as Royce rode ahead to lead the small band of men. She didn't want to violate their truce, but she was going to enjoy this ride with Royce. She urged her mare forward and cantered up to him. "Surely you're not afraid to ride with me?" she asked innocently.

"I'm nay afraid of any woman," he said.

"Really? Is that why you ran away from me last night?" She smiled sweetly.

His eyes popped. "I dinna run from ye, Ailios," he warned.

"It sure looked like it to me," she said tartly.

"Can we ride—or will ye try to talk my ears off this dawn?"

"I intend to talk your ears off. Tell me about Malcolm's wife."

He started and his gray eyes softened—Allie knew she didn't imagine it. "She's the daughter of a Master," he said, surprising her. "An' she has been married to my nephew for nigh on three years. He found her in the new city o' York, in yer time."

So Claire was from New York. They would get along great, Allie thought with excitement.

"Malcolm was hunting a page from the Book o' Healing. Claire had a shop where she sold old books. The chase led him to his wife."

Allie became alert. "The Book of Healing? You mentioned the Book before."

Royce looked grim. "The Cladich gives the holder o' the Book its powers to heal. The Brotherhood has been left with one single page; the rest is missing. An' I worry Moffat has some pages."

Allie stared at his gorgeous face. "Demons destroy. They don't heal."

Royce made a sound. "Moffat's armies have been growin' these past few years."

Allie shivered, suddenly terribly cold. "Royce, in my time, the demons are out of control. Every year there are more pleasure crimes. Every year there are more demons."

She didn't need to read his mind to know what he was thinking. Either the true demons had found a way to radically increase their reproduction rate, or they weren't being vanquished in the same numbers as before. If the latter were true, was it because a very high demon, even Satan himself, had found a way to heal the evil hordes?

"No demon can be allowed to have such power," Allie finally said.

"Aye."

And that meant that if Moffat or another powerful demon had any holy pages, the Masters would have to regain them. "Royce, did my mother use the Book?"

"O' course she did. Centuries ago, when it was enshrined on Iona, she used it all the time." He smiled briefly. "T'was a different world, Ailios. The Ancients had great power an' we could worship openly. Now an' then, the gods would even walk amongst us—or help us in our battles with the deamhanain."

Allie smiled, imagining a near paradise on Iona. "I wish the gods would walk among us now."

"Our scholars claim they have been forsaken by man— an' have lost their great powers because of it. T'is why, they say, they do not come to earth now. But Claire an' Malcolm believe Faola helped them vanquish a great deamhan, the greatest Alba has ever seen."

Allie pulled her horse to a halt, facing Royce, so he halted, too. Everyone pulled up. "They fought together? They vanquished a great demon *together?*"

"Aye, they did." He stared unwaveringly at her. "I feared for Malcolm when he met her. The Code frowns on marriage. A Master must stand alone. But Claire has her own power—an' he's stronger with her than alone."

"Of course they're stronger together," Allie cried.

He gave her an odd look, spurring his charger forward. Allie followed and trotted to come abreast of him. "Wait a minute. Masters aren't supposed to marry?"

"Aye."

"But Malcolm married—and so did you! You said my brother is married, too!"

"Malcolm is an exception to the rule. As for the Black Macleod, I dinna ken him well." His jaw flexed. "My marriage was a great mistake. I was young an' foolish. I married Brigdhe before I was chosen. She paid the price for it." With that, suddenly impatient, he raised his arm. "Ye wish to talk, do so at Dunroch. Otherwise we'll nay be there by nightfall." He spurred his mount into a canter, his men following.

Allie sat still, thinking about everything she had just learned. *His wife's name was Brigdhe.* Pain filled her as she thought about the woman. In that instant, she knew something terrible had happened to her.

"Ailios!" Royce's voice cut through the forest, razor sharp.

Allie jerked back into the present. Royce was dead-set against her, and finally, she was beginning to understand why.

AFTER LEAVING THE HORSES on Morvern soil, they were rowed by six of the men across the sound and to the island of Mull's south shores. As they trekked up a steep, rocky path, Allie saw Dunroch above them, as gray as the rocks it sat upon, shrouded in a thick, swirling Atlantic mist.

A short while later, Royce extended his hand to help her up the last part of the treacherous ascent. They passed through the narrow, high walls of a barbican over a lowered drawbridge and through a large, circular gate tower. Allie found herself inside an inner bailey, the walls of the castle to her left, the walls to her right containing a lower ward. The inner ward was busy and Allie was now used to the sight of Highland men and women coming and going, often accompanied by livestock, the men usually well armed. As they approached another gatehouse, a tall, dark man stepped out.

Royce smiled. "Hallo a Chalium."

The man grinned, striding forward, impossibly more muscular than Royce, and even an inch or two taller. Allie did a double-take because he was so utterly gorgeous. "Ruari." He embraced Royce briefly.

Allie watched Royce and his nephew, gladdened by their obvious bond of affection and caring. He was not entirely alone in this world, even without her, and that pleased her immensely.

"I see yer watch is on their toes," Royce said.

"Aye. Ye wouldn't be happy waitin' for my bridge to go down."

Malcolm turned his dark, interested gaze upon her. "An' who's yer guest?"

Allie was surprised when Royce took her arm, almost possessively, guiding her forward. "Meet Lady Ailios, Malcolm. Ailios, my nephew."

Allie extended her hand. "Hi. It's Allie. Allie Monroe."

Malcolm's gaze flickered and he glanced down at her feet. Allie suspected he knew she was from the future, but wasn't sure why he was looking at her toes.

Royce murmured, "He's looking for some sign—like yer bejeweled shoes."

She was wearing her jeweled Giuseppe Zanotti sandals, as they were the only low-heeled shoes Aidan had brought her. Allie smiled and lifted her skirt, and Malcolm chuckled at the sight of her sandals and jeans. "Welcome to Dunroch. Ye must meet my wife." He turned to Royce, his gaze filled with speculation. "Do ye wish a word with me alone?"

"Aye. I have a great favor to ask ye."

Allie knew what that favor would be and she tensed. He was going to ask Malcolm to protect her from Moffat, so he could return to his dark, solitary, tormented life.

"Ask. Ye ken I willna deny ye." Malcolm gestured at Allie and she walked with both men through the gatehouse and into a small courtyard filled with flowers and shrubs. Instantly she knew the gardens were Malcolm's wife's work.

And the moment she stepped into Dunroch's large great room, Allie saw a tall, auburn-haired woman in jeans. She was thrilled—and relieved.

The woman was at the table—with a laptop computer! The moment they entered, she slammed the lid down, flushing, as if caught in a grave transgression. "Malcolm! You didn't tell me we had guests," she cried, standing.

"Dinna fear," Malcolm said softly.

The striking woman looked at him and Allie knew they were silently communicating. Then her eyes widened and she looked at Allie in surprise.

Allie smiled, her heart racing. "Hey. I'm Allie. You must be Malcolm's wife, Claire." She strode forward and held out her hand.

The woman took it, towering over her—she had to be five foot ten or so—and smiled warmly. "Hello! This is such a surprise." She looked at Royce with some confusion, and then back at Allie, this time dissecting her features. Then she turned back to Royce, her gaze wide with speculation and interest.

"Hallo a Chlaire," Royce said with a genuine smile.

Claire smiled back. "Hallo a Ruari."

"We'll be outside," Malcolm said, and both men left.

Allie stared after Royce and was rewarded with a single, backward glance. She hoped she saw regret in his eyes, but he only nodded.

Then she turned, pulling the god-awful caftan over her head and laying it on the table. Claire made a sound. Allie saw her staring at her skinny jeans and tiny top and trying to hide a smile. "Well…this is interesting. How is Royce, er, doing, these days?"

"Mr. Medieval? Oh, same old, same old—bossy, arrogant, a jerk and a tyrant." Allie smiled at her. "I so hope you and I will get along because I need a friend!"

Claire laughed. "Royce must sweat bullets every time you walk into the room."

Allie blushed. "He's pretty attracted."

Claire just looked at her. "And you're in love?"

Allie felt her smile fade. "Is it that obvious?"

"No, it's not, but Royce is a handsome, powerful man. Men like him and Malcolm do not exist in the twenty-first century, at least, not openly." Claire took her hand. "Come and sit…tell me everything."

Allie sat down with her and Claire called for wine. "I was hoping," Allie said, suddenly nervous, "that you could tell *me* everything."

Claire looked at her, puzzled.

Allie gave in to a moment of doubt and despair. "What is wrong with him?" she exclaimed. "One minute he can be kind, the next cold and even cruel! But I love him—even though no sane woman should love a medieval man, ever!"

Claire sat up. "When I met Malcolm, I was insanely attracted to him. But I've studied medieval history, and I knew—I *knew*—it would never work. It was like he was from Mars, while I'm from New York City."

Allie smiled just a little.

"Even so, it did work. Malcolm and I fell in love and we've worked out our differences—we still do." But then Claire said, "Royce is one of the hardest men I know."

Allie felt a pang of fear.

"I'm not sure," Claire said slowly, "that it's a good idea to fall too deeply for him."

"Too late," Allie said.

Claire took a breath. "Want to start from the beginning? I'll help if I can."

"I fell in love with him in 2007—in the span of twenty-four hours. And then a demon murdered him."

Comprehension filled Claire's eyes. "You must have fallen in love with an older Royce—because he's not dead now."

"His fourteen-hundred-year-old self and then some," Allie said. "He's got exactly five hundred and seventy-seven years left."

A maid appeared with bread, cheese and wine. Claire thanked her and the maid inclined her head, murmuring, "My lady," before casting a quick, curious glance at Allie.

"You seem to have adjusted really well to the whole demonic thing. It took me a while—I was freaked out to learn evil was a *race*," Claire said when the maid was gone.

Allie shook her head. "I've been fighting demons for years, since I was a kid." Claire started. "But I'm a Healer first and last. I only fight because they get in the way of my healing."

"I thought I felt a power coming from you," Claire said, eyes wide.

"Healing is my destiny. I can heal pretty much anyone, anytime," Allie said seriously. "It's what I'm meant to do." Then she thought of the young girl she'd tried to bring back to life—and the modern Royce, dying in her arms. "But I can't raise the dead."

A pause fell. "How did you wind up here?"

Allie sighed. "I fell in love with Royce in my time. When

he died, I conned Aidan into taking me back here, to him in the past. It's a huge coincidence, but when I first met Royce, he'd come from 1430, and Aidan had followed him. So when Aidan went home, I went with him." She added, "Royce was awful when I first got here. But then we saved a boy from a rockslide and we fought demons together and we even made love. Now I don't want to go home. I can't go back to a future without Royce. And I can't leave Mr. Medieval behind, either. He needs me—they both do."

Claire was wide-eyed. "So you are planning to stay in the fifteenth century?"

Allie hesitated. "For now. The only thing I'm certain of is that I have to figure out how to vanquish Moffat so he doesn't murder Royce on September 7, 2007."

Claire gasped. "The bishop of Moffat murdered Royce?"

Allie tensed. "And he may be after me. How bad is he?"

"Bad. Extremely ambitious and well-connected—he claims a distant kinship with the Queen. And he is power-mad. I guess the deamhanain want to turn you—or force you to use your power for their ends."

"I can't be turned," Allie said, meaning it.

"Allie, you don't want to go head-to-head with Moffat."

"No, I don't. You sound as if you're speaking from experience."

"In a way, I am. Malcolm and I vanquished the earl of Moray, against all odds. He'd preyed on Innocence in Alba for a thousand years, but somehow, we did it, together. However, that was after he took me prisoner. It's something I prefer to forget."

"I'm sorry," Allie whispered.

A strange look passed across Claire's face as she reached for the jug of wine. "How about a glass of wine?"

"Sure. What is it?" Allie asked with some alarm. "Why

does the name Moray still bring dread and fear to your eyes?"

Claire grimaced. "I sometimes dream about him. Three years ago I wasn't even sure we'd vanquished him—I expected him to come back. But everyone said that even if he did, he'd leave Malcolm and me alone—we're too powerful and he'd avoid that kind of confrontation again. We're even more powerful now," Claire added. "Three years ago Malcolm was new to his powers, and I didn't even know I had any."

Allie had a bad feeling, too. "You don't believe he's gone."

Claire hesitated. "It's not Malcolm or myself I worry about."

"Then who?"

"Aidan."

Allie jerked. "Why would you worry about Aidan?"

Claire was surprised. "No one told you? Malcolm and Aidan share the same mother, but not the same father. He is Moray's son."

Allie could not believe that Aidan was the son of a demon. "He's a Master."

"Yes, he is. But in case you haven't noticed, he is a bit of a renegade. I worry about him. That charming facade hides a lot of conflict," Claire said. "On the surface he seems like a playboy who can't help gratifying himself, but he will always come through for the gods, for Innocence. He is afraid, Allie, afraid of what his father's legacy to him might be."

Allie absorbed that. "Well, his aura isn't evil and if it's even slightly tainted, I haven't noticed." She was firm. But his power was different—she'd sensed that, but hadn't really understood it. She let it go. It didn't matter—he was her Knight of Swords.

"If you worship the gods," Claire said, "then you believe in Fate."

Allie knew where she was leading. "I do. But it is not Royce's Fate to die in 2007. That was a mistake."

Claire was silent, clearly not believing her.

"I know all about the dumb Code," Allie added. "I'm not a Master and I have no intention of following the rules."

Claire smiled. "I'm not a Master, either, just the daughter of one. How can I help?"

Allie leaned forward eagerly. "Just think about how to best vanquish Moffat now, so he can't murder Royce in 2007. He was dressed in modern clothes—he might have been a modern man, too." And the only reason she couldn't be certain was that the medieval Aidan ran around in Levi's when he chose.

"Let's hope he was from the future," Claire said softly, "so we can destroy him now and save Royce then."

Allie was so relieved to have an ally. "I hate to ask you, but maybe you shouldn't mention this to your husband. I have no idea what happens when a Master breaks the rules, but he might not be on our side."

Claire laughed. "He's always on my side, but don't worry, I won't say anything until I have to."

Allie hesitated. She'd come to Dunroch for assistance, which she was getting, but she also needed answers. "Royce was afraid of your relationship with Malcolm at first."

"He told you that?"

"Yeah, he did."

Claire said, "Royce is a very hardened soldier, Allie. He's lived through centuries, and he's seen it all."

"Is that a warning?"

"You could have picked someone easier to love."

Allie almost smiled. "No kidding." Then she spoke seriously. "Maybe the reason Royce is so hard and cold—and so alone—is his past and his wife."

"I know he was married, but it was long ago, and I don't know any details."

Their gazes met. "Damn," Allie said. "I know that something terrible happened to his wife and he is still suffering because of it."

Claire said softly, "Ask Malcolm."

ALLIE FOUND MALCOLM outside with Royce, standing on the ramparts looking out over the Atlantic Ocean. She paused. The two men, standing above her in their leines and plaids, with the sun trying to emerge from the windswept, gray skies, were a magnificent sight. Her heart turned over a dozen times as she stared at Royce. Why didn't he want to be healed? And she wondered if his pain had something to do with his willingness to die in the future. It was a startling and dismal thought.

He turned and glanced down at her.

Allie hurried up the stone steps. "Hi." She smiled at both men. "Am I interrupting?"

Malcolm seemed bemused, but Royce looked wary. "Lady Allie, we have finished our conversation." He clasped Royce's arm. "Yer woman wishes a word with me, I think."

Royce's gaze slid over Allie's top and jeans. "Dinna think to seduce him to yer cause. He's very fond o' his wife."

Allie smiled at him. "You're my cause. And the only man I wish to seduce," she added.

Royce scowled.

"Besides, I really like it here. I am going to think of this as a vacation. Iona is a mile or two from here. It's holy ground and Claire has already offered to take me there."

They hadn't even discussed it. "So even if you change your mind, I can't go back to Carrick with you," she lied lightly. "Not yet."

Royce appeared alarmed. He flushed. "Malcolm has agreed ye can stay at Dunroch. There'll be no visits to the Sanctuary."

Allie was taken aback. This was odd—and interesting. Why would Royce refuse to allow her a visit? Iona was holy. Her mother had lived there for centuries.

"She stays here," Royce said to Malcolm, as if his nephew were a foot soldier. "Until I decide otherwise." He leapt down the first few steps and then leapt again into the ward.

Malcolm chuckled.

"What was that about?" Allie asked, remaining bewildered. But now, she shivered. It was freezing high up on the walls, exposed to the blasting Atlantic winds.

"He be jealous. Green, in fact." Malcolm laughed again, guiding her down the stairs.

"He's jealous of what? A bunch of monks worshiping the Ancients?"

"Ah, lass, the Masters often sojourn on the isle, an' I think he dinna wish for ye to have a choice of other men."

Allie straightened, keenly interested now. Hadn't her modern Royce mentioned he'd taken his vows on the island? And of course Iona would be the perfect sanctuary, as no demon ever tread upon holy ground. Did Royce really think she'd become interested in another man if she went there?

Allie walked to a stone bench and sat, cross-legged. If she needed to provoke Royce by going to Iona, she just might do so.

Malcolm came and sat beside her. "Yer man has asked me to keep ye here an' to protect ye while he hunts Moffat."

"I know." Allie stopped smiling. "But I'm not staying. Sorry! Dunroch is wonderful, but my place is at Carrick with Royce. He needs me."

Malcolm simply studied her, his gaze searching. "Ye have a good power, Lady. Even sitting next to ye, I be calm an' soothed. I agree—my uncle needs yer light."

"So you'll tell Royce you won't let me stay here?"

Malcolm sighed. "Lady Allie, I canna deny Royce. He's more father to me than uncle. I vowed to keep ye an' protect ye. I must do so."

Allie was dismayed. "Then I have to work on Royce. How long do I have? When is he leaving?"

"He'll leave in the morn. Aye, work yer wiles. T'will be interesting to see who's stronger—I dinna think he can resist ye for too long."

Allie was encouraged. But she said, "I hope he told you why he's hunting Moffat?"

"Aye."

"Did he tell you about his death?"

"Aye. I willna lie, Lady. I have grave worries now. Royce be more powerful than Moffat, but power doesna matter if his Fate is written otherwise."

Allie hugged her knees to her chest. Everyone seemed to think that Royce was going to die on September 7, 2007, no matter what. Well, let them be pessimists. She was an optimist and proud of it, and more importantly, she never gave up. She wasn't going to start now. He simply couldn't die that day.

"I see ye care for my blackhearted uncle."

"I love him," Allie said. "Even when he is in his Mad Max mode."

Malcolm seemed bewildered by that. "An' ye wish to ken what?"

"I want to know what happened to his wife, when it happened and why he is suffering from so much guilt—and if he is in love with a ghost."

Malcolm stood. "Ye need to ask Royce such great questions!"

"He won't talk about her." Grim, she said, "He loved her, didn't he? Royce loved a woman with his heart and soul." She was so dismayed admitting what she'd been secretly afraid of.

Malcolm hesitated. "Royce has never spoken of his wife. T'was long ago."

Allie bit her lip. "Am I a fool to hope he'll ever love me that way?"

Malcolm clasped her shoulder. "Lass, heed me. Royce was a boy of three an' twenty when he wed. He be a man over eight hundred years old now. Why do ye care about the past?"

Allie pulled away and hugged herself. He'd been so young! She hadn't realized. "Royce loved me in the future. Maybe he can't love me right now, but there's a connection, and it's not just sex."

Malcolm flushed.

"He cares. He's proved it—once or twice." She wiped her eyes. "What happened to his wife? Malcolm, please."

Malcolm caved. "A great deamhan seized her, tortured her, raped her—for days, maybe weeks, I dinna ken. Royce finally rescued her—an' handed her to another man, breaking their marriage. Most Masters live alone, Lady Allie. There be a reason the Code requires it. Royce gave up his wife to protect her."

"Oh gods," Allie whispered. "Poor Royce." She sat abruptly, wanting to cry for him. "You have Claire!"

"Aye, an' I love her greatly. But she's the daughter of a great Master."

"I'm Elasaid's daughter!" Allie cried.

Malcolm sighed. "Lass, I be young, just eight an' twenty. T'was easy for me to give over to Claire. I dinna ken if Royce loved Brigdhe or if he cared as any husband should. But I dinna think he will ever allow himself to be too fond of any woman again. Are ye certain that in the future he said he loved ye?"

Allie looked up. She was about to say, "Hell yeah," but she stopped. The realization was dreadful. Royce had never said those three words, not even with his last dying breath.

Malcolm looked at her with pity. "I dinna think my uncle capable of the love ye want, lass. He's hard, aye, but he's older now—an' tired."

And that, Allie thought, explained why he'd wanted to die.

CHAPTER TEN

"DO YE WISH TO GO inside?" Malcolm asked, his tone kind.

Allie was about to refuse. She wanted to sit and think about Royce and his past—and about the present and their future. But before she could even smile at him, a terrible foreboding fell over her.

Dark power.

Allie sat up, alarmed. She had never felt such a huge and impending sense of evil before.

"Lady Allie?"

Allie was on her feet. She didn't look at Malcolm. Evil was coming, like the black clouds blown in before a terrific storm, but this was a cloud of death. The demon or demons had stunning reserves of power. For one moment, Allie was unmoving.

"What happens?" Malcolm asked sharply.

Allie glanced at him and saw that he was alarmed. "There is evil coming. Give me a moment."

"I sense nothing!" he said swiftly.

Allie turned away from him, focusing entirely on the approaching darkness, the foreshadowing of destruction and death. Dark and malignant, steadfast and intent…the shadows were marching…like men, overland…from the north. Allie finally realized what was coming and she cried out.

She faced Malcolm. "Thirty or forty demons are approaching! But they are not alone. Malcolm, I am certain hundreds of humans are with them—all of them possessed, all with demonic power. And there are animals, too."

Malcolm's eyes widened. "A demonic army attacks Dunroch?"

Allie nodded, aghast. "They're coming from the north—and if my senses work in this time the way they do at home, you have a half an hour to prepare."

Malcolm had already turned away, shouting to the watch on the small gatehouse tower, and bells began ringing. The entire compound broke into frenzied activity. Allie had been confronting and fighting demons her entire life, but very rarely had she ever run into a gang of them—and then, she'd wisely fled. Usually they perpetrated their crimes of pleasure and death solo.

Men appeared on the walls dragging large, man-size bows into defensive positions; others began rushing up to the ramparts, while fires were started in her ward and elsewhere. Allie came to her senses—the castle was preparing for an attack, and she had to help. She ran through the gatehouse after Malcolm and into the inner ward.

His knights were appearing, some of the Highlanders in chain mail, others in nothing but their leines and plaids, everyone heavily armed. Now, from where she stood, she saw more archers and knights appearing on the walls and the curtain towers. The outer bailey was a bit below where she stood and she saw a wooden machine being wheeled into position, near a huge pile of large rocks. The machine would clearly catapult the rocks over the walls at the enemy.

The darkness was coming, and rapidly.

"Ailios!"

Allie whirled in relief as Royce rushed toward her, Claire following. "Royce, thirty or forty demons are approaching from the north—and they have an army of possessed humans with them."

He seized her arm, a look of alarm on his face. An instant later it was gone.

"An army of demons is preparing to attack Dunroch?" Claire gasped. "This is unheard of!"

"They want Ailios," Royce said, staring at her.

Her heart lurched, not because of his words, but from the cold, hard look in his eye. But this was the moment they needed Royce at his worst.

"Will they really besiege us?" Claire cried. "Dear God, even the humans can cross the moat and scale the walls with their demonic power, no matter what we throw at them, but the higher demons can leap *inside* the walls."

Instantly, Allie understood that the higher demons could time travel. Right now, a bunch of them were probably leaping ahead by thirty minutes or so and would land within Dunroch's walls as the fight began.

"They intend to distract the entire garrison with a full attack so one of them can take Ailios," Royce said swiftly. "Dunroch canna be defended as if this is a genuine siege. Claire, pass the word to every man—he must watch his back. Our defenses are breached the moment the battle begins."

Claire ran in Malcolm's direction.

Allie realized, in shock, that a huge battle was about to unfold so she could be captured. Her gut roiled. "Are you certain? Royce, why would they go to all this trouble to get me?" she cried.

"Have they not tried to capture you almost daily since the south of Hampton?" he said grimly. "Moffat has planned this since that day, because the march would take that long."

Allie felt ill. "How bad will this be?"

"We canna keep the true deamhanain out o' Dunroch unless we anoint the grounds with holy water an' prayers, but there's no time. If the deamhanain wish to get inside, they will. Sooner, nay later," he added darkly. "Someone will try to seize ye in the midst o' fierce fightin'." His eyes blazed.

"Should I give myself up?" Allie asked in real dread. So many would be hurt and would die because of her! "Moffat wants me alive."

"Are ye mad?" Royce cried, turning white. He grasped her with both hands and shook her, once. "Ailios, dinna speak ever o' givin' up to Moffat again."

Allie wet her lips, which were terribly dry. "I was hoping you'd say no."

He shook his head. "Ye willna fight today," he said softly, dangerously, his grasp tightening.

Allie was about to protest, but no words spewed. Instead she thought about his death at Moffat's hands in the future—and how he'd almost died the other night at Carrick, distracted by her attempts to fight the demons. She needed to admit that her efforts were paltry, no, pitiful. "I won't fight," she said hoarsely.

He seemed surprised. "Good. An' ye'll stay where I put ye, until I tell ye otherwise."

Allie was in disbelief. "I'm a Healer. People will get hurt today, likely people will die. I have to heal, Royce. It's what I do!"

"How can ye be movin' about Dunroch while arrows an' rocks are flying over the walls? When the deamhanain are inside the castle, lookin' fer ye?" Royce said to her grimly.

"I can't wait until the battle ends to heal those who are critical," Allie cried, meaning it. "I'll be careful, I swear!"

"Fer once, just this once, ye'll listen to me. I canna fight with ye running around the keep to tend the wounded, the perfect prey. Yer selflessness is admirable, Ailios, but ye'll stay where I put ye. Ye'll heal when the day is done."

Allie stared in surprise and he stared back, determined. "Are you telling me that I should hide?"

"Nay. Ye'll stay close to me during the battle so I can defend ye if need be."

ROYCE HAD CLIMBED up to the curtain tower closest to the foremost gatehouse, as the north wall defended the moat and the drawbridge. The south walls were not breachable, as they perched on the cliffs dropping hundreds of feet to the Atlantic Ocean below. Allie had asked if she could come up and he'd nodded. She stood beside him, wearing a boy's mail shirt, her hip against his thigh. Every tower and every rampart was occupied by archers, knights, bowmen and the huge, deadly-looking crossbows that fired bolts the size of swords. Barrels of boiling liquids were being brought up. Allie stared to the north, filled with sick anxiety and dread.

This was all because of her. Why was this happening? Why, out of the blue, had Moffat come after her in South Hampton that night?

She glanced at Royce. At least they were in this together. As invincible as he seemed, his death in the future had proven his mortality. If anything happened to him, she'd be close by to heal him—no matter what.

Allie hoped Royce didn't want to die in the fifteenth century, too.

His gaze slid to her and locked with hers. "I won't be dyin' today."

Allie took his hand. His gray eyes flickered with surprise

but he didn't pull away. "No, you won't. Claire has some healing power, too, doesn't she?"

"Some. I saw her heal Malcolm with my own eyes when he was fatally wounded by Moray. She dinna heal him completely, Ailios, but she saved his life by stoppin' his bleeding."

"It's better than nothing. She can help."

"Ailios, her powers are nothin' like yours. An' Claire's a warrior. She fights with Malcolm, although I dinna ken how he fights with his woman at his side."

Allie was impressed. But Claire looked really strong—as if she could seriously kick some ass.

Allie turned to stare to the north; Royce gently tugged his hand free. She let him. If the circumstances weren't so dire, she'd be thrilled that he'd held her hand, even if for a minute.

The isle of Mull was really charming, Allie thought. Other areas were majestic—like Carrick. Facing her, gentle, forested hills rolled into a vivid blue sky dotted with cotton-puff clouds. As she stared, the black cloud so close now that her gut roiled and the hairs on her nape stood up, she saw a herd of deer emerge from the closest ridge, three does and a buck taking flight across the rocky road leading to the barbican.

"They're here," Royce said flatly.

For one more moment, Allie did not move.

From that tree line, the demon army emerged.

A line of giant men, clad in armor and mail, helmets glistening in the sun, their bows on their backs, marched down the ridge toward Dunroch's walls. The foremost men carried large crimson and black pennants.

Allie fought for composure.

More men, pack horses, equipment and machines followed—battering rams with iron heads, catapults like those in the courtyard below, and oddly, plank wood fencing, and carts carrying tall ladders.

"T'is nay fencing," Royce said grimly. "T'is shields fer their archers an' the men who will try to scale the walls." Royce glanced around them. "No deamhanain are inside Dunroch yet."

"Why don't they leap inside whenever they want to?" Allie asked, her mouth so dry that swallowing hurt.

Royce turned a brilliant gaze upon her. "Alba is in chaos now, but it isn't anarchy—yet. We all answer to the King an' Queen. Moffat is a great lord an' bishop, Ailios, an' he canna declare war as he wishes on the King's men. He canna attack Malcolm or me as he pleases. In a way, there's a truce between us. There'd be anarchy if a deamhan dared to invade a Master's home at will, for the Master would have revenge. This," he said harshly, "is the beginning of anarchy in Alba."

Allie shivered. "Yeah, and it's because of me."

He took her elbow. "Ye serve good, Innocence an' the Brotherhood. Any Master would defend ye with his life. Let us go down."

Allie stared as the first horsemen appeared behind the army of giants and equipment.

All the demons were mounted.

So much death wafted from the horsemen.

And the aura of the entire army burned in red.

And suddenly, Allie's gaze went to one of the horsemen on the far right, mounted on a dark beast. The rider was far away, but Allie knew he didn't wear armor because he did not gleam in the sun. For one moment, she couldn't look away, and she felt the demon's terrible, hypnotic pull.

Hallo a Ailios.

She felt his smile.

Come to me, Ailios.

Allie's heart slammed—but she couldn't look away.

"Ailios," Royce said sharply, turning her toward him.

Her relief was crushing. She had not a doubt she'd been staring at Moffat and that he'd greeted her with telepathy, trying to mesmerize her. "Let's go," Allie whispered nervously. *He had almost succeeded.*

"Today he *dies*," Royce said.

THE BATTLE STARTED and the world as she knew it changed.

In one instant, the peace and calm of the day was shattered. Allie stood with Royce in the middle ward, between both gatehouse towers. Flaming arrows whistled, landing not just on the ramparts where most of the men were positioned, but in the ward not far from where she and Royce stood. Allie tensed as rocks and boulders exploded, shards flying dangerously close to them. Men began crying out in agony, shot by arrows or hit by the rocks. A man on fire fell from the walls, landing in the bailey, just across from where she stood with Royce. Shouts of rage began, as the defenders fired arrows and bolts from the crossbows at the attackers, hurling flaming liquids down upon them.

But the wounded increased in number, with every slew of incoming arrows and projectiles. Royce grasped her arm more tightly, as if he knew that it was almost impossible for her not to rush to the stairs and go up to help the wounded. Allie braced herself. She had to stay put for now. Nothing had ever been so hard.

Suddenly a sword-size bolt flew over the crenellations, impaling three men in a row. On the bolt, they fell to their death in the ward.

"I can't do this," Allie screamed, shoving at Royce. "I can save two of those men!"

He pulled her into his embrace and locked her there,

against his chest. "Stay still. They've breached the moat. Giants are scaling the walls—human ones."

Allie went motionless, staring up at him. "How do you know?"

"I'm listenin' to Malcolm," he said.

He was reading Malcolm's mind. Malcolm and Claire were fighting the invaders from the largest tower, which guarded the drawbridge. Allie tuned in to the three men and realized they were all dead. She told herself not to cry—not now, not yet.

Later, when it was over, she would pray for all the sacrifice and bless their souls, and then she would grieve for the human dead.

She focused on the castle around them, but she didn't feel evil inside, not yet.

"He's waitin'," Royce said, "for the right moment."

Allie couldn't imagine when that would be. The arrows, bolt and catapults kept coming. She could now hear the front gates being rammed. Worse, Malcolm's men were shouting more urgently and furiously on the ramparts. With dread, she looked up and saw two giants crawling over the crenellations. They were instantly slain by Malcolm and Claire and two other huge warriors, using both swords and energy. One was dark and swarthy, the other bronzed and golden. Allie seized Royce's sleeve—the two additional men had the brilliant powerful auras that only Masters could have.

He had followed her gaze. "Aye, Malcolm has summoned help."

A slew of giants now began breaching the crenellations. Malcolm, Claire and the two new Masters instantly hurled them back with blasts of energy, but as they dropped, more giants appeared. Allie saw Aidan appear beside them, sword in hand, now dressed like a medieval Highlander in a tunic, mail and boots, his legs bare. She watched him viciously slay four of the giants, making him as much a Terminator as Royce. He no longer appeared affable at all.

Wood screamed, shrieked, exploded.

Allie, now encircled in Royce's arms, her back to his chest, tensed in dread as the gates were breached and the giants rushed in.

"Ye stay here," Royce said grimly. "Ye stay against this wall." He seized her shoulders. "Moffat will try to come now that I fight. Ye ken? I'll keep one eye on ye."

Allie nodded, but she didn't want him distracted. She seized his face in both hands. "Don't you dare keep one eye on me! I won't move. You fight with both eyes on the demons, damn it!"

In answer, Royce handed her a small, deadly dagger and drew both swords, and before Allie could blink, he was striding into the horde, viciously determined, a golden warrior. He entered the fray like a lethal machine, his arms moving at stunning speed, like rotating blades, and the giants fell, one after another, as he strode through their midst. He had become a two-handed killing machine.

The entire inner ward had become a battlefield. Just feet from where she stood, Masters and Highlanders fought the giants.

The pale sand-colored dirt ran with blood.

Bodies lay everywhere—the dying and the dead.

How could she simply stand there and watch, doing nothing?

Allie saw that Royce was on a roll. He certainly seemed invincible now. The huge urge to heal overwhelmed her and she moved just two steps from the wall. There, she knelt beside a very young man, stabbed through his side, half of his tunic covered in blood. The boy's eyes were closed, but he was alive.

Allie sent her white healing light over him and through him. She focused, the terrible uproar of the battle vanishing, and it was only her and the young defender and her white healing power. She didn't move, aware of his severed flesh knitting, of a severed muscle healing. She felt his heart beating normally. She was rewarded when his eyes opened and he blinked at her in surprise. Then he smiled. "Lady, thank ye."

Allie glanced into the melee. Royce was half covered in blood but he was focused and unhurt. Every giant who turned toward him—or that he attacked—fell to his blades. In spite of how horrible such a battle was, the sight of him thrilled and reassured her. He was power and courage, and today, the gods smiled upon him.

The giants kept on coming through the gatehouse, however, never mind that the men above were pouring hot oil on them and shooting them with flaming arrows. A little heat wouldn't stop them, Allie thought grimly. But they were human, and enough wounds would eventually kill their bodies.

She glanced up at the ramparts; most of the battle had moved down into the ward. She was pretty sure that wasn't a good sign. Claire and Malcolm remained above, though, fighting those still trying to scale the castle walls.

Allie turned away. Another man lay unconscious a few feet away from where she knelt. He'd suffered a blow from one of the catapulted rocks and had fallen from the ramparts above. Allie scrambled over to him and began healing him instantly.

"Ailios."

At the silken, seductive, deathly tone, Allie froze. Slowly she looked up at Moffat.

He smiled at her. He truly had the perfect beauty of a golden angel—but he was the harbinger of death. His eyes gleamed with a demonic lust that was so very sexual Allie's tension skyrocketed. In that instant, she knew he'd entrance and seduce her before he was through with her—and that he'd take more than pleasure from her. He'd take power, leaving her the victim of a pleasure crime. "Aye," he murmured.

Allie felt a chill sweep over her—and it was partly sensual.

"You'll never be able to resist me, Ailios. I'll wait while you finish healing him." He chuckled.

In that instant, Allie believed him. His powers of enchantment were terribly strong and she had to somehow keep a shield of white light about herself. Worse, she knew that if he seized her, he'd leap into another time and place with her. He only stood a foot away, towering over her, and that was dangerously close. She had to put more distance between them—but she was so afraid to move now. If she moved, she was certain he'd reach down and grab her. She didn't even dare look toward Royce.

Sweat ran down her body in streams of fear as she tried to think, on her hands and knees, near the wounded man.

"You don't wish to finish the healing?" he murmured, his blue eyes hot and bright.

It was hard to think clearly when the lord of so much mayhem and death stood staring down at her, contemplating all the ways he'd use her. There was so much fear her chest hurt. Allie knew she had to move. She erupted, crawling backward as fast as she could.

His pointy shoes followed her.

Before she could leap to her feet, her heels hit the wall. She looked up in horror.

He knelt so they were almost face-to-face, his features perfect. "You're so much like your mother," he breathed.

His breath tickled her skin. How did he know her mother? "Fuck off."

Her inarticulate response clearly amused him. "Don't you want to see her, Ailios?"

Allie's heart slammed. "She's dead."

"Really? Since when?" His cruelly beautiful smile played.

She could hear herself panting. "I will never heal demons."

His soft laughter came. "Maybe, maybe not. I have vast powers, beauty, and I believe that in the end, you will serve me well." His gaze slid to her mouth. It dropped lower, to her breasts and cleavage, daringly revealed in the tiny top.

"I'll die before healing demons," she said and she spat at his face. "And you'll have to rape me to get me in bed."

He wiped the spittle aside. "I'll enjoy that even more than seduction. If you wish to scream in sexual pain, it can be arranged."

Allie knew he meant it. She realized she was shaking as she slowly sat, still on her knees, her back now against the wall. There was no damned place to go.

He reached for her.

But she had been waiting for his move.

In spite of his magnetic pull, she thrust the dagger through his palm.

He growled, eyes widening in surprise, and he hesitated a fraction of a second.

Allie ducked and rolled beneath his outstretched arm.

Her hair leapt into his hand.

She howled from the pain. But even briefly blinded by it, there was panic. *Could his grasp on her hair be enough to take her through time with him?*

And from the corner of her eye, she saw the blade.

A swirl of silver light.

Royce.

It sliced through her hair and she was free. Allie leapt away.

Royce stood facing Moffat, smiling coldly.

Simultaneously, Moffat and Royce blasted one another with energy, but it was a stand-off. Moffat seized his sword with his bleeding hand, drawing it free of its scabbard. He thrust—as did Royce. The two blades locked.

So afraid the future would be repeated in the past, Allie looked at Royce, his blood-drenched leine sticking to his entire body like a second skin, delineating every muscle he had. His face was a mask of savage pleasure. *He wasn't afraid—he relished the violent encounter.*

"A Ailios," he said softly.

And he stepped back and thrust, forcing Moffat back to the wall. The blades shrieked and screamed, metal hissed and burned, filled with their power. Suddenly Royce drew his shortsword, so swiftly Allie was certain he'd mortally wound the other man.

Somehow Moffat drew his own small blade and parried.

Allie looked at her dagger, which lay on the ground not far from where the two men were furiously engaged. They seemed to be evenly matched, the one exception being the wound she had inflicted on Moffat's right hand. In spite of all the fighting he had done that day, Royce was not wounded, and Allie prayed that gave him the advantage.

The men withdrew and attacked again, each using two swords now. As they did so, Allie darted past them and seized the dagger. She was going to stick it right into Moffat's heart the next chance she got.

Royce and Moffat were braced swords against swords once more, pitting holy strength against demonic power.

Allie estimated she was but two steps away from her target. She needed an opening....

"No," Royce said sharply.

And although Royce didn't look at her as he spoke, Moffat used his shortsword, dropping his hand then raising it savagely, clearly going for Royce's jugular.

For one horrific instant, Allie thought Moffat would slit Royce's throat. But Royce brought his shortsword up in the nick of time, and as the blades rang, Allie leapt at Moffat.

He turned, trying to strike his longsword at her to deflect her dagger, but he was caught on Royce's longer blade and Allie slipped underneath.

Instead of penetrating his chest, she stabbed him deeply in the side, burying the entire blade there up to the hilt. Moffat turned white, dropping his weapons.

He looked at her, his eyes red with rage and hatred, a terrible promise there, and he vanished.

"Damn it," Royce cried in frustration.

Allie sagged against the wall. She could barely believe what she had done—she had almost caused Royce's death again!

He sheathed his swords and took her by the arms.

Instantly she became aware of his power, his rage and his heat. She stiffened with tension, her gaze shooting to his.

His silver eyes blazed with savage bloodlust. But he said, "Are ye hurt?"

"No. Are you?"

"Nay." He wet his lips, looked at her mouth and Allie felt the blood rushing through his veins. She felt the huge pounding pulse in his loins. She felt his murderous rage change, becoming pure, primitive male lust.

He turned abruptly to assess the battle, his jaw hard and flexed. Allie followed his gaze—the giants were fleeing, although a number of Masters and giants remained engaged, both on the ramparts and below in the ward. Their master, Moffat, was undoubtedly calling them off.

She leaned against the wall again, smelling Royce's scent—man and sex, blood and death. He became still, but his grip on her arms didn't ease and his breathing was rapid and shallow. With terrible clarity Allie recalled how he'd taken her on the table after the last demonic attack. Her body quivered in response to both the memory and the man holding her, but it didn't matter. They were surrounded by so much suffering and death.

The urge to go to those who needed healing consumed her. "Let me go," she said quietly, tuning in now to the wounded. A man pierced with three arrows, one through the lung, was closest. He would soon die if she did not attend him.

Royce didn't respond. He turned his silver gaze on her with so much promise Allie swelled and spasmed. And for one more heartbeat, Allie thought he would refuse; she thought he'd pull her close and claim her. Instead, his jaw flexing, his eyes hot and bright, he released her and stepped away.

Ignoring the last of the battles, Allie hurried to the wounded archer, refusing to think about Royce now or what had just happened. She knelt, drenching the man with her healing light. She was aware of Royce standing behind her now. He was guarding her against any sudden, even if improbable, attacks.

She breathed hard. Yes, this was how it was meant to be. He was meant to stand behind her as she healed, vigilant and defensive, maintaining a safe perimeter for her.

She was not meant to be the cause of his death.

When the wounded man was sitting up and breathing

well, Allie hurried to the next man, whose head was bleeding profusely. He was moaning heavily, having lost his entire right ear. She sent a soft rush of white light over him to ease the pain, then began flooding him with her power to stop the bleeding. Then she turned to Royce. "How many wounded are there?"

"Maybe a dozen live, not more."

Allie tensed. Could she possibly heal everyone? "How many are dead?"

Royce glanced upward, to where Malcolm remained on the ramparts. A moment later, he said, "Maybe three times that number. Ailios, yer nay alone. MacNeil has great healing power, an' Claire can help."

Allie inwardly wept for the fallen. She didn't know who MacNeil was, but she'd take any help she could. "If there is someone you want healed first, let me know." She turned to the man prone before her and infused his head with her healing power.

Time began to slow as Allie turned to the next of the wounded—and then the next. So many were burned and the projectiles had caused serious head injuries, but the stab wounds were the worst. Allie had never seen anything like the mayhem caused by this medieval battle, but then, she'd never been in any kind of military conflict before. She healed four more of the wounded when Royce touched her shoulder. "Ailios, Malcolm needs ye to heal his best man, Seamus. Claire has tried an' failed an' MacNeil be with a wounded Master."

Allie simply sat still for a moment. The battle was finally over, the last of the invaders having fled. But the keep was filled with female sobs, quieter, subdued male conversation, as well as the moans of the wounded. A terrible pall hung over the castle grounds. The day had turned dark, as if the Ancients grieved, and death and misery had become tangible, casting a heavy weight upon the grounds, one Allie could actually feel upon her shoulders.

Allie rubbed her temples and blinked. She was feeling weak and just a bit faint, and she wasn't sure her legs would hold her if she stood. She needed a moment of respite, when no real interlude was to be had. The dying could not wait. She took a deep breath, reminding herself that there were more wounded. She hoped MacNeil could heal half of them. She was pretty certain her reserves were dwindling.

"Ye dinna have enough power, do ye?" Royce demanded, his gaze searching.

"I can't argue with you now. Where's Seamus?"

Royce led her through the ward, stepping carefully to avoid the corpses, the wounded calling out to her as she passed. She smiled at each and every man. "I'll be right back," she promised them all, meaning it.

"I can feel that yer tired!" Royce exclaimed. "Ye can't heal all the rest! MacNeil doesna have infinite power, either! Ye'll have to pick an' choose."

"I am not a god, to decide who lives and who dies," Allie said grimly.

"Aye, today ye are," Royce flashed.

Allie faltered. That wasn't fair. She could never dispense life in such a manner. "Don't try to stop me from doing what I have to do," she warned softly. She did not want to waste her time or her strength arguing. Then she saw an ashen Claire, gesturing to her.

Allie hurried over to a big, middle-aged man with iron-gray hair. He was unconscious and he had been bleeding from the abdomen. From the amount of blood staining the ground, she was afraid he'd slip away at any time.

"I stopped the bleeding, that's all," Claire cried. "I can't do more. He's dying, I can feel it!"

Allie knelt, felt his life flickering weakly and drew her white power from within and cast it over Seamus. Then she pushed it into him, through him, seeking his life first, nourishing it with her power, feeding it. When it blazed strongly, she focused on his wound, sweating now. It had become a distinct physical effort to find the power and cast it, much less sustain it. She felt faint again and her stomach was so upset she was nauseous.

Allie found the strength to sustain her power. Eventually Seamus looked at her, blinking.

Allie couldn't smile. The ground was tilting. She sat down in the dirt, gasping for air. She told herself that she could do this—and she would.

Royce knelt, putting his arm around her. "Ye've done enough this day."

"Give me a moment," she said, hoping her tone sounded soft, not weak.

Royce stared at her. When she didn't look at him, he tilted up her chin, forcing her gaze to his. "Ye've never healed like this, have ye?"

"I'm not a war veteran."

He grimaced, clearly not comprehending her. "Can ye hurt yerself? Kill yerself?"

Allie had no idea. "Of course not."

She knelt over another wounded man, ignoring Royce's expletive. He clasped her shoulder. She said quickly, "Please don't interfere. I can do this."

"I dinna think so." But he released her, his face tight and grim.

Allie tried to find her power. It seemed weak and far away and almost nonexistent, like the illusion of an oasis in the desert.

Shit, she thought. The man lying prone in the dirt was

conscious and he was regarding her with wide, hopeful but pain-filled eyes. She sucked up all her determination, all her strength. She found the white light flickering inside her and seized it, somehow. It felt so elusive now.

She pushed it at the man, who had been stabbed many times. He gasped as her warm healing power washed over him.

But bathing him in her light wasn't going to heal him. She needed to flood those wounds, Allie thought grimly. She trembled and on all fours, reached deeper than she would have ever believed possible. The white light was there. She pulled it out, hurting physically now, as if someone was pulling her organs out of her body while she lived and breathed and watched. Sweat blinded her. She wanted to moan—she did. Then she summoned up all her strength and flooded the man with healing light.

The ground spun. The day turned ominously gray. She felt Royce's hands on her as she fell forward into the dirt.

As he lifted her into his arms there was so much relief and even more exhaustion—and then blackness claimed her.

CHAPTER ELEVEN

ROYCE GAZED DOWN at the tiny woman in his arms and felt his fear escalate wildly. She had become as pale as linen before it was dyed. She didn't even appear to be breathing. "MacNeil!" he cried and he heard the desperation in his tone.

The Abbot remained kneeling over the last of the wounded. "Take her in. I'll be up shortly," the Master said, not looking up.

Claire touched his arm, commiseration in her eyes. "Follow me."

Royce nodded, his stomach twisted into painful knots. Ailios was the bravest person he had ever seen, man or woman, and she could not die now. She could not have given her own life to save the others. Terrified, he followed Claire into the hall and up the stairs of Malcolm's tower, Ailios as light as a small child in his arms—and as still as a corpse. Claire shoved open a door to a small, pleasant bedchamber and he laid Ailios on the bed. She didn't stir.

He sat beside her, seizing her hands. He was horrified because they were so cold, and he placed his cheek close to her nose, aware of his racing heartbeat, his rampant fear. At first, he felt nothing, and his fear became terror. *Ailios could not be dead.*

And then he felt her faint, shallow breath on his face. Relief made it impossible to speak clearly. "She's barely breathing," he said thickly. How could this be happening? He had brought her to Dunroch to protect her. It had been his best judgment that Dunroch would be a safe haven for her, with Malcolm to defend her. Instead the deamhanain had followed them there. Moffat had dared to violate Dunroch and he had almost seized her.

He should have never brought her to Dunroch; he should have never thought to hand her over to Malcolm. MacNeil had chosen him for a reason.

"She is selfless," Claire said, interrupting his panicked, racing thoughts.

"Aye, she never thinks o' herself." She had tried to heal too many of the wounded, but that was what Ailios would do, for he knew her now. If another battle came, she would act no differently. But only a true goddess could heal so many of the sick and dying. She wasn't a goddess. If she could not control her need to heal, someone had to do it for her. This was the fifteenth century, where battles were common, a weekly event.

Surely it wasn't written that she would die now, this way. She was going to be his lover in the future!

"How ill is she?" he asked Claire without turning to look at her. He kept Ailios's hands clasped tightly against his chest. They remained as cold as the water in the ocean below Dunroch.

"I can feel her life."

Did Claire take him for a fool? Furious, he looked at her. "Aye, what's left of it! How much life *is* left? Or has she killed herself?" he demanded. His heart raced in agitation. What could he do to help her? He had never felt so powerless.

"I don't know," Claire whispered, ashen. "She's so weak."

MacNeil strode in, his bold red and black plaid swinging against his muscular thighs. "I dinna think to meet Elasaid's daughter this way," he said grimly.

In common circumstance, MacNeil was a man of smiles, wisdom and wit. He was only deadly serious when the situation was dire. He was deadly serious now.

Royce stood so the Master could sit beside Ailios. "She would die to save even the most common life," he said harshly.

MacNeil stroked Ailios's thick dark hair away from her cheeks. "Such a small woman for such a great Healer," he murmured. "Aye, like her mother, she will give to others until the death."

Royce felt like striking the other man. "She willna die. She is small—an' *mine.*"

MacNeil did not bother to glance at him, his gaze remaining on Ailios. He cupped her cheek. Royce fell silent, because he could actually see the Master sending her a white light. A moment later he saw her chest rise and fall visibly; two small spots of pink color appeared on her cheeks. Her lashes fluttered but her eyes didn't open. And for the first time in his life, Royce felt faint. Relief overwhelmed him.

He must thank the gods, he thought.

MacNeil smiled, revealing two deep dimples. Not looking up at Royce, he said, "Ah, Ruari, ye can thank *me* sometime." He ran his blunt finger over the curve of her cheekbone and murmured, "Rest now, Allie Monroe."

Royce became incredulous. He seized the Master's shoulder and whirled him, the chamber suddenly a blaze of red.

MacNeil simply grinned as he stood. "Oh, come, I ken she's yer Innocent, but she belongs to all of us, too. An' ye canna forgive a Master for taking such an opportunity. I'd be dead if I didn't want to touch her."

"Ye had no call to stroke her face!" Royce said, and before he'd even finished speaking, he balled up his fist and struck MacNeil in the jaw.

MacNeil didn't budge, as if an ancient oak. He didn't even vibrate. But his kelly-green eyes widened with genuine shock.

Claire cried out, running between the two men. "Stop!" She looked wildly between them. "What are you doing?" she cried, first to MacNeil and then to Royce.

Royce smiled grimly, briefly satisfied, hoping MacNeil would take the bait—because he deserved a pummeling.

But MacNeil only rubbed his jaw. "What's wrong with ye?" he finally said, puzzled. "T'is forbidden, in no uncertain terms. Masters dinna fight one another. We're allies, not rivals."

"Then ye should have healed her without giving in to the need to caress her," Royce spat.

MacNeil's eyes narrowed. It was a moment before he spoke. "Come to Iona." He vanished.

Royce tensed, because he had just been given an unmistakable command. MacNeil had been the Abbot of Iona for as long as he could remember. No Master outranked him. If orders were to be given, he gave them. If decisions were to be made, he made them. MacNeil's first duty was to the Brotherhood and the Ancients and he left Iona only to battle the highest deamhanain, in the gravest of crises.

"Come downstairs." Claire laid her hand on his arm and smiled. "She'll be fine, Royce."

He glanced at Ailios, now sleeping peacefully in the bed, so small she was dwarfed by it like a child. But she was a lovely, seductive and sensual woman. The sight of her caused his heart to leap, lurch, overturn. "Nay. Leave us," he said. He took a wood chair, brought it to her bedside and sat down beside her.

He heard the door closing.

He had been out of his mind with fear when he'd thought she might die.

And he wasn't quite calm now.

He had never wanted to vanquish anyone the way he'd wanted to vanquish Moffat when he'd seen him with Ailios, taunting her, lust in his eyes.

What had he said? Royce's gut roiled all over again. He had almost finished the task of destroying the deamhan. Had Moffat lived because it was written that he should die by Moffat's hand in 2007?

Many decades ago, he had realized death did not matter to him very much. His life had become impossibly tiresome centuries ago—2007 was five centuries away, almost as long as he had already lived. But…his life didn't feel tiresome now. His duty to protect and defend the little woman lying in the bed had become consuming. Every demonic conflict, chase and hunt had new and higher stakes. How could he die when she needed him?

Her recklessness terrified him!

He slumped in the chair. He *was* tired. He had been tired of the cycle of this life for a very long time. Moray had been the greatest deamhan to ever walk Alba, but he had been vanquished. And then Moffat, who'd existed for centuries, rose up to take his place. For all anyone knew, he might even possess the missing Book of Power, the Duisean, which would explain his ascendancy over all the other dark lords. Moray had possessed the Book before his death. Centuries ago, he'd stolen it from its holy shrine. Many Masters had since searched for it, but it had not been recovered.

When Moffat was vanquished, a new dark power would rise up to preside over all evil. It was the way of the world. The Masters could ceaselessly and tirelessly fight the shadows, but the shadows would always return. There would never be peace, and if there were, the Brotherhood would die.

Still, one thing had changed. This one had become his Innocent in the south of Hampton, and she remained his Innocent now. He could not trust her with Malcolm, and that had become clear this day. And she must live at all costs, even at the cost of his own life, which wasn't worth all that much anymore, anyway. He could not be sure of Ailios's Fate, but it was great. Somewhere, it had been written as such.

He looked at her and thought about taking her back to Carrick. He was a man, and his loins filled. No matter how he wanted her, he had to stay away from her, because his enemies must never think they were lovers. That day had proven that, too.

He felt himself flush. The entire castle had seen his concern for Ailios that afternoon. He had told MacNeil that she *belonged* to him. Claire had witnessed the absurd statement.

MacNeil and Claire could be trusted to be discreet; others could not. He had to keep a firm grasp on his virile nature and his overwhelming attraction to her. But how could he do that, when the moment she was better and they were alone, he was going to want to mount her, pleasure her and have her pleasure him?

The door burst open.

Royce leapt to his feet, his sword ringing as he drew it.

Guy Macleod looked at him and at the woman in the bed. "You willna lust after my sister," he warned.

Royce sheathed his sword. "Dinna ye think to knock?"

The Black Macleod laughed. He was a big, muscular man with dark hair, swarthy skin and shockingly blue eyes.

Except for his eye color and size, he and his sister looked very much like siblings. He wore a red and black plaid over his leine, and thigh-high black boots with huge, spiked spurs. "Yer fortunate," Macleod said softly, "that I dinna take yer head."

Royce braced for a battle of wills and words. "She's sleeping. She needs rest. Step outside."

"Aye." Guy Macleod gave his sister one last look and whirled. Royce followed him onto the circular landing outside the chamber door.

Macleod now smiled coldly at him. "Ye sit and lust after her."

Royce returned his look. "Yer sister is safe with me."

Macleod laughed, mocking him. "No woman is safe with any Master, and we both know it."

"She's not any woman. She's a great Healer—yer mother's daughter."

"Aye," Macleod flashed. His brilliant blue eyes heated. "I will take her back to Blayde."

Royce laughed with no mirth whatsoever. "She stays with me."

The Black Macleod straightened. "So you can use her? I think not. She's my sister and unless she has a husband, I have every right to bring her into my household. I am her lord and master now."

"Yer mother," Royce said, no longer smiling, "spoke to Ailios."

Macleod started.

"Elasaid came to her just days ago, telling Ailios to trust me. MacNeil chose me an' sent me to her. An' we ken he sees what the Ancients wish for him to see. T'is *my* duty— *my* Fate—to protect her now." He added, "I saved her this day from Moffat...not ye, not Malcolm, not MacNeil."

After a pause, Macleod said, "Lady Elasaid is dead."

"Aye, but she came to Ailios from the other world. Ye can ask Ailios yerself."

Macleod was grim, but his eyes flickered with comprehension. "If MacNeil chose you, he must have seen something to make him do so. But I dinna like MacNeil choosing you and not me, her own brother."

"I will tell ye this," Royce said. "I will not use yer sister. I have no wish for my enemies to think us fond o' one another. Today I spared her Moffat. I will die to do so again. There is no one ye can trust as ye trust me."

Macleod stared for a long, assessing moment. "I have never doubted ye would give yer life for her, Royce." He flushed. "I canna argue with MacNeil's will, or the Ancients. But if ye touch her, if ye hurt her, ye will pay—and I will be the one to make ye pay. The Code be damned."

Royce knew he meant his every word. Two hundred years ago Macleod had laid siege to a great fortress to force the lord there to release his daughter—and hand her over in marriage to him.

"Tell her I came. I'll come again when I can. Tell her she is always welcome at Blayde." Macleod vanished before Royce could respond.

Royce seized the door handle and thrust it open. He had expected a confrontation with Macleod, who was both ambitious and hotheaded. MacNeil had chosen Royce, not her half brother, to defend Ailios for the Brotherhood, and no one could argue over such a choice, as MacNeil's wisdom had been proven by time.

He stepped inside and saw that she was sleeping deeply. As he covered her with a fur, he realized he was almost smiling—and that there was a smile in his heart, as well.

He didn't like such weakness and he frowned.

His heart had no reason to feel pleasure. Resolved, he chased the lightness away.

ALLIE AWOKE to a strange chamber filled with shadows, illuminated by the fire dancing in the hearth, and Royce's steady stare.

He sat in a chair just inches from her bedside, his gray gaze intent upon her. She smiled, thrilled to awaken to the sight of him there.

He smiled tentatively back. "Yer awake," he said unnecessarily.

Her smile faded. She thought about the terrible battle of that day, the dead and those who had almost died. She sat up. "I have to pray. I have to go to the closest shrine."

He reached out and clasped her arm. "Ailios. Ye were very sick. There's a chapel at Dunroch, but ye need not leap out of bed as if it's on fire."

Allie sank back against the pillows, sitting up now, acutely aware of his large hand grasping her wrist. His touch sent delicious shivers through her. He let her go and she was surprised when Royce leaned forward to add a pillow behind her back. She recalled him in his battle mode, slaying demons left and right. The same man had not just rearranged her pillows for her. Someone far gentler had done that. "I have to pray for those we lost, Royce," she said quietly.

"I ken. The prayers can wait. How do ye feel?"

She now remembered her last waking moments. She had been healing the blond man who had been stabbed so many times, becoming so weak and ill that she had finally lost consciousness. She vaguely recalled Royce lifting her into his arms. "I fainted?"

"Ye passed out," he said quietly. "Ye pushed yerself well past yer limits." He turned and poured water into a mug and handed it to her. "Ye have limits, Ailios. Yer a powerful Healer, but yer terribly young. Mayhap yer power will grow in time."

Allie drank gratefully, thinking about his words. "Please tell me that the last man I healed survived."

"Ye still think of others." But he answered her question. "Aye, Kirkus lives."

"Thank the gods." Then, struck by an awful thought, she met his gaze. "I must look like hell."

His next smile was deeper, although brief, exposing one dimple. "Ye always look well."

Her heart raced. Oh, did she know that look. They were having a serious conversation, but Allie knew what was in the back of his mind. She could feel his lust beginning to rise and throb in his veins.

The tension in the room changed. Allie thought about his needs and hers—it felt like eons since they'd been together. She ran her fingers through her hair, finally glancing up at Royce as she did so. "Liar," she said softly. Her top was spotted with dried blood. Her jeans were probably in the same condition.

His eyes were as fierce and intent as his expression. "Ye always look well," he repeated, this time in a bedroom tone.

Was he flirting with her? Would he act on his lust? Oh, Allie did like this. "If you want to think so, I won't argue," she said softly. She reached out for his hand.

He just looked at it.

"I don't bite," she whispered. "Not unless you ask me to."

His eyes blazed.

Allie sat up and leaned forward, boldly taking his hand. It was large and strong, just like the man, a hand that could wield a huge longsword with fatal effect—or stroke her body in a silken, cunning caress. From it, she received so much heat—and an incredible sense of security, of masculinity, of power. "Thank you."

He looked away, staring at the bed. "For allowing ye to hold my hand as if I'm a small boy?"

She laughed. His gaze whipped to hers. "For protecting me from Moffat. For standing by me while I healed," she said.

For a long moment, they stared at one another. Allie said even more softly, "You've been here with me the whole time I've been passed out, haven't you?"

He tugged his hand free. "Ye were ill. Ye needed rest. MacNeil healed ye by giving ye his great power. Ye canna ever heal so many at one time again."

Allie smiled, pleased, even though he clearly wasn't going to answer her. Mr. Medieval *cared*. "You know what? You're really not such an ogre, after all. The Terminator, maybe, but not an ogre."

He shook his head. His face was taut.

"That was a backhanded compliment. What is it, Royce? What's wrong?"

"Ye sit there smiling, in jest, when ye could have died. Canna ye not see how serious this is? Ailios, ye canna walk the world as if yer immortal."

"Like you don't?" she asked.

"No one cares if I live or die," he said firmly, standing. "Everyone cares about ye."

"I care if you live or die!" she flashed. Then she softened. "And you know it."

"Aye, but I dinna ken why." He stared directly at her. "There are many men to please ye in bed."

It took Allie a moment. "You think I'm in love with you because of great sex?" And her incredulity faded; she laughed.

He flushed. "Aye, I do." His hands found his hips.

And Allie went still. She focused and saw the uncertainty in his aura—it was a pale, milky, sky-blue. She felt the same uncertainty coming from him in fragile, broken pulses. "Hey." She threw off the fur and slung her legs over the bed. "You are definitely gorgeous and hot. But I admire you, Royce, immensely, more than I have ever admired anyone."

He seemed bewildered. "What do ye see to admire so much?"

"Strength, power, integrity, honesty, loyalty…should I continue?"

He now folded his arms across his chest, causing his biceps to bulge. "Aye," he said.

Allie took a pillow and threw it at him, laughing. "Conceit, arrogance and an utterly tyrannical nature!" she cried.

He caught the pillow, feathers flying, then gently tossed it back at her. "Ye admire my conceit?"

"Take a good guess," Allie said, on her feet and hugging the pillow now. As it was the only thing between them, she dropped it. "I forgot heroic," she whispered, laying her hands on his chest. And she felt his body tense and his heart thunder.

His silver gaze slammed to hers.

"You are a hero," she said, meaning it. She took his hand and placed it on her chest.

His warm palm covered her bare skin. She looked into his sizzling eyes and saw his gaze drop to her mouth. Love consumed her. Desire, already heady, crested. In spite of the day's ordeal, her flesh began an urgent throbbing. She felt like telling him just how much she loved him—better yet, showing him in that bed—but it wasn't necessarily the smartest idea, considering he had rejected her yesterday in no uncertain terms. Besides, she was holding out for three very specific words.

"I'm nay hero." Royce removed his hand and turned, slowly pacing the room like a caged-up lion.

Allie was about to tell him he was not just her hero, but everyone's hero, when he said, "Yer brother was here."

Allie jerked, stunned. "He was here? While I slept?" she cried.

"Aye. Ye may have seen him fighting on the ramparts. He's dark, an' he wore red an' black." Royce paused, facing her.

Allie suddenly recalled seeing two Masters on the ramparts. "That was my brother?" she gasped, utterly distracted now.

"Aye."

That had been her half brother. "I want to meet him," she managed.

"Ye will. He came to take ye to his home, but we discussed it an' he agreed to leave ye with me. He's since left."

A huge disappointment began. Allie sat down on the edge of the bed. "Why didn't he stay until I woke up?"

Royce shook his head. "He's young an' hot," he said. "He's a bold, impatient man. He waits for no one. But he'll come again an' yer welcome at Blayde, his home, anytime."

Allie felt her brows rise. Her brother sounded like another entirely medieval man, very much like Royce. An alarm bell went off. "Guy doesn't sound like he'd discuss very much with anyone, ever."

"He doesna discuss much, yer right. He fights first an' talks later, in spite of having a good wife to rein him in. If yer asking if we fought, we dinna. I wouldn't fight yer brother." He added wryly, "But if ye think me a tyrant, well, he makes me look like a milkmaid. His household wouldn't please ye much."

"Great." She thought about it. "Thank you. I wasn't about to leave you now, anyway."

Royce stared at her.

Allie tensed, sliding to her feet. "You need me—and I need you. I think that's become very clear."

His color rose. "I'll nay deny I need ye in my bed—"

"Stop! I wasn't referring to sex and you know it."

Flushed, he shook his head. "Yer a foolish woman if ye'll start thinking of ways to heal my heart again!"

"Will you ever respect the privacy of my thoughts?"

He gave her a bold look. "Ye like the invasion."

Her body reacted to his deliberate choice of words. "In a way, I do. It makes communicating with you very intimate. But if you knew that, you wouldn't be so eager to read my mind all the time."

"To protect ye, t'is best I ken what ye think."

"Liar," she said softly. "You can't help yourself. You read my mind the way you look at me—you undress my thoughts with a single telepathic thrust the way you undress my body with a single physical glance."

His face hardened. "Do ye wish to ken why they call me Black Royce?"

She hesitated. "I think you intend to tell me, regardless."

"Because my heart was blackened long ago."

"Because of what happened to Brigdhe?"

He paled.

Allie prayed she hadn't gone too far. "I pried. I asked Malcolm about her. Royce, it wasn't your fault."

He had recovered his composure. His eyes were cold. "I willna discuss my wife with ye."

Allie retreated. "I am so sorry about what happened. And I will respect your privacy."

He stared and she stared back. Then he nodded. "Good."

Allie turned away and breathed deeply, in relief. She had better tread with care on that particular subject. She slowly turned and walked over to him, beginning to smile, using all of her feminine power. "Please forgive me?" she asked softly, laying her hand on his chest.

"There's nothin' to forgive. Ye like to talk an' ye like me. So ye spoke to Malcolm. My past is hardly a secret." He shrugged as if indifferent now.

Allie managed not to sigh. Until Royce gave her his heart, he would always try to turn the tables on her. He probably did so instinctively. "In my time, people talk a lot, about *everything,* all the time, men included."

He stepped away from her so her hand fell from his chest. "That must please ye."

Now she shrugged. "It's a different world."

"Ye must miss yer home."

Actually, Allie hadn't thought about home at all since meeting Royce at the fund-raiser. Since the moment he'd appeared in South Hampton, she'd become completely and irreversibly caught up in his life and his Fate.

He smiled, pleased.

But now, she thought about her father and Tabby, Sam and Brie. They had to be worried sick about her! At some point, she had to figure out how to get a message to them. "I need to learn how to read your mind," Allie said. "But I think I can read one thought. You're not still planning on leaving me here, are you?"

His smile vanished. "Nay," he said. "Ye needed me today. Had I left yesterday, ye'd be in Moffat's hands."

Relief surged. "I did need you today." She smiled brightly, a cover-up, for she was trying not to think about Moffat's lust and what he intended for her. But her gut roiled. No demon had ever frightened her so before, but then, no demon had ever made her his prey. She wouldn't mind never laying eyes on Moffat again.

"Ailios." His sharp tone made her meet his hard, uncompromising gaze. "Ye won't be apart from me until Moffat is dead."

More relief arose.

"He won't take ye," Royce said coldly. "I willna allow it."

Allie nodded. "I know you won't."

As she saw his set expression, his warriorlike resolve, a vague image of another woman crept into her mind, followed by the whisper of her name. *Brigdhe.*

His wife had been captured by his demonic enemy.

And the demons wanted to capture her now.

And Allie saw, in that single stunning moment, the truth.

Royce was afraid for her because of what happened to his wife.

Royce strode past her, shoving open the door. "I'll take ye to the chapel," he said, flushed.

And she knew she was right.

ALONE IN THE CHAPEL, Allie reached out to the dead.

Confusion, anguish and sorrow wafted in the air, making it feel thick and heavy. Having been so suddenly and violently killed, their souls lingered nearby, a tangible presence, clearly uncertain as to whether to leave their loved ones behind, unwilling to move on. So much energy came from the recently dead and Allie knelt, trying to sort through the various roiling emotions. She wanted to heal each and every confused soul.

Allie identified the first of the dead, a very young, newly wed man. His name formed in her mind—Thormond—as did his pale, red-haired image. She knew he was afraid to leave his bride, and as she lit a candle for him, she began to pray.

She called out to the Ancients, one by one, asking them to heed her and to help her ease the passage of the dead into the next world. When she felt certain that the old gods had gathered and were listening, she turned her attention back to the dead young man.

She blessed him and his wife, reassuring him and encouraging him to go to the next life. She could feel his youth, not just in physical years, but in soul lifetimes, and she knew he would soon find rebirth. Allie prayed until she felt the confusion and uncertainty subsiding, until she felt his swirling energy soften. A moment later, she felt his presence dwindling, and then it was gone.

She managed a smile and wiped a tear from her face. She would call on Thormond's wife tomorrow. Then she turned to the next hovering soul, this man far older but just as reluctant to leave his family and friends.

Many hours later, Allie stood, feeling shaky. The chapel was empty now, every soul sent on his or her way; two of the dead had been women, inadvertently killed in the attack. Moffat had to be stopped.

She stepped outside into a blushing dawn. Royce was sitting on the stairs leading up to the ramparts, waiting for her. Her heart turned over hard as their gazes met. As she walked over to him, he stood.

She saw the question in his eyes.

"I'm fine. It took some time to get the gods' attention—and to send everyone on their way."

"It took all night," he said flatly, his gaze still searching. "Did ye try to heal every lost soul?"

"Were you listening to me?"

"A bit."

"They all needed me, Royce."

He shocked her by reaching out and putting his arm around her. "Will ye rest now?"

She leaned into his magnificent body, then gave in and turned, wrapping her arms around him, her cheek against the flat, hard lower edge of his chest. He hesitated and then his arms engulfed her. Allie stood still, breathing in his power, his essence, his scent, and relishing being in his arms.

"Does anyone ever pray for ye, Ailios?" he asked softly.

She nuzzled his chest, the linen rough beneath her cheek. "Who on earth would do that?"

His grip tightened.

Allie felt his heart pick up a new, stronger rhythm. "I wasn't put here for myself, Royce. Like you, I was put here to help others."

He was silent.

Allie thought about the intimacy of the moment. They were alone together and she was in his arms, in a silent dawn filled with the light of both the rising sun and the full moon, and his concern was just as evident now as it had been earlier. *I am no longer alone*, she thought, and she smiled against his chest.

They had been through so much in such a short time. They had survived so much together. They weren't quite lovers and they were far more than friends. And no matter what mode he was in, Allie knew she could count on him.

"Tell me about the future," he said hoarsely.

"What?" she asked, surprised, pulling back to look up at him.

He made a derisive sound, releasing her. He folded his arms across his chest and stared tightly down at her.

Allie felt her heart race. "You want to know about the time we spent together?"

His expression threatened to crack. "Aye."

She was stunned and thrilled. "Let's sit," she said. "I'll tell you anything you want to know."

CHAPTER TWELVE

ROYCE SIMPLY STOOD, his arms folded almost defensively across his chest.

So Allie sat on the steps he'd vacated. "What do you want to know?"

His gaze was intense. "Everything."

Allie realized he wanted every single detail of their time together—even the time in bed. Her heart lurched, and her body became terribly hollow. "Where do you want me to start?" she asked slowly.

"How did I find ye?"

Allie wet her lips, his gaze unwavering upon her. "It was as if you knew I was there, at Carrick. I was waiting for you in the hall with a glass of wine. I didn't know you were from the future—I was expecting my golden warrior from this time, the same man who had appeared to help me fight the demons in South Hampton the night before. You drove into the courtyard in a black Ferrari and the moment you got out of the car, you looked into the window at me—as if you could see me, which you couldn't possibly."

His nostrils flared. "I'd ken ye were there. I'd sense yer white power—yer purity, yer beauty…yer heat."

She inhaled, desire pooling. "You knew I was there, all right. You came into the hall like a man coming home to his bride."

Royce stared, his gaze now silver. "I dinna think I'd forget the date."

Allie was bewildered.

"I left ye in my home on September 6, 2007. I wouldn't forget such a day, ever."

She stood and hugged herself now, terribly serious—and acutely aware of the tension throbbing between them. It was so easy to feel his pounding pulse. "Now I understand, because when you came in, you greeted me without a pause."

"And ye were pleased to see me?"

She nodded, smiling briefly. "I couldn't wait. I couldn't wait to see you, to make sure you were real and to be in your arms—and in your bed," she said softly.

His eyes blazed. "Ye dinna ken I was my future self?"

"I was confused—but your aura was the same. Still, you had such short hair—you looked older—but I knew it was you."

"And?" he demanded when she paused.

"You asked me if I wanted supper. I said no. You dismissed the housekeeper. I asked you if you had a brother and you said no. And then I asked if you had rescued me the night before."

He stood so still he might have been a marble statue, but he was hardly made of stone. His aura blazed with red desire, and his leine billowed, exposing that desire.

She whispered, "You said you rescued me, but not the night before. You said you'd helped me over five hundred years ago."

Royce didn't move.

She felt moisture dripping between her thighs. "You took my glass of wine away and told me I talk too much." Allie trembled. "And you told me you'd waited five hundred and seventy-seven years for me."

He made a harsh sound. "And?" he demanded.

"You took me in your arms—you kissed me with your tongue in my throat—and then I was against the wall, and you lifted my thigh and your trousers ripped," she managed.

He stared and she stared back. "How much pleasure," he finally said, "did I give ye?"

"So much," she whispered. "More than any man ever. We had sex in the hall, there against the wall, and then you took me to your bed, and we made love all night." Her heart raced madly now. "I must have come a dozen times. So did you."

He breathed hard.

"And in the middle of the night," she said, "you held me and smiled and we talked about the Masters and the Brotherhood."

His eyes went wide. "I talked to ye while we were in bed?"

She nodded. "For quite some time."

He turned away from her, as if shaken.

Allie tried to find some composure. It wasn't easy when she was now so acutely tuned in to his lust, which seemed to match hers completely. "You were very talkative—compared to now. And you weren't afraid to smile, either."

He faced her, eyes wide and searching. "'T'is the truth!" he exclaimed.

She nodded. "Surely I'm not the first woman you've had a conversation with during sex?"

"The bed is for sleep or sex, nay for speeches."

Allie felt bug-eyed. "You've never cuddled and chatted with a woman in bed before?"

"Never," he snapped. Then, cheeks flushed, he asked, "Did I tell ye I love ye, too?"

Allie went still.

And he knew. His color diminished. "I dinna say the words."

It was hard to confirm the terrible truth. "No, you didn't, not even while dying. But you didn't have to. Because I saw the love in your eyes."

He shook his head fiercely. "I couldna become such a fool in old age!"

Allie didn't like this. "For God's sake, Royce, falling in love is wonderful, not foolish."

"Aye—for an ordinary man."

It took Allie a moment to respond. "Malcolm has Claire."

"And I pray every day she willna suffer for it. Every day, I pray Malcolm willna regret his choice."

In that moment, she felt his thoughts go to a featureless woman with titian hair. "This is about Brigdhe!"

His eyes blazed. "I took vows. I follow the Code. There's no room in my life for foolish sentiment."

Allie shook her head. "Earlier I realized you're afraid for me because of what happened to her. But I am not her! I am stronger! And if this is why you are trying to avoid a relationship—"

He cut her off. "Yer nay my wife—or my love—and ye'll never be either," he said savagely.

Allie recoiled, hurt to the quick. He had loved his wife. And even though Allie felt terrible for what Brigdhe had been through, and even though that had been eight centuries ago, she couldn't stand how much he had loved her— and that he refused to open his heart to her now.

"Ye'll never have my heart," he said.

She covered her aching chest with her hand. Did he know how cruel he was being?

Then he said harshly, "Yer a Healer, Ailios, an' ye belong to the world, not to any one man."

She trembled. Even she knew that was her Fate.

With that, he whirled, leaving her alone in the dawn.

IONA SPARKLED in the midmorning sun, its gleaming beaches as pale as pearls.

Allie stepped from the galley without help, trembling with excitement. She'd spent the few hours since dawn torn between despair over Royce's determination to avoid her, and her own determination to break through the walls he'd erected around his heart. She had despaired over the apparent depth of his love for his dead wife, too. Apparently Brigdhe was a rival after all, even as a ghost.

But then they had taken their leave of Claire and Malcolm, boarding a single-masted galley, and they had been rowed the few miles to the small island. Royce was not on her mind, as she took in the rolling green hills behind the beaches. Even the ocean sparkled like sapphires that day.

Allie stared toward a walled compound, within which were several medieval buildings, including a church. She knew from her previous tours to the island that a medieval abbey had once stood there, as had a Benedictine monastery. In fact, the chapel bells began ringing as she focused on the compound to determine which it was. She felt the soft, serene, giving presence of women, and realized she faced the abbey.

She slowly turned. Up the pale dirt road was another fortified compound, this one far larger. So much power came from behind those solid walls that she became breathless. Testosterone and strength wafted from the fortress, so strong that she paused, aware of a new tension, gathering within her, tightening her, calling to her womanhood. Masters were there, and she was acutely aware of it.

The Ancients were nearby, too.

She felt their power and their majesty most of all. "Ailios? Come."

Royce stood on the pier, waiting for her. She smiled at him, another rush of excitement consuming her. "I have been drawn to this island many times! I've felt so much holiness here—and I always thought I could feel people, power. I'd hear voices and then I'd laugh at that and tell myself the island was haunted."

Royce met her gaze. "Ye sensed us in other times."

"Damn right I did," Allie cried. Happy, she seized his hand. "Let's go. And smile—it doesn't hurt."

He pulled his hand from hers, his mouth remaining in a rigid line. Allie felt some of her joy vanish, her excitement fade. He'd been deadly serious since boarding the galley. His tension was huge, none of it sexual. His aura roiled, as if with distress that bordered on anguish. She wished she could read his mind so she could understand what was tormenting him now.

She was fairly certain it had something to do with their conversation about the future. As they started up the road, the men leaving the galley at anchor by the pier, she said, "It's a beautiful day. What's wrong?"

He glanced at her, his strides swift enough that she had to break into a trot to keep up with him. "There's nothin' wrong. I have affairs to attend with MacNeil. I dinna ken what he wishes of me now."

"You seem sad."

He gave her a dark look. "I dinna have time to be sad. We'll stay an hour or two, then we'll return to Carrick." And he outdistanced her.

Allie followed, aware that on some level he was hurting. She hesitated, then gave in to her urge. She showered him with her healing white light.

He whirled, his aura sucking up the white light like a sponge. "What do ye think to do?" he demanded.

"Let me try to ease the pain, Royce," she said quietly, coming up to him. She reached for him.

He swatted her hand away. "Ye can ease my pain with yer body, not with yer power," he said furiously. "My pain is between my legs—nowhere else!"

"Of course," she said, not meaning it. "I want to heal you and you turn the discussion to sex."

He leaned close. "I dinna need healing," he said, hard. "An' when ye change yer mind about love, ye can ease my pain anytime." He walked away from her, jerking open the heavy, studded door set in the monastery's thick walls. It wasn't locked or bolted, but of course, no demon would ever set foot on the island. It was too holy.

Allie hesitated, telling herself not to be hurt. He still grieved for his lost love, and he still carried that crushing guilt, although he would never admit it. She wondered what kind of woman his wife had been. She had to have been some kind of saint.

She was competing for Royce's heart with a saintly ghost. That was just great.

Allie walked after him, and as she did, some wounded anger began. No matter what he said, he was hurt and he needed her. She flung a bolt of white healing light at him, through him.

He whirled, eyes wide with disbelief.

"Try to tell me that doesn't feel good!" she cried, closing the door behind her.

He breathed hard. "Ye do so again, I'll lock ye in Carrick's tower."

"You would never treat me that way." Allie had no doubt.

He flushed. "Dinna try yer healin' on me again," he warned.

"Do you feel better?" she asked.

"I feel fine," he snapped. "An' yer power has naught to do with it."

Allie decided not to argue. And then it didn't matter. Her eyes widened as she saw three heavenly hunks crossing a path beyond them, each one golden and gorgeous, clad in Highland garb. Her glance moved from broad shoulders to bare thighs and then up to three nearly perfect faces. The Masters started, looking her way. Interested smiles followed, as did bright, gleaming gazes.

Royce made a sound.

Allie didn't have to look at him to know he was aggravated. She laughed. "Ooh la la. Introduce me."

"I think not," he snapped. Then, "Ye prefer blondes, do ye not?"

"Very much," she said with another laugh. The three Masters veered her way. Allie knew they were checking her out in her tiny pink tee and supertight jeans. She smiled invitingly at them all.

Royce took her arm and hauled her up the road. "Brian wasn't blond."

"Brian was just a nice guy."

"Who never pleased ye in bed."

"True." She twisted to take one last look at all that eye candy. "Who are they?"

"Doesna matter. Ye won't see them again. They're leaving."

Allie sighed with mock disappointment. "Jealous?"

"Why would I be jealous? Ye dinna belong to me."

"I sure don't." She craned her head to eye a dark, towering man with extremely short hair who was leaving a nearby, long, low stone house. He did a double take, glancing at her and then nodding at Royce. "You know, you could leave me here, couldn't you? Moffat won't step onto holy ground." She kept a straight face.

Royce turned an incredulous gaze on her.

And she knew why he'd changed his mind about sending her to the island. Once he'd started caring, he couldn't handle the idea of leaving her there with so many supersexed hunks. Allie shrugged. "I do like Carrick a lot, but I don't mind spending some time here while you hunt Moffat," she said as innocently as possible. "I mean, I could spend all my time praying." She batted her eyes at him.

He choked. "An' whose bed will ye climb into?"

"Bed? Do you *ever* think of anything else? I want to stay and *pray.* Why are you talking about *sex?*"

Royce had halted; so had she. He stared unhappily at her. "I ken yer game. Ye wish to excite me, provoke me. Ye want me jealous!"

She touched his hand. "Yes, I do, and it's pretty easy to accomplish."

"I'm nay jealous."

"Really." She hid a smile. She'd never known any man as jealous.

His mouth twisted. "If ye play me, ye'll be sorry."

"How sorry?" Her heart raced. She couldn't help imagining Royce staking his claim.

He nodded. "Ye want me to take ye here, now? An' what about yer foolish need for my love?"

His words ended the game. "I know you care. You've proven it time and again. And I care—and I'm not afraid to say so. I care enough to suffer your awful temper, your rude behavior, your medieval *nature.* I care enough to stick around for the long haul—and help you let go of the past."

His eyes widened. "I only want to fuck."

"Maybe. Maybe that's what you want right now, on this particular autumn day in 1430. But you wanted more than that in my time. And, Royce? I think you lie. Not to me, but to yourself. I think you want more than sex, right now, in 1430. I think that's why you suck up my white light like a starving man devours his last meal. I think you care a helluva lot and it *terrifies* you."

He paled. Then a furious flush began. "I'll show ye how I care." He seized her arm and started to pull her away from the road.

Allie tensed. "If you are thinking of changing the subject with sex, forget it!"

He faced her. His gaze blazed. "Ye want to ken how I feel, what I want, how I care? I care about yer body an' yer face. Nothing more!" he shouted. "An' it will never be more. Stop pushin' at me!"

"Where is the man who sat up with me all night while I slept? Where is the man who sat outside the chapel at Dunroch all night, while I prayed? Where is the man who asked me about the future—and listened to what I had to say?"

"He's gone!" And with that, Royce strode away, leaving her standing there beneath a huge tree, alone.

How had such a terrible, heated argument arisen? Allie hugged herself. She had meant to provoke his jealousy—she had meant to play him—but it had backfired. She had set him off like a keg of dynamite.

She stared after him and saw him greeting MacNeil. Royce didn't look her way, but the tawny-haired abbot did. Allie somehow raised her hand toward him in a greeting.

Royce had become a lit fuse, ready to combust at any moment. What did that mean?

She didn't want to have doubts about them or their future. But suddenly it felt as though if she pushed any harder, she would lose him after all.

She just wished she knew what had changed since last night, to make him so volatile.

"CAN YE CALM YERSELF?" MacNeil asked.

He almost felt as if he couldn't breathe. She was ogling all the Masters, and even though she meant to thoroughly irritate him and provoke him, her admiration was genuine. He had read her thoughts—she liked every hard body, every pretty face. She liked it far too much—the way she liked being in his bed, ridden by him, in the throes of rapture.

How long would she remain without a lover? he wondered. She was a woman with strong sexual needs.

And while she had succeeded in making him angry and jealous, he was acutely aware of Ailios, standing a distance away, trembling and hurt and, for the first time, filled with doubt about him.

Good, he thought savagely. Let her have doubts! She should have doubts! He was a Master and he would never be more, not to her and not to anyone.

And in the middle of the night you held me and smiled and we talked....

He could not imagine being in her bed and holding her and talking. It was absurd!

And he was as weak as he was a liar, because he wanted nothing as much as he wanted to do just that, not even the rapture they could give one another.

What was happening to him?

Should he leap again and remind himself how Brigdhe had suffered at Kael's hands because of him?

Royce smiled grimly at MacNeil, who stared closely.

"She's an annoying, provocative woman. Disobedient," he added quickly. He kept his mind closed so MacNeil would not lurk. "She's nay easy to protect, defyin' me at every turn."

MacNeil gave him a mildly disbelieving look. "Dinna make the mistake ye made with yer wife."

Royce stiffened, stunned. "Do ye dare to read my mind?"

"I dinna have to. Ye look at her like a boy starving for his first girl. Yer heart is written on yer face. Ye give her yer heart an' yer doomed, an' maybe she's doomed, too."

"I dinna have a heart," Royce snarled. "It was cut from my chest long ago." He was so shocked and angry he turned away, and by gods, he was trembling.

You came into the hall like a man coming home to his bride.

Well, if he had waited almost six hundred years for her, the way he waited now, of course he had come into his hall that way. But she would never be his bride, or his wife, or even his lover. Bedsport, yes, one day—in the future, in her time—if he could somehow wait that long. And that no longer seemed likely, either.

Not a moment went by that he didn't feel the need to be with her, in her; not a moment went by that he did not have, in the back of his mind, a knowledge of the rapture that was so close—and so far.

"Well, that's pleasing to hear, as she belongs to the Brotherhood, an' she always will," MacNeil said. "I want her safe an' protected. If ye canna keep a distance from her, I will choose someone else." There was disapproval in his tone.

Royce met his gaze. "Ye said yerself, any man would want her."

"I would have never guessed ye'd turn into a randy boy over her. I willna have her death on yer head, Ruari," MacNeil said sharply. There was nothing affable or charming about him now.

"I willna allow her to die," Royce exclaimed, glad the conversation had been turned to firm, safe ground. "I saved her yesterday."

"Aye, ye did yer duty, an' the Ancients be pleased."

Calmer at last, Royce glanced toward Allie and saw her walking away, clearly heading for the sacred shrine. He was glad and he felt himself soften. He knew how much their gods meant to her. He wanted her to find peace and joy at the shrine. No one deserved peace and joy more.

"Moffat has declared war on us with his actions," MacNeil said. "I'll be goin' to court to see if the King can bring him to heel."

Royce walked into the meeting house with MacNeil, where they settled into chairs before the hearth. "Have ye been told about the future?"

MacNeil looked carefully at him. "The Ancients," he said slowly, "have let me see the future."

Royce became still. MacNeil had a great power of sight, which he claimed was not his, and that the Ancients allowed him to see when they so chose. Royce had once believed him; now, he believed MacNeil saw what he chose when he chose, and used the device of the power being controlled by the gods as an excuse to avoid fortune-telling. It was hard to breathe— so much was at stake. "So ye dinna speak to Aidan."

MacNeil shook his head. "I saw the future the day I summoned ye to Iona to tell about Ailios—the day I sent ye to 2007."

Royce inhaled. "Are ye saying ye saw my death?"

"Aye."

He shouldn't be shaken. He was old and tired and worn and it was more than time to die. But he stood, shocked.

MacNeil also stood. "I'm sorry, Ruari. But 2007 is a long time from now."

Royce turned away quickly so MacNeil would not see his expression. But what about Ailios? Who would protect her, defend her, when he was gone? Who would guard her while she healed? Who would share her bed?

He had thought about his death for centuries. He had never worried; he had accepted that one day, his Fate would be death. Now, he turned. "Are ye certain ye saw my death?"

"Aye, at Moffat's hands—ye were protecting Ailios. Aidan was with ye."

So it was written, he thought, walking over to the fire. He stared blindly into the flames. Ailios had hunted him down in the past to prevent his death in the future, but his Fate was engraved in stone.

It didn't matter. No one would care.

I care!

Her voice resounded as loudly as if she stood beside him, crying out.

Ailios would weep for him. She had already wept over his dead body—and she would do so again.

He trembled, uncertain.

MacNeil clasped his shoulder. "We all go, eventually."

Royce somehow smiled. No one knew MacNeil's age, but it was said he was well over a thousand years old. "Ye'll never die. Who will manage the Masters if ye do?" His voice cracked.

MacNeil stared sympathetically at him.

"Swear to me," Royce said roughly, "that when I'm gone, ye'll see to her care yerself. Yer the most powerful among us. Swear to me, now, that she'll be yer Innocent."

MacNeil nodded. "I give my word."

Royce turned away, sickened now, for he saw them in bed. It was inevitable.

MacNeil said quietly, "I shouldn't say so, but she loves ye deeply, Ruari. She'll never love another man."

He whirled. "Did ye see that, too?"

MacNeil hesitated. "Nay. I canna see past the day ye die."

Royce thrust himself into MacNeil's mind, and realized he was telling the truth. Clearly he had lurked on Ailios. Did it matter? Eventually MacNeil would seduce her. He would never think to deny himself, not with Royce gone.

Royce walked away. His temples pounded. He was supposed to wait five hundred and seventy-seven more years for her? For what—a single night?

One night was not going to be enough.

And if there was only going to be one night, he wanted it to be sooner; he wanted it to be now.

"Ruari, dinna give in to such temptation."

Royce jerked. He was so agitated he'd forgotten to shield his thoughts.

"Moffat hunts her. I dinna ken what to make o' the fact that she's here now, in this time—an' ye dinna die for almost six hundred years. A long war lies ahead."

And in that moment, it truly sank in.

Moffat would not die tomorrow, or the next day, or the day after that. He had to hunt him—but the hunt would last almost six hundred years—and in the end, he was to be the one vanquished.

And the burden of such an endless war, added now to the burden of the past eight hundred years, crushed him down.

"Yer strong. Ye can protect her for such a long time. I'm sure of it."

Royce couldn't answer.

For the first time in his life, he had entered a war knowing the outcome. It wasn't war—it was a journey to his death.

And then he rallied and recovered. There was no choice. It was a journey he had to make, a war he must fight, because he had been chosen, and Ailios must live.

ALLIE WAS BATHED in holy light. She no longer prayed. On the floor of the knave, before a sacred shrine containing the holy Book of Wisdom, the Cladich, she knelt before all the gods. Their holy blessings washed over her, through her, and she wept, carried away on a tide of religious rapture.

When the communion was finally over, she became aware of her surroundings. The gods had gone. Long, dark shadows had crept into the chapel. Allie sat on the floor, dazed. She'd come into the chapel in the morning, instinctively finding her way to the shrine, and she had begun to pray. The Ancients had come closer and closer, and finally she had been the one showered with their holy, healing powers. The tears of rapture had dried on her face and now, they stung. She felt empowered and weakened at once.

Allie stood and became dizzy. She reached out to a pew and waited for the chapel to stop spinning.

She'd never had such a religious experience in her life, but she was pretty sure every Ancient had come to her. It had been mind-blowing.

Allie took a deep breath and turned, her mind starting to clear. She thought about Royce, who had said they'd leave the island hours ago. Before she could decide what his mood might be at the delay, she saw the woman standing at the end of the knave, as if she had just walked through the door.

Her heart slammed. *"Mother?"*

Elizabeth was dressed in a long, pale gown, and she looked as corporeal as anyone. But the moment Allie spoke, Elizabeth began to fade. Through her body, Allie could see the chapel walls.

"Mother! Wait!" she cried. She rushed up the knave, toward her.

Elizabeth did not smile. As Allie came closer, she realized her mother's expression was haunted. No, it was *frightened*. Allie paused before the translucent apparition, terribly alarmed. Elizabeth started to speak urgently to her—but Allie could barely hear her whispers.

"Mom! What is it? What's wrong?"

"Danger…you…Ruari," she seemed to say. And then she swiftly faded into nothingness.

Allie gasped in shock. *What had just happened?*

Her mother had reached out to her from the dead, again. And she had been frightened. Had she been asking for help? Had she been trying to warn her? What did this mean?

Allie stepped from the chapel, shaken to the core. She glanced around, but it was a dark night, filled with shadow, clouds clearly having come in that afternoon. The various buildings beyond the chapel were lit from within with fires and torches, but she saw no one moving about. Even though the grounds were holy, she strained her senses. The night was vacant of all evil.

A man materialized from the dark shadows, striding purposefully toward the chapel.

Allie knew it wasn't Royce from his far lither silhouette, just as she knew he was a Master, his aura filled with holy power. But it was also filled with uncertainty, which surprised her—as if he did not quite know himself. His strides suddenly faltered as he sensed her.

His gaze turned instantly to her, and he paused, not entering the chapel.

Torches had been lit by the monks and the garden and path outside the chapel were illuminated. Allie saw a very young, golden Master. His wide gaze turned to very smug, male appreciation and he undressed her with a look. "Ye must be the Healer."

Allie put her thoughts of Elizabeth aside. "Yes, I am Allie. You are?" She had to smile. This man was probably no more than twenty-one, but he was pure beefcake. Sam would lick him up, all over.

"Seoc." He grinned and approached. "Ah, they said yer beauty is unrivaled, but I dinna quite believe it."

Allie smiled with some amusement. "I'm hardly unrivaled in beauty. You should see my two best friends. Not only are they beautiful, they're blond and *tall*."

"I dinna mind someone so small," he said with deep dimples.

"I'm with Royce," she said softly. Better to head this one off at the pass, she decided.

He sighed. "Aye, I heard that, too. I heard he canna stand ye lookin' at another man." He grinned. "I dinna care. Ye can look at me anytime. Are ye certain ye wish to be with such an *old* man?"

Allie had to smile. "How old are you, Seoc?"

"Old enough to please you very well."

"Twenty-one? Twenty-two?"

He shook his head. "My age doesna matter, lass. An' I'm glad to prove it to ye."

"Royce will take yer head—at least," Allie said flatly.

"Probably," Seoc agreed affably. "But I have nay doubt it will be well worth it."

Allie laughed. "I think you were on your way to pray?"

"I'm newly chosen. My brother has ordered me to some penitence."

And Allie saw the resemblance to MacNeil in Seoc's vivid, long-lashed green eyes, but otherwise, his features were far prettier. "MacNeil?"

"Aye." He held out his hand. "Let's converse some more. I can pray for guidance later." But he turned to glance over his shoulder.

Allie had already felt Royce approaching and her heart leapt in excitement. She saw him striding up the road and she went still. His aura was an inferno of crimson and gold. Not rage—just burning desire.

Although she didn't move or breathe, her pulse exploded, beginning to pound in unison with the blood rushing in his veins and filling his loins. He was coming for her—and there was no mistaking his intentions.

She didn't know what had happened, what had changed. Suddenly it didn't matter. He wanted her now and he was going to take her. And suddenly she could feel the rapture awaiting them. It was so close…and every inch of her body expanded, heating impossibly.

Royce came out of the shadows, and the first thing she saw was his hot, silver gaze. Then she saw how terrifically his leine thrust out. Desire made her feel faint. Her flesh began a distinct throbbing, swelling and already seeking his.

"Well," Seoc said. "Well."

Allie didn't even notice him slip past her, into the chapel. She somehow wet her lips, trying to regain some control over her mind. Royce was on the rampage for her now. Her own body was rejoicing—and joining him in that rampage. She needed him, hot and hard, inside her small, tight body. But she needed the words, too, didn't she?

He reached her, grasping her shoulders, his hands uncompromising. His gaze locked with hers, and so much lust burned there, she spasmed.

He knew. His face tightened.

Allie gasped at the torturous wave of pleasure.

He pulled her close. "I canna tell ye I love ye," he said thickly. "Not now, not ever."

It was a warning. Allie tensed. She tried to breathe—tried to think. Instead her hands clasped his hips. Her pulse drummed frantically now everywhere—he pulsed between them, against her. "What is it?" she managed to ask.

"Ye can heal me," he rasped, his blazing eyes holding hers. "Here, now, tonight."

She tried desperately to understand. "With sex?"

His mouth came closer. "Aye. Ye can heal me with yer body."

She stared into his eyes and saw more than lust. She saw urgency, even desperation—and fear. She started, touched his rough jaw. "What is it? Please, what's happened?"

"Everything's different now." His arm swept behind her back, his hand cupping her buttock. "Just let it be." But his gaze was searching.

"Ailios, I need ye," he said.

Allie reached for him.

CHAPTER THIRTEEN

ROYCE SEIZED HER JEANS by the waistband, above the fly, and covered her mouth with his.

Allie gasped at the urgent onslaught of his mouth, while his knuckles pressed low and hard, beneath her denim and the lace of her thong. His tongue swept deep and Allie moaned, pressing her belly outward, against his hands.

Around her, in her, she felt his hot pulse racing in his body, frantically pounding in his veins.

Her own desire soared in tandem with his and she felt his excitement intensifying. He felt her every response, too. Suddenly he tore her jeans down her hips, kneeling. Allie's body went still as his mouth moved over the lace covering her throbbing flesh. He hooked a finger beneath the thong and swept the scrap aside. His tongue swept the length of her, down one wet crevice, up another.

She held on to him and gasped with pleasure.

Allie felt him stiffen to incredible proportions and she felt him throbbing; she felt his need to explode. She began to crest out of all control. Clinging to his shoulders, she gasped his name. "Royce—let me come."

In answer, he pulled her down to the ground, his mouth still on her sex, his fingers in her now. And he said, "I have to taste yer light."

Allie was briefly confused. And then the strangest thing

happened. Something touched her deep inside herself—and it wasn't physical.

Royce went still—and deep inside her, he somehow touched her again.

His pulse changed. She felt a sudden rush of power expanding in his veins. It heightened her excitement; he cried out again, his grasp on her hips tightening. The wave of pleasure spiraled wildly in him, in her.

And Royce strained inside himself, as if fighting his need to climax. Allie wanted to scream at him to let go, because she needed to let go, when he touched her on some other plane again.

It was a caress between souls.

He had never been as strong, as virile; his power had become huge. He knew it—she knew it.

She felt him start to come.

The climax was unlike any she'd ever had before. He was overcome with the power in his body, but with it was the greatest lust she'd ever felt, an excitement so vast it was blinding for them both. There was only pleasure, power, pain and ecstasy. His climax became hers.

Royce moved over her, seizing her face. She met his wide, blazing eyes, aware he was as shocked as she was. He surged deep, stretching her tight body wide. He roared with pleasure. She wept with her own release, riding far and wide, higher and higher still. The climax intensified for them both, in unison. They were somewhere above the earth now, shooting through and exploding in the stars. Allie knew she never wanted to touch ground again.

And he delved deep again, not just into her hot, wet body but into her power, her light, her soul, and Allie embraced him, shattering in rapture and joy.

HOURS LATER, Allie held hard on to Royce's big body as they both finally became still. Although stunningly spent, she was spinning mentally, physically, emotionally. Every time she slept with him, it was off the charts, and better than the time before. But this time, Royce had made love to her. She was sure of it. This time, there had been a connection, a union, that wasn't physical. She felt as if he had somehow reached into her, entwining her soul with his.

His arms tightened around her.

Allie smiled against his slick chest. He probably didn't know it, but he was hugging her. And she became aware of how exhausted she was.

For one more moment he held her, and then he moved away, onto his back, beside her. Allie was too tired to move.

They lay outside the chapel on his plaid, staring up at the dawn, for a long time. He finally said, "Did I hurt ye?"

Allie sighed, gathered up her wits and will, and turned onto her side and touched his hard rib cage. His gaze was on her, wide and searching.

She smiled at him. "No. That was incredible. What happened?"

For one moment, he didn't answer. Instead he sat up. "How do ye feel?"

"Sort of beat." And she moved closer to snuggle, not really wanting to fight to sit up.

His hand closed on her shoulder. "Can ye sit?"

Of course she could sit. Allie did so, with Royce putting his arm behind her back, as if to prop her up. Instantly she snuggled against him. "I'm cold," she said. It was probably freezing out, as it was almost dawn, but she hadn't noticed yet.

He hesitated, then lay back down, pulling her down with him, close to his big, warm body, his arm around her.

It was another victory and Allie smiled, somehow refraining from kissing the skin covering his ribs, his chest, his neck. Love burst in her heart.

He reached past her and covered her with half of the plaid they lay on. "Is that better?"

"Yes, much." She snuggled even more closely. "What happened, Royce? There was a union between us that was apart from that of our bodies."

"La Puissance," he said abruptly.

She had to peer to look up at him. He wasn't smiling. She wanted him to be as happy as she was. "The Power?"

"Aye." He gazed down at her. "I told ye, I can take power from anyone. I tasted yer power, Ailios. It was *good.*"

Shockingly she became entirely aroused again, never mind how weak she felt.

So did he.

His lids drifted down. "T'is forbidden, to take power fer pleasure." Then he gave her a very male look. "But power makes the pleasure so much better."

"It sure does. Who cares if it's forbidden?" she cried. "It was the best."

He suddenly sat up and looked away, appearing dark and unhappy. "The gods gave us the power to take life so we can defend ourselves from evil or heal ourselves if mortally wounded. They dinna give us such a power to use it for common bedsport."

"What they don't know…" Allie said, sitting up with an effort. Aware of the cold now, she tugged her half of the plaid over her shoulders.

He met her gaze. "A Master can lose his mind when the power floods his veins. He can easily take too much life— a maid can die if he does."

"You didn't take too much from me," she said, stroking his chest. "I'm not dead, just beat."

"I have control," he said. "I'm nay young an' hot."

Allie laughed. She couldn't imagine what he had been like when he had been "young and hot."

He gave her a long, strange, intense look. He was serious when he spoke, his tone hushed. "Yer power is so *pure*. I dinna ken any power could be so good."

Allie became as serious. She recalled the way his aura and his body soaked up her white light the few times she'd dared to try to heal him.

"Yer holy. Yer power is holy. I dinna think the Ancients will be pleased with me," Royce said flatly.

She didn't like the sound of that. "They won't know."

"They ken all. So does MacNeil," he added darkly. He seemed very unhappy now.

She grew nervous. "Royce, what happens when a Master violates the Code? Does he go to jail?" she quipped. But she didn't smile now.

"A fall, or worse."

"A fall—like the way an angel falls?" She was incredulous—and then, finally, alarmed.

"I willna fall, but aye, Masters have been turned to the dark by tastin' such power, by takin' what doesna belong to them, by discovering La Puissance an' needing it time an' again."

Like a drug addict, Allie thought. And in that instant, Allie got it. It was the exact flip side of a pleasure crime. "The demons take all the life from their victims during sex. Obviously it turns them on. Oh my God. Taking power…life…during sex…it's a huge turn-on for a Master, too."

"The more power, the grander La Puissance." His gaze was steady on hers. "The temptation when ye start becomes terrible to resist. I had to touch yer light. I only meant to touch it, Ailios. Just a single time." He suddenly cupped her jaw, his hands stunning her because they were so gentle. "An' then I tried a sip. A small sip o' pure white power. I needed ye, lass."

Allie felt his pulse pounding all over again. He was thinking about her healing power running in his veins. He was thinking about the violent yet beautiful ecstasy they'd shared. "And my power in your veins felt good. I know—because everything you felt, I felt, too. You became stronger, you had more stamina, you were insatiable—and if there'd been a battle, you'd have been invincible, too."

"I could have stayed in ye fer days. But ye'd likely be dead." He stood. "T'is fortunate I can control the urge. Others cannot. I willna take yer power again. It belongs to all of man, an' I have no rights." He was fierce as he spoke.

Allie stood, as well. Her power did belong to mankind and there was no point in arguing that. "So what else can happen now? What did you mean when you said you could fall—or worse?"

He made a sound. "There's suffering an' death, Ailios. Even Masters pay for their crimes."

She inhaled, thinking about his death in the future—which they were going to undo. "I am fine. And the Ancients know it if they were spying on us."

"Are ye?" He reached for his leine and shrugged it on.

Allie bent and wrapped herself in his plaid, worried that he might pay some price for having tasted her power. "Of course I'm fine." But the moment she spoke, she realized her senses were dulled.

She was still in tune with Royce. But the night around her felt stunningly vacant, when she should have felt the life force of every cricket, every bird, even every leaf and every tree, as well as all the human energy in the buildings beyond them. She strained and finally sensed the power coming from the Masters and monks in the monastery, but it was muted.

Panic arose as she faced Royce.

"What?" he asked sharply.

"I can just barely sense the men in the monastery. I can't feel all the life that I know is around us, right now!" She strained anew and finally felt the barest whisper of energy coming from the insects, flowers and fauna in the woods.

Royce took his dagger and sliced his thumb.

Allie stared as the blood welled from the thick pad there.

"Heal me," he said.

She hesitated, then reached for her white light.

To her surprise, and then to her dismay, it took a vast effort to find it and bring it forth. And then it took even more effort to stop the bleeding from the paltry cut. By the time she'd stopped the cut from bleeding, she was perspiring and out of breath. Slowly she looked up. How could this be happening?

"T'is forbidden with an ordinary maid—but I took power from ye, a great Healer." He bent and began retrieving her clothes.

She touched him. "We won't tell anyone. How long will this last?"

"I dinna ken." He straightened, handing her the garments. "Neither one of us was very quiet, Ailios."

She felt herself blanch. Royce had been roaring his head off in triumph after triumph—and she had been weeping mindlessly in ecstasy, too.

"Dress yerself," he said.

THE SUN WAS EDGING upward into the sky, amidst many dark, ominous clouds, as they walked together toward one of the longer buildings, centered in the monastery. Royce was so grim that Allie had become very worried, too. And as they passed several Masters, also heading toward the rectory where they would eat, no one looked at them.

The contrast from the day before, when every Master had smiled invitingly at her, was glaring.

Allie's unease increased.

Then she saw Seoc standing on the porch, arms folded, his gaze hooded but directed toward them. Allie sensed his speculation, his curiosity, his interest, and she felt herself blush. Seoc turned and walked inside. "Are we in big trouble?" Allie asked, low.

Royce didn't have the chance to answer. MacNeil walked out of the rectory door, his face set in hard lines. He stepped down to the ground and asked Allie, "How are ye?"

She smiled brightly, falsely. "Fine—perfect, in fact."

He made a sound. "Yer power's compromised."

Allie tensed. "It was my fault. You know—Adam and Eve, the whole bad woman thing."

"Ye need rest. I'm hoping ye'll be fine in a few hours." He clasped her shoulder and gestured toward a small bungalow. "Ye can take my bed."

Allie expected Royce to go ballistic, but he stood there, his face perfectly impassive, not uttering a word. "It really was entirely my fault and I am not going anywhere without Royce." She shook his hand off.

MacNeil's expression hardened. "Yer mother was nay so difficult."

Allie shrugged.

MacNeil looked at Royce. "The Queen is on her way to Carrick."

Royce started. "Yer sure?"

"Seoc arrived last night—he encountered her retinue on the highway."

Allie looked back and forth between both men. "The Queen—as in the Queen of Scotland?"

MacNeil glanced at her. "Aye." Then he said, "Royce needs to return to Carrick. Ye will stay here."

Allie was in disbelief.

"Aye," Royce said grimly.

"I'm going with you!" Allie retorted.

MacNeil firmly grasped her shoulder. "Ye canna be hurt again."

She wrested free. "No one has hurt me. And certainly not Royce!"

Royce looked at her, his face so tight now, it might have been made of plaster. "MacNeil is right. I compromised yer power. T'was not my right. Ye'll be safe here. Yer Fate is here, Ailios."

Allie was furious. She stepped closer to Royce, facing MacNeil. "You do not control me. You do not own me and you cannot order me around! Where Royce goes, I go."

"One night like last night an' ye will turn yer back on the gods an' Fate?"

Allie tensed in dismay. "It is about more than one night and you know it."

"Aye, I ken ye love him deeply. Did ye not take vows—the same vow as yer mother did? Can ye turn yer back on any pure creature, human or beast, if in need?" MacNeil asked seriously. "Are ye not sworn to heal those who suffer? Can ye heal a broken bird now?"

She didn't know what she could or could not do, and the lack of power was frightening. "I have never turned my back on suffering, and I never will," she finally said.

MacNeil nodded, satisfied. "Then he leaves an' ye stay."

"No!" A terrible alarm filled her. "You don't get it. I need Royce with me when I heal. He can guard me while I heal, MacNeil! And I swear, we will never cross the line in bed again!" She was panicking.

"There's hundreds o' Masters to guard ye," MacNeil said bluntly. "I will summon Aidan to do so."

Allie felt Royce's heart rate surge. She turned and looked at him in despair. But he said, "Aidan will defend ye. I approve of the choice."

This can't be happening, Allie thought. "Why are you agreeing to this?"

His color rose. "I dinna ken what might happen the next time I bed ye."

"What does that mean?" she gasped.

"He means he doesna ken what he will do when he canna think at all," MacNeil said bluntly.

Royce didn't trust himself. "I trust you," she said. She stared and he stared back. "I have always trusted you. I always will."

"No good," Royce said slowly, "can come of yer being in my life."

She cried out. "You're turning away from me *now?*"

His face hardened, and that was answer enough.

Her heart seemed to break apart. She had not expected this. And it was hard to think clearly, when she was beginning to hurt so much. Royce was trying to protect her once again. In a way, they were right. She and Royce had compromised her destiny last night. She needed all of her powers back. But as soon as they were back, she could join Royce. She would simply make certain he never took any power from her again.

And an image flashed in her mind's eye, a terrible recollection of how his aura and his body had rapidly soaked up her white light the few times she had tried to heal him.

She faced MacNeil. "How long will you keep us apart?" she demanded.

MacNeil turned his intense green regard on Royce. "Until he forgets what yer power can bring him."

Allie cried out. "What does that mean?"

Royce now refused to meet her eyes.

Allie knew she was never going to forget the passion of that night. Neither would Royce. "Like hell," she spat. "This is *temporary*. As soon as I am better, as soon as my power is back, I am going to Carrick!"

"Ye canna have both worlds. Ye belong to mankind or ye belong to love. And we both ken yer choice."

Allie felt dazed. The ground under her feet felt skewed. Her entire life she had known her Fate was far bigger, far grander, and far more significant than finding a romantic or true love. She'd never dreamed there would even be a choice. But damn it, secretly she had dreamed of someone like Royce; she had dreamed of finding her soul mate.

"I'm sorry, lass," MacNeil said. "I must think o' the greater good, not worldly passion an' not worldly love. Say yer farewells." He smiled grimly at her and walked back into the rectory.

Allie couldn't move. Her heart shrieked in protest. Her mind, however, began reminding her that people needed her. The world would be a horrific place without her white healing powers.

Royce smiled sadly at her. "Ye'll see me again. This is best for us all."

"No! It's not best! What's best is having both worlds— you and me together—and my powers as strong as ever!" she cried, seizing his hands, afraid if she let go, it might be forever. "When will I see you again, Royce? When?"

He grasped her hands firmly. "Have I ever told ye that yer light is the most beautiful part of ye?" he asked softly.

She was crying. "That's because you need my healing," she whispered.

"I have lived this way for hundreds of years. Save yer healing for those who truly need it," he said quietly.

She shook her head. He needed her healing—he needed her—and she needed him. But mankind needed her, too. "We have just started, Royce. This cannot be the ending," she implored, sliding her hands up to his chest. "Please, fight this stupidity with me. Help me find a way…why did you have to take power from me last night?"

"I dinna mean to," he exclaimed. "I wanted yer body, Ailios, an' then, it wasn't enough."

Allie leaned against him and he embraced her. "This is not the ending. This is the beginning."

Against her hair, he said, "MacNeil is the wisest of men. And he must think of the gods, the Brotherhood an' Alba. I'm no ordinary mortal man—an' yer nay an ordinary woman. Ye belong to Alba, Ailios." His tone had become strange and thick.

She looked up at him and saw that his gaze glistened. "Will you admit now that this saddens you? Will you admit now how much you care?"

He took her face in his hands. "I care."

She inhaled and began trembling wildly.

Royce let her go. A moment later, she was staring at him as he walked through the buildings and out the monastery gates, upon the road that would take him away from her.

ALLIE SAT BENEATH a towering fir tree, her knees clasped to her chest. She had been left alone for the morning, which was just as well. No matter how many times she told herself that she and Royce would be together—for a lifetime—and that they would get past this dreadful dilemma, just then, her optimism refused to arise. Her heart hurt. She wanted to cry. She was uncertain and hope eluded her. She just didn't want anyone witnessing her grief and sorrow.

It began, finally, to rain.

She was wearing a plaid over her jeans and T-shirt and she pulled it closer. Worse, she was worried about Royce, and it was more than fear over his hunting Moffat, the man who would one day kill him if they did not change the future. She had a strong sense of unease, even of dread. Something was wrong—she could feel it—and whatever was happening, it was about Royce.

She was never going to forget the look in his eyes when they'd said goodbye, or the sound of his voice when he'd told her he cared.

"Allie?"

At the sound of Claire's voice, Allie leapt to her feet, whirling. Her senses were still dulled, she realized with some panic. She should have sensed Claire's power as she approached.

Claire smiled hesitantly at her. "Come on. It's cold and it's about to pour."

Allie moved toward the closest building with her. "When did you arrive?"

"We just got here." Claire stepped into the meeting house, Allie behind her. It was vacant. "I heard Royce left for Carrick."

Allie told herself she would not grieve openly now. "MacNeil has decided he can't protect me and that we should be apart."

"MacNeil is usually right. How are you feeling?"

Allie started. "Do you know everything?"

Claire nodded. "I've been there, Allie. When I first met Malcolm, he was struggling with temptation—and we fought for his soul. I'm pretty sure Royce's soul isn't in danger, but we all need you with all of your power. That kind of sex is really dangerous."

"So you're taking their side," Allie said, anger rising.

"No." Claire pushed a piece of wet hair from her cheek. "I'm on your side. I'm a hopeless romantic. I can't believe you made Royce lose control—and his head—the way you did. That says everything to me. I thought Royce was always in control!"

He hadn't been in control last night, she thought. And then she smiled to herself, thinking of how easily he became jealous. "What does that mean to you?" Allie asked.

"I think he's pretty smitten with you. And Royce is as cold as a man can be. Or, he was that way."

"He cares—he told me so." Allie went to a cane chair and sat down by the small fire, trying to warm her chilled body. It was impossible. "I feel like I am back to normal. My senses were so dull after we made love, but everything is sharp as can be now."

"Really? Because you didn't feel me approaching."

Allie flushed, caught in her lie. "My senses have come back—mostly."

Claire pulled up another chair. "I know your mother was an all-time great Healer and a Priestess. Maybe your Fate is bigger than you know. Everyone was against Malcolm and me at first. But we're so much stronger together—and every day makes us even stronger than the day before. Maybe, in the end, it will be that way for you and Royce."

Allie grimaced. "Royce needs to let go of his pain, his past. Until he does that, he won't let me close enough to make him stronger."

Claire was surprised. "Royce is hurt? Over what? What past are you talking about?"

Allie waved dismissively. "Forget it. Right now I need to get off this island. To hell with MacNeil. I have a bad feeling about Royce. He needs me. He may be in trouble."

Claire's eyes widened.

Allie stood, staring. "What aren't you telling me?"

Claire flushed and stood, too. "Actually Malcolm and I don't come to Iona without cause. We wanted to warn Royce that Joan Beaufort was on her way to Carrick."

Allie's heart lurched. She did not like Claire's cautious tone or her expression. "Are you talking about the Queen of Scotland? Because MacNeil told Royce she's on her way there."

"Yes, I am," Claire said very quietly.

"What's up?" Allie demanded.

Claire bit her lip.

"What aren't you telling me?" Allie cried.

Claire hesitated. "Allie, we came here to warn Royce. I don't want you to even think of going up against Joan Beaufort."

Something was going on. "That's the second time you said you came here to *warn* him. Is the Queen a demon? Is he in danger?" But even as she spoke, her sense of dread and urgency escalated.

Claire said, "Well, he's only in danger if he refuses her. I know you're not familiar with our world, but no one denies the King or the Queen. Here, a royal can decide to execute anyone without reason or cause. Here, there's no judge or jury and very little law."

Allie breathed hard. "Frig! Spill it."

Claire said, "Royce was—and maybe still is—the Queen's lover."

Allie was shocked. And then the anger began. "Like hell!"

HE RODE INTO CARRICK'S inner ward, finally finding some distance from his heart. All day a sense of loss had sickened and saddened him. All day he had grimly fought every such sense—and too many images and recollections of Ailios to count. Now, he had other, far more urgent matters to attend—like his Queen.

In all the years he had known Joan Beaufort and been her lover, she had never once come to Morvern. When she wished for him to service her, she summoned him to court. Sometimes he came; usually he ignored the summons. Not because he had ever been averse to bedding his liege—she had many lovers, and she was pretty and hot—but because his vows always came first and her summons were usually inconvenient. And although few men would dare to deny her, he'd never cared how irate she became. He'd been aware that she could tire of such arrogance and order his head placed on a pike—without his body beneath it. But in the past, he simply hadn't cared.

And when they were together, it had been easy to remind her of why he was valuable to her alive. In bed, Joan was insatiable, wicked and easy to control.

Now, however, he cared about his head. He simply could not depart this world with Moffat hunting Ailios. Unfortunately his sudden lack of indifference to his Fate weakened his position immensely.

But Joan hadn't come to Carrick because she missed his prowess in her bed. He had not a single doubt she had come to Carrick to see firsthand if the rumors of a Healer with amazing powers were true.

Had MacNeil not ordered him back to Carrick alone, he would still have chosen to leave Ailios behind. Joan must never know how powerful the Healer truly was. And he felt certain Ailios would never be able to hide her abilities for long from anyone, even someone as dangerous as the Queen.

For Joan's cunning and ambition knew no bounds.

Donald came running up to him, a wide smile on his young face. Royce slid from the charger, handing the boy the reins. He tousled his hair in greeting, looking past him at the royal Household guards blocking his own front door.

But then, he'd already seen the royal pennants waving from his towers. Joan Beaufort had moved in.

"How are ye, lad?" he asked.

"The Queen is here!" Donald cried, his tone hushed with awe. "When I bowed before her, I was so close I could touch her skirts!"

Royce hid a smile and said sternly, "Yer liege is English, lad, dinna forget it."

Donald sobered. "But the King is Scot."

"Aye." Royce nodded to his men as he strode toward the heavy, paneled door. Both guards stepped before it, barring his way with their lances.

"I am the earl of Morvern. Put yer weapons down afore I take them from ye," he said pleasantly enough. But he was furious that she had put her guards in front of his door. That was Joan, flaunting her power over him—except that power wasn't absolute, and in bed, she would quickly be reminded of it.

The guards hesitated.

Royce drew his dagger so swiftly no one had even breathed, and as swiftly, his shortsword. The latter he shoved beneath both locked lances, lifting them high. The dagger found the larger soldier's throat. "I am lord here," he said.

Lances were lowered.

"Stand aside," he snapped, irate now. He did not care for the mere notion of bedding the Queen. Once, he had enjoyed her rather depraved passions. Now, he thought it might be an effort to amuse her—and him. The woman he wished to bed that night remained far from Carrick—and was forbidden to him now.

He strode into his hall, sheathing dagger and sword.

Joan sat in a chair by the hearth, her back to him. Her ladies surrounded her and six more guards lined the chamber. Of medium height, buxom and pale blond, renowned as a great beauty, she did not turn to greet him. "You have displeased Us vastly, Ruari." Her tone was ice.

He shoved all regrets and apprehensions aside. He refused to think of Ailios now. "Then I beg yer pardon," he said firmly, striding to the front of the chair to face her.

Joan had startling blue eyes and fine features. She looked angelic; she was anything but. King James had fallen in love with her at first sight, while a prisoner at the English court. He loved her still—and had no notion of her shocking faithlessness.

Royce noticed that she wore a court gown in the French style, excessively fitted across the bust and shockingly low-cut. If she took a deep breath, she might expose her nipples, and she was well aware of that.

"You may beg for Our pardon," she said.

His temper flared and he struggled with it. He got down on one knee and stared at the floor. "If it pleases Yer Majesty, I beg now."

"It pleases Us greatly," she snapped.

He did not look up, as she had not given him permission to do so. His temper took over at last. Outside of bed, Joan was a tyrant. If he did not take her to bed, how could he recover his power over her? But Ailios, he was certain, would be furious if he bedded his Queen.

Joan said, "Everyone leave Us, now."

His heart accelerated. He had no wish to think of Ailios now. They were not lovers, or even sworn to one another. And in spite of his ambivalence toward Joan and the coming night, hot blood began gathering in his loins as if realizing what must transpire. But then, anger was so easily confused with lust.

"We arrived here yesterday with no proper greeting," Joan said. "Your housemaids are fools—but We are certain that is not their real task in this household. Have you fucked them all? You may look up."

He lifted his head and met her bright, angry gaze. "Aye, I have."

She flushed. The stain spread from her cheeks to her neck and breasts. "Where have you been, Ruari?" she demanded. "What is more important than Us?"

"I have been at Dunroch. Nothing, Joan, is as important as ye." He always knew when to strike and calling her by her familiar name was just that.

"I spent the night alone," she whispered in heat and hurt.

He found that impossible to believe as he stood. "Then I am truly sorry," he murmured, taking her hands. "Let me show ye, Joan, how sorry I am." Images flashed of Ailios in his arms, riding him into the eternity of La Puissance. Somehow he shoved them aside.

"You are not sorry—you are never sorry. You do as you will, never mind I am your liege!" She stood, her gaze moving to the fluttering skirt of his leine. She licked her lips and said, "I summoned you to court six months ago and you did not even reply."

He stepped very close to her, purposefully becoming entangled with her skirts. Her breath caught. Amused, aware that her need for him was reducing her to the beggarly status he desired, he murmured, "Ye must have been enraged, waiting for me to *come*."

Slowly she dragged her gaze away from what rose between them. "I was enraged last night—waiting for you to make *me* come."

He smiled. "Maybe yer tired o' giving so many commands. Maybe ye need a man to command ye. An' maybe waiting is good fer ye, eh?" He clasped her waist, turning her away from him.

She cried out in excitement. "Never," she whispered hoarsely. "I will give the commands."

He laughed. "I dinna think ye can command much now, Joan. But that's why ye have come back to me. I'm the man ye canna control, ever. Ye'll do as I say, when I say." He spoke softly, his breath against her ear, but he pulled her firmly against his heavy loins.

She breathed hard, and it was a moment before she succumbed. "Fine, yes. Fine!" Then she said, "Ruari," and it was a woman's plea.

Royce tensed. He had no plan except to survive the Queen's stay. He hesitated, so aware of his ambivalence now—and the cause for it. It was almost as if Ailios were present and filled with hurt over his behavior.

But by damn, this was politics.

He seized her wrists, restraining her with one hand, and rubbed his lips against the side of her neck. "Ye need patience, Joan," he whispered, his mouth moving against her ear. She trembled. He splayed his other hand low on her belly and she gasped. "I think tonight I'll teach ye patience." And he let her go abruptly.

She gasped in surprise, turning to face him, but he walked away. "What was that?" Joan cried.

Because he was a virile man, his body was more than ready, and he was aware that she knew it. Worse, his failure to acquiesce was uncharacteristic. He collected his wits.

Joan *liked* his arrogance and tyranny, and he turned. "I'll be the one to decide when we fuck," he said coldly. "I said I'd teach ye patience. I meant it. Ye can start the lesson now."

Her eyes went wide. Her color rose.

"That's a taste," he said, "o' what I may decide to give ye later."

Her eyes glazed with lust. "Damn you."

"And, Joan? Ye may summon me to court, but Carrick is for Maclean affairs. I dinna like ye calling on me—ever."

Her flush became mottled, anger and lust becoming one. "Sometimes, Ruari, I hate you."

He laughed at that. As if he cared.

"And maybe, this time, you go too far."

"Ye like it. If I served ye like the others, ye wouldn't be here."

"One day you will go too far," she panted furiously. "And, Ruari? Tonight the lesson continues."

He smiled tightly. "Tonight, I'll be the one to decide if ye have learned any lesson at all."

She flushed all over again.

He was aware that his triumph was momentary, and he wondered how he was going to manage her that night. Sooner or later he'd have to play the stud. But she enjoyed other women as well as men—he might orchestrate an orgy for her, making certain she was so preoccupied that he was the one left out of her bed.

And then he saw Ailios.

Not in his mind, but standing in the corridor behind the hall, as pale as a ghost, except for the two bright spots of crimson on her cheeks.

She was furious and in that moment, he knew she had been spying on him.

CHAPTER FOURTEEN

SHE TURNED AND VANISHED into the corridor.

He glanced at Joan, but she had paced to the other side of the hall, calling for her maids. She hadn't seen Ailios. *Ailios had seen him with the Queen. But it had been a matter of politics....* He composed himself and it was not an easy task.

"I have matters to attend," he said flatly. He wanted to explain his actions to Ailios, although he could barely comprehend the overwhelming need. He never explained himself to anyone. "But we also have grave matters to discuss." And he was thinking about Moffat's attack on Dunroch.

She looked at him. "We have *very* grave matters to discuss."

He stilled, focused and intent, and lurked. As he had suspected, Joan was thinking about a powerful Healer—and how she could best use such power for her and King James. "Yer Majesty, yesterday Dunroch was attacked by Moffat."

Joan widened her eyes, feigning surprise. "Surely you jest!"

Royce wasn't surprised to realize Joan not only knew of the attack, but she had supported the bishop secretly. His tension rose but he spoke casually. "Moffat be yer cousin, but we have been at odds for many years. I believe he attacked Dunroch because o' me, not my nephew. He has no conflict with Malcolm."

"I will see into this. I will have the Chamberlain of the Realm investigate the matter. As dear as Moffat is to me, he cannot attack my vassals at will." Her gaze narrowed. "Is it possible that you provoked my dear cousin, Ruari? After all, you and Moffat have been warring for years over land and cattle. I almost regret his having lands in the north, bordering yours."

He decided to retreat and he shrugged. "Perhaps some o' my men raided one of his villages. I dinna ken. I will look into the matter, as well."

"Good." She stared at him. "Rumors have reached the court. Have you a powerful Healer at Carrick?"

"I have a guest from the south. Lady Monroe be kind an' caring. She takes it upon herself to nurse those who are ill."

Joan made a sound. "So you claim she is not a powerful Healer, one who can give life back to a boy crushed by dirt and stone?"

"Yer Majesty, she attended the boy, as did I. He wasna crushed to death. When we dug him from the rockslide, he was alive. T'was a miracle—God's work."

"Where is Lady Monroe?"

"I dinna ken," he said, and finally, there was some truth in his words. But he suspected Ailios had gone to her chamber. She must have found someone, perhaps Aidan, to leap with from Iona to Carrick. There was no other way she could have arrived at his home so swiftly, when he had left the island before her. He had ridden hard and fast to make Carrick as soon as possible.

"Find her and bring her to Us," Joan said imperiously. "Do so now." She turned her back on him.

Royce strode from the hall, very displeased.

He tried to sense where Ailios was. The moment he came close to the narrow spiraling stairs leading to her chamber in the north tower, he felt her pure, light power. Something soft and warm, as bright as she was, seemed to wash through his heart. It felt more than good; it felt like a huge relief.

He bounded up the stairs, dismissing such absurd feelings.

Her chamber door was open. He saw Claire with her and he started.

Claire looked at him, her regard cool and accusing.

Both women condemned him for the interlude with the Queen, he thought grimly. And he hadn't done anything except make empty promises and play her. "She was to stay on the island," he told Malcolm's wife.

Claire shrugged. "If Joan had come to see—and use—Malcolm, I would stop it."

"Yer husband would do what he had to do to save his head—an' yers," Royce said coolly.

Claire smiled grimly. "Good luck. You need it." She walked out.

He finally looked at Ailios. She threw a mug at his head.

He ducked and it clattered on the floor. "So ye disobey even MacNeil?"

"Were you going to tell me that you and the Queen are *lovers?*" she cried, flushed.

He felt his own color rise. "The affair is purely a matter o' politics," he began.

"Oh! Forgive me! Screwing her brains out is so very political!"

"I haven't been in her bed in months—in almost a year," he said grimly.

"I saw *everything,*" she cried.

He softened because she was so hurt. "Then ye saw nothing at all," he said flatly.

She made a sound.

He just looked at her and saw tears rise. Impossibly he wanted her to understand; impossibly he wanted to take her in his arms. "Ailios, I dinna wish to bed her. Yer the woman I want in my bed."

She made another sound. "That's not what I saw."

"I dinna do anything except play her!" he cried. "She's my liege. Do ye think I can refuse her easily? If yer King wanted it, ye'd go to his bed an' act pleased about it!"

"We don't have a King!"

"Then yer fortunate. Here, there are royals, an' even now, Joan may decide to take my head. She's nay very pleased."

Ailios hugged herself. "You're with me," she finally said, trembling.

He hesitated, almost ready to agree. "We canna be together. Last night was the proof. I willna hurt ye, ever, an' I willna take away yer great power again."

"You've already hurt me, Royce," Ailios said.

He trembled, very close to crossing the room and sweeping her into his arms. "I dinna do as she wished. I dinna want her. I was thinking of ye, Ailios, not her, but I dinna wish to enrage her. I wish to keep my head."

She stared, her dark gaze searching.

"I have never lied, not once in all my life," he added softly.

She turned away, wiping her eyes, and she had never appeared as fragile or as vulnerable. The urge to protect her overcame him. She did not belong in this miserable time. Why did she have to love him? It was impossible, forbidden, and he was unworthy of her.

But even knowing all of that, he cared. He cared that she didn't really understand what he had done and why he had done it, and he cared that she understand how much he wanted her and that he had been acutely aware of her, the entire time during the encounter with Joan. He gave in and crossed the room.

She started.

He cupped her elbows. "Lass, I wish to avoid Joan. But again, I willna lie. To save my head, I will go to her bed."

Ailios inhaled. "Can she really execute you for refusing her?"

"Ailios, the Queen has ordered many beheaded for far less. Her will is law in Alba. I dinna ken yer world, but t'is the way of this world."

She trembled and reached for his shoulders. "I can't stand this. I *won't* share you."

Her words made his heart leap with what felt like exultation. He already knew he could not, would not, share her—but a liaison between them was forbidden. Eventually he would have to let her go. Eventually she would want to go.

But just then, he was fiercely pleased to hear her possessive statement. Just then, he wanted her loyalty and love. And what did that mean? He had already admitted a truth he had no wish to ever admit again—that he cared. To care was dangerous—more dangerous, in his view, than denying the Queen.

"I will try my best to divert her tonight," he said softly, aware that they had just weathered a very personal crisis. And that left him standing alone in her chamber with the most beautiful and pure woman he had ever known, a woman whose mere presence brightened any chamber and any soul—even his. His heart began a new, insistent beat.

She stiffened, aware of his sudden change of interest. "Royce—it's only been a few hours, but I missed you so much."

He tried not to think about the shocking fact that he had actually missed her, too. As importantly, he must not think of her small, hot body beneath his while he drove into her tight warmth and wetness. And he must forget her extreme passion, which matched his exactly. But she took his face in her hands and stood on tiptoe.

"Ailios, dinna."

"Tough," she breathed. "You're mine." And she kissed him.

He tried to remain still, but her words undid him. *You're mine.* His hard body jerked and became fully attentive, clamoring for union and release. He fought the need to be with her, the urge to take her, dominate her. But she plied his lips sensually, seductively, inflaming him impossibly. Still, he refused to move or participate; he would not kiss her back.

She suddenly nipped his lip. The demand was unmistakable. And then the pressure of her mouth increased. He felt her blood screaming in her veins. He felt her need, acutely, as if it was his—which it was. *She needed him driving inside her. He needed to drive inside her.* Against his very will, he opened for her. She moaned and her tongue went deep. He thought of taking her to the bed, mounting her, teasing her. He thought of thrusting deep. He thought of La Puissance.

His mind turned blank; he wrapped her in his arms, bent her backward and took over the kiss.

"Hurry," she gasped.

Somehow, a degree of sanity left, he pulled away.

She gasped, shocked.

He walked to the far side of the chamber, trying to recover his composure and control. He leaned against the wall, waiting for the violent urge to move into her to dull and subside. He heard her panting behind him and thought about how this woman affected him as no other ever had. Was that why the Ancients had chosen him, because he would not think twice about dying for her?

He said roughly, "After last night, I truly dinna trust myself, Ailios." He finally looked at her, mouth hard and tight.

"I trust you." She hesitated, trembling. "But I have my powers back, Royce, and I can't lose them again."

"Aye." He glanced away, with guilt. "Calm yerself, quickly. She has asked fer ye an' we need go down to the hall."

"What?"

That truth was like ice water. He took a few deep breaths and faced her. "She's heard about Garret."

She stared, then said, "What does this mean, exactly?"

"It means ye willna heal a single soul, a single beast— not even a fly—while she is here."

Her eyes widened. "Why?"

"She'll take ye with her, back to court. She'll want yer powers for herself an' ye'll be a hostage at court until ye lose yer powers—or until ye die."

She paled. "Royce, you're kidding, right?"

"Do I appear amused?"

"No. You seem really worried—and you're worrying me."

He knew he'd kept his expression impassive, but Ailios seemed able to read his thoughts. "If she wishes to take ye from here, I canna stop her. Ye'd have to go, or we could leap to another time, when she's nay royal—or when she's dead."

"Why don't we do that now?" she exclaimed.

"Ailios, I'm lord o' Carrick an' all of Morvern. I'm a Master, but my people need me here an' now. And the Code demands a Master live in his time. We canna pick an' choose where to live." He smiled briefly. "If we leap forward a dozen years, I willna stay with ye. My place is in this time."

"Oh," she said with dismay. "Damn."

"Aye, damn." He said, "I told the Queen yer a kind, caring woman an' ye prefer to attend the sick like any midwife."

"Okay," Ailios said. "When will this wonderful meeting take place?"

"Now."

She slipped to her feet. "Absolutely not. I have to get dressed."

He did not understand. "Yer dressed."

She gave him a very sidelong look, one arch and sultry. "Oh, no, this is not dressed."

ALLIE HAD PUT ON HER bombshell red Escada evening gown for the meeting. It was a strapless chiffon sheath that floated down her curves, except for the corsetlike bodice, and it was slit up the back. It was sexy, strong, seductive. Ceit had supplied medieval hairpins, and she had managed to pile her hair on top of her head, while leaving many loose tendrils skimming her neck, shoulders and face. She'd stained her lips with her lip gloss and crushed berries—and added that concoction to her cheeks. This was *war*.

She was upset and she felt threatened as she never had before. But she had never been in love before—and she had never come up against a woman with so much power. She was even jealous, never mind that Royce's affair had occurred before she'd ever known him. There was a bottom line—there was no way Joan was ever going to get her clutches on Royce again.

As she reached the threshold of the hall, she saw Royce standing grimly by the hearth. The Queen sat alone, looking to be in a snit, but her ladies surrounded her, clearly waiting on her every whim. Unfortunately she was blond, pretty and young. Fortunately no one had told her that dark red was an overpowering color for her. However, she was wearing some very real rubies. In the twenty-first century, Allie guessed that necklace was worth a half a mill, easy. As determined as she was, she was also nervous. In the Middle Ages, she didn't count for much. The Queen was going to *hate* being outdone. But that was the point, and it was too late to have second thoughts.

Royce turned.

Allie tensed, unable to smile, waiting for him to react to the sight of her prepared for a more subtle version of an all-out, hair-pulling, nail-stabbing catfight. She wanted to blind him to the other woman. She needed him to look at her and become oblivious to Joan.

His gray gaze widened. Then it turned bright and hot, sliding from her head to her toes.

She smiled at him, just a little, relieved that he appreciated her in the dress. But he met her gaze, his face turning hard with disapproval, all male appreciation gone. He knew she'd chosen the dress to outshine the Queen.

Are ye mad to provoke Joan so?

Allie started, for an instant thinking she'd heard him speak. But he hadn't spoken and she had been imagining it.

The Queen had seen her. She stood, her gaze going wide and incredulous. And she looked at Allie almost exactly as Royce had. A flush of anger began.

She wasn't happy about being bested, Allie thought. She trembled. She had won this round, but it didn't feel so great and there was a long battle ahead.

"Yer Majesty, this is Lady Monroe." Royce had reached her side, and he sent her a warning glance. He also clasped her shoulder, urging her to get down on her knees.

Allie got it. She was to behave. Well, her behavior depended on the oversexed Queen. Allie knelt. It had become surreal, as if she were in a fifties movie.

"Ah, well, now I begin to understand your lack of performance, Ruari," Joan said with cool disdain. "You did not mention to Us that your guest is young and somewhat pretty. You may rise, Lady Monroe."

Somewhat pretty? Allie tensed impossibly. Those were fighting words. She reminded herself that she was a lot prettier and slimmer than the Queen. Allie rose, and met the Queen's direct, seething gaze. In that instant, she knew Joan Beaufort hated her as much as she hated Joan.

"In fact, your guest is pretty enough to wait on Us." Joan smiled triumphantly at her.

"Like hell!" Allie gasped, stunned. Did the Queen think to turn her into an actual servant?

Royce seized her arm, his jaw hard.

"What does the wench mean?" Joan demanded.

"She means that serving Yer Majesty is her greatest wish," Royce said flatly. "She would be honored, but Lady Monroe has been sent to me by her guardian. I canna release her into another's care, not even Yer Majesty's. I am sworn as her guardian now."

Joan laughed. "Then perhaps We will take over as guardian," she said bluntly. "Oh, Ruari, do you think Us a fool? You have taken her to your bed, and you do not wish to give up such temptation."

His face never changed. "I have been so involved with estate affairs, I dinna have time for temptation. I have barely spoken to Lady Monroe since she came to Carrick, but a few days ago."

"We did not ask if you had spoken to her— We are certain you barely speak to her. You are a man of few words. But

We are *certain* you are enjoying Lady Monroe's attentions in your bed," Joan said with displeasure. "And you will have to find a new mistress, if We decide she will serve Us instead."

Royce's smile was cool. The deference vanished from his tone. "Do ye come to *my* home to ask about *my* privy affairs?"

Joan stared at him. Her blue gaze sparked. It was a moment before she replied. "We ask now. We do not care for another lover to interfere in Our stay here."

"Lady Monroe willna interfere in yer stay, Yer Majesty. I would hardly be such a fool," Royce said flatly.

"But We think she has already interfered, as your greeting was lackluster, after such a long absence on your part," Joan shot, and the powerful woman was suddenly peeved in a completely feminine way.

"Then I haven't understood," he said softly. "For I believed ye got a very proper greeting. But then, I am a *patient* man."

Allie felt like kicking him, hard.

Joan flushed. "We are very patient, as well—when it suits Us."

"Ah, well, patience may be a small price to pay for what Yer Majesty truly desires."

Tension sizzled in the room.

Allie choked. Joan was as hot as a woman could be, and Royce was promising her a night of passion. She knew he was treading a fine line and that he had to promise her what she clearly wanted—because this made Joan a woman, not a royal. But there wasn't going to be a repeat of what she had witnessed earlier. Somehow she was going to thwart the damn slut first.

Joan stared at him for another long moment, and then

turned her gaze to Allie. "You will not interfere with Our desires."

Allie felt her blood pressure soar. She somehow smiled sweetly. "I can hardly compete with the Queen of Scotland," she said. "After all, I am only *somewhat* pretty."

Displeasure crossed Joan's pale face.

Royce stepped between them. "Lady Monroe means her words, Yer Majesty. She willna cross Yer Majesty."

"Lady Monroe needs to learn how to speak to her Queen," Joan said tightly. "We do not care for her tone of voice—or her gown. We should like it for Us."

Allie blinked. *What?*

Royce took her arm firmly. "She is pleased to give ye the gown as a gift."

Allie choked. The damned Queen was going to take her dress!

"What did she say?" Joan demanded.

"She said, 'With pleasure,'" Royce returned.

Allie told herself to count to ten. She did not even get to two. "It won't fit her," Allie said, meeting Joan's gaze.

Joan turned red. "Come before Us, Lady Monroe," she snapped.

Allie knew she had to obey, even without Royce's glare. She held her head high and walked forward, feeling as if she were on the way to the guillotine. If Joan wanted the dress, there was no way to refuse. But then, why not give her the gown and watch the seams burst as she struggled to put it on? And how had Royce ever wanted that nasty woman? "I am very pleased to give you the dress," she began.

"We have not given you permission to speak," Joan said.

Allie shook with anger. Behind her, she felt Royce trying to silently tell her something. *Ailios.* Had she heard him thinking her name?

"We do not care what pleases you," Joan said, two spots of pink on her cheeks. "And We take what pleases Us, whenever it pleases Us."

Dinna speak.

She started. Had she really heard that?

Aye, ye listen closely to me.

Royce was communicating with her. A thrill began, never mind the witch bitch Queen. Somehow, she kept silent.

"Tonight, we will take *your* lover to *Our* bed." Joan smiled maliciously at her.

Allie lost her desire to try to be subservient. She opened her mouth and heard Royce before she got a word of protest out.

Dinna speak.

She breathed deep.

I willna bed her.

He meant it, Allie thought. It was a promise. She was so relieved that she trembled.

"Speak," Joan ordered.

She inhaled, trying to control her temper. She knew she had to play along with Joan's need for power and control, no matter how humiliating it was, but Joan needed a little come-uppance. "Then you are in for the time of your life! There is nothing and no one as good as Royce in bed, is there?"

Joan's eyes widened.

"I mean—" Her fists clenched. "He pleasures you all night, doesn't he? Again and again and again, from supper to dawn? And even when the sun is up, he still wants more?" Allie hoped Royce did not screw the Queen the way he did her. She was counting on it.

And when Joan's gaze flickered with more displeasure, she knew she was right. "We are always too pleased to care about the time."

Allie smiled grimly again. "And afterward, of course, is the very best part." She turned her smile sugary sweet.

Ailios, cease.

Allie ignored him. "The *very* best part!"

Joan seemed incapable of smiling. "What do you mean?"

She blinked innocently. "I mean that the best part is afterward, when he holds you and whispers how much he loves you."

Royce choked.

Joan was red.

Allie just kept smiling. Take that, you witch! He loves *me.*

Joan became enraged. "How dare you speak to Us in such a manner! How dare you claim that Ruari cares for you— and not for Us! We are his liege! He has sworn homage to Us on bended knee! Have you no care for your Fate, Lady Monroe?"

Dinna speak a single word!

And as Allie heard his warning, she felt his tension. And she didn't blame him. She had gone too far, but this woman was impossible. Tyranny or not, it went against her nature to simply take her abuse and grovel at her feet. But that was what she had to do, damn it, because there were no civil rights here. And what did outshining the Queen really accomplish except to piss her off? *I should have held my temper,* Allie thought.

Aye, ye should have, and ye must grovel now!

Allie inhaled. "I am sorry if I have offended you. I have foolishly fallen in love with Royce. But I understand he's your lover and how I feel doesn't count." She now felt Royce slump in abject relief. "And I lied. He doesn't hug me when we're done and he never talks in bed. It's only sex. When he's not with me, he's with one of the housemaids. I want to be special, but I'm not."

Royce actually inhaled loud enough for Allie to hear him.

Joan, however, did not soften. "We do not accept your apology. You are the most disrespectful creature We have ever met. Only the rumors that have reached Us keep you alive."

Allie tensed with dread. She finally looked at Royce and he gave her a warning stare. She turned back to the waiting Queen.

"Show us your healing power," Joan commanded. "Now."

Allie stood very still, recalling Royce's admonition that, under all circumstances, she must not reveal her powers to the Queen. How she wished she could show this woman who really had power now. Carefully she said, "If you had a fever, I would sit by your bed and wash your forehead with cool compresses, to lower the temperature of your body. If you hurt your wrist, I would place a tight bandage there, to speed the healing. Do you have an ailment I can soothe?"

Joan stared with anger. "We have heard how you saved a dying boy." She turned and signaled to one of her ladies.

A moment later, a solider in uniform came into the hall, carrying what looked like a dead puppy in his hands. Allie cried out, for the pup wasn't dead, but it had been clubbed and it was unconscious. It was badly hurt and eventually would die.

Ailios, no!

She shook with horror, overcome with compassion for the suffering dog, the urge to rush to it and instantly heal it overwhelming. She'd heard Royce, but could think of nothing other than how she must heal the black and white puppy.

"Heal the mutt," Joan commanded.

Dinna do it.

Allie trembled, moving toward the soldier with the pup as if entranced. How could she turn from the vows she'd taken, before the Ancients and her mother?

She'll take ye far from here. Ye'll be her prisoner.

Allie stopped in her tracks. The spotted pup's lashes flickered and she felt tears gathering as its pain washed over her, around her. And she folded her arms tightly around herself. "I can put the puppy in a soft bed, inspect it for broken bones and try to splint any," she managed hoarsely. "May I take the dog to my chamber and try to ease its pain?"

"Heal it now, before me and all the witnesses in this room," Joan demanded.

Allie felt the tears falling down her cheeks. It was hard to speak. She hated Joan—she hated the soldier—for cruelly beating this tiny dog. "I can't."

Livid color diffused Joan's face.

Royce stepped forward. "She canna heal such a wounded animal, Yer Majesty."

Joan looked ready to break something—or order someone broken. "Get the animal out of here," she snapped.

Allie gasped. "Let me take it to my room, please!"

But the guard was leaving and Joan turned a narrow blue gaze on her. "We will have the gown now."

Allie froze.

Joan smiled cruelly. "Give Us the gown."

Royce said tightly, "Ye canna treat my ward in such a manner."

Joan looked at him. "You mean, your mistress? We will take her to court anyway, where she will learn respect. And We will treat her as We choose. Be pleased, Ruari, that We do not take her head, and that, mayhap, We will send her back to you sometime."

He stood there breathing hard.

Allie looked at him. *Don't do anything. Let her have her moment of power.*

Royce stood there, fighting his fury.

"Give Us the gown."

Allie swallowed hard. Joan wanted to debase her, and she was succeeding. It was unbelievable that she had to obey this monster of a woman. Suddenly aware of the fact that several guards stood by the front door, she jerked on the zipper. Then she let the red dress fall to the floor around her ankles.

Everyone stared.

Allie only wore a white G-string and she flushed with embarrassment. Somehow, she held her head high as she stepped out of the circle of fabric.

She felt Royce's outrage.

She looked at him. *It's all right,* Allie tried. *I hate the stupid dress anyway.*

His aura was the dark, deep, violent red of a man ready to erupt in fury. But he unpinned his plaid and whipped it about Allie's bare body. Allie had never been more grateful for anything. Then he retrieved the gown and handed it to Joan.

Joan stared at her and then at him. "Tonight you will come to me, Ruari. And you will not be thinking of Lady Monroe. She will go to the Tower."

Royce didn't speak. Incredibly his face was now a mask of indifference. He inclined his head.

Joan clapped her hands. A lady ran to her and Joan handed her the dress, then she and her women marched out.

Allie turned into his arms. "Bring me the puppy," she cried frantically.

ALLIE HUGGED THE PUP, who licked her cheek enthusiastically. Healing the dog had taken about three minutes, an indication that she had her powers back.

Then, the pup nestling in her lap as she sat in her bed, stroking it, she thought about the bitchy Queen. There was no question as to what she must do.

She was a Healer and her power was white. Just then, she wished it were black and that she could cast spells like Tabby, or even Sam, who was not that good at them.

But she wasn't a witch and she had never cast a spell in her life. However, she was the granddaughter of a great and powerful god. She had to try to use her power to incapacitate Joan.

It went against her very nature and even her every instinct. She had been put on this earth to help people. Joan was a very unpleasant, power-mad woman, but she wasn't evil. But Joan had made herself clear. She was going to use Royce as if he were a gigolo. Allie wasn't going to share her man.

As Allie stood, leaving the puppy napping on her bed, unhappy with what she had to try to do, she suddenly saw her mother in the mirror over a chest. Her reflection was frightened.

She whirled, but no one was standing behind her. She faced the mirror, breathless, but the image of Elasaid was gone.

So much had happened since yesterday afternoon, when she had thought she'd seen her mother at the shrine on Iona. She'd forgotten to mention it to Royce—she'd pretty much forgotten it herself.

"Mom, what is it?" she cried. Oddly she was starting to think of her mother by her Gaelic name—her real name, not the English translation.

Elasaid did not reappear.

This was the third time her mother had visited her since the South Hampton fund-raiser. What did that mean? Allie was certain she'd been warning her last time, but this time, her message, if there was one, had been impossible to decipher. However, there had been no mistaking her expression of fear.

Allie scooped up the pup, which wriggled happily, licking her cheek. She hugged it, wishing she could communicate with Elasaid, when she felt evil.

It stopped her in her tracks.

It was coming from the hall below.

Not the great, overpowering evil of someone like Moffat, for this presence was weaker, far different, and very human. Allie felt so much depraved lust. Not for power and pleasure, but for physical pain and monetary gain.

Allie hurried downstairs toward the great room. There she faltered in surprise, because Aidan was with Royce. They were standing by the table, a small, slender man clad in English dress with him. His black stench turned her stomach instantly and Allie knew he was the source of the evil she had sensed.

He had seen her, too. As he stared at her with dark, soulless eyes, she knew he could not wait to find someone or something to torture. She knew he'd done so a thousand times, and would do so again.

Royce strode to her, his face hard and grim.

Allie looked toward the table and saw a document there. Their visitor's presence was disconcerting her, but like smoke, true evil wafted from the page. It was a hundred times more powerful than their human guest. "Who has called, Royce?" she asked, putting the puppy down.

"Godfrey Speke. He brings a missive from the south." Royce's tone was noncommittal.

Allie stared into his gray eyes and froze. Instead of Royce, she saw the bishop of Moffat, tall, golden, sinfully handsome, sitting at an ebony desk, a crystal glass of wine in hand. He was clad in crimson velvet robes. A quill and more parchment were upon the desk in front of him. She did not have the power of Sight, but the image was so vivid and strong, she was certain that Moffat sat at a desk somewhere just then, thinking about her—reaching out to her with telepathy. And the bishop lifted the glass and saluted her with it.

Allie jerked herself back to the hall, shaken. Her gaze moved to the small man standing by the table. It was hard to focus on Speke, when Moffat had just sent his version of a greeting to her, over hundreds of miles and perhaps, hundreds of years.

Wait here. I'll send Speke on his way. Royce communicated with her silently.

A good idea, Allie responded. *I don't think he should spend the night inside Carrick's walls.* She walked over to Aidan, who appeared entirely unperturbed.

Speke smiled obsequiously and greedily at Royce. "What reply shall I bring His Lordship?"

"This is my reply," Royce said. He took the parchment and ripped it in two, then handed the parts of the page to Speke. "A guard will see you off Morvern lands. If the dawn finds any man, woman or child missing, hurt in any way or dead, I will dispatch ye to hell myself."

Speke snarled. "I have ridden hard for two days. You do not offer me a meal, wine and a bed?"

Royce ignored him. "An' if I find mutilated sheep, cattle or horses, I'll hunt ye down, as well. I'll enjoy mutilating *ye,* Speke." He strode across the hall and jerked open the door. Six of his men appeared. "Get him off my lands. Guard yer backs."

Speke looked at Allie. His gaze glittered with anger and demonic lust. She stepped back, as if that might deter whatever horrific thoughts he was having. Aidan touched her shoulder reassuringly, while saliva appeared on Speke's thin lips. He licked them. Then he left the hall. Royce slammed the door behind him.

But evil remained, and it was coming from the parchment.

Allie's gaze went to the halves of the page, now on the floor. Speke had dropped them—he'd left them purposefully, she had no doubt. Her heart lurched and her body tensed.

Moffat leaned back in a carved, thronelike chair. He lifted his hand, as if toward her, and a ruby signet ring winked in the firelight. *Soon, Ailios, soon.*

Allie leapt, hearing his silken tone as clearly as she'd just heard Royce. "What does Moffat want?" she cried.

She saw Aidan and Royce exchange looks. Aidan turned to her. "Ye listen to Royce," he advised. Then he leaned close. "Ye left Iona in a great rush, lass."

Allie couldn't dissemble. "I had to go. I had no choice."

"Aye, I see ye did. Well, ye won't have to worry about the Queen after this night." He smiled arrogantly and left the hall, heading up the stairs.

It took Allie a moment to comprehend him. She whirled to face Royce. "Wait a minute! You asked him to go to Joan!"

"He doesna mind. An' she willna be thinking o' me in another moment."

"It's not right!" Allie cried.

Royce said softly, "Aidan is very young an' very hot, Ailios. If he wasna in Joan's bed this night, it'd be someone else's. Do ye think she's the only royal who uses her power to take lovers at whim?"

Allie stared searchingly, but realized he was right. As

little as she cared for history, she did know the story of
Henry VIII. He was surely not the only King to use his
crown to acquire lovers. Before she started feeling sorry for
Aiden, she remembered he was a big-time player. The
Queen was young, pretty and lush. He was probably eager
to jump into her bed and amuse himself. "We owe him."

"Aye."

Allie met his serious gray gaze. His tension filled the
room—and it had nothing to do with Joan.

As she stared, words tried to form in her mind. She
realized she was on the verge of reading his thoughts. Surprised, she strained to make sense of the jumbled language.
She couldn't.

But she saw an *E* in her mind's eye, drifting upward like
smoke, followed by an *L* and an *A*.

"You're thinking about my mother!" she said.

He started.

"What has happened?" she cried. "What did that letter
say?" She inhaled. "It was from Moffat!"

Royce stepped away from her. "The missive is a ruse."

Allie didn't like his avoidance of her question. "What did
it say?"

His nostrils flared. "It doesna matter. I will protect ye.
Dinna worry, not now, not ever. Let us discuss the next few
days." He softened slightly. "While Joan is with Aidan, I can
take ye far from here."

"Into another time? So I can hide there while you return
here?" Allie shook her head. "Royce, we have to talk. I had
a visit from my mother yesterday at the shrine. She was
really distressed, even frightened. I think she was trying to
warn me about something. And I just saw her a moment ago,
upstairs, in my room. Something bad is happening—or
about to go down!"

His eyes flickered. He quickly looked away.

She gripped the edges of his plaid. "What aren't you telling me?"

He cursed, finally meeting her gaze. "Moffat plays games, Ailios, that is all. Elasaid is dead."

And Allie had a horrific inkling. "You are linking Moffat and my mother in the same breath!"

"T'is a ruse," he repeated firmly.

"You had better tell me what Moffat said—what he wants!"

Royce breathed hard. "He wants to trade ye for Elasaid."

CHAPTER FIFTEEN

ALLIE CRIED OUT.

Royce steadied her. "I dinna believe he has yer mother, Ailios. I believe yer mother is dead—an' has been so for centuries."

She reeled, barely hearing him. Was Elasaid alive? Had she somehow escaped death with her great white power? Had her death been feigned in the twenty-first century? Or had she been captured from a far earlier time?

"Could she somehow be alive? Could she be Moffat's prisoner?" she gasped.

"He's playing ye," Royce said sharply. "Yer mother canna be alive."

As terrible as her plight might be, Allie could barely think—but she could feel, and hope burst forth. "Maybe she cheated death the day she died in 1992! Maybe she appeared dead—but her power brought her back to life! Oh gods! It would explain why she is frightened and what I have been seeing!"

"Ye have false hope," Royce cried. "An' that plays into Moffat's hands."

"So this is a cruel trick?" she demanded, shaking.

"If yer mother lived, why has she nay come to ye—to me—to Iona, to the shrine? No one has seen her in over two hundred years!"

Allie hugged herself, reeling. "Maybe she's been a prisoner—or on the run! Maybe she is alive now—and communicating with me telepathically!" Allie covered her face with her hands. She was suddenly sure her mother was alive— and imprisoned by Moffat. But if Elasaid was a captive, her powers had to have been greatly reduced—she had to be hurt! She became so frightened, her mind went blank. "We must accept this offer!" she cried. "I am young and strong— we have to save my mother! I'll take her place! Royce, she must be ill or hurt!"

Royce blanched. "There will never be such a trade!" he said harshly. "Not as long as I live!"

She shook violently, terrified for Elasaid.

"She's dead," Royce said harshly. "An' ye allow Moffat to toy with ye like a cat with a mouse."

"I have to assume she lives," she said. "I cannot assume she is dead. If there is any chance that she is alive and in Moffat's power, we have to rescue her."

"Ailios." He took her into his arms and spoke quietly and firmly. "We will go to Blackwood. He's a few hours from Moffat's hall. He's had spies on Moffat for a long, long time. I will learn the truth o' this matter. Ye must trust me now. An' ye must think o' the facts."

Allie stared into his eyes, gripping him tightly. The fact was that her mother kept reaching out to her after so many years of silence. The fact was, Elasaid was afraid. "And if Elasaid is alive? If she is Moffat's prisoner?"

"We will free her."

She nodded fiercely. "Yes, *we* will free her, you and me, *together.*"

He pulled away. "I will free her with the help of Aidan, Malcolm an' a few other Masters. Ye will stay safe where I put ye!"

She smiled grimly. "I am coming with you—and sticking

to you like glue! I am not about to be dumped in some future time while you play hero! Too much is at stake!"

Royce hesitated.

She didn't have to read his mind to know he was concerned about her being in the vicinity of Moffat's base of power. "Royce," she said softly, taking his face in her hands. "Please, please, hear me now. If she is alive, she is hurt, otherwise she'd leap away. If she is alive, *she* needs healing! I can heal her! And have you forgotten we are going after the man who caused your death in 2007? What if *you* need healing?" Panic began. "I cannot stay behind. I won't. I love you too much! We are in this together, no matter what."

"Yer too brave for yer own good," he said gruffly, walking away from her.

Allie trembled and watched him pace. "Actually I am scared out of my mind."

Royce turned to her. "I want ye with me, Ailios. That way, I can watch over ye. But first, ye'll make a vow."

Allie tensed.

"Ye swear to me on yer mother's soul that ye'll obey me. This is war an' my word is the final law. I dinna trust ye at all," he added.

Allie cringed. "How can you not trust me?"

"Ye have the kindest heart—an' the most reckless soul. I'll turn my back an' ye'll think to heal, to fight, God only will ken. An' when I turn back, ye'll be hurt, or dead."

He only wanted to protect her. "As long as you are reasonable," she began.

He strode to her, eyes ablaze. "Nay! I may be reasonable, but we both ken ye'll think me medieval, aye? Mr. Medieval? Nay. Whatever I command, ye'll obey, be it reasonable to ye or not."

"That is not fair," Allie said harshly.

"If Elasaid is alive an' in Moffat's control, that's unfair, as well."

That took away her hesitation, fast. "Okay. You have my word. I won't disobey you."

Hard satisfaction covered his features. His tone softened. "Come here."

Allie hesitated, then walked to him and was surprised when he pulled her into his arms. He held her tightly against his big body and her heart dropped with sickening force as she realized what he intended. "Now?" Dread began.

He laid his cheek against her hair and held her more closely. She felt the strong, steady beat of his powerful heart. "Remember, the pain will end. It seems to last forever, but it's just a moment."

Allie closed her eyes. "I was really hoping to avoid this, somehow."

"Aye." He kissed her hair. "I willna let ye go, lass."

Allie turned to look up at him and he covered her mouth with his.

And in spite of what was about to happen, her heart exploded with sudden, impossible excitement. Too late, as they were flung with the speed of light through the hall, she knew it had been a distraction.

His mouth moved to her cheek, resting there; she screamed.

PANIC MADE IT IMPOSSIBLE to breathe as they were hurled through space. She saw the stars, shockingly close, stunningly bright. She saw moons and more than one sun. Her stomach, her other organs, even her heart were jamming against her muscles and bones. Allie wept and wept, sure that this time her insides would be torn from her body by the velocity necessary for time travel. This time, her brain would be scrambled like eggs.

His grasp somehow tightened. As she sobbed, he did not make a sound.

They landed.

Pain exploded in her head. The stars and moons blinded her. Finally Royce grunted.

She couldn't breathe. But the excruciating torment of traveling at the speed of light was rapidly lessening, leaving only the terrible stabbing pain in her head. Allie wondered if they had landed on concrete.

Royce gasped thickly, "T'will soon pass."

Hot tears staining her cold face, Allie realized they lay on wet ground. But now, she began to breathe, rapidly and shallowly, frightened. As she did so, Allie became aware of Royce's huge body enveloping her.

His powerful arms enclosed her, holding her tightly to his broad, hard chest, and one of his rocklike thighs was thrown over hers. And the moment she became aware of him, her senses fired wildly.

His pulse drummed, hot and male, through his entire body, and she realized how swollen he was. Dazed, she could not begin to imagine how such pain could bring such lust. But her body began to throb and ache in response.

His large hand tipped up her face. His eyes were blazing and he smiled so seductively at her that her heart stopped.

I need ye.

He hadn't spoken but she heard him, soft and seductive, a murmur of his thoughts. It crossed the back of her mind that something unknown and different was happening. He nudged her thighs apart, sliding one massive leg between hers. She felt him ease up her denim skirt, high over her buttocks. The broad head of his shaft found the silk covering her sex. Allie gasped, their gazes locking.

Ye need me now.

Yes, Allie thought.

Royce grasped her bare buttocks, moving her higher. Allie gasped as he drove past the thong, easily brushing it aside with his slick, hot flesh. Allie wrapped her thighs around his waist. Looking at her, he lowered her slowly onto him.

She gasped and flung her head back, stretched wide and tight. Her muscles clenched him, instantly spasming. He grunted with pleasure and moved deeper. The sensation of his hard body impaling hers blinded her. Her contractions did not cease.

He wrapped her in his arms, his thrusts urgent, determined, deep. *Ailios.*

Allie felt more than his body plunging into hers. The pleasure was almost unbearable. She felt his blood heating impossibly, his climax so close—and she felt his relief and his love. She cried out, shocked to feel his emotions as if they were her own, the rapture so intense now it hurt even as it pleasured her. And he came, crying her name aloud.

She managed to look at him. Although his face was strained with the release and his eyes were burning silver, he smiled at her. She felt his pleasure and even pride, the savage triumph, and her body gave over yet again hurling her into a million pieces. She wept with the pleasure now.

I need ye.

Yes, take more.

She felt him climax again, his seed hotter now, burning inside her, and her ecstasy intensified.

He paused over her, breathing hard, sweat dripping.

She clasped his shoulders, somehow smiling. "I love you."

His eyes brightened. He bent, lifting her jersey tee, lowering the cups of her bra. Allie moaned as he tugged on her nipple with his teeth. Still inside her, he throbbed dangerously.

White power.

A softer pleasure had come over her, a prelude to another terrific climax. Allie lay still, her senses firing, but she had heard him, somehow.

Without even thinking about it, she lifted her power from inside herself and showered it over him, into him.

He lifted his head and their eyes met.

He needed her healing so much. Allie gave him more white light and saw his surprise turn to pleasure, relief, and even more pleasure. He began to move in her again, his gaze now locked with hers, softer but as intent and determined. Helplessly, she spiraled into the universe with Royce.

And even in the throes of her climax, Allie gave him more white light. He gasped in rapture. Allie held on, never wanting to let go.

"Ailios?"

Royce's voice somehow penetrated thick, dark clouds. Allie started, realizing she'd fainted or passed out.

Royce cradled her in is arms, his worried gaze on her face. Somehow, she smiled at him. *My God,* she managed to think, *what had just happened—and after a leap?*

"I hurt ye," he said thickly.

"No, you didn't." Allie touched his cheek. She realized she was incredibly weak. Her hand was shaking, her arm almost incapable of rising. But then, she'd been giving him her power while in the throes of too many orgasms to count. She hadn't been thinking and there'd been no control. She let her hand drift to his strong neck and chest, over his leine. She wasn't surprised that he remained hard. She would have laughed, except she was so tired. "I'm not sure why that happened, but it was great," she murmured. "How do you feel?"

He took her hand and clasped it. "Ye gave me yer healin' power. Ye shouldn't have done such a thing. Yer weak now— while I am stronger than I should ever be."

"I wanted to…you needed it…and it felt good, didn't it?"

His eyes darkened. It was a moment before he spoke. "Ye need to save yer power for the ill—and mayhap, for Elasaid."

His words were like ice water being thrown over her. She shivered and started to sit. He helped her. As he did, she became aware of the power coursing in him. "I was hoping to heal you," she said softly.

He hesitated. "I can break down stone walls with my bare hands right now." He grimaced. "Ailios, never again."

She reached up to touch his beautiful face, wishing he'd tell her if the burden of guilt and grief he lived with had eased. "It just happened. You were hot, I got hot and one thing led to another."

He gave her a look. "That was La Puissance."

She felt a frisson of worry. "Yeah, no kidding. Are we in trouble?"

"I dinna ken." He folded his massive arms across his broad chest. He was clearly unhappy now.

"What happened? Does leaping always make you so horny?"

He almost smiled. "A leap makes any Master randy, Ailios. It's weakenin'. My body sought yers afore I could think clearly. My body wanted yer body, an' it wanted yer power."

Allie understood. The desire after a leap was reflex, and taking power was sexual. "But the first time we leapt, you didn't touch me. And when I leapt with Aidan, he didn't touch me."

"Ah, well, I'd have killed Aidan had he given in to his urges." Royce smiled grimly at her. "Ye were weak the first time. Ye passed out. An' ye dinna belong to me then."

Allie went still. Did Royce know what he had just said? She felt certain it had been a slip, because he suddenly flushed, glancing away.

"Can ye stand?" he asked more quietly. "We're at Black-wood Hall. I can carry ye." He nodded toward the rising sun.

"Can I rest a bit more?" She did not want to be carried down the hill like an invalid, but she was really exhausted and felt certain her legs were not up to the task of even a minor stroll. How much power had she given Royce? His aura had never been as brilliant.

She finally glanced around. They were in a lightly wooded grove on a rolling hill. Through the birch trees, she saw a walled castle below, the stones striking red. A village lay below its curtain walls, which were surrounded by a moat where swans floated. It was beautiful. She wondered where, exactly, Blackwood Hall was.

"We're north o' Dumfries," Royce told her.

He bent and swept her into his arms. Allie sighed, giving in. They had to find Elasaid and she was too beat to do anything physical now...even walk. She clung, enjoying being in his arms, as he walked down the hill, leaving the woods behind. His heart beat steadily, powerfully, beneath her cheek. She became aware of the extent of her love. Impossibly it had grown.

She looked up at him. "You never answered me. Do you feel better?"

He hesitated. "Yer light takes the chill out o' my heart," he finally said.

Tears came to her eyes.

The sun was just rising and the morning was cold. Villagers were leaving their huts. Cattle and sheep grazed on the commons. As they walked past the first shelters and a common well, the peasants turned to glance curiously at them. Everyone looked at her short skirt and legs, mostly with pity.

Royce growled, "They think ye too impoverished to wear a long garment."

Allie had to laugh. "I'd rather be thought of as poor than wear what the maids at Carrick wear."

He gave her a look. "Ye need English an' French gowns."

Allie's heart leapt. "You mean, like the Queen was wearing?"

"Aye." He glanced ahead, his strides lengthening.

"You want to clothe me in velvet and jewels?" She was amazed.

"I dinna say any such thing."

"Admit it!" She didn't need to hear a confession, because she knew that he wished her outfitted like royalty. In spite of the circumstance, her heart filled with joy. She kissed his throat.

"Ye'll catch an ague the way ye dress. Mayhap Blackwood can find ye a gown."

Let him make excuses. She was happy—until Allie saw the drawbridge lowering and thought about why they were there. "Blackwood knows we're here."

"Aye. I sent him my thoughts last night."

A few minutes later, they were crossing that bridge in a serious silence. Blackwood Hall was smaller than Carrick and Dunroch, and the main building looked like a manor house, with a single tower above. Blackwood was standing on the landing above the stairs leading up to the hall's great door as they approached.

She hadn't paid much attention to him the first time they'd met, when she had been so stunned by Royce's rejection. Now, she saw a tall, powerful man, too handsome for his own good, his hair as dark as midnight. He seemed to be amused, although what he found amusing, she had no idea. He was dressed in black boots that covered his knees, dark hose and a black wool jacket with a narrow, nipped-in waist, puffed skirt and full sleeves. The skirt did not cover his hips; instead, it exposed his loins. A very large pouch had been sewn into the hose, over his manhood, as if he wore a jockstrap below. Allie had never seen such a sight and she stared. Royce's manner of dress, in a leine and plaid with no underwear, was sexy as all hell. But this was almost, and maybe even more, revealing.

Royce took her arm. "Dinna ogle."

"Is that the fashion?" she managed to ask, ignoring him.

"T'is called a codpiece, an' aye…the English are pleased to strut their manliness with their frivolous surcotes and hose."

"Well," Allie said, smiling, aware of her heart rate accelerating, "I won't be the one to object."

Royce gave her a dark look. They'd reached the bottom of the stairs and Allie dragged her gaze upward. Sam would go nuts for this one. She whispered, "Is he single?"

Royce looked at her blankly, clearly not understanding. Then, as clearly, he lurked. He flushed. "He's nay wed an' he'll never be wed. He's the worst rake—as bad as Aidan."

"I bet he'd love my friend Sam," Allie said.

"Ye forget why we be here," Royce said furiously.

"Not really. Can you put me down?"

When he did, clearly intent on keeping an eye on her, Allie preceded him up the stairs. "But good humor usually helps. Or would it be better if I moped around all day and wept all night, worrying about my mother?"

Royce was silent.

Blackwood greeted her with a smile, glancing lazily at her from head to toe. "Good morning, Lady Allie. T'is my pleasure to have you at Blackwood Hall."

She met his blue gaze and found it hard to look away, acutely aware that he wished to charm her. "Thanks. We're imposing, and I am sorry for that, but we really need your help."

His gaze flickered, and he nodded for them to go inside. His hall was sparsely furnished, very much like the great room at Dunroch. In spite of that, the long table was beautifully carved and gleaming with wax, and the chairs in front of the hearth were upholstered in a rich wine-hued wool fabric. Aidan was standing by the fireplace, and he smiled at them. He did not seem any worse for wear.

Allie couldn't help it. "That was fast," she teased.

He gave her a very male look. "I have leapt into the past."

She got it. If he had come from the future, he'd spent some time with Joan. She was dying to know some details, but didn't dare ask if Joan might be a new, nicer person now.

He grinned. "She's in very high spirits," he said, laughing.

Allie went across the room and hugged him. "I felt awful yesterday. I didn't think it right for Royce to ask you to divert Joan."

"Ah, lass, she's my liege. If she needs my services, I'm more than eager to oblige," he said, amused. Then, with a glance at Royce he said, "O' course, that might change, if I'm ever so fortunate as to have a maid like ye to love me."

Allie met his gaze, wishing she could lurk. To her surprise, graphic images formed, and she saw Aidan with the Queen and two other women! Instantly she realized he'd sent her the little mental note. "Really?" She felt herself blush.

He just laughed at her. "Yer terribly curious about my privy affairs."

She patted his arm. "Thank you for getting Royce out of hot water."

He grinned at her. "Well, if ye touch me again, I mayna live much longer." He gestured toward Royce.

She didn't bother to look back, as she knew her lover well now and he'd recover from a brief bout with jealousy. "I can manage him. Don't worry about it. Will you help us find Elasaid?"

"Aye." Aidan's smile faded. "If she's alive."

Royce and Blackwood joined them. "Lady, I have had spies at the cathedral, in the village and town, and at Moffat's Hall for many years," Blackwood said, all business now. "Last night, Royce told me you would come and why. I have summoned my spies and most should return to Blackwood by this evening. We will have some word then."

Allie felt like pulling out her hair. "That's an entire day away!"

"Ailios, the spies place their lives in danger every day they betray Moffat. T'is no simple task for each man to simply pick up an' walk out of his place," Royce said.

Blackwood smiled slightly at her. "But know this. Until last night, there has been no word, nor even any rumor, of a woman prisoner or guest. If the bishop has Elasaid, I am certain she's not in his hall or the Cathedral."

Allie hugged herself. "You said you have spies in villages and the town."

Blackwood nodded. "His lands are vast. She could be hidden in one of the villages easily enough. The town of Moffat is large. She could be hidden in a cellar there."

Allie looked at Aidan, and then at Royce. No one was jumping up and down with optimism or excitement. "Why don't we just say it? We're searching for her here, now, but she could be in any time and any place."

Royce clasped her shoulder. "We will find her if she lives."

So much despair began. "How? How will we do that when he could have her imprisoned in ten hundred, twelve hundred, fifteen hundred, or even two thousand six? The possibilities are infinite!" And she thought that maybe the only way to find her mother was to agree to a trade.

"I will never trade ye," Royce snapped furiously.

Allie wasn't surprised by his passionate outburst, but clearly, Aidan and Blackwood were taken aback. Blackwood said carefully, "A trade and treachery combined might give us what we want."

"Never," Royce said fiercely. "Ye think to offer him Ailios—an' then we'll follow her to Elasaid, when she's Moffat's prisoner? An' then what? What if we canna free her? Nay! We wait to hear from yer spies. Then we begin our own search. We'll follow Moffat night an' day an' let him lead us to Elasaid—*if* he has her. *If* she lives."

"Ye dinna wish to be convinced," Aidan said so softly Allie almost missed his words.

Allie turned away. Aidan was right. Royce didn't want to believe that Moffat had her mother, and she knew why. Because the only real way to locate her was through a trade.

Royce's plan to follow Moffat to Elasaid might take forever. And if Moffat had her mother, she was pretty sure they did not have forever.

THREE DAYS LATER, Allie wandered over the drawbridge, but didn't go down the dirt road to the village. Green hills rolled into an eternity, framed by a blazing sun and an azure-blue sky, spotted with fluffy white clouds. Fat, woolly sheep dotted the pastures and the scene was picture-postcard perfect.

But nothing was perfect. Allie walked along the moat, head down, aware of the swans and ducks floating in the slow waters. Blackwood's spies had not uncovered any information about a female guest or a prisoner. They continued to search each village and town under the bishop's control.

Royce, Aidan and Blackwood had been tailing Moffat for three entire days and as many nights. Moffat had not left his lands. By night, he was at Moffat's Hall, by day, at the Cathedral, managing affairs in his bishopric. Allie sat down on the grassy ridge, knees drawn to her chest. How ironic—the master of the Scot demons pretending to serve God.

It was an Indian summer day, surprisingly warm, and Allie had shed her long-sleeved T-shirt. She still wore her tank and mini. Now, the sun warmed her shins and knees. Nothing could warm her heart.

How much longer could they wait for some real facts? Last night, she'd dreamed of Elasaid. It had been a nightmare.

Elasaid had been scantily clad, as if in a modern nightgown, and she had been behind bars—or in a cage. Tears had stained her pale, gaunt face. Allie had woken up, determined to communicate with her, but the moment her eyes had opened, the vision had been gone. She spent hours trying to summon her mother back to her, to no avail.

She had not a single doubt that her mother was alive, in some kind of jail, and being treated terribly. This had to stop—and it had to stop now.

She sensed Royce approaching and glanced up. She hadn't seen him since the night before, as he'd been gone by dawn. A pair of riders were cantering through the village and she instantly recognized Royce's powerful crimson and gold aura. She focused, praying he had a found a clue to her mother's whereabouts.

We dinna have news.

Allie hugged her knees tightly to her chest, despairing.

Royce and Blackwood galloped to a halt before the edge of the moat where she sat. Royce leapt down from the chestnut charger he rode, handing the reins to Blackwood. Allie managed to smile at their host, while Royce removed an oilskin from the back of his saddle. Blackwood nodded at her and left, trotting over the drawbridge, leading Royce's mount.

Allie just sat there, unsmiling.

Royce strode over, his face shadowed with his version of her pain. "We dinna learn anything, Ailios. Ye must be patient now."

She shook her head. "I have no patience left." She refused to look at him, despair clawing at her. Royce was her hero, but this wasn't working for her. They weren't going to find her mother like this. Why did he have to be so damned protective? Why couldn't he agree to a trade—even if a phony one?

"Will ye begin to hate me for doing what I think best?" he asked seriously. "Will ye hate me for protectin' ye?"

She stared, trembling. Although he had insisted on separate rooms, not a day went by that he didn't look at her with so much heat, she began a total meltdown. But his will was stronger than hers, and he didn't come to her room. She knew he was guilt-ridden over taking her power, but that had been days ago. She'd been healing the villagers in the valley since the morning of their arrival, so he hadn't hurt her at all, not really.

She knew he was afraid of caring for her—and she also knew it was too late. He was in denial. That was okay. Allie intended to focus on their relationship—*after* they found Elasaid.

Allie slowly stood. "We will never find my mother this way."

He tucked the package under his arm, his face hard. "Yer way will see ye raped an' murdered."

"Stop reading my mind," she cried.

"Ye keep thinking o' trading yerself for yer mother," he accused. "That's insane, Ailios. Elasaid wouldn't want ye in her place!"

"So do you finally admit that she is Moffat's prisoner?"

He hesitated. "I lurked while ye slept last night."

She tensed.

"I was in yer dream with ye. Aye, I believe yer mother may be alive—an' in Moffat's cage."

Allie went to him.

He tossed the package aside and wrapped her in his arms.

"Please," she begged. "Why can't we do as Blackwood first suggested? Why not pretend to trade—and use that pretense to find my mother? I am strong! If he hurts me, I will heal—and quickly!"

Royce breathed hard, gripping her arms. "I'll nay see ye in Moffat's hands—ever. I'll nay see ye burned an' beaten, filled with his seed, an' maybe with his spawn!"

Allie recoiled. Brigdhe's shadowy image washed through her mind. "Is that how you found Brigdhe?"

"Aye!" His stare was as bright and as hard as diamonds.

And Allie saw him kneeling over a hurt woman with titian hair. Suddenly she felt so much pain. And she saw the woman recoil. She saw her rejection, her revulsion and hatred. And she saw Royce backing away, ice-cold in his heart, his soul. Except for the guilt that began to sink its claws into him.

Stunned, Allie realized she had just seen into Royce's mind. She slid her hands to his chest. His heart thundered there. "But you left her," she whispered. "You blessed her marriage to another man."

His face was hard. "Aye."

Allie shook her head, sympathy flooding her. "Oh, Royce. Tell me that was my imagination—tell me she didn't hate you for what happened."

He stared down at her, his face twisted beyond recognition. "She hated me. An' I willna rescue ye from Moffat an' have ye hate me that way, too."

She trembled, wanting to cry for him. She clasped his face. "I could never hate you. I love you too much."

"Ye'd hate me if he raped an' beat ye an' chained ye like a dog. Ye'd hate *me,* Ailios, yer *hero,* for failing to keep ye safe."

"No," she tried, meaning it. "I would love you still."

He flinched. Then, stepping back he said, "Well, I hate myself now for failin' ye this way. I hate seeing yer eyes black with sorrow, instead of light with joy an' laughter."

"I'm scared," she cried.

He took her by the shoulders. "Aye. But we have only begun the hunt. I mean my words, always. Ye must have patience now."

"I can't be patient. What's he doing to her, right now?"

"Dinna allow yer mind to wander so freely," he said, his grasp tightening. "It serves no one but Moffat."

Allie felt the tears begin to run. "I'm out of all patience and I'm scared sick," she whispered, running her hands over his linen-clad chest. He tensed—and then his heart thundered. She smiled weakly and slid her hand into the neckline of the leine, over the hot skin there. She felt his pulse explode with excitement.

But he caught her wrist. "Our union remains forbidden," he said.

"I don't care," she cried, her urgency blinding. Beneath her skirt, wet heat trickled down her thighs. The little scrap

of silk lace suddenly hurt her oversensitive flesh. And she
slid her free hand beneath his tunic, scraping the hot, turgid
skin of his erection with her nails. His eyes widened; she
traced the bulging vein running on the underside of the
length there.

Dark color suffused his cheeks. "The watch is above and
it's the light o' day," he said roughly.

Allie caught him in her hand. "As if you care."

He didn't move, except for his manhood, which leapt and
quivered beneath her fingers. Their gazes locked.

Allie smiled and stepped closer, and she guided him
toward her.

He seized her bottom beneath denim and lace, lifting
her. Allie cried out, exultant, as he whirled, impaling her.
She wrapped her thighs around his waist and begged for a
climax. He caught her mouth, covering it, pumping deep.

She felt him come violently, hot and deep, and she wept
in her own release.

Somehow he laid her down, never leaving her, his mouth
fused with hers. The pressure was incredible, and just when
she thought he'd break her body apart, another orgasm broke
over her, in her.

"Come with me," he said, moving slowly now. "Another
time, Ailios."

Allie wept and strained for him.

He tested her slowly, paused, rubbed her cleft and
stroked deep.

Allie sobbed his name, shattering all over.

"Aye," he moaned, and his body contracted violently a
dozen times.

When they lay still, the sun remained high, but huge
clouds had cast long shadows over the grass and the moat.
Allie blinked, aware of his weight. He shifted and moved

off of her, then jerked her clothes down, glancing upward toward the watchtowers.

Allie flushed. "Is anyone up there?" she asked in a whisper.

"Ye whisper now?" He was incredulous but he smiled. "Blackwood's men are soldiers, an' the towers are for the watch."

Allie grimaced and sat up.

Royce knelt, staring, and their gazes locked.

He was simply so beautiful—as beautiful as he was strong, powerful and virile. She had never loved him more and now, her heart wanted to shatter the way her body had done so many times.

He turned and walked to the oilskin he had dropped, retrieving it. Then he knelt beside her again, handing it to her.

Allie became still. "What is this?" she asked, but she knew. *It was a gift.*

Poker-faced, he said, "Open it an' see."

She couldn't move or breathe; she couldn't speak. *Royce was giving her a gift.* Allie took the package, her hands shaking, and then she tore at the strings. Royce smiled.

She didn't see, she felt it.

She pushed the skins aside—and the finest, softest emerald-green velvet spilled into her hands. She breathed hard, standing, holding up a long, beautiful velvet dress, trimmed in darker green and gold. Jewels were sewn into the trim. She thought she saw citrines and emeralds. She looked up, stunned.

Royce stared expectantly at her. "Do ye like it?"

She hugged the dress to her chest. "I love it." She started to cry.

"Then why do ye cry?" he asked. "Ye hate it!"

She shook her head, overcome. "It's the most beautiful dress I have ever seen."

He smiled. "Really?"

"Read my mind," she cried, and she rushed into his arms. "Thank you." She kissed him. "Thank you." She kissed him again.

He laughed. The sound was stunning—warm and rich but light and bright—and Allie realized she'd never heard Royce laugh before. "If a gown will make ye so hot, I'll buy ye dozens," he teased.

She somehow smiled, clutching the gown. "I'm not hot. I'm happy."

"Yer always hot," he said quietly. "Yer always happy. I have never known anyone as happy."

Allie just stared.

He smiled ruefully. "We have amused the entire watch enough for one day. Let's go in, lass."

ALONE IN HER CHAMBER, Allie put the gown on and paused before a looking glass. It had a low, square neckline and then fell softly to the floor, skimming her body, and it fit very well. The color made her appear radiant. But then, she had been well loved—and she was in love. And there was no more doubt that Royce loved her in return.

He could deny it and pretend whatever he wanted, but his actions, his behavior, his concern, said it all. Her heart ballooned. She would treasure this dress forever…her very first gift from him. Then she tensed, fear stabbing at her, and she looked up into the mirror.

Moffat smiled at her.

Allie froze. Her heart beat hard, swiftly. In real alarm, she slowly turned—but the golden demon did not stand behind her.

She glanced at the mirror again. Only her own reflection greeted her.

She inhaled and began to shake. Had Moffat just tried to communicate with her?

Elasaid was in great danger, and she couldn't go on this way.

The beauty and joy of what she had just shared with Royce had vanished, slipping into a cherished memory. Allie felt ill. She loved Royce with all of her heart and all of her soul, but he wasn't going to agree to a trade, even if it was a trick. He was simply too protective.

She hated defying him. She had even given her word to obey him. But he hadn't forbidden her from finding her mother.

He was going to be very angry if she did what she felt she had to do.

Allie went to the window and focused on the devil's right hand. Instantly Moffat's smug, smiling image filled her mind, as if he had been waiting for her. He stood in the same room she'd seen before, but he looked out a window that faced south.

She instantly understood that Moffat was to the north of where she now stood.

Hallo a Ailios.

Allie breathed hard. Royce would be so angry, but this wasn't a betrayal—this was a necessity. *Hallo a Thormond.*

His smile flickered with surprise. *You know my given name?*

She hadn't. His name had simply come to mind. *Where is my mother?*

Come to me tonight and you'll learn what you wish.

Allie tensed, acutely aware of his lust. Was there any point in asking what he'd do with her? He would either use her for his pleasure or not, but he would certainly try to use her as a Healer—that much was clear. *I will come to you if you release my mother.*

He smiled widely. *Ah, beauty, t'is easily done.*

Demons lied. Demons cheated. No demon could be trusted. *If you give me your word, if you keep it, I will heal for you— once.*

You have my word.

Allie was violently ill now. Their bargain was almost sealed. This was the best she could do, as she had nothing else to offer. Besides, Moffat didn't want Elasaid; he wanted her. The gods only really knew why.

Speke will meet you after midnight outside the south wall. He will bring you to me.

Allie hesitated. Speke was depraved and evil, and she had no wish to go anywhere with him. But Moffat was even worse, and if she couldn't bear to be led to him by Speke, how would she face the bishop in the end? And while she desperately wanted to find her mother and be reunited with her, maybe she shouldn't be bargaining with the devil's own. Maybe she shouldn't go through with this plan.

And suddenly she heard her mother sobbing.

Allie jerked and saw Elasaid on a stone floor, naked and hurt. Bruises mottled her back. She wept in despair, but she was in physical pain.

"Damn you!" Allie shouted.

Moffat smiled cruelly, locking gazes with her. *Tonight.* And then his image vanished.

Allie began to shake. What she had just seen was proof that she had no choice now. She hugged herself.

She had just made a pact with the devil.

CHAPTER SIXTEEN

ALLIE SPENT the entire evening thinking of inane things—
like a fantasy shopping spree at Saks, *X-Men 3,* Tiramisu's
thin-crust pizza, Godiva chocolate and matchmaking her
three friends with Masters. Halfway through supper, Royce
had started looking at her with suspicion. She'd turned her
thoughts to hot, off-the-charts sex, instantly distracting him.
What she must not think about was meeting Speke later that
night; at all costs, she must not think about the bargain she'd
made with Moffat.

She knew Royce would read her mind.

Now, she lay alone in her bed, a small fire in the hearth,
listening for Royce. His chamber was next to hers, and
about an hour ago she had felt his power still and soften. She
was pretty sure he was asleep.

She hated betraying him this way.

Allie slid from the bed, clad in the medieval Highland
version of a nightgown, and she knelt before the fire. She
wished Tabby were with her, because she needed a cloaking
spell. But her friend was far away in the future, and hopefully
well on her way to recovery from her broken heart. She didn't
do spells, so she prayed to the Ancients for their protection
and guidance. If she was very lucky, one of the gods would
take pity on her and cloak her power from any who could sense
it. She was afraid that, even asleep, Royce would feel her

leaving Blackwood Hall. She was pretty sure he slept with one sense on her.

After praying for some time, Allie blew out the candles, certain no one had been listening to her. It was late and she couldn't delay. Her mother's Fate was at stake. She slipped on the emerald velvet dress, trying not to think about how furious Royce would be when he discovered her gone. Hurting in advance for them both, aware that reconciling him to what she had done would not be easy, she took her dagger and soundlessly left the room.

She paused outside of Royce's closed door, listening for him. She sensed that he lay still and motionless, and while his power filled the chamber, it was quiet, making Allie certain that he remained asleep. But he wasn't at peace. Tension emanated from him. Allie wondered if he was suffering from unpleasant and disturbing dreams.

She was afraid to open the door and check. On the other hand, if he was awake, she had to know, because the moment she went downstairs, he'd surely appear and prevent her from meeting Moffat. Stiff with anxiety, she grasped the door handle and gently pushed. The hinges creaked loudly.

Allie tensed and glanced into the chamber. Royce lay motionless on his back, one arm flung out, the covers pulled to his waist. He slept in the nude and his bare chest rose and fell in a steady, even rhythm.

Allie breathed hard and backed out, amazed he hadn't awoken. Then she turned and ran barefoot down the corridor and downstairs. She let her senses drift behind her, but he wasn't following her. She sensed no one near, anywhere, and she crossed the hall. She unbarred and opened the front door, the wood groaning, and instantly, she felt Speke's soulless presence in the near distance.

Lust for pain and pleasure wafted from outside the walls, evil and potent, lying in wait there for her.

Allie bit her lip, feeling very much like a small prey, and she had to remind herself that Speke was the least of her problems. He was inconsequential, the messenger and the guide, and she was going to have to deal. She stepped outside, leaving the door ajar so as not to make more noise. She had become somewhat of an expert on castles in the past week, and she knew that every stronghold had a small door that could admit a man on foot or a single horse and rider. Every castle also had secret exits, to be used in the event of a siege. She did not know where the tunnels were at Blackwood, but earlier, she'd found the sally-port.

Allie crossed the bailey at a run, keeping close to the buildings and the walls. She did not intend to be spotted by the watch. The sally-port was on the eastern wall, and she unbolted it and stepped through. Then she ran alongside the moat, which gleamed black as velvet in the starlight, heading south. Still keeping as close to the wall as possible, she finally turned the corner. No watch shouted in alarm.

Her heart pounded. She had made it, but she was hardly pleased. Speke's sick lust was stronger now. Allie slowed, pretty sure he was thinking about her and just as certain she didn't want to know what he was thinking. Her gaze veered to the darkest place beneath the south wall. She couldn't see him, but he was there, and as she approached, her feet began to drag. When she was a few yards away, she saw the outline of a small dinghy. His form emerged from the shadows.

Speke must have smiled, for his teeth flashed, glistening with saliva.

Her heart thundered now. Her grip on her dagger tightened. "Speke."

"Lady." He stepped forward and his gaze met hers. It was intense, bright, maddened.

Allie looked away, uneasy.

He dragged the rowboat to the moat and slid it silently into the water.

Allie didn't move. His lust was hotter now, and she felt his energy roiling. She didn't have to read his mind to know he was thinking about her in some very grotesquely sexual and sadistic ways.

How was she going to get into the rowboat with him?

How else would she cross the moat?

She could swim.

Except, her long gown would make swimming almost impossible. And she wasn't about to strip down to almost nothing in front of this evil man.

"Come, Lady." His teeth flashed again. Spittle dripped from his lips.

Allie could not believe she was such a coward, when she hadn't even reached Moffat himself. She rushed past him and stepped into the rowboat, then held up her dagger threateningly. "Stop thinking about me," she warned softly. "You touch me and you're dead."

His teeth flashed—as did his eyes. He stepped into the stern and picked up the oars. "So pretty…so small. So much skin to cut and taste. Have no fear, lady. I obey my master. He has forbidden me from cutting you, from tasting your blood. I'm not allowed to touch you, alas."

Allie was not reassured. And Speke did not look upset. He looked pleased—too pleased. In that moment, she had a terrible foreboding that she would not make it to Moffat Hall in one piece.

AIDAN AWOKE.

He had been chosen ten years ago, even though his father, the earl of Moray, had been the most powerful deamhan in

Alba for a thousand years. He hadn't understood why the Brotherhood chose him, and even though MacNeil had claimed it was his Fate, Aidan hadn't truly believed it. He wondered if he had been chosen because of his devout mother. In truth, he hadn't cared to be turned into an avenging hero of any kind, as he enjoyed his life far too much. But once chosen, Moray had been hunting him, determined to turn him to evil.

Moray had been vanquished three years ago by his half brother, Malcolm, and his wife, Claire. Aidan hadn't believed it then; sometimes, in the midst of a nightmare, he did not believe it now. How many nights had he awoken, a lover at his side, wet with sweat, oddly afraid, only to rush into his son's chamber to make certain Ian lived and was still at Awe? But his powerful deamhan father was dead. Otherwise, he would have long since come back to destroy everyone—his own son and grandson included.

The vows were usually inconvenient. Rushing through time to protect the Innocent often interfered with his affairs, especially his love affairs. The Code he rarely bothered with. He hated rules in general, especially those handed down by the Ancients thousands of years ago.

But, oddly, he cared about Innocence, and he had done so even from the Choosing, when he was so ambivalent about the Brotherhood. He could not comprehend why, as he was well aware that his nature was a selfish and hedonistic one, except, of course, when it came to his small son. His greatest love, after little Ian, was beauty, and the pleasure that came from it in bed. Every time he turned around, another beautiful woman awaited his attentions, or so it seemed. And while he'd rather seduce Innocence than protect it, in the last decade, he had become a great defender after all. He'd even heard bards sing

his praise as if his powers were legendary. That had amused
him to no end.

In the past few years he had come to care about his vows,
too, although he would never openly admit it, and he was
certainly not as fervent as the great Masters, men like his
best friend, Royce. Ruari Dubh had never condemned him
for the fact of his paternity, he had never objected to his hedonistic ways and he had never criticized his failure to truly
embrace the Code. Most importantly, he had been more of
a father to him than anyone. Royce had even begged
Malcolm to be a true brother to him, when Malcolm had first
hated him, because of what Moray had done to their mother.
Aidan owed Royce more than he could ever repay and was
acutely aware of it.

And his powers kept growing, month by month and
year by year. At first, there had been the stunning strength,
the impossible stamina, the endless virility and the ability
to leap time. Then a healing power began—at first
awkward and elusive, then increasingly steadfast and
strong. In the past years, his senses had begun to hone and
sharpen in the most amazing manner. He could sense evil
from great distances, and identify its source. The other
week, he had sensed evil in the future, and he had leapt to
1552 in a faraway land to battle a horde of demons, in order
to save a beautiful widow and her child. The widow had
repaid him handsomely in her bed. The child would one
day be a King.

Now he sat up, fully awake, aware of evil very close to
the castle walls. He focused. A relatively weak but sickly
evil human was at the south walls.

And instantly he felt the Healer's white power there, as
well. Aidan tensed, surprised. Her power was usually
blinding, for it was such a huge healing light. But now, it

was faded and weak, almost imperceptible. He knew she had disguised it.

Alarm filled him.

What ruse was this?

But hadn't she wished to trade herself for her mother from the start?

Where was Royce?

He leapt from the bed, seizing his belt and swords, which lay on the floor by the head of the bed, in easy reach. He was buckling the belt as he strode into the corridor. At the far end, Royce's door flew open and he came out, his face hard. "Evil comes," he said tersely.

And Royce flung open the Healer's door. He froze.

Aidan felt his shock and then his disbelief. He hurried to him. "She's nay there. She's at the south wall—with the blackened human."

Royce turned to him, the terrible comprehension filling his eyes.

Aidan said urgently, "She's disguised her power, mayhap with a spell. But I can sense her." His focus sharpened. "She's with evil named Speke, a henchman o' Moffat."

Royce shook. "She gave me her word that she would obey me."

Aidan already knew his friend was in love with the Healer, even if he would never admit it. It still surprised him that Royce, a true soldier of the gods, a man committed to his vows, had become smitten by a woman, for it was against the foolish rules. But he was gladdened, for he liked Allie and knew how deeply she loved Royce. It was pleasant to see actual expressions on Royce's face, to sense his happiness and even see him smile. Now, he feared for them both. He grasped Royce's arm. "We need to hurry."

Royce looked at him, his gaze as cold as ice. "She betrayed me."

And Aidan knew that comprehension was the knife in his heart, severing their bond and sealing their discordant Fate.

Sorrow crossed Royce's features, followed by a terrible look of anguish, and then all emotion was gone. He strode down the hall. He slammed his fist on Blackwood's door but did not stop. Aidan followed him, wishing the Healer had thought about what breaking her word would mean to a man like Royce. She was in trouble, but when the trouble was ended, Royce would turn from her. Aidan felt sorry for them both.

And then he felt her pain.

So did Royce, for he paled—and he began to run.

THEY HAD BEEN TREKKING across the rolling, wooded hills for about twenty minutes, Allie clutching her knife, her palms wet with sweat. She was acutely aware of the pressure building in Speke. He didn't look at her, but his energy had been roiling ever since they had rowed across the moat together. It had been growing hotter and hotter by the minute. His head was down now. She didn't like what was happening. She felt his mind racing in frantic circles. It was as if he was tormenting himself with his thoughts of her.

She sensed him losing control. She prayed it was her imagination. She walked several steps behind him now, ready to defend herself at the slightest provocation.

He stopped.

Allie almost crashed into his back. She halted and leapt away from him. Past him, below in a small valley, she saw the light from the fires of a small village. But she did not sense Moffat's huge black power there.

Speke turned, his eyes gleaming red in the starlight. "You're afraid."

"Not at all," she lied thickly. She held up the knife, pointing it at him.

He licked his fat lower lip. "You're the purest of them all—purer than a virgin."

"Keep walking," Allie said tightly, her heart slamming.

"But you're not a virgin. You like to fuck. I saw you this afternoon, in broad daylight." His smile curved.

"Your master has forbidden rape."

Speke smiled widely and reached into a jacket pocket. His energy had become explosive, as if he was ready to find a sexual release from whatever thought he was having.

Allie tensed, certain he was about to assault her.

And he threw a rope around her neck, laughing.

Allie went to cut it.

He kicked her wrist so hard that pain blinded her and she dropped the knife.

"I did not touch you," he crowed, and the noose tightened around her throat. He jerked on it cruelly, so she was hauled abruptly forward. She seized the noose, starting to choke, and he jerked again. Allie fell face-first into the dirt and grass as he pulled, strangling her.

Panic overcame her and she could not think. The noose was so tight, she couldn't pull it away from her neck. Frantically she clawed at it as she rolled onto her back, incapable of drawing any air into her lungs. *She was going to be strangled to death*.

Suddenly he released the pressure.

Allie gripped the noose, loosening it, breathing hard and deep, blood seeping down her neck, sobbing in relief.

"Oh, yes," he said. And he jerked on the line, hard. Immediately the noose tightened, cutting into her flesh, threatening to break her fingers, so she couldn't breathe yet again. She felt blood against her knuckles, and she was blinded by panic.

She couldn't breathe.

He jerked tighter.

He was going to break her neck.

She clawed at the rope, at her skin, the night growing even darker, her lungs burning.

He laughed in sheer excitement, releasing all the pressure.

Allie gasped for air, sucking it in, the night blackening around her. She gulped raggedly, her throat on fire, knowing she must not faint, not now. Somehow she tore the rope to her collarbone, gasping. "Stop!" Her tone was raw.

"But I can't touch, or cut, or taste!" He jerked so hard and abruptly on the rope, she went face-first into the ground and pain exploded in her neck; something snapped.

A roar filled the night.

And Allie felt Royce's fury. Before she could even assimilate that he had come to defend her and that she'd been too hurt to even sense him approaching, Speke was blasted off of his feet and across the wood.

Choking, Allie seized the rope, loosening it. On her back, frantically sucking in air, she saw Royce standing not far from her, enraged, his murderous fury directed at Speke, his aura like the fires of hell, shocking her. Aidan and Blackwood were with him, but Allie barely saw them.

Royce glanced coldly at her.

As if on cue, Aidan ran to her, kneeling. Instantly Allie felt sick, but not from being strangled and choked. Her gaze locked with Royce's; she knew he was very, very angry with her. But she had to stop him from killing Speke, who might have information about Elasaid.

Aidan removed the rope, flinging it aside. "Yer bleedin'. Ye clawed yerself. Be still."

Allie tried to speak, to tell him to keep Speke alive, but it hurt to do so.

"Hush," Aidan said, encircling her throat with his hands. She started, stunned to feel his healing power entering her body, warming her throbbing neck, realigning her spine, and finally easing the terrible pounding in her skull. It felt so *good*.

But she couldn't stay still and her gaze lifted to Royce, who watched her now. Her heart thundered in response to the cold look in his eyes. She wanted to beg him to understand, but he turned away dismissively, lifting his hand, before she could try to use her voice.

Speke was flung across the wood again, into a tree, so hard she heard his bones crack.

She shoved Aidan aside, somehow standing. She tried to speak, but her throat hurt. "Royce, stop! He may know where Elasaid is!" she rasped.

Royce didn't look at her. His expression ruthless, he blasted Speke again, his energy lifting him high and sending him into another tree.

"Royce," Allie cried hoarsely. "Stop, please!"

Aidan said, beside her, "He canna hear ye." He touched her to restrain her.

She somehow glanced at Aidan and saw kindness and pity in his eyes, which she did not understand. "Stop him," she begged.

But Royce now lifted Speke and sent him whirling back, toward them. He crashed not far from where Allie stood with Aidan, his body broken and mangled. He would not live much longer.

But he was still very much alive. His red eyes were filled with fear. "I didn't…touch her…."

Allie shoved free of Aidan, running toward him. "Where is my mother? Where is Moffat keeping her? Where is Elasaid?" she cried.

Speke didn't look at her. He only had terrified eyes for Royce, who strode toward him. "Ye die," he said ruthlessly.

"No," Allie gasped. "Royce, I am begging you!"

But Royce ignored her, staring at Speke. And Allie saw the man's power, blacker than the night, spiral upward from the creature's body like a small cyclone. Aidan gripped her arm and Allie cried out in despair. The evil swirled upward into the skies and Speke lay sightless and dead.

"Royce," she whispered, choking on a sob.

Royce stood still, breathing hard. If he heard her, he gave no sign.

Aidan said quietly, "I lurked. He dinna ken where Elasaid is."

Allie heard him, but could not take her gaze from Royce. For she felt his fury escalate and his aura turned to flames. Like a forest fire out of control, it raged.

And then his aura contracted as he willed himself into a state of control.

He suddenly looked at her, his eyes silver and hot with restrained wrath.

She went still.

Aidan stepped in front of her. "Yer angry, Royce. But think. She's yer Innocent," he said tersely.

Royce didn't look away from her. "Dinna interfere, Aidan."

As afraid as she was, as tense and stiff, she managed to speak. "It's all right." Their gazes remained locked, his frighteningly hard. "We have to discuss this."

Royce gave her the coldest, most condescending look she'd ever received. "Talk?" He was scathing. "I dinna wish to speak with ye ever again."

Allie cringed. "Royce!"

"Ye broke yer word."

She tensed, her pulse hammering. Carefully, aware of how monumental this moment was for them, she breathed and said, "I promised to obey you—but you didn't make me promise not to trade myself for Elasaid."

His eyes widened. "Ye ken I would refuse a trade! I said many times I wouldna trade ye for yer mother. But ye stand before me an' claim ye dinna disobey?" His eyes blazed.

She inhaled. "Don't do this."

"We're finished." He turned and gestured furiously at Aidan. "Get her out o' my sight."

Aidan dragged her away.

WHEN ROYCE FINALLY returned to Blackwood Hall, it was close to dawn. Allie had sat in the hall, waiting for him, chilled by her fear. The moment he came in, she leapt to her feet. He didn't look at her, striding from the hall and upstairs.

She hugged herself. She hadn't meant to betray him— she had done what she thought right. Yet she had known he would think her agreeing to a trade, behind his back, a betrayal. But she hadn't imagined this kind of reaction—as if, in one instant, he could cut her out of his heart and his life without ever looking back.

And then she heard thunder booming.

It was directly above her and she jumped up, crying out, the thunder reverberating again from directly above her. Just as she wondered if they were in the midst of an earthquake and the castle walls were coming down, she felt his rage explode, turning into pain.

Allie ran up the stairs, hearing that terrible sound again. As she came to the small passage leading up to the tower, she realized that there wasn't a storm and there wasn't an earthquake. Stone was crashing down.

Aidan seized her from behind. "Ye'll nay go up unless ye wish to die!"

Allie turned and fought him. "He's hurt! He needs me!"

"He's in rage because o' what ye did."

Stone sheared off and crashed down. And she saw him vividly, as if she could see through the walls, breaking apart the window embrasures with his bare, bloody hands, heaving slabs of stone onto the floor. She leapt, facing Aidan, terrified for him. "Let me go to him! He'd never hurt me!"

Aidan's grasp tightened, becoming cruel. "He hates ye now."

Allie went still, staring at Aidan's cold, hard face. She realized he was angry with her, too. She watched Royce destroying the stone tower with energy blasts and his bare hands. "I did what I had to do—what I thought was right. Aidan, you of all men should understand!"

"I understand ye broke yer word."

She inhaled, trying to pull away from him. In the end, he was as medieval as Royce—as ruthless, as uncompromising. He let her go. Allie hesitated, because Royce remained in a furious fit, destroying the tower. "Don't leave him," Allie whispered, afraid he might hurt himself. She trembled, tears finally falling. "He will never forgive me, will he?"

"Ye crossed him," Aidan said. "He'll never forgive ye."

ALLIE WENT DOWN to the hall for breakfast, exhausted from a sleepless night. She hadn't lain down even for a few hours—she had been on her knees, praying for Royce, asking the gods to heal him now. All the while she had been acutely aware of his pain and rage. She had tried to communicate with him telepathically, but he hadn't tried to speak to her in return, not even once. His power had finally quieted, to seethe softly in the tower above the hall.

She stumbled into the hall. Soon, he would come out of the prison he had chosen for himself, and they would be face-to-face. And then what? He was dead set against her.

She would never forget the way he'd looked at and spoken to her last night. Surely, sooner or later, he would begin to understand why she'd done what she had. Surely his love for her would allow him to reason—even though he was the least reasonable man she knew.

It couldn't be over. He was the love of her life.

We're finished.

Allie trembled with dread as Aidan stepped inside. He didn't smile at her, and he looked tired. But then, he'd undoubtedly sat up for the rest of the night with Royce to make sure he didn't hurt himself. Eyeing her expression, he said, unsmiling, "I willna ask how ye slept."

She bowed her head, sitting stiffly on one of the benches at the table, her knees bruised from the hours spent kneeling on stone. Aidan was against her now, too, when he had fast become a treasured friend. "How could I sleep when Royce was so upset? I know you macho guys think if a woman does her own thing, if she acts independently, it means we don't love you. But you are so wrong."

Aidan gave her a long look. "I ken ye love him an' ye always will." He sat and poured mead into a cup and drained it before glancing at her. "Blackwood has gone to the town of Moffat. A spy has sent him word he wishes to meet. Mayhap there's news o' Elasaid."

Allie started. "Any news would be great."

A housemaid stepped into the hall. "My lord, my lady?"

Aidan glanced up, noted that she was young and blond, and sent her an automatic smile. "Aye?"

"Kenneth from the village has come to the kitchens. His wife is very ill an' he has heard Lady Allie is a Healer. I told him I heard no such thing, but he insisted I come to you an' ask if she can attend his wife." The blonde shifted nervously.

Allie stood, not having to think about it. "Of course I'll help."

Aidan stared thoughtfully. "An' how would the villager ken that Blackwood's guest heals?"

"I don't know, my lord."

"It doesn't matter," Allie said. "If someone is ill, I have to heal them. I took my own vows, Aidan."

Aidan stood, but glanced upward in the direction of the tower room where Royce had spent the night. "He broke down an entire wall. Blackwood is furious."

Allie hated the idea of leaving Royce alone, even though he was far calmer. "You should stay with him. I can take an escort of knights to the village. I won't be long." She didn't think she needed much of an escort, as the village was about five minutes on foot from the moat. On the other hand, it couldn't hurt to play it safe.

Aidan appeared relieved. "I dinna think it wise to leave him. He's quiet now, but I have never seen him so enraged. I wish to stay with him."

Allie took a long glance at his handsome profile. He was a medieval playboy, with all the charm a man could possibly have, but he was as loyal as a man could be toward Royce. Last night had shown her that. "Thank you."

He finally smiled as he walked with her to the front door. "I'm yer Knight of Swords, lass. I haven't forgotten."

He had forgiven her! Allie was relieved. She did not want to lose his friendship, not now, not ever. Impulsively she faced him so they halted. "I wish I could undo what happened last night. I wish I had understood better that the standards I live by are not valid here, in this world, for men like you and Royce. I wish I hadn't gone behind Royce's back!"

Aidan's gaze was searching. "We live by our word, Lady Allie."

There was no possible response to make to that.

He guided her outside. Allie found herself in the midst of six English knights. They were clad from head to toe in armor, and even with their visors up, they looked like mean fighting machines. She hadn't expected a fully armored escort.

She had just mounted a small gray palfrey when she felt Royce's power. She tensed and glanced up at the tower.

Instantly she saw Royce standing at the embrasure, staring toward her. Her heart turned over with so much love and fear, and real, clawing despair. *Don't do this,* she thought silently, begging him now. *Don't turn away from me. I love you!*

He vanished from the window.

She inhaled, because no answer could be more eloquent. She hadn't felt any emotion at all—not anger, not pain, not even the flicker of male desire. He was closing himself off from her completely.

"Godspeed, until the afternoon, then," Aidan said. He nodded at the foremost knight, and the small retinue moved out.

Shaken, Allie let her mare follow the chargers, glancing worriedly back at the tower. Royce remained gone from her sight.

A moment later, they were trotting over the drawbridge, the first wattle huts ahead. Children appeared, dancing about the edge of the road, calling out to the knights.

Allie couldn't smile. If Royce remained set against her, she might never smile again.

They halted before one of the huts, a gray-haired man pacing before the doorway. Allie slid down from her mare, trying to focus on the task at hand. Instead all she could think of was Royce and how he was determined to blame her for a betrayal she had not committed.

"Lady, thank ye fer coming," Kenneth cried, his face ashen with fear and worry.

Allie shoved all thoughts of Royce aside. "It's my pleasure." She touched him and this time smiled with warmth that she meant. "Don't fear. Your wife will be fine."

His color became even paler.

Allie glanced into the dark interior of the hut, but saw nothing but shadows. She became aware of a woman's suffering. It was slight, and blended with a small pain. The woman was hardly ill at all.

"I'll only be a moment," she told her escort. She smiled and faced the husband. "Please wait outside."

He nodded, ghostly white now, shaking.

"She will be fine," Allie said, and she strode across the dirt yard and entered the hut.

It was dank and dark inside. Smoke made it difficult to breathe. It took her a moment to adjust her eyesight to the darkness. Then she saw the woman, lying on the floor, her hands and legs bound.

Evil began swiftly filling the hut.

Allie realized it was a trap. The woman wasn't sick—she'd been hurt and tied, so Allie would feel her suffering. The woman was *bait*.

Kenneth wasn't afraid for his wife—he was afraid of the lord of darkness.

Allie turned to flee.

Moffat materialized before her, smiling.

She tried to duck, too late.

He seized her—and as they were hurled through mud and wattle, past stars, she screamed for Royce.

CHAPTER SEVENTEEN

HE DID NOT KNOW WHERE Ailios was going with Blackwood's knights. It was not his affair, and he reminded himself that he did not care—that he would never care again. Aidan had remained behind, and of course, he knew why. Still, Aidan should not have let her go.

The urge came to leave his prison and find her and protect her. Then it vanished.

Aidan could protect her now.

Aidan could *have* her now.

He felt sick at the thought. He had spent the entire night raging at Ailios for her treachery, at himself for his folly and at the gods for their capricious ways. He had torn a dozen stone blocks from the walls, smashing them into shards in sheer frustration, haunted by her smile, her laughter, the light of joy that was so often on her face and in her eyes.

How could she have betrayed him?

He had admitted that he cared!

The chamber was destroyed. The round room was littered with broken blocks of stone and gravel, filled with dust. Two of the walls were in ruins. He was ill in his heart, in his soul.

He saw Ailios healing the boy as they pulled him from the rockslide; he saw her healing old Coinneach; he saw her as she lay beneath him, gasping with pleasure and weeping with rapture.

And he saw Aidan with her in his bed, the two of them in the throes of the same damned rapture.

He roared and wrenched another stone block from the wall in more frustration, more fury, not caring that his hands were raw. *He would kill Aidan if he took her to bed.*

He leaned against the broken wall, heard himself choke on a single sob. He hadn't shed a tear since he was a boy of four or five. But his chest pained him terribly, and it was unlike anything he'd ever experienced in his life. He had never felt this kind of anguish before. *What was happening to him?*

She had reduced him to this pathetic moment, where he wept over the personal loss of a woman. Royce trembled. He was a Master, committed to his vows and the Code until he died. She was unimportant! He had a duty to her, as every Master did. He must forget their brief, forbidden love affair.

But how would he forget her laughter and her joy, her kindness and her grace?

He sank to the pitted stone floor amidst boulders and rocks. There, he rubbed his face, his eyes. He must think like a soldier, not a fool. This was for the best. He had known all along that she threatened his vows. The wrenching conflict in his mind and heart continued to prove how dangerous she was. His heart shrieked at him in protest. If he heeded it, he might listen to what she had to say.

She had betrayed him.

He could never forgive such disloyalty and he would never trust her again.

The pain in his heart, his entire being, increased. He felt crushed by its weight. Worse, the sun that had begun to shine in his life was gone. It would never shine again. He was going to spend the next six hundred years in thick fog and black clouds, lost and alone.

She was all that was good in this world.

She would forgive him if their roles were reversed.

Shaken, he strode to the broken window opening and stared out, but she was gone and out of sight now. He was relieved; he was disappointed. He should go downstairs and ask Aidan where she had gone and why. That much he could do.

He fought the urge. He would pretend he didn't know she had left Blackwood; it was not his affair, not ever again.

Royce!

Her scream of terror pierced through the tower room as if she stood beside him. He jerked, alert and alarmed.

She screamed again.

And he shoved all emotion aside. He focused his every sense upon her—and knew Moffat had captured her at last.

THIS TIME, as she lay on cold stone, the pain of the leap finally subsiding, she was nauseous. She clawed the floor as the torment dulled to an intense soreness in her entire body. Leaping again, so soon, had hurt more than ever and she felt certain she would not be able to do so in the near future. But she'd worry about that later. Where was Moffat?

He no longer held her. Afraid to move, she lay impossibly still, straining to sense him. As she focused, she became aware of how dank it was around her, the stale odor of refuse assailing her now. Thick smoke hung in the room, making it almost impossible to breathe. Where was she?

Moffat was not present. Evil was everywhere, encircling the place where she had landed, and Allie guessed she was within a perimeter guarded by Moffat's human soldiers. And she was not alone.

A woman was present, just a short distance away. Allie reeled, not from the pain in her battered body, but from her fear and despair.

Cautiously, alarmed, Allie opened her eyes.

The room was dark and filled with shadows. The floor she lay on wasn't stone—it was rough, splintered wood. A small fire burned in a very rustic stone hearth. Allie sat up, her gaze moving to the form wrapped in the blanket there.

The woman stared back at her, unmoving. Her eyes were huge in her pale face.

Allie took in her long tangled hair, and the dark bruise on her cheek. Gaunt hollows were beneath her eyes. But nothing compared to the woman's emotional torment. Her heart swelled with compassion for her.

But she didn't go to her yet. Allie glanced quickly around the rectangular room, noting a table, a bench and that the floor was covered with straw, most of it dirty. Her gaze moved to the closed wooden plank door, and then to the shuttered windows on each side of it.

"Where am I?" she said roughly, hoping that the woman spoke English.

She did. "Eoradh."

"Where is that?"

"The far north."

Allie tested her body and stood. Her limbs trembled, weak from the leap through time. She hoped her healing powers were unaffected by the strain of time travel. "Have you seen Moffat?"

"I dinna ken Moffat."

The woman was clearly Scot, although her accent was different from Royce's and everyone else she'd met so far in the Highlands. While her impulse was to rush to her and heal her, Allie walked quickly to the door. As she reached for it, the woman said, "T' is bolted from without. And there are guards everywhere."

Allie tested it anyway. The woman was right; it was

securely locked. She tried both shutters, but they were locked, as well. Where the hell was Moffat? And why had he taken her to this primitive hut in the far north?

She turned and walked closer to the fire. "Are you a prisoner, too?"

The woman laughed bitterly and pushed the blanket aside. She was naked beneath, her hands and legs bound, and she had been beaten.

Allie tensed in sheer dismay at the sight of the cruelty she'd suffered. But the firelight now played over the woman, and Allie was close enough to note that her hair was a mass of dirty titian curls. And the name formed swiftly in her mind—Brigdhe.

Brigdhe had been captured and tortured.

No, it was impossible, she thought with some panic. Moffat couldn't be so clever and so cruel to do this to Royce again.

"I can heal your pain," Allie said softly. "May I?"

The woman's eyes were wary. "Why would you do so?"

"Because I am a Healer."

The woman stared, considering her words, and finally she nodded.

Allie knelt beside her, showering her with a strong, healing white light. The woman did not have major injuries, but she'd been beaten and raped. As Allie felt her physical pain recede, she focused on the terrible anguish in her heart. She dared and sent a white light there, as well.

The woman pulled the blanket up, her eyes wide, brighter now. "You have a great magic," she gasped. "My body no longer hurts."

"Are you Brigdhe?" she whispered, meeting her blue gaze.

She started. "Aye. How do ye ken?"

Allie hesitated. "I am a friend of your husband's."

Brigdhe's face tightened. Her expression was hard to decipher—Allie decided it was partly anguish and partly anger.

"He will rescue you," Allie cried, touching her reassuringly. "I am certain."

Brigdhe hugged herself. "I have been here for days and days. At first, I *knew* he would come. But he didn't come for me. And day after day, Kael did as he pleased, cruelly, openly telling me how he wished to hurt Ruari. Now I know how powerful Kael is. Ruari may never find me, and if he does, he will die. I will grow old in this dungeon. I will grow old being raped and beaten. And why? Why? Because Kale hates my husband. He uses me to torment Ruari. I am naught but a pawn in the affairs of men!"

"No, Ruari will find you! He will take you from this place, and Kael will die," Allie said fiercely. "You will be freed!"

Brigdhe looked away, crying. The torment in her heart hadn't eased. Allie knew she didn't just cry with hopelessness, but she wept for the loss of her love for the man she had married.

She had been told too many times to count that the past couldn't be changed. But she had to try. For if Brigdhe could forgive Royce when he rescued her, he would not have to suffer the burden of guilt for so many centuries. "This isn't Royce's—Ruari's—fault," Allie said, taking her hands. "He loves you. He would die for you. Your disappearance is killing him. Please, don't blame him."

Brigdhe tore her hands away. "Are you in love with him?" she cried.

Allie hesitated.

Brigdhe's eyes widened. "Are you lovers?" She was both shocked and accusing.

"No!" For they were certainly not lovers now, in this time.

Brigdhe was angry again, and that was a good sign. "Leave me alone," Brigdhe said bitterly. "If Ruari does come, you are welcome to him. If I ever escape this hell, I will never return to him as his wife."

"He loves you so," Allie tried again. "Don't lose hope— don't let go of your love for him. Please, try to hear what I am saying. If anyone is to blame, it is Kael."

Brigdhe shook her head and as she did so, they both heard the bolt outside the door being lifted. Brigdhe jerked up the blanket, consumed with so much fear that Allie felt it wash over her. Anger arose. She stood, wishing she had a weapon. Somehow she had to defend Royce's wife from his demonic enemy.

The door opened and Moffat stepped inside, smiling. "Hallo a Ailios."

It was hard to think. Clearly this was the sixth century. A very young Royce would soon appear to vanquish Kael and free his wife. Moffat had captured her and brought her to this terrible time and place. Why?

And what would happen when "Ruari" appeared to rescue Brigdhe? Could the past be rewritten after all? She was terrified Royce might die when he was only twenty-three years old.

Allie realized she was defensively hugging herself and she dropped her arms and straightened her posture. "We agreed to a trade," she said coldly. "Where is my mother?"

Moffat grinned at her. "Your mother is dead."

Allie felt like clawing his eyes out. "No, she's not. She's alive!"

"I sent you every thought you had of her caged and hurt," Moffat said with gleaming eyes. "In truth, I have never met the great Elasaid. I was born many years after the massacre of her family at Blayde."

She had been duped, Allie thought furiously. Royce had been right—her mother was dead and Moffat had tricked her. Elasaid had been trying to warn her not to fall for such treachery from the afterlife. "I won't heal for you."

"Really?" He smiled widely. "I have promised Kael you'd heal his brother, who is dying. In return, he has allowed me to keep you here—with her." He gestured indifferently at Brigdhe, who huddled beneath the blanket, listening to them. "It is in your best interest to heal Kael's brother—and wait for Royce to arrive." He laughed then, triumphant.

Allie stiffened with dread. In that moment, she had the dreadful comprehension that Moffat didn't want her—that this was a trap and it was set for Royce.

Moffat was reading her mind, because he said, "Aye, beauty. T'is a trap and you are the bait."

ROYCE TENSED in the high tower at Blackwood Hall, filled with alarm and sick with fear. In that moment, every memory he'd ever had of what Kael had done to Brigdhe filled his mind, paralyzing him. Moffat would use Ailios to torment him as Kael had used his wife, he had no doubt—unless he could save her in time. It was the past repeating itself. It was his worst nightmare come true, his most ancient fear rekindled and reborn.

Now, he heard nothing but the wind whispering in the trees outside. But he had heard her calling him.

He fought the gut-wrenching fear. Instead his mind calmed and he readied for the battle of good and evil that was to come. A terrible savagery stole over him. This time, Moffat had dared too much and gone too far. He would suffer a horrendous death. And Royce listened to the universe.

At first, he heard nothing but the vast, eternal silence. He strained and remained intently focused. A ripple went through the eons of time

He breathed hard and refocused. And slowly, the tormented passions of humanity reached out to him from the many ages of time. First he felt fear, and then waves of extreme anger and hatred, followed by lust, sorrow, vengeance, jealousy…

He breathed hard again. Somehow he was tapping into the emotions of too many victims to count. He did not want to feel the horrors of a thousand strangers, unjustly destroyed by demonic hands or the capricious will of Fate. There was only one person he wished to find. Sweat poured down his body in streams.

The roiling mass of turbulent human emotion receded. The vast silence of eternity came yet again.

And then he felt a vague ripple of fear, followed by the nearly intangible rush of anger.

It was Ailios. He had little doubt. He closed his eyes, controlling his breathing, his mind. *Tell me where you are.*

At first there was no answer. The fragile sense of her fear and anger vanished. His heart wanted to panic. He would not let it do so. And then her fear slithered through him, intensified, and this time it was followed by the heavy weight of evil.

Royce straightened. He knew without a doubt that he had found her and she was in Moffat's control. But where were they?

Ailios, hear me. Where are you?

There was no answer, although he waited hours for her to respond. All the while, he strained to sense her again. And when he did, the anger was gone; there was only fear and alarm. *Ailios, feel me, hear me. Where are you?*

It remained an incredible feat to feel her, and that told him that she was far away, in another time. How would he find her? She could be anywhere....

He was ready to give up. She was too far away for him to contact her with telepathy. He had to make contact with Moffat. He would offer a trade—himself for Ailios. And then he must pray that Moffat wanted him, not Ailios.

He whirled to go to the door and came face-to-face with Elasaid.

Royce froze. Her shimmering face was strained with worry. He hesitated and instinctively reached out to touch her, certain she was a ghost. "Elasaid?" His hand drifted through her shape and form, for she was just an image etched onto the air.

She said, "He has taken her to Eoradh."

He was shocked. Moffat had taken her back in time to the place where Brigdhe was imprisoned. He could barely assimilate what this meant. He was about to leap when she seized his wrist. She had no corporeal form, but he felt her touch, like the caress of a cool breeze on a chill winter night.

"The gods bless you, Ruari. Go with caution into your enemy's trap."

SHE WAS BAIT.

"You're frightened for your lover," Moffat murmured. "Well, I cannot reassure you."

Allie felt her heart hammering in alarm. "Why bother with such an elaborate trap? Why lure him here to this time? Royce dies in 2007. You murder him."

Moffat's brows lifted in surprise. "Is that a ruse on your part, Lady Ailios?"

He didn't know, Allie thought, her heart jackhammering. And that meant that a modern-day Moffat had murdered the modern-day Royce. *It meant that they must kill him now and forever remove the menace he posed to them.*

He seized her and pulled her close. "Ah, well, it doesn't matter. He murdered my favorite lover. Ever since, I have been planning his destruction. My trap is perfect now. I will not sit by and let him live after what he has taken from me." Moffat let her go.

Allie backed away, rubbing her bruised arm. This was a burning vengeance, a crime of passion.

"He hates me. He won't come."

Moffat gave her a long look. "Oh, he'll come."

Allie didn't bother to ask why he'd chosen this time and place. She already knew. He wanted to emotionally destroy Royce. He would be devastated to return here, to see his wife again, this way, in Moffat's hands. And she knew Moffat was right.

Royce would never leave her here. Their affair might be over, but he would rescue her. He would die to do so.

She was so afraid for Royce. She did not like Moffat being there with Kael, allied against Royce. She didn't have to understand the rules of the universe to know that if young Royce failed to destroy Kael, Royce would be killed. But everyone kept insisting the past could not be changed. She prayed now that it was written in stone.

"Let us go."

Allie stiffened. "Go where?"

"I promised Kael you'd heal his brother. I can hardly walk into another man's home and take it over for myself." He took her arm. "Not even in this primitive time."

Allie twisted to free herself, but to no avail. "I am not healing a demon!"

He mocked, "You gave me your word."

"I lied," she snarled at him.

"Then I will encourage Kael to spend the day with Brigdhe. You've healed her—she won't be healed when he is through."

Allie cried out. But she met his demonic gaze, already knowing he would love to sick Kael on the injured woman. "Fine. Take me to him."

He laughed at her and shoved her outside.

Allie saw that they were in a very primitive wood fort. High wooden stockade fencing surrounded the interior courtyard, a wooden watchtower on each corner. The building she had just left was the largest structure within the fort; the rest of the buildings were mere huts.

Many armed men were on the walls, wearing leather helmets and carrying leather shields. Others sat outside a group of huts, drinking and gambling. Everyone was human—and evil. She was certain the only Innocent ones in the fortress were her and Brigdhe.

A huge dark man hurried toward them. He was as evil as Moffat; a true demon from the highest level. Usually the highest demons had the appearance of golden male angels, but not this one. He was as ugly as Moffat was beautiful. Allie cringed. She was in the hands of two of the most powerful demons she had ever encountered.

His gaze swept her with demonic interest. "Bring her," he ordered Moffat. He was barefoot, clad in a roughly woven tunic, a wool mantle over his shoulders, and he made Moffat, in his fine velvet robes and pointy shoes, seem the epitome of elegance.

Allie felt even sicker than before. She was about to defy her very Fate by healing a demon. It was unbelievable, but she had to spare Brigdhe any more pain.

Moffat shoved her forward and she followed Kael into another hut. Instantly she sensed death.

Kael looked at her with pure malice. "Heal my brother."

Allie walked past him, the dying demon's aura thick with the blood of his innocent victims. He was pretty and golden, like Moffat, and he looked at her with his red eyes as she knelt, no fervor present. He had been stabbed dozens of times in a battle, and any one of his wounds would have killed a mortal man instantly. But he was a demon and he still lived. Still, he had lost too much blood, and a raging infection had set in. He would die if not healed.

Allie couldn't breathe. This man had taken hundreds of Innocent lives, enjoying every sadistic moment of seduction, pleasure, torture and rape. She felt all of their souls, crying out for justice—begging her to desist. She couldn't do this.

Moffat knelt over her, so close his body spooned hers, his thick manhood a terrible and threatening presence against her back. "Heal him. Otherwise, while Kael enjoys the woman inside, I'll show you how much you've been missing while in Royce's bed."

Allie bit her lip. She hardly cared about herself, but she did care about Brigdhe. She lifted her hand, and without enthusiasm, reached for her white light. To her surprise, it eluded her grasp.

She reached more determinedly for it. There was only a thread to seize.

She seized the fragile wave and showered it at the demon. But she had nothing in her hand but air.

Her powers had been compromised by the leap, or the Ancients were near, refusing to allow her to heal their mortal enemy.

She tensed, trying to feel any holy presence within the general area, and she was not surprised to feel grace and majesty nearby.

"What happens?" Kael asked, interrupting her. The demon's eyes were closed, his face white. "He still dies!"

Allie hesitated, knowing she was in grave straits. "I don't have the power," Allie tried. "I lost it during the leap."

Moffat hauled her cruelly to her feet. "You will pay for this!"

"The gods won't let me heal a demon!" she shouted in desperation.

Kael knelt over his brother. "He breathes, but barely! Make the bitch heal!"

"I am warning you," Moffat snarled, his face so close to hers his breath feathered her cheek.

"There is nothing in me," Allie cried. "My powers are gone."

Moffat pulled her from the hut. He let her go and she stumbled. "Don't take this out on Brigdhe," she begged. Fear arose and consumed her. Could she somehow find the courage to sacrifice herself for the other woman? "Do with me as you will…but leave that poor woman alone."

"You're about to pay a terrible price for your refusal," he said softly, furiously. "I will enjoy hurting you."

Her fear escalated. She didn't want to die, but maybe death would be preferable to what Moffat would do to her. Allie told herself she must survive. Royce needed her—the world needed her. *Royce, where are you? I am in so much trouble!*

And suddenly she thought she felt him, somewhere far away, listening to her.

Royce?

Suddenly Moffat stiffened, his head up, as if he scented Royce, too.

Allie wet her lips, praying. She did not want Royce walking blindly into Moffat's trap. They needed the Ancients' help. Weren't the gods stronger in this time? "I am glad the gods wouldn't let me heal that bastard," she said with heat, in an attempt to distract Moffat.

"Be silent." He remained poised like a hunting hound sniffing the night. Then he finally looked at her, emanating a terrible tension. "He comes, Ailios."

She trembled and cried, "What do you intend?"

"After I am done with Royce, I will bend you to my will—and enjoy doing so. You had better beg the gods to return your powers to you." He jerked on her and hauled her roughly back to the building where Brigdhe was imprisoned.

Moffat shoved her into the hut. She tripped and almost fell, but he caught her and dragged her across the room. "What are you doing?" she cried in alarm.

He seized a trapdoor she hadn't noticed, set into the floor, and flung it open. Then he pushed her over the edge.

Allie fell into cold, wet dirt.

Above her, Moffat laughed and slammed the trapdoor closed.

And that was when she felt something hot, dry and scaly slither over her hand.

She became still.

The snake hissed.

Slowly Allie turned her head, adjusting her eyes to the darkness. And when she could see, she met dozens of small, glittering eyes. Dozens of snakes writhed in a mass just feet from where she lay, hissing and seething, angry at the invasion of their den.

Raw terror began.

Royce, help me!

CHAPTER EIGHTEEN

THE MOMENT HIS POWERS returned to him, he felt her.

Royce sat up. He was in the woods on the same ridge where he'd last been when he'd come to remind himself of Brigdhe's pain. He froze. Ailios's terror rolled through him in chilling, gut-wrenching waves.

She was never afraid.

He leapt to his feet and heard her.

Royce.

He couldn't imagine what was being done to her. The Code no longer mattered. He wasn't sure exactly when his younger self would appear, and he didn't care. Before Ruari arrived, while he still had power, he was going to rescue Ailios and destroy Moffat once and for all.

He started down the ridge, focusing on her, savagely determined. Her image formed in his mind. She was pale with fear, as she crouched in a black hole. *She had been put in a pit.*

He halted, focusing with all of his being, and it took him but a moment to realize she was alone. Moffat wasn't there.

He was so relieved. He had been terrified that Moffat or Kael was raping and torturing her. But now, he could not understand her terror. Ailios wasn't afraid of the dark and he was fairly certain being in a pit wouldn't frighten her, either. He reached out to her. *I'm here. What frightens ye?*

There was no reply.

He strained to see.

Instead he heard her weeping.

He started to rush down the ridge. Her image came another time, as forcefully. She crouched against an earthen wall, and he saw the snakes seething about her feet.

Royce.

She'd been put in a pit with snakes. And in that moment, a shocking memory returned, a memory he hadn't recalled in over eight hundred years. When he had vanquished Kael and rescued Brigdhe, he'd heard a woman crying out to him. He'd tried to find her, but failed.

In that exact instant, he remembered it as if it were but yesterday. He recalled leaping into a pit filled with snakes, only to find it empty.

Yet he'd heard her calling to him.

He'd heard Ailios through the centuries.

Royce reached the tree line, so enraged he could barely see. Ahead lay Eoradh, and he threw all of his power at the huge front gates. Nothing happened.

In dismay he turned and saw Ruari coming down the hill, intent on rescuing his wife. Furious, he turned back and blasted the front gates again. They did not even shudder.

His power was gone, taken by the holy laws of the universe, and he roared in rage. Ailios needed him, but he was powerless to help her. Still, damn the Code now! He'd free her as an average man would with ordinary human power. There was nothing ordinary about his will.

Royce, help me.

He went still, filled with a sense of helpless rage. How could he get past the archers on the walls without his powers? And even if he did, how could he get past the giants with their lances?

Ruari had reached the front gates and Royce thought he faltered, as if hearing Ailios, too. But then Ruari wrested them off their hinges, flinging the huge doors aside. The barrage of arrows began.

Ailios needed him *now*. He could not stand aside. He was about to run forward, behind Ruari, when he saw Moffat standing in the courtyard.

The deamhan was grinning, waiting for him.

This was Moffat's plan.

Moffat had lured him here so he would be powerless, so he could be destroyed.

And then he would mercilessly use Ailios for his own demonic ends.

His mind raced. He would gladly die if he could free her. But dying and leaving her to Moffat served no one, not even Ailios. And in that moment, he knew he needed Ruari to rescue her. Raw frustration, the rage of sheer helplessness, overcame him.

Ailios needed him, but now, he had to depend on Ruari to hear and heed her cries.

ALLIE HAD MANAGED to finally calm herself. She had done so with prayer. In fact, she felt certain she was not alone now. One of the Ancients was nearby and he was most definitely male. But even that could not truly comfort her. She was acutely aware that the snakes were very close to her sandal-clad feet, and she remained frozen, her back digging into the earthen wall. If there was any one thing she despised and truly feared, it was snakes—even the nonpoisonous ones.

Where was Royce?

And if he did come, what did Moffat plan?

She didn't dare move. The mass of snakes continued to writhe not far from her feet.

She felt the majestic presence hovering near her somehow increase. The air seemed to caress her skin. Some of the chill in her gut, her bones, receded.

And she heard men shouting.

Allie was afraid to focus on what was occurring above her, afraid to take her eyes from the snakes. But she had to know what was happening, and she tried to listen, to feel.

The shouts were faint and they were cries of alarm.

She felt pain.

She jerked, finally forgetting the snakes, worried about Brigdhe. But instantly she realized that men were being wounded and dying. A violent battle was in progress. Her heart leapt with hope. Had Royce come? If he was above, why couldn't she feel him?

She now closed her eyes, pushing her fear of the snakes aside. She strained. *Royce? Are you there? Please, tell me!*

In reply, there was only the pain and cries of the wounded and dying.

And then she thought she felt him.

She felt a vague ripple of his power, but it wasn't the huge power of a Master who had mastered his karma long ago. It was uncertain, raw and perhaps even new.

It couldn't be Royce and tears of dismay fell.

A snake hissed, dangerously near her right foot.

Allie didn't even cry out. She met the blazing eyes of the serpent as it coiled and began lifting its head. Its eyes seemed demonic. She sensed it was about to strike and she prayed the creature was not possessed.

But it boldly detached itself from the writhing mass, and seemed intent on her. Fear clawed at her. She stared at the glowing eyes of the serpent.

It hissed, its tongue flicking out.

Allie gasped. She was the granddaughter of a god. If ever she could cast a spell, it was now.

"Gods! Peaceful and quiet," she breathed. "So peaceful and so quiet, now serpent lie still, peaceful and quiet, so peaceful and so quiet, now serpent at rest, no battle here, no one to kill."

The head began lifting higher, as if to strike, and its eyes gleamed.

"Serpent lie still…peaceful and quiet," she whispered, her lips feeling as if they'd turned to wood. "Ancients, please, harken. Lug, greatest of all Ancients, harken."

For one more moment, the snake stared with almost human hatred at her, and then it recoiled and lay still.

Allie almost collapsed, and only the snake lying inches from her toes prevented her from doing so.

AS HE RUSHED THE FORT, the horns began blowing. He tried to use his new powers to sense Brigdhe, but he could not feel her presence, even though he knew she was within.

Royce, help me.

Almost at the barred gates, Ruari faltered, certain he had heard a woman's cries for help—a woman calling him by his English name. Did his mind play tricks with him now?

He hesitated. In spite of the men now shouting in alarm from the watchtowers, he sensed the presence of a woman who was not his wife. She was so afraid.

Was this his imagination? If not, what did it mean?

Arrows began hailing around him. Coming to his senses, he tore the barred doors from their hinges, relishing his new power, throwing them aside. An arrow stung him, another went deeper; he pulled them out, feeling no pain. He drew his sword and rushed into the fort. Instantly he saw a deam-

han clad in long, elegant robes, far finer than any he had ever
seen, grinning at him. His evil was huge and dark.

Giants began rushing from the huts, spears aloft. Ruari
wanted to rush the hall, but he veered his course, intending
to dispatch the golden deamhan first. Before he could take
a stride in his direction, the deamhan vanished.

Which was just fine; he would hunt him later. He turned
to the giants, and as they threw their spears at him, he tried
his power, blasting them with it. The giants fell back as if
pushed by huge winds, their spears falling.

Royce? Are you there? Please, tell me.

He was shocked to hear the woman crying for him again.

One of the giants stood, lunging for him with his studded
club, and the blow tore the skin from his arm. He took the
giant's head with a single thrust of his sword, realizing he
must not heed this strange woman. Perhaps she was a deamhan, intending to soften him so the enemy might destroy him.

He lunged up the steps and into the darkened hall where
Kael waited, grinning evilly at him.

And even as he saw Brigdhe, horror arising at the sight
of her naked body, half covered by a blanket, he felt another
power present with them.

It was pure and bright and light, feminine and alluring.

It was a power beckoning him. Confused, he looked
around to espy another woman.

The blow took him by surprise, sending him flying
through the air. He landed hard on his back by the door, but
did not drop his sword. And as Kael's sword descended, his
own weapon yielded uselessly and Kael's blade rent his
shoulder, all the way through muscle and bone.

He knew if he let the ghost-woman distract him another
time, he might very well die. A terrible battle began, in
which there would be but one victor. He rolled away as

Kael blasted him with more energy, the second blow as stunning as the first. Pushed against the wall, he felt Kael's sword coming, and this time, he struck viciously upward and steel met steel. Metal screeched, rang. He leapt to his feet, bleeding heavily but in no pain.

He was hurled backward into the wall again. As he crashed there, he gathered his wits at last. For now, there was only him and Kael—the deamhan who had tortured his bride.

"A Brigdhe," he roared. And he struck at Kael with all the power he had.

Kael was hurled backward across the entire hall. He landed not far from Brigdhe. Ruari pursued. As Kael rose, he struck hard and deep into the deamhan's inhuman heart.

Brigdhe screamed.

Savagely triumphant, he dropped the sword, lifted Kael by his neck with his two hands, and he snapped it easily, cruelly, in two.

His head hanging uselessly, Kale snarled at him. "Your suffering just begins." His red eyes ceased glowing, becoming lifeless.

He could not understand the words and did not even care to. A terrible pain finally arising in his shoulder, he ran to his wife. But now, the demonic evil gone from the hall, he became aware of the pure power that was taking over the space within the four walls. He still did not understand it, but it was tangible and intense, somehow beckoning. It somehow pulled at him; he wanted to turn and discover it…her.

Royce.

He turned all of his attention on his wife. *Brigdhe* needed him, not the ghost-woman. She had needed him for days and he had failed to rescue her until now. He had failed in his duty to his wife. Nothing was as reprehensible. She sat with her back to the wall, and when he knelt, she recoiled. He stopped himself from reaching for her. She cried, "Don't touch me!"

Now wary, he eased back. Of course she was frightened still. "T'is over now. I'll take ye far from here," he said.

"No."

He tensed, searching her eyes, but she wouldn't look at him now. "I'm sorry, Brigdhe," he said grimly, meaning his every word. "I will find a way to make ye forget this terrible time."

"Sorry?" Her tone was scathing and hatred filled her eyes. "Get away from me. He did this to me because of *you.* Stay away from me!"

Her words delivered the blow that Kael had not been able to wield. He tried to breathe and failed. *She was right.* Kael had used his bride against him. He had vowed to protect Innocence, but he hadn't even been able to protect his own wife. Being a Master was now irrelevant; what kind of man did that make him? Guilt came, crushing him with its terrible weight. *He had done this to her.*

In that instant, his marriage ended. Brigdhe must never be endangered by him again. He did not blame her for hating him; if he dared to think upon it, he might realize he hated himself, too.

"Can ye stand?" he asked roughly. He refused to tolerate any sorrow now. He would only allow the guilt.

"Dinna think to help me now," she cried furiously.

He stood and stepped aside, allowing Brogan, who had just appeared, to lift her and carry her from the hall. He followed them, but only to the door, and stared after them. Although he was determined to be a soldier, shame began and joined the festering guilt. How could he make this up to her? He watched Elasaid kneel beside Brigdhe, Brogan having placed her on a pallet on the ground. Reassured she would be well cared for, he slowly turned to the empty hall.

Royce. Help me. Please.

His eyes went wide. He'd heard the woman as clear as day. Now that the battle was over, Brigdhe safe at last and being attended, he felt her wrenching fear.

My spell won't last much longer.

His eyes widened. It was as if she was speaking to him directly. Was she a witch?

"Ruari," MacNeil said tersely, his tone one of command.

Ruari was certain he was in for a severe set-down, as he had been warned—ordered—not to hunt Kael alone. "Nay now," he said, not even looking at him. He scanned the hall slowly, looking into every shadowed corner. "Did ye hear the woman?"

"Aye."

And he saw a trapdoor set in the floor. He rushed to the door and lifted it, hearing the hissing of snakes. "Get me a torch!" he called.

MacNeil ran outside.

Ruari didn't wait; he leapt down into the black hole. The woman's fear consumed him, and with no difficulty, he turned and found her huddled against one earthen wall.

"Royce!" she cried.

Before he took a step toward her, she flung herself into his arms.

He did not move, shocked by the feeling of her small, soft body in his arms. He did not even know what this woman looked like and he wanted her instantly, with a terrible urgency. Something was terribly familiar, yet he knew he'd never met—or held—this woman before.

She was a Healer. In spite of her fear, he could identify the strong healing force of her power.

She clung, shaking, and whispered, "The snakes."

He realized they were seething about his bare feet—and hers. He held her close with one arm and reached up. "MacNeil?"

MacNeil handed him a burning torch. Ruari took it, waving the torch, scattering the snakes away from their feet. Then he looked at her.

His heart vanished. The loveliest woman he had ever seen smiled at him, and love was shining in her dark eyes. *She loved him.* What was this?

He was almost certain he knew her; still, if they'd met, he'd have taken her as a lover, and he knew he had never had her in his bed. As his shock began to fade, something primitive, possessive and triumphant arose, while blood rushed into his loins. He smiled back at her.

Her eyes widened. "Oh," she breathed as if she'd just made her own discovery.

He didn't understand. "Let me get ye up."

"You're not my Royce," she said, her eyes now huge.

Again, her meaning was so strange. Did she belong to someone else? He did not care. Soon she would find out that he was very different from other men, but not strange or exotic. He waved the torch at the snakes again, and then laid it carefully down. He grasped her by her tiny waist and handed her up to MacNeil. A moment later, he gave MacNeil his hand and was hauled upward to stand beside the small woman and the Master. He stepped closer to her, so Mac-Neil would understand he would not be allowed to poach.

"Are ye hurt?" he asked her. Real concern arose. "Did Kael touch ye?"

She shook her head. "No." She glanced at MacNeil. "Where is Moffat?"

"I dinna ken Moffat."

She tensed, paling. "Is Kael dead? Is Brigdhe okay?"

Her speech was odd—she was a foreigner. "Kael is dead," Ruari said. "My brother is takin' Brigdhe from here."

She faced him, breathing hard. "Go to your wife. Do whatever you have to do to make her forgive you. This was not your fault!"

"My marriage is over," he said.

She whirled back to MacNeil. "Moffat is hunting Royce—in the fifteenth century! Please, find him and warn him."

MacNeil seemed to understand her, but astonishment rose on Ruari's part. Did this woman mean that *he* was being hunted in the future? Her dress was very fine, very strange. Did she belong to him in another time? Oh, that did please him. But he thought of the deamhan in the robes he had seen earlier, and he instantly knew that had been Moffat.

"Moffat was here when I first broke into the fortress," he said. "He leapt."

She cried out. "I have to find Royce!"

MacNeil said, "If he is here, he has no powers."

She blanched.

"I will make certain he goes safely back to his time—an' you must go back, as well," MacNeil said.

Ruari stepped between them, fury beginning. "The maid belongs to me," he warned.

"She belongs to the future an' ye'll let her go," MacNeil said as firmly.

"I dinna think so."

"Stop," she cried. She stepped between them and said urgently, "MacNeil, please warn Royce now. Moffat has murdered him in 2007—I am so afraid for him!"

MacNeil nodded, then said to Ruari, "Ye have but a moment with her." He strode out.

She wrung her hands and then, slowly, turned to him.

Their gazes locked. Looking into her dark eyes, he wanted to possess all of her, not just her body. "Are ye mine? In what time?" he demanded. "The fifteenth century?"

She nodded. "Yes, we're together in 1430."

He was dismayed. "That's in eight hundred years!"

She nodded, staring at him as if soaking up every detail of his face and hoping to memorize them.

He went still. How could he let this woman go back to the future? So much desire roared. But even as it did, he thought that he must not have any real involvement with any woman, ever again. Still, he hardly needed to be fond of her to spend the night with her.

His mind was made up. They would share one careless night. "I need ye, lass. I canna wait eight hundred years." He pulled her close, so she could feel his very swollen shaft as it pulsed between them. "Tell me yer name."

"Ailios." Tears rose. "I love you so much. You're so different—you're the same! Royce, you're so young!"

He started at her bold declaration, then even more triumph began. He was loved by this brave, pure woman! "I'm nay too young, Ailios, an' I'm glad to show ye."

She smiled and touched his face. "But I'm not yours yet. And you don't love me yet. You love Brigdhe. You're married still."

Had the day been less grim, her words would have amused him. "Ailios, I'm a warrior. Warriors dinna have soft hearts. I'm fond of Brigdhe—t'is my duty to be fond o' her. But it doesna matter now. My marriage ended the day Kael captured her." And just so she did not get the wrong idea, he added, "I willna marry again."

Her eyes filled with tears. "I thought you loved her," she gasped.

"Ye speak so strangely," he exclaimed, finally smiling ever so slightly. "Ye may ken me in the future, but ye dinna ken me now."

She flung her arms around him and buried her face in his chest, as if what he had said had pleased her greatly. His heart thundered. The pressure increased in his loins. This was very different. It might not be so easy to walk away from her when they were done.

"Then I am the only woman who has ever had your heart," she whispered, looking up at him, her smile saucy. But her gaze remained moist.

"Ye talk too much," he said, tilting up her chin. He felt her tense.

"Ruari, let me heal you." Even as she interrupted him, he felt a wonderful warmth seep into his shoulder. It was so pleasing he went still, surprised.

She smiled, her small hands on him now. "Hmm, you like that, don't you?"

He looked at her, having heard the very sultry note in her tone, his cock so stiff now it truly hurt him. "Very much," he said softly, answering her smile with one of his own. And it felt good to smile after the anguish of the past weeks.

She sent more warmth into his shoulder, and he was aware of her blood pounding with stunning force inside her small, beautiful body. He allowed himself the pure enjoyment of being attended by her, of having her purity heal him, and of sexual anticipation. It must happen sooner rather than later. He needed her—and he was not a patient man. In fact, he wasn't sure he had ever been so hot.

She began working on his flayed arm. He looked at his shoulder and saw only the bloody leine, in scraps there. He pulled at the linen and saw his flesh knitted together, the scar vivid and red. The skin on his arm was pink and new.

She had dropped her hands. "I had better go," she said thickly. "It's forbidden to change the past."

He caught her and reeled her in. "How can ye go when yer body is hot an' wet, achin' fer mine?"

She inhaled. "This is so hard. But what I feel for you now is half of what I feel for you in the fifteenth century. Ruari, you need me in that time. I won't let Moffat murder you! And…you don't love me yet."

He stared, perplexed, his gaze searching hers. "Ye have said twice that I love ye in yer time. I ken ye believe it. Did I say so? Because this day I have decided to never allow myself affection again."

She was dismayed. "I am getting the feeling that the past won't change—and you are going to beat yourself up with guilt for the next eight hundred years, no matter what!"

He tensed, displeased. Did she read his mind? How else would she know he was consumed with guilt? "I'm tired o' talk," he warned. "An' I willna wait eight hundred years to take ye to my bed. I want one night. Surely ye can give that to me?" And he let his new power of enchantment free, seducing her with his eyes and his will.

He felt an urgency arise in her. He smiled, leaning close, stroking her back, her hip. "Can ye really resist me? I want to pleasure ye till ye beg me to stop."

She inhaled and he felt how close to capitulation she was. "I don't know what would happen if we slept together. I'm afraid it would change everything that's happened in the fifteenth century—and I might not want to leave you, Ruari." She clasped her temples, pulling away. "Right now, you don't love me and you don't need me—you want a night of fun. I have to go back. We belong together in the fifteenth century. You have no idea what we've been through in a few days! And you are in danger, not as you stand here before me, but as your eight-hundred-year-old self!"

He sobered. He had never imagined being cared about and loved this way. What kind of man would he become in the next eight hundred years, to earn such a woman? A terrible internal battle began. Could he wait so long to seduce her to his will and take her to bed? Was she speaking the truth? Did he need her in the future? Because she was right—he wanted her insanely, but he did not need her.

He thought about his vows. The day he'd made them, they had become his life. He was only just studying the Code, and it was long and complex, but one rule was clear. Changing the past or the future was forbidden. And in the future, he was being hunted by Moffat with this woman at his side.

He must not detain her. "Do ye love me even now, when we're strangers?"

She smiled. "Yes, I do."

His heart leapt with an excitement he could not recognize. Oddly he wanted this woman's love and loyalty. "An' ye'll go to me now, in the future?" he asked. He had to make certain.

She nodded and touched his cheek. Her hand lingered; she did not speak.

She was so beautiful, her light so bright, a beacon of hope and joy. His manhood raged, hardly heeding his will. But he had no time for joy and she had her duty to his future self. "I'll let ye go, Ailios, but with terms."

She started, smiling. "With terms?"

"I want ye in my bed more than ye ken, but I'll settle for a kiss."

She went still. "Yes," she breathed.

And it was the one word he needed. He crushed her in

his arms, hard, and opened her mouth with his lips. Instantly his head swam with desire, passion and lust, but the joy tried to rise up, too. *She was an angel of light and hope.* He plied her mouth and used his tongue there, while rubbing her mound with his shaft, so she would be sure to know what she missed.

She kissed him back and in unison, their pulses soared.

He wasn't sure who pulled away first.

Panting, he stared. He was senseless. He had never wanted any woman this way. And that was the best reason to send her back to her time.

"Don't worry. I'm your destiny."

He remained too stunned—and too inflamed—to speak.

She smiled at him, then turned and walked outside.

He went to the window to watch her. And his eyes widened.

A man was coming down the ridge. It was himself, but hardened by centuries of war.

Ailios cried out and began running to him.

CHAPTER NINETEEN

ALLIE SAW ROYCE striding toward her, on the other side of the fortress's open gates. She thanked the gods that he was alive and started to run. He was hurrying toward her, his eyes ablaze with his own relief.

Moffat materialized between them.

Allie screamed in warning, but even as she did so, Royce vanished, leaping into time. Moffat vanished as if on his heels.

She halted, stunned. *Moffat was hunting Royce with a vengeance.*

She realized MacNeil had come to stand beside her just as she saw Aidan beyond the clearing, on the ridge. As she spoke, Aidan vanished into time, apparently following Moffat and Royce. "Go after them! He can't survive Moffat without his powers!"

"As soon as he leaves this place, he'll find his powers," MacNeil said, clearly meaning to soothe her. But his words were barely spoken when he vanished, too.

Allie clasped her cheeks. She needed to be with Royce, but he could have gone anywhere!

A huge white power fell over her.

She tensed, stunned, and turned to face Elasaid.

Allie couldn't breathe. *Mom.*

Her mother smiled gently at her, but not with a mother's

affection. Her expression was impersonal. "You are a Healer," she said softly. "And you are so afraid for Ruari."

Allie realized that she was face-to-face with her mother centuries before she had been conceived. Elasaid was dressed simply, in a long, belted gown, and Allie somehow knew she was very young, at least in immortal terms. To make sure, she whispered, "Is this your time?"

Elasaid seemed slightly bewildered. "Yes, I remain in my time. You are favored by my father," she added. "He came to watch over you this day."

Allie's heart raced wildly. "I felt an Ancient nearby. Who was it?"

"Lug," she said with a smile. "You are very blessed—and so very young."

Allie reeled. Her grandfather was the most powerful of the gods, although some might say he was second to Dagdha. And he had been with her while she was in the pit. He had reached out to touch her and comfort her.

"Your destiny is written," Elasaid said. "It is decided by the Ancients."

"Can you see it?" Allie asked.

She hesitated. "Yes, I can."

Allie tried to think. Did her mother know that one day she would give birth to her? "Your Fate is written, too, isn't it?" Allie finally asked.

"Of course. I am here to heal, as you are. And one day, I will bequeath the world another Healer." Her gaze searched Allie's and then she smiled. "You are my daughter, aren't you?"

Allie's heart leapt. Tears arose. She managed to nod.

"I can't see my own future," Elasaid said, "but Lug is your grandfather and he is my father. You have the power I had at your age. You are from the future—my future."

Allie started to cry. "You taught me everything I know."

Elasaid slipped her hand into Allie's. "You are so beautiful—your light shines like a holy beacon. I look forward to the day I hold you in my arms. Now, may I send you back to your time?"

Allie held her mother's hand tightly, knowing that when she let go, it was probably forever. "I have to find Royce," Allie said hoarsely, and she let go. "I will not let evil kill him."

"I don't know where he has gone, but, my darling, his Fate is also written, and what is written cannot be changed."

Tears fell. "I'll never give up. Can you send me back to October 5, 1430?"

Elasaid nodded. "Go with the gods," she said.

HE CHOSE TO LAND a hundred years later, in the French city of Paris, a place he had never visited once in his entire life—a place he could not be—a place where he was sure to have his powers. Pain exploded in his skull as he hit the ground, and he heard Moffat cry out, while feeling his evil nearby.

He needed all of his powers now, but he was powerless for a moment and acutely aware of it. In those first minutes, had a living being come by, man or woman, he would have ruthlessly taken all of his or her power to replenish his own. Fortunately, the deamhan suffered the same loss of power in the first few moments after a landing and Moffat was as helpless as he was.

He felt the power flooding into him as the pain in his skull dulled. Royce sat up, reaching for his sword.

Moffat, who had followed him, lay still.

Royce leapt up to kill his enemy.

He raised his sword; Moffat's eyes went wide. Their gazes locked as they blasted one another with energy. Royce brought the blade down on Moffat's neck. But the deamhan vanished just as his sword met corded tendon and taut flesh before slicing through.

He screamed in rage and followed.

HE FOUGHT THE PAIN of the landing, blinking at the stars exploding in the sky, reaching out to feel Moffat. Instantly, as the purple blackness lightened and became gray, he felt his evil presence. A moment later he stared up at a terribly familiar wall. Dread arose—he was at Carrick.

His mind blazed and he decided he had followed Moffat to the early eighteenth century. He managed to sit up, aware that his powers were beginning to return, and knowing he must flee this place immediately. Surely, somewhere on the grounds, he would find his older self.

He had landed in the southern outer ward, which was now cobbled stone. Potted flowers were near the interior gatehouse walls. He was astounded, because he saw so few men on the ramparts, as if this was not a time of incessant war. And then he saw that the drawbridge was down, the portcullis open in the first gatehouse. A fine gilded carriage drawn by six black horses was entering the castle.

Where was Moffat? He stood, searching for him, but instead of sensing evil, Ailios's great white power flowed over him, through him.

Royce jerked, stunned. His gaze and senses were drawn to the carriage, for she was within the vehicle. As he stood, the carriage crossed the drawbridge and he heard her laughter—and the squeal of a child, followed by more childish voices.

Amazement stunned him senseless.

The carriage was passing him now.

He strained to see within—and saw himself seated beside Ailios, three small children with them.

What did this mean?

But he knew. *Ailios had given him those children. Ailios was his wife.*

Remaining stunned, he turned to stare after the carriage as it vanished into the next gatehouse. And so much intense yearning consumed him.

Moffat materialized beside him, sword in hand. He grinned.

Royce didn't think, he leapt—and so did Moffat.

HE BECAME AWARE of fires raging, an inferno. He had leapt forward another one hundred and seventy years into a place called St. Petersburg. This time, the knives in his skull remained even as his powers returned, and in the back of his mind, he knew his body was beginning to suffer from so many leaps. He realized a huge palace was in flames. A mob was besieging the walls, which were guarded by a very few frightened soldiers. The mob wielded pikes and logs, and had destroyed every carriage and vehicle in their path, while the soldiers wielded strange weapons with swords sticking from them. Loud bangs sounded. Men screamed in fury, in agony. As he stood, he saw the palace gates had been breached.

"You will die today," Moffat panted.

Royce still gripped his sword as he whirled to face the deamhan. "So ye lust for me, not Ailios," he hissed. He hurled his energy at him, but Moffat blocked it.

Moffat laughed, thrusting. "I will kill you for taking Kaz from me. Then Ailios will bend to me—in my bed—and she will heal for me as I choose."

Royce met the thrust, enraged. Moffat wanted revenge on him after all. Their blades rang. Did he have the holy Book of Healing?

"I have many pages from it," Moffat replied. "How else would I keep so many giants alive in these wars?"

Royce roared his answer and thrust many times, so swiftly that Moffat was driven backward, able only to defend himself. Royce laughed, feeling triumph at hand.

Moffat laughed back—and leapt.

Royce roared and followed.

HE CRASHED, no longer caring about the pain in his racked body. The knives had gone entirely though his brain, or so it seemed, and he howled from the pain. As he struggled to see past the shooting stars in his mind, searching for Moffat, he was dismayed—for he was at Carrick once more. Horseless carriages filled the courtyard. Laughter drifted from the open doors of the hall. He recognized Ailios's voice and he had one coherent thought. *She was still his wife.*

He heard himself speaking, for a strong breeze was carrying sound that day.

"Die," Moffat panted.

Royce felt the blade caress his jugular, a whisper of razor-sharp steel. He leapt.

HE LEAPT FAR into the future, centuries farther than the date of his death. And this time, even before crashing, he searched for Moffat and felt him on his heels. He grunted as he landed again on his back. Somehow, he had kept a grasp of his sword. This time he wept from the torment of the leap. He wanted to faint from the agony and knew he must not. He was certain he could not withstand time travel many more times.

He heard Moffat gasping beside him. His head exploding, he managed to see a strange, starless sky. He tightened his grasp on his sword.

Above him were a thousand huge towers, all brilliantly lit from within. He was lying on a smooth, gleaming, ebony road, one that seemed to be made of seamless and endless black stone. There were no stars, no moon, just the light from the towers. He sat up. Silver horseless vehicles moved on the road, hovering just above it, filled with people whose faces he could see through the windows. Others flew high in the sky, like birds without any wings.

But he could not think about this strange world. Power had returned to his muscles, flowed in his veins. He stood. "A Ailios!"

Moffat sat; Royce seized him, so he could not leap. In that moment, he felt the deamhan's black power returning. He struck, intending to behead him this time.

And Moffat leapt anyway.

But Royce was ready. Anticipating the leap, he went with him, his blade cutting into his throat and jugular artery as they were hurled past the huge towers and into the void of timeless space.

Moffat howled in rage and pain.

Flying through the stars and moons, through meteors and rock, past suns, the force now threatening to tear him limb from limb, Royce finished the thrust, slicing through Moffat's neck.

For one more instant, their gazes remained locked.

Royce felt savage triumph. He released his sword and watched it spin away into infinity.

Moffat's gaze became incredulous, and then his head and body separated and were hurled away toward other galaxies.

Royce gave over to the leap with his body, and, suddenly exhausted, he willed a landing, any landing, anywhere…in any time.

WHERE WAS ROYCE?

Allie huddled in one of the two large chairs in Carrick's hall, sick with fear and despair. She'd arrived home in the late afternoon of the exact day she'd been seized by Moffat at Blackwood Hall. It was almost midnight. Royce had vanished into time, pursued by Moffat, over twelve hours ago, if she dared count the hours in a normal way.

Where was he? What was happening? Why hadn't he returned to her?

Allie was so afraid, and no matter how Ceit and Peigi hovered, how kind they were, how attentive, the sick feeling in the pit of her stomach would not subside.

She felt power approaching and cried out but it was Aidan who strode into the hall, his face hard and grim.

Allie gasped, "Where is Royce?"

"I dinna ken," he said.

Allie shivered, a terrible cold stealing over her already chilled body. "What does that mean?"

He paused by her chair. "I followed them to a French city in the seventh century, but they leapt so quickly, I landed after them. I managed to chase them to the eighteenth century but they were long gone by then—an' I could not find their trail."

Allie choked on more fear. Moffat was hunting Royce through the centuries. "Try again!"

"I canna," Aidan said fiercely. "Ye dinna think I wish to find the man I love as a friend, a brother and a father, all at once? They're gone, Allie, long gone, an' they could be anywhere, in any time."

She felt her tears finally falling. "It's been hours and hours. Oh God. What could be happening?"

Aidan did not answer, laying his large hand on her back.

"Have ye eaten? Have ye taken some wine? Ye need to do so an' get rest."

"I am not resting," she flashed furiously. "I am sitting right here, waiting for Royce to come home!"

His expression grave, he left her to go to the table, where he poured a mug of wine and began sipping it. Allie stared. She had never seen him so somber. In that moment, she knew he thought Royce dead.

She would never believe it.

But when midnight came and went, she curled up in her chair and wept.

FIVE DAYS LATER, Allie was standing on the ramparts of the southern walls, staring listlessly across the ravine and adjoining lands, wishing Royce would miraculously appear before her very eyes. She was so afraid he would not. As she stood there, one of his heavy plaids wrapped around her green velvet dress, she saw three riders approaching. Not a one was Royce, although they were Masters all, and she let the tears freely fall.

She wasn't going to believe he was dead. She would never believe it. But why didn't he come home?

She didn't move as the riders galloped closer, finally crossing the drawbridge. A moment later she turned and saw MacNeil, Seoc and another Master whom she did not know dismounting in the bailey below. MacNeil glanced up and raised his hand. Allie could not wave back.

She turned away, her back to the men. She prayed to her grandfather that MacNeil brought good news, but his expression had been severe.

Power approached. It was a power she had yet to feel, hot and impatient, battle ready. She turned and stared at a dark, blue-eyed man clad in thigh-high boots, a red and black plaid worn over his leine. In spite of his intense presence, his searching blue gaze was soft with sympathy.

Allie tensed.

He was reading her mind, because he smiled. "Aye, lady, I'm yer brother, Guy Macleod."

Allie breathed hard. She looked at him, thinking about the fact that he was a powerful man she could depend on— her only family in this time. Aidan had stayed at Carrick, but she knew he was ready to go home to his small son. Guy was a stranger, but she needed him. "Thank you," she managed to say, realizing she might break down at any moment. "Thank you for coming."

He studied her for a moment. "Do ye wish for me to call ye Ailios or Allie?"

"Allie," she said, because there was only one person whom she wished to hear the name Ailios from. "I need Royce," she heard herself say brokenly.

His slight smile vanished. "It has been five days since he was last seen outside Eoradh in the sixth century. T'is time to grieve."

"No! Is that why you came? To tell me to give up hope?"

"Yer my sister. I came to invite ye to Blayde. I have a wife an' she can comfort ye."

"I am not leaving Carrick," Allie cried. Tears fell. "I appreciate your offer. I can't leave...not yet."

He said carefully, "If Royce could return, he would."

Allie began to cry.

Guy Macleod laid his large hand clumsily on her shoulder. "Ye need to come with me to Blayde," he said. "Yer my sister. T'is my duty to care for ye now."

Allie shook her head, backing away.

He became coaxing. "My wife is very kind. Ye'll like her." He hesitated. "She's from yer time."

"I have to wait for Royce," Allie tried desperately.

"Then wait with me and Lady Tabitha at Blayde."

She shook her head to clear it; she couldn't have heard him correctly. "I beg your pardon. You didn't say your wife's name is Tabitha?"

He seemed perplexed. "Aye, I did. Ye'd like her greatly—everyone likes Lady Tabitha," he said.

She was in disbelief. "Not Tabby…my Tabby?"

"I dinna ken."

"Is she dark blond and beautiful, a good hand taller than I am? Does she cast spells?" Allie cried. "Does she use Tarot? Did you find her in New York?"

Guy's eyes went wide. "Keep yer voice down. She's no witch. But aye, I found her there in the year 2008."

Allie simply stared, stunned.

ALLIE STOOD at the canopied entrance of her Park Avenue home.

The city hadn't changed. Park Avenue was bumper to bumper with yellow cabs and luxury black sedans. Horns blared. Pedestrians rushed up and down the sidewalks. The center of the street was abloom with flowers. No litter marred the clean, swept sidewalks.

It was September 21. She could have returned home at any time, but it had seemed appropriate to return two weeks after Royce had been murdered by Moffat at modern-day Carrick—because she'd been waiting in the fifteenth century for two weeks for him to return.

Royce's Fate was engraved in stone. Moffat had been meant to murder him, and apparently, he had done just that in 1430.

It was hard to grasp the fact that Royce was dead. Worse, she was convinced she had caused his death a second time. If she hadn't gone back in time to save him, none of this

would have happened, would it? And he would have lived
another six hundred years.

Her heart shrieked at her in protest. Her heart would
never believe him dead. Her heart would wait for him
forever.

She was deeply depressed, grief-stricken. She had even
considered going back to Ruari in the sixth century, but what
if she caused his death then, too? It had become time to be
sensible. He was dead, for there was no other explanation for
his absence. She would mourn forever—but her place wasn't
the fifteenth century. Of course it wasn't. Her place was the
twenty-first century.

Her father and her brother, Alec, had to be sick with fear
over her disappearance. But Allie just stood there, unable
to move forward, staring at the glass doors of the entrance
to her apartment building. Aidan touched her elbow. He had
insisted on taking her home. "Maybe I should wait a
moment," he said. "To make certain ye find yer family well."

"You don't have to wait," Allie said hoarsely. She suddenly
turned and wrapped her arms around him in a bear hug,
clutching the velvet dress Royce had given her in her arms.
"If Royce comes back, you'll come for me?" And then she
realized what she'd said. She needed a miracle, desperately.

His blue eyes flickered oddly. "O' course."

Allie turned away. He had been grieving, too. She'd caught
him weeping when he thought he was alone. He didn't think
Royce was ever coming back to them.

Wiping her eyes, she marched up to the front door. She
tried to smile at the doorman and failed. "Hi, Freddie."

He barred her way. "Hello." He was a flirt and he smiled
at her. "Who are you here to see?"

Allie was bewildered. "Are you joking?" She started to
go past him; he took her arm.

"Lady." His tone changed. "No one goes up unannounced. Who are you here to see?"

She gaped at him while he stared firmly at her. "Have I changed so much?" she finally asked. "This is where I live."

Instantly she saw a wary look in his eyes—a look she was very familiar with, being a New Yorker. He thought her *nuts*. "If you won't tell me who you wish to see, I can't let you in. You have to be buzzed up."

This was insane. What was wrong with him? "I'm really tired and this isn't funny." Freddie never joked. "I *live* here."

"Unless you're a new tenant, you don't live here. And there are no new tenants—there haven't been in years."

He didn't know her. "Buzz William Monroe—or Alec," she cried. She looked past him at Aidan, who was listening closely, his eyes wide and alert. *What is this?* she asked him silently.

He shrugged.

"Are you kidding?" Freddie said incredulously.

Before Allie could argue, she saw her brother coming through the lobby toward the front doors. As sad as she was—and as bewildered—it was great to see him and her heart leapt. Freddie opened the doors and Allie rushed into his arms.

Alec's eyes went wide, then he grinned at her with an odd, very male look. "Wow. Do we know each other?" His grin played.

Allie released him, shocked. She opened her mouth to blurt out that he was her brother. *But he didn't know her, either.*

What was happening?

"Hey, don't be insulted. Did we meet each other last night at Ciprianni's?"

She inhaled. How could her own brother not know her?

She glanced at Aidan, and he shook his head with a warning she did not understand.

"Hey, I'm sorry, I made a mistake," she said.

"No, I'm the sorry one." His seductive smile played. "How about a drink?"

"Another time," Allie managed to say.

He shrugged and walked to the curb for a taxi.

Allie stared after him as Freddie rushed to hail a cab for him. If Alec didn't know her, if she wasn't Alec's sister, what did that mean? What could it mean?

And Royce's image came to her mind, flooding her senses with yearning.

And she heard Elasaid. *Embrace your destiny, darling.*

Freddie had returned to his post before the two doors.

"What happened to the Monroe Heiress?" Allie asked, trembling.

"I'm going to call the cops now," he said. "Lady, you are cute as hell but you are nuts! There is no Monroe Heiress. Mr. Monroe has three sons."

Allie gasped and had to sit down on his stool. "He has three sons?"

"You just met the oldest," Freddie snapped. "Then there are the two boys."

She reeled.

"His wife had the twins two years ago," Freddie added. "Mr. Monroe is nuts about those little boys."

Her father had remarried after all. But what about her, Allie Monroe? Who was she—and was William Monroe her father or not?

IN THE NEW YORK CITY Public Library, Allie found exactly what she was looking for.

William Monroe had married the socialite heiress Laurel

Cady-Benton two years ago. The moment Allie saw the
pretty blonde's picture, she sensed that she was a kind,
centered woman and perfect for her father. In their wedding
photos, she and her father were clearly in love.

He had never been married to her mother, Elizabeth.

There had never been a Monroe Heiress.

Allie looked at Aidan, shocked. "This is not my time,"
she said. "I have to go back."

CHAPTER TWENTY

TABBY AND SAM shared a two-bedroom loft in Tribeca. There was no doorman to ring her up and Allie pounded wildly on their door. It was 5:00 p.m. and if Tabby was still in the twenty-first century, she'd be home, school having let out at quarter past three. Allie was half expecting her to be there, because Guy had found her in 2008.

Aidan took her wrist. "Ye have to calm, Allie."

"How can I calm? Apparently I was never born! What the hell does that mean?"

Aidan was as relaxed as she was not. "It means yer meant to go back to Blayde, to live with yer brother—the last place yer mother was seen."

"My mother was last seen here—except, suddenly she doesn't exist in this time, either!" Allie banged on the door again. Her mother must have fled the massacre and leapt directly to 1982, the year she'd met William Monroe, the year Allie had been born. But clearly that hadn't been meant to be. "I almost feel as if I am going to go up in smoke at any moment."

Aidan smiled. "Ye belong to the Brotherhood, lass. Ye willna vanish from time."

Allie stared at him, thinking that he had to be right. Somehow, what her mother had done had been wrong. But if that was the case, what did it mean about her relationship with William Monroe? Had the Ancients taken his memory of her away so that he wouldn't suffer when she went back? He was her father, wasn't he?

The door opened, revealing Sam standing there in a tiny top and low-slung fleece shorts, her short hair soaking wet, most of her midriff bare. She looked annoyed—and then her eyes went wide in disbelief and relief. "Allie!" She embraced her hard.

"You know me!" Allie said hoarsely, choking in relief.

Sam glanced at Aidan and her eyes went wide and then narrowed. Aidan smiled the kind of smile that would instantly put most women on their backs, undressing her from head to toe, an easy enough task as Sam barely had any clothes on. Sam checked him out as quickly and as boldly, then dragged Allie inside. Aidan followed and she shut the door behind him.

Allie made introductions. "Is Tabby here?"

"She's at a PTA meeting. We have been so worried!"

Allie just stared. So Tabby still existed—even though she'd eventually go to the past and live there. Or would she stay here?

"Allie!" Sam grabbed her. "We need to talk!"

"We can talk in front of Aidan," Allie said.

Sam gave him a glance and then said, "The morning after the party, Tabby called you because you took off. And no one, *no one,* I mean frigging *no one*—" her voice rose shrilly, when Sam was as cool as Royce all of the time "—knew you! Not the housekeeper, not your father, not your brother. What the hell happened?"

"But you didn't forget me," Allie whispered.

"We've been freaked! We were afraid it was demons, and that Fate decided to make a few adjustments to the situation. But the gods never intervene when someone is murdered and you know it."

"I've been in the fifteenth century, Sam. The CDA rumors are true."

Sam stared at her and Allie stared back. Then she looked at Aidan. "He has power, lots of it—and it's not demonic."

"Yeah, he has power. There's a secret Brotherhood filled with guys like him who have taken vows to protect Innocence no matter what," Allie said. "The Masters time travel as well as vanquish evil. They are descended from the gods, Sam." She almost added, so was she. "They're almost immortal—and almost invincible."

"Holy shit." Sam then said, low, "There's a spell in the Book we never understood, Allie. It's about Fate interrupted, and Fate corrected."

Allie hesitated. Sam had referred to the Book she and Tabby lived by, handed down to them by their mother, a book only a Rose woman could use. It was filled with wisdom, magic, myths and spells. "I don't exist here anymore. And that means one thing—my Fate is the past."

Sam appeared dismayed and she hugged her, another totally uncharacteristic action for her, as she was the least touchy-feely person Allie knew.

The door opened and Tabby walked in. She saw Allie and rushed to embrace her. Allie realized she was crying. "It's all right."

"No, it's not. Sam, Brie and I have spent nights trying to figure out what happened to you and what it meant. Brie said you weren't coming back! Thank the gods she was wrong!"

Allie hesitated. "This is temporary, Tabby. My life is the fifteenth century now."

Tabby gaped.

Allie whispered, "I found him. I found the Emperor."

Tabby gasped. "Then why do you look as if someone has died?"

Allie tried not to cry.

"Oh my God," Tabby whispered. "I'm sorry, Allie. I'm so sorry."

Allie sucked it up. "I need Brie. I have been trying to summon her, but I don't think it's working. Can you call her? I have to speak to her before I go back."

Sam was already on the phone.

"Aidan? This is my other best friend, Tabby." Allie realized Aidan was staring at Tabby in surprise.

Tabby did a double take and appeared confused. "Do I know you?"

"I dinna think so—Lady Tabitha."

Tabby started. She glanced at Allie but before Allie could divert her—she didn't think she should tell Tabby she was going to meet her destiny in another year and that he was very medieval—Sam said, "Brie left the office, like, ten minutes ago."

"How do you know me," Tabby asked uncertainly, "and why are you addressing me as 'Lady'?"

The words weren't even out of her mouth when a soft knock sounded on the door. Allie gave Aidan a warning look and ran to it, knowing it was Brie, her heart leaping wildly. She needed a final, definitive answer about Royce. She needed to know that he was alive and out there, somewhere.

Brie stood in the doorway in a shapeless brown suit, looking flushed, as if she'd walked the twenty blocks from CDA to the loft, her brown hair pulled tightly back, tendrils sticking to her damp skin. She wore her heavy black I'm-A-Brain glasses, but they were crooked. They embraced and clung.

"I heard you calling!" Brie exclaimed breathlessly. "What are you doing here? You can't be here!" she cried.

Then she looked past Allie and saw Aidan. She turned redder and glanced aside. Then said, "I have missed you so. I have thought about you so much!"

"Everything has happened so fast and I didn't know how to get word back to you guys." Allie held her by the upper arms. "Everything Tabby saw in the cards was right. And you were right—he was there, that night at the fund-raiser. Brie, please. *Is Royce alive?*"

Brie shifted her weight, as she usually did when nervous. "Allie, you know I can't see on demand."

"Please!" Allie cried, and instantly, she knew she was on the verge of hysteria. Her grip on Brie tightened. "Try to see…try for me. I can't believe he's gone forever!"

"I don't know," Brie cried back, strained. "I only know that I saw him coming for you. A big, golden, beautiful man, a warrior. You were meant to heal his heart—and he was meant to take you to your Fate. That's all I know!"

"Allie," Aidan interrupted. "Yer hurting the lass."

Allie released her. "I'm so sorry!"

Brie wiped one of her cheeks with her knuckles—she'd started to cry. She was terribly empathetic. "I know your heart has been ripped out. I'm sorry, so sorry!"

Allie fought not to weep. "How can this have happened?"

Brie put her arms around her. "You can't fight Fate."

Allie looked at her. "After eight hundred years, he was finally coming around. I was healing him."

Brie didn't seem to hear her. "Allie? You need to go to a place called Carrick—you need to go now!"

HE AWOKE, not for the first time, aware that his strength was returning. And as he did, he heard the woman as she pounded food with a stone, and he sensed the man outside of the cave where he had been taken. He could smell meat roasting.

Saliva gathered.

He began to recall what had happened.

Moffat had chased him through the ages. The many leaps had exhausted him. He had landed without thought in this long ago, primitive time. He opened his eyes and adjusted his gaze to the dim light in the cave.

The woman wore a deerskin and she did not look his way, grinding leaves rhythmically with her stone. Her face was strange, with huge cheekbones, a wide, flat nose, small eyes. She was small, too, like Ailios, but so was the man.

He had gone so far back in time he did not know the date. But then, these people had no calendar.

She looked at him and smiled.

He read her mind. She thought him a god; so did her man. But now, he remembered appearing in their midst. Just before losing consciousness, he had sensed their shock and fear.

The man appeared, also clad in a skin, grinning. He was pleased with the tribal kill—two deer.

More saliva gathered—he was starving. He recalled the woman feeding him some kind of bland gruel while giving him sips of water. He sat up. Both people turned to stare.

He smiled at them, testing his body, searching it for strength and power. He sent a blast of light energy through the cave and was pleased when the dirt and leaves lifted and swirled.

The cave people's eyes widened.

"Thank ye fer carin' fer me," he said. His strength and power were rapidly returning. He flexed his hands, standing.

They got on their knees submissively.

They were in awe, still afraid. It didn't matter. He had lain in exhaustion for days—he wasn't sure for how long—and he had to go home. But before he did, he'd make sure they had enough stores to last the winter.

Royce stepped out of the cave.

"I DINNA THINK WE SHOULD be here," Aidan said. "I think ye should go directly to Blayde, yer brother's home."

Allie paused outside Carrick's twenty-first-century front walls, which were covered with blooms. Why had Brie insisted they go to Carrick?

"He's nay here," Aidan said sharply. "Ye have yer hopes up."

She did have her hopes up, but Allie wasn't going to admit it. They'd taken a commercial flight to Scotland, to avoid the physical stress of leaping. Allie had no funds, so Tabby had paid for the airfare. Their goodbyes had been tearful. While Allie knew she'd see Tabby again, she'd probably never see Brie or Sam. On top of losing Royce, it was simply too much.

"Stop being so brave," she had told Sam fiercely. "Find someone to help you hunt the demons so you don't have to do it alone!"

Sam had been amused. "I have Tabby and Brie," she said flippantly. "Besides, maybe I'll join CDA."

In a way, Brie was her best friend, even though she was so shy, introverted and bookish. Allie had hugged her, not meaning to say anything. But then she'd whispered, "Stop hiding behind your job, those glasses and those awful suits."

Brie had smiled sadly. "I'm not you.… I love you, Allie."

It hurt terribly leaving them behind, even more than leaving her father and Alec, but nothing hurt as much as facing the final truth about Royce. Why had Brie sent her here? Was this supposed to somehow help her move on to a life without Royce in it? She glanced down the hill toward the two large garages, which looked like small manor homes. Royce's cars were housed there, unless the estate had already sold them.

She breathed hard. "I guess we can leave the rental car

here. I doubt anyone will tow it." She started toward the bridge, which spanned the ravine.

Aidan came abreast of her. "Why did yer friend send ye here? T'is cruel—but she's nay cruel at all."

"She's an empath, Aidan, and she also has the Sight. I don't know why she sent me here, but I've learned over the years that Brie is always right. There's a reason, and I guess we're about to find it."

He was silent.

Unlike the fifteenth century, the portcullis remained raised and they started to walk through the first gatehouse. Allie saw a gardener tending several of the potted plants in the courtyard. She realized that the estate was being kept up, probably because it was for sale. The gardener suddenly straightened and tipped his tweed cap at her.

Allie smiled politely back. They knocked on the front door.

Mrs. Farlane opened it. She beamed. "I thought you'd be gone for the day, Lady Maclean!" Then she glanced past her, puzzled. "Did you leave the Aston-Martin by the garage and walk all the way up?"

Allie gaped, so confused she could barely comprehend the housekeeper. Royce was a Maclean—but so was Malcolm. Had the housekeeper confused her with someone else? "The Aston-Martin? I don't have an Aston-Martin," she stammered.

Mrs. Farlane looked bewildered. "His Lordship gave it to you last year for your anniversary!"

Allie reeled. Aidan steadied her. "His Lordship?" he asked.

"Is Her Ladyship ill?" Mrs. Farlane became distressed. "Lady Maclean, come inside and sit down. Let me summon His Lordship!"

Allie somehow followed the housekeeper into the hall. *She was being mistaken for the lady of Carrick.*

Mrs. Farlane had rushed off.

Allie stumbled, facing Aidan. "Oh gods," she whispered. "Is it possible?"

And then she heard a man's footsteps. She whirled—and her heart sank.

A tall man who very much resembled Royce had come into the hall, his aura reeking of power. He wasn't Royce, for his hair was dark, but those silver eyes were unmistakable. He was Royce's son or grandson. Was this His Lordship?

His face was concerned as he approached. "Mother, are ye okay?"

Allie cried out.

"Mother?" Bewilderment crossed his face.

And Allie realized it wasn't over.

Then Royce stepped into the hall.

Their gazes locked.

Allie took one look at him and knew he was fourteen hundred years old. The modern Royce lived. He had not been murdered on September 7. And that could only mean one thing.

Royce had vanquished Moffat as they fought through the centuries after leaping from Eoradh.

"Royce!" Allie cried, her knees buckling.

Royce's eyes widened with disbelief. He whirled. "Thors, I need a privy word with yer mother."

Thors said slowly, "That's not my mother. At least, it's not Mother now. She's come from another time. My mother is visiting at Blayde. An' Aidan has leapt from the past, too." He gave Allie another serious look and left the room.

Allie ran to Royce and threw herself into his arms.

He held her for a moment. Then, "You are so young!"

"You lived—you vanquished Moffat!" She clasped his beautiful face.

"Aye! I leapt through many ages, fighting with him the entire time, an' I was too ill to come home to ye. But I am returning to ye, Ailios. Ye canna stay here. We have children—grandchildren—great-grandchildren! Ye must go back to me in the fifteenth century so we can have this future!"

Allie nodded, overcome. "I love you."

He smiled. "I ken—for ye have suffered my medieval ways for six centuries. Now go, darling. I willna lose this life of ours."

Allie turned and gave Aidan her hand.

SIX DAYS HAD PASSED since she had been seized by Moffat outside of Blackwood Hall. Allie stood on the ramparts, mindless of the drizzle, wrapped in one of Royce's plaids. Autumn had settled over Morvern and the leaves on the Scot oak trees were red and gold, while the grass and shrubs were turning brown and barren. She knew Royce was coming back, but until he did, she was suspended in a state of breathless anticipation, tinged with real fear for his safety and welfare.

And then she felt his hot, hard power below.

She whirled, crying out.

Royce was leaping up the steps to the ramparts, his gaze burning and bright.

It was her Royce—Mr. Medieval—and he had clearly been in his Mad Max mode. His leine was spotted with dried blood, as if someone had dipped a paintbrush in it and then shaken it at him. Allie wasn't sure she wanted to know what had happened. She ran toward him.

Royce ran, too, and on the top step, he swept her into his embrace and held her, hard.

She breathed in his scent—Highland pine, rain, sex, man.

She sensed for his injuries, but there were none. In fact, his power was as great as it had ever been.

"Aye, I was hurt, but I'm fine now." He took her face in his hands and smiled warmly at her. "Hallo a Ailios," he said softly.

She touched his cheek. "Hallo a Ruari."

He clasped her hand to his cheek. "Moffat's dead."

"I know."

He started.

"I saw our future, Royce. I saw our wonderful future!"

His puzzled gaze softened. "I saw it, too. We will have many fine children, Ailios."

She nodded and realized she was crying.

"I'm sorry I scared ye so. I was so weakened from the leaping. I landed in a distant time and I dinna have the power to come back to ye for days."

She somehow nodded.

"I could never leave ye," he whispered, his tone suddenly rough. "I love ye too much."

Allie went still. His words reverberated through her body, her heart, her soul.

"Ye win," he added with a smile that revealed his single dimple. "Don't I get to take ye to bed now?" he added, his gaze gleaming.

Somehow she said, "Damn right."

He swept her into his arms and started down the stairs, his strides rapid and determined.

She felt his pulse roaring, gathering in his loins. "I have missed you so much!"

"Aye, I ken. Ye were scared an' ye went to yer time, to find ye dinna exist there anymore."

They entered the hall. He was lurking—she loved it! "The gods want me with you, Royce."

"Ah, well." He ran up the stairs to his tower. "That's a very hopeful statement." His grin flashed, wicked, and he laid her on the bed. "I'll fight the gods to be with ye, Ailios," he said seriously, but he looked at her legs.

She had dressed for his return every day. She leaned back against the pillows in the green jersey dress. The slit fell open. Royce sat and slid his hand up her thigh, high. "I like the pink thong best," he said roughly.

She looked at his fiercely tented leine. "I know. Take that off."

He smiled and stood, dropping his belt and pulling off his boots. He tossed the plaid aside—and then the leine.

Allie breathed hard. He was the most magnificent man, and her heart soared. I am the luckiest woman on this earth, she thought. "I'm going to pleasure you, Royce," she managed.

"I dinna think so," he said roughly and tugged the thong off, pushed her dress up to her waist, then reached for the wrap top. Then he looked at her. "I love yer body, yer face, but I love yer kind heart the most," he said.

Allie felt more tears gathering. "Royce."

"I love ye, Ailios."

She laid her hand on his thundering heart. She wanted to fly to the stars and then back again—a hundred times—but she fought to sense his guilt, his pain. And he knew, because as ready as he was, he waited for her now.

It took a long moment and she felt only a faint echo of the guilt that had consumed him for the past eight hundred years. She had at least five hundred and seventy-seven years to finish healing his heart.

He was lurking, because he smiled roughly and said, "Aye, I may not be called Black Royce for much longer."

"Come to me, love," Allie whispered.

He did.

TWO DAYS LATER, Allie stepped out of a steaming bath and wrapped herself in her favorite plaid, which she'd claimed possession of from Royce. She and Royce had definitely had a honeymoon. He'd barred the door, only opening it for food and drink. She was exhausted from the several days they'd just spent together, filled with passion that had been at times mindless and at other times amazingly gentle, peppered with conversation, cuddling, affection and intimacy. She was deliriously, ecstatically, joyfully in love.

She dried her hair with a linen towel and stepped into her jeans and a cashmere sweater she'd been given by Sam. She went to the mirror—no, looking glass—over the chest, thinking about how she'd have a servant nail it to the wall in a more convenient position. She'd taken a dozen lipsticks from Sam and Tabby before leaving, too. But before she could decide on a shade for her lips, Elasaid appeared in the mirror.

Allie tensed, stunned. She was afraid her mother would vanish the moment she turned. But she did turn, cautiously murmuring, "Mom?"

Her mother stood smiling at her, her eyes soft with love. Allie could see the bed through her figure and knew she was a spirit from the afterlife. "I didn't think I'd ever see you again!" she cried.

Elasaid whispered, "I am so happy for you, darling."

This was goodbye, Allie thought. But before she could begin to barrage her mother with questions, a dark man appeared beside her—and he was the spitting image of her brother, Guy, except that he was in his forties and silver streaked his temples. And she knew she was looking at Guy's father, William the Lion, the fifth baron of Blayde.

Her heart thundered. "William Monroe isn't my father," she whispered.

"No, darling, he's not. I was afraid—I had you to guard

and protect. I asked Lug to send me to the safest place. He sent me to Will Monroe."

Allie trembled, staring at her father, a handsome man who reeked of mortal power, even being dead.

William Macleod smiled at her. "I am proud of you, daughter," he said.

He took her mother's hand and Allie saw the white light coursing between them, happiness and love. "Father," she managed to say. She wanted to know this man.

"You will know me through your brother," he said.

Allie smiled through her tears. It was a command. She nodded. "I sensed the truth the moment Royce told me about you and Mom."

"I know."

Allie started. "How much can you see from the other side?"

Elasaid's beautiful smile played. "Darling, that is not a just question. The gods bless you and Ruari and your children and their children." She blew a kiss.

Allie saw her and her father fade. She lifted her hand. They continued to smile at her, their love so evident and consuming. They slowly receded, until she was left standing alone in the room. She wiped her tears. They were together for eternity—and she would get to know her father through Guy, as he had *ordered* her to do.

Wow, Tabby was in for a *huge* ordeal. Allie bit back a smile. She'd manage. It would be worth it in the end.

She found Royce in the hall, in a deep conversation with his steward. But he instantly looked at her, his eyes warm with deep, undying love.

Allie's own heart swelled with delirium and joy.

She sat down to eat, ravenous. When the steward was gone, Royce came over. "Did ye enjoy yer bath?"

"Yes. What's wrong, Royce? Did I tire you out?"

Annoyance flashed. "I was being kind by not coming to yer bath! We made love for two days!"

She laughed at him. "Gotcha."

He smiled back. Then he sobered. "Three Masters have gone to Moffat Cathedral an' retrieved six pages o' the Book o' Healing."

"That's great!" Allie cried.

"Aye, but I had hoped they might find the Book o' Power there." He sat down beside her.

Instantly Allie knew he wanted to ask her something. "What is it?"

He smiled at her, his expression so beautiful and open, so unguarded, her heart ached. "Ye met me at Eoradh."

She blushed, recalling that sexy encounter with his younger self. "Oh, yes. We met."

His smile faded. "I remember the day so well. In one moment, ye changed my world. I wanted ye so badly—an' dinna wish ye to leave. I still dinna ken how I let ye go, but I understood I needed ye more in this time than then."

She was stunned. "You remember what happened?"

His smile returned, and his gaze flickered. "Ye told me how much ye loved me, even my young self—an' ye let me take a kiss."

His memories of that terrible day had been changed by her arrival in the past. She was stunned. "But it's forbidden to change the past."

He eyed her oddly. "Did we change the past?"

"You do remember that the first time you met me was in the future—in 2007—three weeks ago."

"Nay, lass," he corrected softly. "I met ye the day I rescued Brigdhe. An' I never forgot ye, not in eight hundred long years." He smiled and stroked his hand over her hair and then down her back.

Allie breathed hard. What had Sam said about an incomprehensible passage in the Book? "My friends never understood some spell about Fate interrupted and Fate corrected."

Royce's brows lifted. "From time to time, something happens that is not meant to be. In the Code, it tells us that Fate will always adjust such errors in history."

Allie met his gaze. Fate had done just that in her case, because she should have been born in the thirteenth century. "I need to go to Blayde," she said suddenly. She had a new family to meet and learn about—and she had a best friend to visit. Boy, would they talk up a storm!

Royce smiled. "I'll take ye so ye can gossip with Lady Tabitha."

"Lurker! Have you met her?"

"Nay, but I'm glad ye have friends in our time."

Allie met his gaze. "*Our time.* Oh, Royce, I am the luckiest woman in the world."

"I'm the most fortunate man." He stood. "We can leave in two days. I have many matters to attend before we visit yer brother an' his wife."

Allie nodded happily.

"I will be back to sup with ye." He surprised her yet again by brushing her cheek with a kiss, his hand lingering in her hair. Then he strode across the hall.

Allie watched him go, loving him so much it hurt. "You know, you do have a way with words."

He glanced back at her. "That's ye, Ailios. I prefer action, but ye love to talk—even in bed." His eyes gleamed. "I dinna mind."

"You *love* talking in bed—don't you dare deny it. Mr. Medieval has a soft side after all."

"There's nothing soft about me in bed," he returned, but he was smiling.

And even though he was so light and happy now, Allie loved him so much she lifted her hand and sent her white healing light deep into his bones—and his heart.

He started and turned.

She waited for his reaction.

And he simply laughed at her before going out into the light of a new Highland day in *their* time.

Dear Readers,

I hope you have enjoyed Allie and Royce's story as much as I have. They swept me away from the very start and I was sad to let them go, because I am a sucker for a super Alpha hero like Royce. For me, the harder the hero, the better!

I am currently working on *Dark Embrace,* Aidan's story. He is not the man you met in *Dark Seduction* and *Dark Rival.* His son's murder has turned him into something very dark, very tormented; an anti-hero teetering on the brink of evil. On the day that he committed evil in the hopes of saving young Ian, he turned against his vows, the Brotherhood and the gods. Now he is a Highlander with no clan, a mercenary with no soul, relentlessly hunting the deamhan responsible for his son's murder. It is what he lives for and nothing more. As I am sure you have guessed, that deamhan is none other than his own father, back from the vanquished—and Moray is hunting him as relentlessly and will stop at nothing to get even.

But Aidan's torment is even greater than the loss of a child. Ian has haunted him for sixty-six years. Not a day goes by that he doesn't glimpse his ghost—but only for a scant second, and then little Ian is gone. To make matters worse, no one has ever seen Ian's ghost except for Aidan—until he takes Brianna Rose back to 1503 with him.

Brie, as you know, is a techno geek who hides behind baggy clothes and big eyeglasses, who has no personal life, and is probably the only twenty-six-year-old virgin in New York City. But she doesn't care, because she is a Rose, and her life is fighting evil with her cousins, Tabby and Sam, and her friend Kit Mars, while working for the HCU. She has had a very secret crush on Aidan ever since meeting him for all of five minutes in *Dark Seduction*. She has other secrets, of course—all the Rose women do. She has the Sight and is a powerful empath.

One September night, her life forever changes when she is awakened by roars of pain and anguish. Brie instantly knows it is Aidan being tortured, repeatedly, by a great evil. The torment is unbearable. Her cousins take her to CDA's hospital unit, where she is sedated—and where she first sees a small boy, standing at the foot of her bed. When she is finally released, she rushes to her computer to try to find out what happened to Aidan. Instead of delving into HCU's extensive database, she goes to old-fashioned history books, and quickly learns about the merciless Wolf of Awe, a Highlander with no clan, a man universally feared and despised, who was hanged in 1502. His name is Aidan—but history claims he is so ruthless and savage, she knows this cannot be *her* Aidan! And in that very moment, she has a crystal-clear vision of *her* Aidan in a stone effigy on his tomb. Brie is so distraught she leaves her loft. And evil is waiting for her....

Aidan has not rescued Innocence in sixty-six years. But when he hears Brie calling out to him in fear and pain, he does not hesitate to leap into the future to protect her. The moment he does so, his life will never be the same....

Brie is stunned by the changes in him. She is afraid of him. But she is determined to help him redeem himself, no matter that he doesn't want redemption....

He only wants to hunt Moray, and the shapeless woman with the ugly eyeglasses is in his way. She insists he has a soul—and he knows he does not. Even worse than that, she is in love with him—he has lurked. He only takes her into the past to annoy her boss ay HCU. He intends to send her back to her time as soon as she is strong enough to withstand another leap. But when he realizes she can see Ian—and communicate with him— she becomes the bridge to his son and his soul.

To learn more about Aidan, the Wolf of Awe, and the very brave, determined Brianna, and their tempestuous love story, visit www.mastersoftimebooks.com.

Have you ever read one of my historical romances? If you like the strong, sexy heroes, you simply have to check out *A Dangerous Love,* on sale April 1, 2008. Emilian St. Xavier is one of Derbyshire's most powerful noblemen, but he is an outcast and an outsider. Wherever he goes, there are scornful whispers behind his back. His past is no secret. His mother was a Roma, and he was raised by her until the age of twelve. Then a rumor abruptly tore him from her side, and brought him in shackles to Woodland, where he was told he was going to become an Englishman and the next viscount....

He is as English as any half-blood can be. He graduated Oxford with the highest honors, and three years after inheriting the ruined estate, all debts have been erased. Woodland is, in fact, prosperous and thriving. Immersing himself in estate affairs, he has no personal life except for casual sexual liaisons. But then he learns of his mother's murder at the hands of an English mob and his world implodes....

Ariella de Warenne is eccentric. She is a great heiress, but she has been allowed to spend her life in libraries and museums. Now twenty-four years old, she lives in London at a family home, often alone. She has no interest in marriage or men—she can think of little worse than becoming a broodmare like most wives of the day. Besides, no husband would allow her to dress as a man and attend her favorite lectures at Cambridge, or have lawyers and radical dissidents as friends. Ladies are expected to be pretty ornaments, and she has no intention of ever being an ornament for anyone. But when gypsies set up camp at Rose Hill, she is instantly intrigued by their enigmatic, dangerously seductive *vaida*. And even though he warns her to stay away, she is drawn to Emilian like a moth to a flame. Only when it is too late does she realize she has been his revenge....

Theirs is an epic romance of great tragedy and even greater triumph. I was shocked to learn of how the Romani were treated over the centuries, of the bigotry and hatred directed at them, even in Britain.

I've been writing about the de Warenne family in different centuries for many years now. This is a great dynasty where the men are powerful, privileged and passionate—and to love once is to love forever. To learn more about the de Warenne men and women and their passions and scandals, their tragedies and triumphs, please visit www.thedewarennedynasty.com.

I look forward to seeing you again on Loch Awe in the fall of 1502!

Happy Reading!

Brenda Joyce

*Turn the page for an exciting preview of
Brenda Joyce's dramatic new
de Warenne family novel,
A DANGEROUS LOVE.
Two worlds collide in this epic story of
love and redemption to be released
for the first time in paperback
from HQN books in April 2008.*

"I WAS HOPING your temper might have improved with a few hours of sleep."

He straightened and faced her, his gaze deeply penetrating. "I did not sleep, Miss de Warenne."

"Then that makes two of us."

His face hardened.

She trembled. "I was hoping we could reach an understanding."

"And what kind of understanding would that be? Oh, wait. You will rendezvous with me tonight at our next camp. You will claim it is to talk and debate, but we both know there will be little talk and no debate."

She breathed hard. "And would that be so terrible? Should I lie and tell you I haven't thought about your kisses—and your touch?" She flushed. Her body had responded to the memory.

"Are you trying to provoke me? Was last night not enough provocation?" He was incredulous.

"You make it sound as if I wanted to lead you a merry chase, when I had no such plans!"

He shook his head. "Last night, you wanted me to pursue you, and do not dare deny it. You wanted me to take you into my arms and you wanted my kisses. I know when a woman sends such an invitation, Miss de Warenne. I did not mistake your desires last night." He stared.

She stared back, aware now of what the hunger in her body signified. "But that was still not intentional on my part, Emilian," she said slowly. "You are the first man who has ever made me think of kisses, the first man to make me feel passion. I never understood what the fuss was about. I never understood why my brother and male cousins were such rakes, going from conquest to conquest. I don't think I even knew what I was doing last night. But when we met, something happened to me—and it is wonderful!" she cried passionately.

He was silent.

She hugged herself. "I am an honest person. I don't care for proper conversation. When I have something to say, I say it. Otherwise, I prefer my daydreams. You were kind and respectful to Margery, my cousin. Can't we discuss this without accusations and anger, but with honesty? Don't I deserve that much after the passion we shared last night?"

"I am not lusting for your cousin," he said flatly. "And we shared a simple kiss, nothing more."

His words seemed to signify that he wanted her still. She was so relieved. "It was far more than a kiss, Emilian."

"For you, a woman without experience."

"That's right. I have no experience when it comes to kisses and lovemaking. What happened last night was hugely important to me."

He stared at her, his eyes dark and unhappy.

She breathed. "Do you still desire me?"

His eyes widened and then turned hard. "Stay longer, and you might find out."

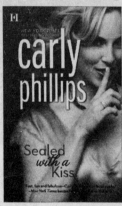

REQUEST YOUR FREE BOOKS!

2 FREE NOVELS FROM THE ROMANCE/SUSPENSE COLLECTION PLUS 2 FREE GIFTS!

YES! Please send me 2 FREE novels from the Romance/Suspense Collection and my 2 FREE gifts. After receiving them, if I don't wish to receive any more books, I can return the shipping statement marked "cancel." If I don't cancel, I will receive 4 brand-new novels every month and be billed just $5.49 per book in the U.S., or $5.99 per book in Canada, plus 25¢ shipping and handling per book plus applicable taxes, if any*. That's a savings of at least 20% off the cover price! I understand that accepting the 2 free books and gifts places me under no obligation to buy anything. I can always return a shipment and cancel at any time. Even if I never buy another book from the Reader Service, the two free books and gifts are mine to keep forever.

185 MDN EF5Y 385 MDN EF6C

Name	(PLEASE PRINT)

Address	Apt. #

City	State/Prov.	Zip/Postal Code

Signature (if under 18, a parent or guardian must sign)

Mail to **The Reader Service:**
IN U.S.A.: P.O. Box 1867, Buffalo, NY 14240-1867
IN CANADA: P.O. Box 609, Fort Erie, Ontario L2A 5X3

Not valid to current subscribers to the Romance Collection,
the Suspense Collection or the Romance/Suspense Collection.

Want to try two free books from another line?
Call 1-800-873-8635 or visit www.morefreebooks.com.

* Terms and prices subject to change without notice. NY residents add applicable sales tax. Canadian residents will be charged applicable provincial taxes and GST. This offer is limited to one order per household. All orders subject to approval. Credit or debit balances in a customer's account(s) may be offset by any other outstanding balance owed by or to the customer. Please allow 4 to 6 weeks for delivery.

Your Privacy: Harlequin is committed to protecting your privacy. Our Privacy Policy is available online at www.eHarlequin.com or upon request from the Reader Service. From time to time we make our lists of customers available to reputable firms who may have a product or service of interest to you. If you would prefer we not share your name and address, please check here. ☐

BOB07

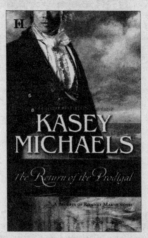

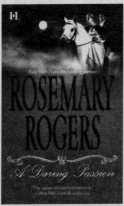

BRENDA
JOYCE

| 77233 | DARK SEDUCTION | ___ $7.99 U.S. ___ $9.50 CAN. |

(limited quantities available)

| TOTAL AMOUNT | $ _____ |
| POSTAGE & HANDLING | $ _____ |

($1.00 FOR 1 BOOK, 50¢ for each additional)

| APPLICABLE TAXES* | $ _____ |
| TOTAL PAYABLE | $ _____ |

(check or money order—please do not send cash)

To order, complete this form and send it, along with a check or money order for the total above, payable to HQN Books, to: **In the U.S.:** 3010 Walden Avenue, P.O. Box 9077, Buffalo, NY 14269-9077; **In Canada:** P.O. Box 636, Fort Erie, Ontario, L2A 5X3.

Name: _____

Address: _____ City: _____

State/Prov.: _____ Zip/Postal Code: _____

Account Number (if applicable): _____

075 CSAS

*New York residents remit applicable sales taxes.
*Canadian residents remit applicable GST and provincial taxes.

HQN™

We *are* romance™

www.HQNBooks.com

PHBJ1007BL

BRENDA JOYCE

is a *New York Times* bestselling author of thirty-six novels and four novellas.

She has won many awards, and her very first novel, *Innocent Fire,* won a Best Western Romance award. She has also won the highly coveted Best Historical Romance award for *Splendor* and a Lifetime Achievement award from *Romantic Times BOOKreviews* magazine. There are over 13 million copies of her novels in print and she is published in over a dozen foreign countries.

Currently Brenda is focused on the de Warenne Dynasty, a series of books about one sprawling family, set in historic England and Ireland, and the Masters of Time, a paranormal series about medieval Highlanders sworn to saving mankind through the ages.

A native New Yorker, Brenda now lives in southern Arizona. She divides her time between her twin passions—writing powerful love stories, and showing her horses at regional and national levels. For more information about Brenda and her upcoming novels, please visit her Web sites at www.brendajoyce.com, www.thedewarennedynasty.com and www.mastersoftimebooks.com.

HQN™

We *are* romance™

www.HQNBooks.com

PHBJBIO07P

THE MASTERS OF TIME

HIGHLAND WARRIORS SWORN TO PROTECT INNOCENCE THROUGHOUT THE AGES...

A golden man, he is called Black Royce—a battle-hardened soldier of the gods. His vows are his life—until he is sent to New York City to protect a Healer from those who would use her powers for themselves. The moment Royce sees beautiful, feisty Allie Monroe, he knows she will be his only weakness—and he is right.

DESTINY IS A DANGEROUS THING

Allie Monroe is more than an heiress. She is a Healer, willing to do anything to save victims of the evil that lurks in the city at night. But alone, she can do only so much—until destiny sends her the darkest Highlander of them all. Then evil strikes and Royce is destroyed before Allie's eyes. Now Allie will do anything to save Royce—even if it means going back in time to a dark, dangerous world. Confronting their enemies could cost not only their lives, but their love—for all eternity.

"The incomparable Brenda Joyce soars to new heights....
A passionate, original paranormal romance!"
—**Romantic Times BOOKreviews**

www.mastersoftimebooks.com

ISBN-13:978-0-373-77219-3
ISBN-10:   0-373-77219-X

50799

9 780373 772193

EAN

HQN™
We *are* romance™
www.HQNBooks.com
$7.99 U.S./$9.50 CAN.